An author of more than ninety books for children and adults with more than seventy-five for Mills & Boon, **Janice Kay Johnson** writes about love and family and pens books of gripping romantic suspense. A *USA Today* bestselling author and an eight-time finalist for the Romance Writers of America *RITA*® Award, she won a *RITA*® Award in 2008. A former librarian, Janice raised two daughters in a small town north of Seattle, Washington.

New York Times and *USA Today* bestselling, award-winning author **Lisa Childs** has written more than eighty-five novels. Published in twenty countries, she's also appeared on the *Publishers Weekly*, Barnes & Noble and Nielsen Top 100 bestseller lists. Lisa writes contemporary romance, romantic suspense, and paranormal and women's fiction. She's a wife, mum, bonus mum, avid reader and less avid runner. Readers can reach her through Facebook or her website, lisachilds.com

WILDERNESS HOSTAGE

JANICE KAY JOHNSON

HOSTAGE SECURITY

LISA CHILDS

MILLS & BOON

First Published in Great Britain 2025
by Mills & Boon, an imprint of HarperCollins*Publishers* Ltd
1 London Bridge Street, London, SE1 9GF

www.harpercollins.co.uk

HarperCollins*Publishers*
Macken House, 39/40 Mayor Street Upper,
Dublin 1, D01 C9W8, Ireland

Wilderness Hostage © 2025 Janice Kay Johnson
Hostage Security © 2025 Lisa Childs

ISBN: 978-0-263-39701-7

0225

MIX
Paper | Supporting
responsible forestry
FSC™ C007454

This book contains FSC™ certified paper and other controlled sources to ensure responsible forest management.

For more information visit: www.harpercollins.co.uk/green

Printed and Bound in the UK using 100% Renewable Electricity at
CPI Group (UK) Ltd, Croydon, CR0 4YY

WILDERNESS HOSTAGE

JANICE KAY JOHNSON

In memory of my parents, who were ardent mountain climbers. They spent the early years of their marriage in Olympic National Park, where Dad served as a ranger often involved in mountain rescue. I loved picturing those early photos.

Chapter One

Trouble could erupt with little warning. If she weren't so aware of that truth, Cadence Jones could in theory have let herself relax into a day that, so far, had been remarkably trouble free.

An EMT and law enforcement ranger in the wild and mountainous Olympic National Park on the western edge of Washington state, she'd made it through most of the morning without a single alert on her radio. She hadn't so much as issued a ticket for speeding or to campers for lacking the required permit. Plus, once she'd turned off the busy Highway 101 a few minutes ago, she was traveling on a narrow gravel road that plunged into the filtered green light inside some of the most magnificent temperate rainforest in the world as well as offering regular glimpses of the swift-flowing Queets River.

She always remained conscious that she didn't dare let herself be lulled into complacency just because this was part of one of her regular patrol routes. This week, she'd been assigned to the west side of the park. She'd already driven slowly through the parking lots for several of the spectacular Pacific Ocean beaches that drew tourists like flies. This being midweek, even Ruby Beach, with magnificent stacks and rock formations, hadn't been quite as crowded as it would be in another few days. There'd only been a few cars parked in lots for one of the other beaches. That would change in the next weeks once schools were out for the summer.

The current peace didn't mean she wouldn't get a call about a drunk driver, a domestic dispute, an attempted suicide, a stolen car or any other crime, most of which were as common in the national parks as they were in major cities. Staying alert was her *job*.

Truthfully, it was the knot of dread in her stomach that kept her fingers flexing on the steering wheel. She should have already called Garrett. Procrastination never helped, but the talk she had to have with him felt big. No matter how she tried to convince herself that she'd be fine whatever he decided, the pressure squeezing her chest and balling greasily in her stomach didn't relent. She had tomorrow off—barring a major callout for a search and rescue, say— but couldn't remember his schedule. Maybe he could take time to meet her for lunch—it might be just as well if he couldn't afford time for more than a quick meal.

Between one blink and the next, she saw his face, lean, handsome, with blue eyes that too often looked remote. That expression alone had been fair warning that it would be a mistake to get involved with him. She should have known herself better than to think she could enjoy a relationship that was never meant to be lasting.

Cadence took a quick swallow from her water bottle. A deer with two spotted fawns appeared on the road ahead, tugging Cadence's attention back to the here and now, where it belonged. How could she not smile? With their incredibly fragile legs, the fawns bounded after their mother and disappeared into the dense, vividly green undergrowth.

The campground at the end of the Queets Road, her current destination, one of the most remote in the park, was small and primitive, hardly worth checking out, but Cadence liked to keep an eye on trailheads, too. Car prowling was less common than it once had been, given how many vehicles had alarms, but people too often left tempting items lying in plain sight instead of at least tucking them away in the trunk. At the campground, she'd wander to check out who was here and whether everyone had permits and was following regulations and spend some time answering questions.

Knowing the landscape as well as she did, she slowed further at a section of road that occasionally washed out. No problem right now.

An alert sounded on her radio, sending a prickle of electricity through her. Dispatch, seeking *her*.

She acknowledged receipt and gave her current location.

"That's good news," a dispatcher she knew well said, urgency in her voice. "A child is missing at the Queets campground. The parents assumed at first that she wandered away, and other campers are helping look for her, but the mother started getting uneasy about a man who walked by their campsite several times and once started a conversation with the girl when the parents were distracted. The kid is five years old," she added. "The father looked for the man, but can't find him. Every campsite is occupied, and a couple of other people also noticed the guy wandering. They say he wasn't a camper and didn't look as if he'd come back from a hike, either."

Cadence thought immediately about the car that had just passed, but there'd been at least two passengers as well as the driver in it, and her snap impression had been that they *were* hikers or climbers heading out of the park. They'd had that scruffy, several days past a shave look.

Still, she felt enough uneasiness to describe the car and suggest that if a state trooper or county deputy was near enough to stop it once it emerged onto 101, they do so.

At that moment, she saw another vehicle bearing down on her at a speed that far exceeded safety on a narrow gravel road with potholes and often nonexistent shoulders. What's more, the driver had to have spotted her vehicle by now and identified it as law enforcement, but he wasn't slowing down as she'd expect.

Damn it. None of her options were ideal, but she couldn't help making a mental leap to the man who had been too interested in a young girl who had since disappeared. She *couldn't* let this vehicle pass, or depend on county or state law enforcement waiting out at the highway. They were all spread too thin over vast territory.

Gritting her teeth, she made her choice and braked sharply even as she wrenched the steering wheel to steer into position to form a roadblock. She flipped on lights and siren to accentuate her point.

For an ugly moment, she thought the oncoming car might slam right into her SUV. There wasn't room for it to brush by her, or she was sure it would have. It rocked as the driver slammed on brakes and slid to a stop, inches from her passenger door.

The driver, the only apparent occupant of the vehicle, fixed a blistering stare on her. She went on the radio quickly, described the situation and the make, model and color of the car before requesting backup. No license plate number; she couldn't see it from her current angle.

It would be pure luck if a county deputy was close enough to reach her before the situation was resolved, but she could hope.

She used her microphone to order the driver to exit his vehicle. "Now," she commanded sharply. "Keep your hands where I can see them!"

He didn't move. Cadence opened her door and slid around

it so that most of her body was protected by the engine block of her SUV. Then she drew her weapon and aimed it at him.

He was still glaring when, a full minute or two later, he finally opened his car door and stepped out. His head and upper body started to bend, and she suspected he was leaning forward as if to reach for something on the seat or the floorboards.

"Hands in the air!" she yelled. "Back away from your vehicle, sir. I need you to lie on the ground, face down. Do it now!"

There was a noticeable hesitation. Her mind worked furiously. Even if he complied, then what? He was a big enough man that she didn't dare get within reach, which meant she couldn't cuff him. If he didn't offer his wallet, she wouldn't be able to reach for it.

"Write me a ticket," he growled, as he took a step backward, leaving his driver's side door open. "Yeah, I was speeding, but there wasn't any traffic to worry about."

"There is abundant wildlife." His sneer didn't improve her mood. "And *I* happened to be on the road," she added.

"Let me get my registration. My wallet is in my back pocket."

"Lie down on the road. This is not optional."

"You've got no right to treat me like this. What are you, some kind of pseudo cop?"

"I'm a federal law enforcement officer, with all the authority held by an FBI or DEA agent. There is nothing pseudo about my uniform or my authority. *Now lie down*." She waggled the gun.

She hardly dared blink as he slowly lowered himself to his knees.

"Shut the door," she told him.

"Shut it yourself," he snapped with a few ugly words thrown in.

Dispatch informed her that a Jefferson County deputy had turned onto Queets Road and was approaching with all possible speed. She responded, "Copy."

What if it was Garrett? She'd count herself lucky, that's what.

Did she dare approach close enough to kick that door shut? Cadence reluctantly decided not.

"Down," she repeated.

He got as far as his hands and knees, let his head hang for a second, mumbled under his breath, then lunged suddenly toward whatever he wanted to get his hands on so badly.

Cadence fired a single shot underneath the car door, aiming to skim the surface of the road. He fell back, screaming at her. No blood.

"Do as I say!" she snapped. "That was your last warning. Down on your face! Hands in plain sight!"

He complied at last, hate in his eyes. If he held a weapon, she'd be dead, she thought. She evaluated him, guessing him to be in his forties with the muscles of someone who worked out on a regular basis. A tattoo showed above the collar of his white T-shirt. He wore cargo pants and boots meant for kicking butt, not climbing or hiking.

What if it turned out speeding was the total of his offenses? Would she be in trouble for firing her gun? Her gut said she'd done what she had to—and that they'd find he had a handgun stashed beneath the seat of his car.

Out of nowhere, nausea struck her, as it had erratically the past week or ten days. With unpredictable bouts of misery and an occasional knees-down visits to toilets, this had to be a flu bug. She wouldn't let herself believe anything else.

She was sweating now, even in the relative cool in the shade of the giant trees, and her hands trembled. She kept her elbows locked and resolutely swallowed the bile that wanted to rise. *Not now,* she told herself desperately.

If only she could move on him, cuff him, look inside the car and especially open the trunk of his car, but the risk was too great. Especially now that backup would be arriving within the next five or ten minutes.

Those minutes crawled. Her nausea slowly receded. She prayed no innocent camper would appear. Onlookers were prone to getting out of their vehicles, asking questions, distracting an arresting officer, even ignoring orders to stay back. Instinct told her this situation was genuinely dangerous, no misunderstanding. A few birds called, making her realize they'd been silent initially during the confrontation, but life was resuming around her. There was another sound, too. She cocked her head. Thin and high. Her certainty hardened.

A few minutes later, she heard an approaching engine. *Let it be the deputy.*

The crunch of gravel and a single blast of a siren were incredibly welcome. A green-clad deputy appeared beside her. Not Garrett, but she'd worked before with Gary Vickers.

"Thanks for coming." She sounded steadier than she felt. "The suspect keeps trying for something on the floorboard of his car. I'd appreciate it if you could cuff him."

"My pleasure." Maybe in his late forties, Vickers was solidly built and had always appeared sharp and competent when he'd backed her up—or, once, when she'd backed him up.

The man's hate-filled stare never left her face even as the deputy walked around the back of her park service issued SUV and approached the prone man from his blind side. With her having already demonstrated her willingness to fire her gun, there was no fight when Vickers cuffed him and ordered him to stand. Within minutes, the suspect had been searched and shoved to the sheriff's department vehicle.

Turning to watch as he was locked in the cage, Cadence let her arms sag before she holstered her gun. That she'd fired it meant a whole new level of paperwork, but right now she didn't care.

She hustled to the open door of the car, joined by Vickers, whose eyebrows rose as he saw what she did—a semi-automatic pistol lying almost under the driver's seat. Then Cadence yanked a thin latex glove from her pocket, donned it and said, "You're my witness," as she pulled the lever to unlatch the trunk lid.

They both heard the whimpers even before Cadence made it far enough to see the little girl curled around a spare tire.

GARRETT WYCOFF HAD stiffened when he heard the request for backup. Jefferson County stretched across the Olympic National Park, which meant deputies policed a stretch of the county on the ocean side, but most operations were east of the park instead, including Hood Canal and other waterways. The two parts of the county were severed by the park, the drive from one side to the other lengthy. Right now, he wasn't where he wanted to be.

He'd just responded to the report of a theft in the tiny community of Brinnon along Highway 101, which almost circled the peninsula. A resident had returned from a long weekend visiting family to find a window broken and a new smart TV stolen. Nothing else was obviously missing from the log A-frame, which made Garrett suspect the burglar was an acquaintance and very possibly a local resident who knew about the new flat-screen TV.

After taking the report, he'd been about to turn onto the highway to resume patrolling when he heard the request for backup from a park ranger and the subsequent communications. He'd never heard such stress in Cadence's voice, and his whole body had tightened with a need to be where he could help. Vickers was good, though, which was a relief. That didn't mean Garrett could make himself do a damn thing but listen and wait. A child had gone missing, but he didn't know how that connected to a speeding driver on Queets Road who wasn't complying with orders.

He reassured himself that Cadence was sharp, fit and experienced. As a slender woman who didn't even top five foot five inches, she had a vulnerability he didn't. And yeah, that scared him, an admission he didn't want to make. He'd been enjoying their casual relationship. He didn't think he'd ever had better sex in his life, and their jobs gave them a lot in common. They both loved getting away into the backcountry. They'd climbed a couple of peaks together. Conversation never flagged when he was with her, but because of their conflicting schedules days went by between them meeting up even for a meal. He frowned. He hadn't seen her in nearly a week, which he'd been unhappy about.

Yet another acknowledgment to make him edgy. He wasn't even sure he was capable of seriously falling for a woman, but never intended to let that happen. He'd drawn a line at the beginning, which she had respected. He couldn't, wouldn't, let that line blur.

No, he'd be tense when something like this was happening that involved any of his coworkers or the park rangers he'd gotten to know.

Vickers spoke briefly on the radio to report the suspect was in the back of his vehicle ready for transport to the jail in Port Hadlock. Long drive knowing someone is drilling the back of your head with a death stare.

Moments later, he identified himself again and said that the suspect had had a semiautomatic beneath his driver's seat and had apparently been going for it when LE Ranger Jones had fired her weapon to force him to return to his prone position. The deputy sounded exultant when he added that the missing child had been in the trunk of the suspect's car. She was terrified but appeared uninjured.

Cadence came on to say that she was transporting the girl to the Queets campground to reunite her with the parents, and that she'd escort them to the hospital in Forks for the child to be evaluated. A special agent chimed in that he was on the way to the scene to examine the car and would also arrange a tow.

Garrett let out a long breath and bumped his head on his steering wheel a couple of times. All was well. Nothing for him to get worked up about, and no excuse for him to have wasted the past twenty minutes. He'd call Cadence tonight and congratulate her for recovering the girl who'd been snatched and arresting the kidnapper. Maybe she'd be free in the next couple of days.

He'd barely merged onto the highway when he saw that the car in front of him was weaving subtly. License plate… he looked it up and was unsurprised by the confirmation that he'd had more contact with the driver than he'd like. Lyle Kellam was drunk more than he was sober. Alcoholics Anonymous always did temporary wonders for the man— until he relapsed. He'd looked good the last time Garrett had seen him at the grocery store in Quilcene, up the road a ways. Given that this was midafternoon, you'd have thought he could hold out for his first drink of the day until he made it home, but apparently temptation had overcome him.

Garrett used lights and siren to get Lyle's attention, and then rode his bumper when that didn't initially work. Once Lyle pulled over, his right front tire turned halfway into a ditch, Garrett walked up, tapped on the window and bent over to see a man who always made him think of an elf with oversize ears, a tuft of white hair and eyes as blue as his own.

Lyle rolled down the window and peered owlishly at him. "You again? I'm almost home."

It's true that he was. Lyle hadn't actually crossed the double yellow line. He gritted his teeth and made a decision.

"I'll follow you home," he said, "but you know what the consequences will be the next time we verify that you're driving under the influence." Significant jail time was what he meant.

Lyle slumped. "I know. I'll call my sponsor. I swear I will."

Maybe. But Garrett didn't renege on his decision to let this slide. He did follow closely as Lyle drove the half a mile to the turnoff to his ramshackle house. Then Garrett blinked his headlights and accelerated to highway speed.

The next hour was uneventful enough to have him wondering if his grandfather really needed him anymore. Seattle PD would take him back, he knew. His goal had always been to work as a detective, not to spend a career pulling over speeders or investigating the theft of a single item from a home. He hadn't minded while his grandfather had depended on him, but that didn't mean he had ever intended to move to this rural county permanently. Yeah, there were rewards, like really getting to know residents, but—

His phone rang and when he saw Cadence's name, Garrett pulled onto the shoulder of the road and answered.

"Hey," she said.

"Exciting day."

"You could say so." The smile he had no trouble seeing sounded in her voice. "Scary, too. Still, you should have seen the expression on her parents' faces."

"Yeah. That makes the job worth it."

"It does." There was a pause. "I'm off tomorrow. Can we meet for lunch?"

Her tone had changed, but he couldn't put his finger on how. "I'm not," he said, "but sure, if you can make it over my way."

"Blue Moose?"

"Perfect." The café in historic Port Townsend, once a logging town and the customs stop for any ship entering the

Puget Sound, was a favorite of his and Cadence's. Food was good, there were plenty of vegetarian choices for her, and the quaint atmosphere included smoothly polished wooden booths.

They set a time and she ended the call abruptly, leaving him…wondering. Telling himself he'd imagined there was anything odd in her tone.

Chapter Two

Cadence was the first to arrive, sliding into one of the smooth wood booths so that she faced the entry. Garrett would try to persuade her to switch, since like most cops, he preferred not to have his back to the entrance or other diners. It had become a lighthearted competition between them, whoever got there first winning, although in truth she didn't care that much.

On a pang, she thought maybe today she'd surprise him by voluntarily giving way, since the chances were good this would be their last meal together.

When he walked in a couple of minutes later, effortlessly dominating the space with his broad-shouldered, six-foot-three frame along with sheer magnetism, only one other booth was occupied. He'd needed to take his break early. Cadence had been glad. She wanted to get this over with.

His gaze locked onto hers, giving the impression that he saw only her. Maybe that was true; in the initial split seconds, he'd undoubtedly already evaluated the quaint restaurant and the few customers and staff, all of whom she knew were watching him. He'd grab attention no matter what, but today he was in uniform besides, wearing a vest that added bulk and the belt that held his holstered gun and a bunch of other paraphernalia. *She* certainly couldn't look away.

As always, the sight of him made her instantly breathless, a little dizzy. When he reached the table, he stood gazing down at her for a minute. A few lines she didn't recognize creased his forehead.

"I listened to your stop yesterday," he said. "I hear you had to discharge your weapon."

She made a face. "I did. After that, I was left thinking about the uproar if I'd risked shooting a guy who hadn't done anything worse than drive recklessly."

"But you knew better," he said, as if he'd never doubted her. His calm and faith in her let her breathe again, although her smile was probably more a grimace.

He slid into the open side of the booth without comment on their silly competition. A waitress hustled up, offering menus neither needed. Both ordered. Once they were alone, he reached across the table for her hand.

"You okay?"

"Of course I am."

He nodded acceptance.

"How's your grandfather?" She always asked, even though she hadn't met the man, had never been invited to the hundred-year-old house where Cliff Wycoff had lived for his entire lifetime. The house where his grandson now lived, too. She'd been so tempted to drive by just to see it, but always resisted.

That house and knowing how important his grandfather was to Garrett were a big part of why Cadence had made the decision to talk to him now. Garrett had never invited her home or to meet the man who he had described as his only family. Their sexual encounters took place elsewhere, including her substandard trailer on occasions when her two roommates were working, tents when she and Garrett backpacked and climbed, even motel rooms a few times. How sleazy was that? Better question: how had she convinced herself she didn't mind?

"Better enough to be getting ornery." Garrett half smiled. "Doesn't like me telling him he's doing too much." She knew his grandfather had had a heart attack followed by a four-way bypass.

"I imagine that's normal."

"It's a good sign," he admitted.

Subject closed.

Their food arrived, and she discovered she was ravenous. Breakfast had been half a toasted bagel, dry, to quell the queasiness that vanished an hour later. The swing between nausea and sharp hunger had characterized this week. Perhaps it was mild food poisoning. Right? Nothing else... In any case, it was not pleasant.

They talked in a desultory way about politics in the sheriff's department, a couple of concerning crimes that had happened in neighboring counties and the expected flood of visitors in the upcoming week or two when summer season really took off.

Finally, he asked, "This the only day you're free?"

"I'm not entirely free." She pretended to concentrate on the last bite of her giant cookie. "Dan Becker—do you know him?—is leaving us. Not the usual time of year, but he's wanted to work at Denali and they had a sudden opening. We're throwing him a party."

She could invite him, but he rarely accepted when she suggested this kind of event, even though many of her co-workers had seen them together. She'd been foolish enough to convince herself that he didn't love the heavy drinking that often ensued, or the fact that he was an outsider. Another waving red flag, she thought; God forbid he appear too much like an actual boyfriend who wanted to get to know her friends. Even if he didn't enjoy himself, it wasn't as if they couldn't have made a brief appearance and then left.

Disappointment showed on his face, but he didn't say, *Maybe I could get there*, even though he knew Dan. Nope, he was disappointed because he wouldn't get laid tonight.

Too bad, so sad.

Except, she loved the passion they shared, the extraordinary sense of intimacy she'd never felt before. The tenderness that flavored the lust.

He shifted on his seat and produced his wallet. "Let me get this one. I'd probably better get back to work."

"There's something I wanted to ask you about first," she made herself say, "but why don't we walk out together?"

His vivid blue eyes narrowed slightly, but he only nodded, tossed a few bills on the table and gestured her to go ahead.

Cadence waited until he'd walked her to her car, an aging Toyota Corolla. Her chest felt tighter and tighter. Oh, this was hard. *I could wait and see instead of pushing*, the coward in her thought. Maybe she was expecting too much, too fast. But then she pictured him saying one day, *Hey, I'm sorry but I've met someone else*. They'd been dating—okay, sleeping together—for four months now. If he hadn't started falling in love with her in that length of time, it wasn't happening.

Get it over with.

She unlocked, opened her car door to facilitate a quicker getaway and folded her arms on top of the door. "You made it plain when we started seeing each other that you weren't interested in any commitment. That long-term wasn't for you."

He recoiled, even taking a step back.

Cadence tried not to flinch. Instead, she lifted her chin. "I'm asking now if you've changed your mind. If there's any chance—"

"You're not happy with how things are?" he asked roughly.

"No. I'm sorry to put you on the spot like this, but the

truth is, I never should have agreed to this. I'm…not really into casual. I've started feeling too much. If I keep seeing you, I'll get hurt." *More than I already am.* "We're good together, Garrett. Really good. I wanted to be up-front with you, see if you feel the same."

Was that panic in his eyes? She couldn't tell, but whatever it was didn't bode well for her.

"I don't want to lose you, but I can't go there," he said. His hands had fisted at his sides.

Pain roared through her, but she held on to her dignity and nodded. "That's what I thought you'd say. In that case, I need to call it quits." She shrugged. "I'm sure we'll run into each other as long as we're both working here. Let's not make it a big deal, okay?" She threw in a "Thanks for lunch" without looking at him again. Instead, she lowered herself into her car, pulled her door shut and shoved the key in the ignition. From her peripheral vision, she saw him backing up but not turning away. In fact, when she turned onto the street, he still stood in the middle of the small parking lot, watching her go.

Which meant she had to zigzag several blocks before she could pull to the curb, set the emergency brake and let herself give way to grief.

It was a good half an hour before she pulled herself together enough to know what she had to do next. If she was wrong about the flu bug, if she were pregnant, she had to face reality. It would change her life in ways she hadn't yet let herself detail, but she had time to come to terms with all that.

And yes, if that was true, she'd tell Garrett. She owed him that much, and he'd owe her some support, too. But now she knew: however much obligation he felt toward her and his unborn child, he didn't love her, couldn't love her. She'd needed to know in case he'd reacted to the news of a pregnancy with a sense of obligation that led him to say things he didn't mean.

She was getting ahead of herself. She'd been trying really hard to convince herself that she was feeling cramps, her period would start any minute, she really had a virus responsible for the icky stomach.

But she knew. She knew.

WHAT IN HELL had just happened? Garrett had the surreal feeling that a car had just hit him and his body was flying through the air. That he'd slam to the ground any minute.

Instead he stood stock-still in that damned parking lot even after Cadence's car was gone.

How had this blown up? She was right; things *were* really good between them. Making love with her wasn't like anything else he'd ever experienced. When they weren't getting together, he thought about her. He made excuses to call just to hear her voice. Something had happened to him the minute he saw her the first time. It wasn't just her looks, although she was beautiful and in a distinctive way. Slender and fine boned, she had skin that was tinted gold, deep brown eyes that tilted up slightly at the outer edges and thick dark hair—not black, but close—that flowed almost to her waist when she released it from the usual braid or knot at her nape that kept it out of her way. He had wanted to put his hands on her more than he'd wanted much of anything in his life, which was something.

He groaned and let his head fall forward, reaching up to knead taut muscles in his neck. He'd let himself get lulled into complacency, damn it. He knew better. Even his grandfather had been asking about "that woman" he'd been seeing, and when Garrett was planning to bring her home to meet him. He'd avoided saying, *Never*, partly because integrating her more into his life would have been natural even if he couldn't see marriage on the horizon.

Was she insulted because he *hadn't* introduced her to the man who was his sole family?

Of course she was.

Honestly, until a few years back, he'd never had family, so that hadn't been an option. He'd disliked bringing women home to his apartment. Instinct had always insisted he compartmentalize. There was the job, there was sex and then there was his stark, lonely home life—although he'd never identified it to himself as lonely.

After his childhood, lonely was a synonym for peaceful.

Things had been different since he tracked down the grandfather he hadn't known he had, and particularly since he'd willingly quit his job with Seattle PD to come to this barely populated county on the edge of the world because he was needed by someone. First time in his life. Maybe that's what had softened him, let him start feeling too much for Cadence Jones. More than was safe.

He'd already known that was a problem, just…hadn't dealt with it.

Well, she'd taken care of that, hadn't she? She'd asked an honest question, and he'd answered honestly: he wasn't ready for anything like what she was suggesting.

Garrett realized how conspicuous he must be, standing here like an old-growth tree in the park that had been blasted by lightning but refused to fall. He retreated to his department SUV, fired up the engine but sat unmoving behind the wheel.

Had something in particular happened to make Cadence confront him like this? She'd met someone else? Had an opportunity to transfer to another park, as her coworker had? Maybe yesterday she'd been hit by the knowledge of how quickly a scene like that could turn sideways. Truly seeing her mortality might have made her reevaluate a relationship that wasn't going anywhere.

Or she could have been saying, *I'm falling in love with you.*

If he'd asked her, would she have answered? And did it matter, anyway?

Garrett had always known that he was protecting himself, but he didn't know any other way and couldn't see baring his belly for some woman to savage him.

Would Cadence do that?

He shook his head hard. Didn't matter. Except he knew that the next time he heard her on the radio when she was making a frightening stop, or rappelling off one of the rock faces of an Olympic Mountain crag on her own to try to save a climber who wouldn't survive until other help arrived, he'd hate it every bit as much as he had yesterday.

CADENCE GROCERY SHOPPED, made a separate trip to a pharmacy for a pregnancy test, but after seeing a couple of people she knew at QFC, decided instead to pick up a uniform she'd had dry-cleaned and, once she got home and found both roommates there. So she bundled up her dirty clothes and sheets for a trip to the laundromat. Better to stay busy. She could slip away this evening to be alone. Bethany and Tierra loved parties and were likely to hook up with guys and not make it back to their own beds tonight at all.

She wouldn't stay any longer than she had to tonight, and she could surreptitiously pour out any drinks she was handed. Booze of any kind didn't sound good at the moment anyway.

She browsed news on her phone while she waited to move her laundry to the dryer and then spotted a couple of several month-old magazines that she could at least pretend interest in until the two dryers stopped. Lugging the baskets of folded clean clothes and sheets out to the car, she was grateful to have completed a chore she too often put off. Honestly, the hours she worked, she rarely managed a real day off. It was a miracle she hadn't been called to join a rescue.

Midweek, she reminded herself. Just wait until this weekend, and then July and August when the park really got slammed with visitors. This and all other national parks were always understaffed, which was a real problem when life-and-death crises arose so often. Glacier melt–swollen rivers, serious climbing rock, powerful ocean waves with an undertow and inadequately prepared tourists kept her too busy to sleep or eat sometimes, far less think about the heaps of dirty laundry at the foot of her bed.

Could she *do* the job if—?

Too soon to worry about.

She changed into a cute sundress and went to the party whether she was in the mood or not. She smiled for all she was worth, while surrounded by boisterous coworkers—rangers and concession workers both. The concession workers especially were a hard-drinking bunch—their pay was lousy, many were college students who liked the idea of a summer job in a spectacularly beautiful piece of this country—and because Dan Becker was an ardent mountain climber, a bunch of climbers who somehow never quite held jobs showed up, too.

Cadence gave Dan a big hug, admitted that Denali was not on her wish list—too much snow and ice, too many times rangers had to fly in small planes and helicopters—and unobtrusively separated herself from the cluster around her before slipping away into the darkness, finding her car and retreating to her not-so-cozy home away from home.

Sad to say, given that she was in her thirties, the word *home* still brought to mind a 1940s bungalow where she'd grown up, where her parents and Oliver still lived in Idaho.

Certainly not this cramped, shared space where she slept and not much else. But as much as she loved her family, she didn't really want to go home.

She wanted her own. Seeing Garrett in her mind's eye and knowing she wanted that home with him, a knife blade of pain plunged into her chest.

She'd get over him. She would.

Cadence carefully hung her sundress back up in the minuscule closet and put on the pajama shorts and T-shirt she wore to bed. Then she locked herself in the bathroom even though no one else was here, read the instructions on the box and followed them. The short wait after she peed on the stick was excruciating.

The answer…not really a surprise. But it was as terrifying, as life altering, as she'd known it would be.

Chapter Three

A pair of cop killers, on the run.

Utilizing lights and siren, Garrett drove too fast for narrow roads, set on reaching Highway 104 to block the SUV speeding away from the crime scene from being able to cross on the Hood Canal Bridge. Grimly determined to prevent them from escaping, he swore under his breath every time he had to swerve around a slow-moving vehicle driven by someone who managed to be oblivious to the lights and siren.

This week, Garrett was filling in for an absent sergeant in the patrol division. Technically, he'd been hired as a patrol deputy, but because of his background, he was used for a variety of other roles, including filling in for or backing up the two detectives and the detective sergeant. He expected to be out on the road today, too; there were never enough bodies to cover multiple shifts and the miles of Jefferson County as well as the waterways. Plus, while the largest city in the county, Port Townsend, had its own police department, after hours and on weekends Dispatch diverted those calls to the sheriff's department, too.

Unfortunately, early morning was the worst time of day to have a crisis. Night shift, already scanty, would be heading for the station to sign off; day shift might not be there yet.

He'd gotten into the station at the crack of dawn. He hadn't been sleeping anyway, so why not? He needed distraction from the hamster wheel of thoughts about the woman who'd dumped him. He'd just sat down to look at the night's activity when the phone rang. He recognized the number right away. He'd gotten to know the Clallam County chief criminal deputy, and felt sure a call this early in the morning wasn't meant to exchange chit-chat.

"Wycoff," he answered.

"We have a problem that's heading your way," he was told tersely. "There was a break-in at a gun shop between Port Angeles and Sequim. An explosive was used to blast a hole in a cinder block wall."

Garrett absorbed that. "What if ammunition had been stored on the other side of that wall?"

"The fact that it wasn't is one reason I assume they'd cased the shop. We'll be examining security footage." The chief deputy continued, "The alarm went off. What's more, the owner of the tattoo parlor that's attached to the gun store was sleeping there. He ran out to see what was happening and got shot. A deputy who happened to be close by responded to the alarm and was gunned down, too." Anger simmered in the brief pause. "Didn't even have a chance to get out of his vehicle or draw his weapon. He's dead. The tattoo shop owner is badly injured, but he was able to tell us that while he lay on the ground bleeding, he saw two men throwing guns and boxes of ammunition into the back of a big black SUV. Tahoe, is his best guess. They took off maybe ten minutes ago, speeding east on 101."

Unless the men were locals, what had they been thinking? The only real highway was pinched between the mountains and the water—the Pacific Ocean to the west, the Strait of Juan de Fuca to the north and Hood Canal to the east. Did they realize the problem with their escape route, or had they assumed they could load the guns and be on their way, anonymous?

Shaking his head, he said, "I'll see to setting up road-blocks. We can't let them get to anyplace more populous."

"I was hoping you'd say that."

"License plate?"

"No outside security camera. Washington state plate, the witness thinks."

The chief deputy promised to keep him updated as they searched the scene.

Garrett spoke to Dispatch to reposition deputies already out on patrol, then made calls to get more out of bed. He assumed Clallam County deputies were on alert in case the pair changed their mind and thought they could do a U-turn and head west instead, to join the tourists traveling through Forks and down the Pacific Coast.

He called the sheriff, who agreed with his intentions, then leaped into his own vehicle to be part of the blockade where Highway 104 turned east from 101. This would be a dangerous stop, if it could be made at all; the two men were apparently in possession of a virtually unlimited number of weapons and all the ammunition they wanted. They'd killed a cop, which meant they had nothing else to lose.

Even as his attention stayed on the road ahead, he listened to radio traffic and calculated tactics. He tensed when national park law enforcement was brought in, but thought it unlikely they'd have reason to get involved in this mess. Even the air force base on Whidbey Island received a notification. The base provided a helicopter when one was needed for either the Olympic or Cascade National Park. They agreed to have one ready to go when needed.

One deputy after another checked in, unfamiliar tension in voices. Garrett wasn't quite in position when one of his deputies came on.

"Black SUV just blew past me. It went by the turn to 104 and is continuing south on 101. I repeat: it's continuing south, and I am in pursuit, although by the time I got up to speed, I lost a visual."

"Did you get a license plate?"

"No, sorry."

Garrett ordered urgently, "Pursuit only, do not attempt on your own to pull over this vehicle." He looked at his dashboard clock. Damn. More time had passed than he liked. As the day advanced at high season, Highway 101 on the scenic Olympic Peninsula could rival stretches of I-5 in Seattle with rush hour approaching. Climbers and hikers wanted to get an early start. Unfortunately, 101 was mostly two-lane, which made a vehicle exceeding the speed limit beyond dangerous. A high-speed chase was too risky. Anyone who'd seen the result of a head-on, high-impact collision never forgot it.

"Have you regained a visual?" he asked a minute later.

"No. Traffic is picking up."

He made a decision he didn't like, but the only one he could make. "Discontinue pursuit." Several deputies were already south of the sighting, and he instructed them to set up where they could see the highway and wait. There were a few turnoffs, but not many; one led back north to Highway 104, and he placed one deputy in a place to watch for just that as he accelerated again on a back road that would connect with the highway at the town of Quilcene.

Since for now the sheriff seemed to be leaving the logistics in his hands, Garrett asked that he contact neighboring jurisdictions, just in case. He was sure he'd heard about a couple of hits on gun shops in surrounding areas. He always made a mental note about crimes that stood out. One had been in Bremerton in Kitsap County, if he remembered right, and another down toward Olympia, the state capitol. Shelton, maybe? He didn't think either had resulted in deaths, but a break-in this bold didn't have the feel of a first attempt to him. A number of previous successes would explain this hit, both brazen and poorly thought out. Apparently, it hadn't occurred to the men that there'd be a glitch that would mean trouble escaping.

Word filtered in from deputies. There were no sightings of a vehicle that matched the description given, certainly not one speeding. There weren't any real alternatives to the highway, not with how close the water was on one side and wilderness areas to the other. That didn't mean the men, running scared, hadn't taken a minor road or even a dirt one with the intention of hunkering down long enough to make law enforcement relax the intensity of the hunt. Several small towns hugged the highway and isolated homes could be vulnerable right now.

Primitive logging or forest service roads offered access to wilderness and national forest areas outside the park, too. Those tended to wind around like a pile of yarn dumped on a floor, but blocked by the national park and the formidable mountains to the west, those roads didn't *go* anywhere. Sooner or later, the hunted men would be dumped back out on Highway 101. The number one priority for sheriff's department deputies was to watch for that reappearance.

He stayed on the radio, adjusting deputies and praying nobody else committed a crime this morning. If so, the victim wouldn't get a prompt response—unless the caller reported a home invasion by two big guys waving guns.

Quilcene was the largest of the few tiny towns that hugged Dabob Bay, a long finger of water separate from Hood Canal. Highway 101 took a sharp bend here that required traffic to slow down, but the town was also the radius of a number of residential streets and, south of Quilcene, Penny Creek Road, which narrowed to one lane that eventually turned to gravel and split several times without any directional signs.

Like every other road heading west into the wilderness, all were dead end.

Where the hell had those men gone, and what would panic drive them to do?

SHOCKED BY THE unfolding manhunt that was dominating radio traffic, Cadence was almost surprised when an alert regarding an injured hiker cut through the intense, strained orders and responses. She was sent to North Shore Road on the southern boundary of the park. Within the park, the road split and became narrow and jarring to drive as she followed the north fork of the Quinault River until she reached the necessary trailhead. Families who wanted a short hike could go only as far as Irely Lake, but the trail continued, eventually connecting with others deep in the interior of the park. It provided access for climbers to a number of peaks, too.

In the back of her vehicle, she always carried an advanced life support bag as well as miscellaneous other medical supplies, a folding gurney on wheels and a more typical backpack that she'd have to carry on a rescue deeper in the park. This hiker, however, had twisted or broken an ankle before the party had reached the lake, not a long walk by her standards.

Assuming, of course, that the information was correct. Too often, what really had happened was garbled by the time it reached her, if it hadn't been in the original telling. She parked, glanced at the cluster of empty vehicles from a Volkswagen Bug to a camper, got out and decided to take only the most necessary medical supplies. She could jog back to get the gurney if necessary.

Her radio crackled. Dispatch directed all deputies to maintain position. Despite an even tone, the voice carried unusual tension. She should be out there, too, but had to wait for orders.

The men who'd committed a gun shop break-in, killed a Clallam County deputy and injured another store owner had vanished somewhere between the turnoff to Highway 104 and Leland, a mere dot on the map where a deputy waited tucked almost out of sight off the highway.

Kitsap County deputies hovered on the far side of the Hood Canal Bridge in case the fugitives succeeded in breaking that way. Clallam County deputies, especially angry after the murder of one of their own, were spread to the north. Mason County, to the south, was on alert. State patrol troopers put themselves under the direction of the Jefferson County Sheriff's Department.

Early on, Cadence had heard Garrett's voice, calm and decisive. Unless someone else had taken over, *he* was directing this manhunt. Somehow, that didn't surprise her; he exuded an air of command. Plus, she also knew that he filled in for sick or vacationing people in the department. Heaven knows, she thought, not quite facetiously, maybe he'd become sheriff for the day.

She felt sure that he wasn't issuing those orders from the safety of the department headquarters in Port Hadlock. No, if there was any conceivable way he could achieve it, he'd be in on the takedown.

She wanted to be able to dismiss her fear for him, which was completely unfounded at the moment. What were the odds he'd be the one in position to see the fugitives when they reappeared? Even if he happened to be, he was capable.Having seen him in action, she knew that. Coming from a major urban police force, he was likely the best trained member of this rural sheriff's department.

But telling herself to knock it off didn't accomplish a thing. She was scared and couldn't wipe from her mind a picture of him reeling from a blast of automatic gunfire.

The shock, the loss of his powerful personality until only vacancy was left.

She couldn't seem to find her usual confident, centered self. It had to be an aftereffect of her close call last week. Where normally she put a tense encounter behind her, she kept reliving this one. Things could so easily have gone wrong. She knew all too well that it took only a split second. If kidnapper Raymond Miller had ducked and grabbed the gun initially and come up firing, or later completed his lunge for the weapon beneath his car seat despite her warning shot, she could be dead. Unlike him, she'd been wearing a vest, but she couldn't return fire without lifting her head above the hood of her vehicle. He could have—

Damn, damn, damn.

He hadn't. Even if he had gotten his hands on that gun, she excelled at her job. She trained regularly at a range, something he was unlikely to do. He was a pedophile—who she'd interrupted from being able to hurt that little girl—not a sharpshooter. And the incident wasn't the first time in her career she'd been threatened. It wouldn't be the last, either—unless this pregnancy derailed that career.

And, yes, for all her self-denial, last week she'd strongly suspected she was pregnant. The awareness made her feel more vulnerable than usual. She wanted this baby with a ferocity she hardly recognized in herself.

Caught up in her thoughts, she stumbled over a half-buried rock. As she recovered her footing, she lectured herself. How about paying attention to her surroundings, a concept that was usually second nature to her?

At a shout from ahead, Cadence saw four people approaching, two men and two women. One man and the taller of the two women were supporting the other guy, who was managing to walk while putting little-to-no weight on his right leg.

For once, the information she'd received was correct, except the hikers had decided to start making their own way down to the trailhead and their vehicle. All four looked to be in their early twenties, one couple wearing hiking boots, the other two only athletic shoes. Naturally, the injured guy lacked the boots that would have better supported his ankle.

Approaching, she smiled, pushed back her anxiety and introduced herself. She helped as they gently lowered the man to a seat on a fallen log, after which she crouched, pushed up the leg of his trousers and eased down his sock. There was definitely significant swelling and the beginnings of discoloration.

She gently probed, had him rotate his foot and decided to crack open an ice pack.

Placing the ice, she said, "I don't think your ankle is broken, but I can't be sure. You need to get an X-ray. I suspect a strain, which can be almost as slow to heal as a break."

Noticeably sweating, he grimaced.

"You expected back at a job soon?"

"Next week, but I work on a computer and mostly remotely."

"Ah." Cadence raised her gaze to the others. "Have you given him any painkillers?"

"Tylenol," said the woman staying close to his side.

"Okay. Well, once the ice does its part, I'll help you get him the rest of the way down the trail. Then I recommend you drive him to a clinic or hospital. Unfortunately, you're going to have to go a distance."

The whole time, Cadence listened with half an ear to the occasional terse comments on the radio. Nothing new.

Eventually, she wrapped the ankle with an ACE bandage to give it additional support and took the place of the obviously exhausted girlfriend to help the injured man hobble the rest of the way. He was placed in the back seat of a Subaru

Forester, his ankle elevated on his girlfriend's lap. Cadence collected enough information from them for her required report, gave them directions to the nearest medical clinic, and as she watched them drive away, radioed in so Dispatch knew she was once again available.

Why wasn't she being sent as reinforcement in the on-going search for the cop killers? But she knew the answer. This was a busy week in the park, and there'd be plenty of calls on her time. *Someone* had to be available to look for straying children, provide medical services to folks who overextended themselves and more. Plus, there were few park entrances south of Quilcene, and since the washout at the Dosewallips River, no entrances could be driven up to until the Staircase Ranger Station. It could be reached by a couple of roads leading to Lake Cushman, which lay outside the national park and thus was surrounded by rustic resorts, vacation rentals, boat launches and campgrounds.

Getting trapped on a dead-end road in one of the wilderness areas or the national park would mean the two men on the run would have to abandon their vehicle and most of the stolen weaponry. Why would they do that? No, since they'd already missed their chance to cross Hood Canal, their goal had to be continuing south toward Shelton, a good-size town, and beyond that the city of Olympia—whatever they had to do to elude the net being cast by law enforcement.

Garrett was clearly intent on *not* letting them escape. In fact, of bottling them up in a rural area where hiding for any length of time would be difficult.

Cadence had to believe the men would be spotted any-time. What worried her most was how a stop would be made. Could even a couple of deputies working together persuade desperate, heavily armed men to pull to the side of the road and docilely submit to an arrest?

Chapter Four

The day was incredibly frustrating. In the next few hours, there were a couple of possible sightings that didn't pan out. Nerves stayed on edge. At length, the sheriff took over as incident commander while Garrett set out to hunt down background on the two men—assuming his instincts concerning them were good.

He spoke again to the deputy chief in Clallam County, who reported that it appeared the burglars had tried to disable the alarm before they set off the dynamite. They might have believed they had succeeded, which meant the blaring alarm had thrown them. Their decision to go ahead with the burglary despite the alarm said a lot about them. If they'd ever looked at a map, they had to have known fleeing was tricky, given the lack of alternative routes. Too, they'd responded to witnesses with instant, deadly violence, no apparent hesitation.

Garrett pursued his memories of previous, similar crimes by making multiple phone calls.

"If it's the same guys," a Bremerton detective told him, "they've made some changes. The gun shop that was hit here is only technically in the city limits. It's actually pretty isolated, which allowed it to have an outdoor range as well as an indoor one."

"This one was outside town, too—and the city of Sequim is pretty stretched out along the highway. The only other business close was the tattoo parlor that shares the building."

"Your injured man."

"Yeah."

He grunted. "We got them on security camera, for what good that did us. They drove a Hummer with a blade mounted on the front. Smashed right through the wall. I learned later that a National Guard armory was broken into that way, too. Years ago, but you have to wonder if that's not how they got the idea. Anyway, they did disable the alarm, but we could still watch them on the security feed. Not much help, as you can imagine. They wore something dark over their heads, gloves so they left no prints. The blade on the Hummer hid any license plate, and once they'd loaded as much as they could get in, they backed away just far enough to keep us from seeing the back plate. Once they swung around and took off, the picture just wasn't good enough for us to make out that kind of detail on the plate, even though the techs really worked at it. All I can tell you for sure is that two men did the job. Both were big and noticeably bulked up. We made some calls to gyms in the area, but nothing panned out."

"That fits the description of these two we have from the neighboring shop owner who survived being shot."

"I can have someone send you our footage, for what that's worth."

Garrett thanked him, and said, "The shop owner is out of surgery and the prognosis is good."

"That's something," the detective said, "but the cold-blooded murder of a deputy?"

What was there to say about that?

"Not so surprising they're driving something different,"

Detective Jacobsen continued. "You kinda look when a Hummer passes. You know?"

Garrett knew.

"I remember hearing about a gun shop robbery in the Shelton area maybe a year and a half ago, but there's been another similar heist since that caught my eye because of our open case. I want to say down Hoquiam way. Aberdeen, maybe?"

"If we drew a circle to encompass these hits," Garrett said, envisioning a map, "what do you want to bet the perpetrators live somewhere in the middle?"

"Wouldn't bet against you," Jacobsen said. "As it happens, Shelton was first, if I remember right. Makes me wonder if they aren't locals there. If so, it would have made sense for them to go farther afield the next time they decided to restock their merchandise."

Garrett's sense of humor was at a low edge for a lot of reasons, but he grunted a laugh. How *were* these guys selling the weapons? Online? What if they owned a gun shop themselves?

Still sounding steamed, a Mason County detective spoke freely about the armed robbery that had happened in his jurisdiction. An armed robbery was what it had been, only there'd been three participants, one of them a woman. They'd rushed in at closing, heavily armed, yelling orders, spraying a few bullets when an employee behind the counter reached for his weapon. He'd been wounded but survived; the woman had held a semiautomatic on him and the remaining man in the shop—a customer—while the two big guys grabbed and loaded. Then all three backed out and they fled at high speed.

"They were in a black SUV. We got a license plate, but it turned out to have been taken from a stolen vehicle that never was located. Neither were they. They had to have known the area well, maybe had a bolt-hole close by. Use a remote to raise your garage door, close it behind you and you've disappeared. Man, I'd like to get my hands on them."

Garrett ended that conversation by saying, "I'll keep you informed," although they both knew that even if he arrested these two slugs, tying them to the other robberies would be possible only if one of the cooperating law enforcement agencies succeeded in tracking down where they stored the stolen weapons and found some with serial numbers from guns taken in the Shelton or Bremerton heists.

Or with a confession, but that seemed unlikely in the extreme.

It was an hour before he got a call back from Hoquiam, in Grays Harbor down the Pacific Coast, where events had transpired much as they had in Bremerton. No woman, and from what little they could see on a poor security camera recording, one of the two men was big and muscular, the other noticeably leaner. Vehicle? A pickup truck.

Wonderful. Garrett still had no doubt that these crimes were all linked, but now had to consider the possibility that there was a ring of crooks, not just a pair. Impatient with himself, he had to ask what difference it made. If they got their hands on the two men who'd killed a cop while stealing one hell of a lot of weapons, they'd be able to trace where they lived and anyone else who was involved. One reason to do their damnedest to make sure at least one of the two survived.

Garrett took a deep breath and rolled his shoulders before he let his head fall back. He was sitting in his department vehicle at this point, positioned south of Quilcene. He'd moved several times as the day went on, waiting. Just as too many of the law enforcement officers on the Olympic Peninsula were doing. His muscles were starting to cramp up.

He got out now and again to walk a few feet and stretch, but that wasn't enough.

Unfortunately, with radio traffic still sporadic even if it remained tense, he had had too much time to brood about Cadence.

Last night he'd gotten into it with his grandfather, resenting what felt like judgment. Or maybe it was that Granddad had said a few things that struck closer to home than Garrett wanted to admit.

He'd been closemouthed about Cadence, but his grandfather had been well aware he was seeing a woman. There were those nights he hadn't come home. And yes, he'd answered a few questions: she was a law enforcement ranger in the national park and she enjoyed hiking and climbing, as Garrett did.

"Something happen?" his grandfather had asked while they ate.

He had managed to shrug. "Just wore down, I guess." He'd pushed the bowl of green beans across the table.

Instead of reaching for them, his grandfather had studied him with shrewd blue eyes. "You seemed happy while you were seeing her."

"The relationship was never meant to be anything long-lasting." He'd heard the edge in his own voice.

"Huh." Granddad slowly dished up a few green beans—he wasn't fond of most vegetables Garrett pushed on him—and took a bite. Garrett had almost relaxed when his grandfather spoke again. "Doesn't seem like your bad mood is letting up. You sure you didn't make a mistake?"

Garrett growled something inarticulate that shut Granddad up, but that didn't mean he wasn't still thinking, his eyes seeing more than Garrett liked. That was a serious downside to actually letting yourself care about someone, open up to him.

Grimacing now, Garrett told himself his problem where Cadence was concerned was that *he* hadn't lost interest. He would have eventually; he always did, but she was right when she said they had a good thing going. They did.

Make that past tense.

She wasn't the only woman he'd been involved with who wanted more from him. He'd just thought Cadence was different. She certainly hadn't shown signs of nesting in the shabby trailer that was her current home. She was a federal law enforcement officer who shrugged off the daily risks, same as he did. She'd talked about other national parks she might like to work in, which suggested moving on was part of her mindset. He knew she'd originally been interested in being a naturalist, the kind of ranger who gave talks and happily staffed backcountry stations. She'd done that kind of thing for several summers, but getting taken on full time by the National Park Service wasn't easy. Eventually she'd attended the law enforcement academy at Skagit Valley College here in Washington state and gotten certified as an EMT and a structural firefighter as well. When an offer for a permanent position came, she jumped on it, even if it wasn't quite what she'd wanted in the first place.

He tended to keep things shallow when he was seeing a woman, but he had asked once if she regretted her choice or was still looking for a chance to shift away from the law enforcement track.

They'd been having lunch beside Lake Constance on their way to climb the mountain. With an oddly pensive expression, she'd glanced around at a beautiful spot that was undoubtedly once pristine, but had become almost as crowded as a park in Seattle in summer, and said, "The trouble is, it's gotten so all of us, no matter what our job title is, are mainly occupied protecting the land and animals from the visitors, and the visitors from each other and even from themselves."

He knew what she meant. She'd found a suicide victim the previous week and had to tell the man's fiancée about it. And it seemed as if half her time was spent on rescues involving climbers and hikers both. Too often the injured were people who hadn't prepared adequately for the outing they'd set out on.

That day, Cadence had given a one-shoulder shrug and said wryly, "There's not much time left over for anything else."

He could see her point. Spending time with her had given him insight into the challenges the national parks faced. The Grand Canyon, for example, was popular for anyone willing to commit suicide by jumping, with no thought given to the ugliness of the job rangers had cleaning up after what had likely been carefully planned acts. Yellowstone in particular had to contend with tourists who thought they ought to be able to set their kid on a buffalo's back for a picture or take a selfie with a grizzly. Here, tragedies on the beaches predominated, along with mountain rescue deep in a park that had virtually no road access.

He'd learned from her, as she had from him when he told her selective stories about policing a major city. What they hadn't done was share backgrounds. He knew she had parents and a brother who, while younger than her but still an adult, lived at home. No, he also knew that camping and traveling to scenic places had been part of her childhood, thus her interest in America's remaining wilderness areas. The few mentions of her family had told him that she loved them. He hadn't caught a hint of resentment or distancing.

It went without saying that he'd kept quiet about his own childhood. Maybe she thought he'd been raised by his grandparents. If so, he hadn't corrected her.

What difference does it make? he asked himself now, angry at having to acknowledge his grandfather was right:

having Cadence walk away from him had done a number on his mood. He needed to put her out of his mind, start looking for someone else who'd be satisfied with good sex and occasional companionship.

Too bad Garrett hadn't seen another woman who remotely interested him in months. Probably since he first set eyes on Cadence during a tricky traffic stop when she'd been his closest backup.

He swore under his breath. What could he do but accept her decision…however much he regretted it?

Putting a ring on her finger, turning now into forever, wasn't possible for a man who didn't believe he was capable of that kind of commitment—or that any woman would keep a commitment to *him*.

The urgency of a voice coming from his radio had him straightening. He was almost grateful for it.

A BLACK SUV driven by a man with a male passenger was spotted just north of Quilcene. When Deputy Herrera accelerated to close in behind it, the driver sped up in turn. Herrera turned on lights and siren—and the driver of the SUV must have slammed his gas pedal to the floorboards. By the time he flew by Garrett's position, the Tahoe—yes, Garrett recognized the lines—exceeded ninety miles an hour. It swerved around slower traffic in front of it; northbound vehicles fled for the shoulder.

God, Garrett didn't want to let it go, but he spoke up and said, "We need to abandon pursuit. I repeat, abandon pursuit. If we don't, we'll have a head-on collision any minute."

The sheriff came on. "All units, cease pursuit. Units farther south, watch for vehicle."

Garrett had gotten the license plate number and shared that on the radio. A state patrolman closer to Brinnon spoke up moments later. "Confirm license plate number. Black

Tahoe just blew by me, but I don't believe the driver saw me off the road. He has slowed considerably. I estimate sixty-five to seventy miles per hour. I'll follow, but keep a distance."

Garrett drove only slightly over the speed limit to keep in touch. Other deputies farther south spoke up, as did deputies from the next county south.

"Saw me," a Jefferson County deputy said suddenly. "Vehicle is speeding up. Swerved and right wheels skidded in gravel."

"Hang back and watch only," the sheriff ordered.

It went on. Evidence of panic showed, which made the pursuit increasingly dangerous. The last deputy lost visual again. Last seen passing the turn to the Dosewallips Ranger Station, a dead end. Somewhere in the next few miles, the vehicle once more disappeared. They got lucky when a Mason County deputy reported a few minutes later that a motorist had stopped and pinpointed a forest service road also leading west, probably into the Brothers Wilderness area. He'd seen the SUV slamming on brakes and spinning and swerving off the road, raising a cloud of dirt that hung in its passage.

Yet another dead end, but this one was more complicated as the forest service roads in varying conditions intersected, and it would be possible to emerge back onto the highway farther south—or potentially north, although that seemed an unlikely choice on their part.

Once again, deputies were ordered into position. Half an hour later, it reemerged. Two deputies set up a roadblock.

"Shots fired!" one of them yelled. "Windshield is shattered." Garrett's heart damn near stopped as he continued driving. The sound was muted, but he could hear the *bang, bang, bang* of gunshots. "Returning fire! Aiming for a tire!" And then, "They're gone."

The men had once again fled the highway, but to Garrett's

alarm, onto a road that actually went somewhere. Worse, to Lake Cushman, a long body of water outside the park boundary. In summer, scattered resorts, rentals and campgrounds would be full. The lake was easily accessible from Hoodsport on the canal—and from Olympia not that far south. The chances of disaster grew by the minute. In flashes behind his eyelids, Garrett saw a multivehicle accident, bodies thrown onto the pavement, or a hostage situation once the men realized that they were perilously close to being trapped. From Lake Cushman, there weren't many alternatives for escape, the principal one Highway 119.

This wouldn't have been his choice for where to draw the line, but he couldn't see that they had any options now. It was time for major roadblocks.

Fortunately, he didn't have to say a word. The sheriff would be looking at the same maps. He issued orders that would pen the two fugitives at Lake Cushman—along with far too many tourists.

Garrett had never been tenser

…until a man's voice took advantage of a break in radio traffic concerning the fugitives to identify himself as Ranger Chaffee with a report on a potential heart attack victim up the trail from the Staircase Ranger Station.

"Doing well with just oxygen. Ranger Jones and I are transporting the victim back down the Wagonwheel trail. Want to confirm request for an ambulance to meet us at the trailhead."

Ranger Jones.

The steering wheel creaked when Garrett's hands tightened. If Cadence and Chaffee reached that trailhead…there wasn't the slightest doubt she would jump right into the drama playing out so close to her current whereabouts.

Chapter Five

Sweating uncomfortably, Cadence especially regretted the necessity of wearing the broad-brimmed Stetson that immediately identified her as a park service employee. She currently anchored one corner of the wheeled gurney carrying a man in his seventies who'd become short of breath taking a particularly strenuous trail that left from the Staircase Ranger Station. After he collapsed, the youngest member of the party had run for help. Both the ranger on duty at Staircase—a likable, stocky man named Tom Chaffee—and Cadence had responded. The hiker had gotten farther than she'd have expected, reaching a stretch that required some bushwhacking on this return trip across an open avalanche slope.

She felt reasonably confident that the guy, who'd regained consciousness before she arrived, hadn't had a heart attack despite his admission that he'd previously had one. Lucky for him, given how long it would take to get him down to meet an ambulance.

"Angioplasty made me feel like a new man," he'd said breathlessly just before she fitted an oxygen mask over his face. He momentarily lifted it to add, "Guess I got too excited."

"There are a lot of hikes in the Olympics that I suspect

you could take without difficulty," Cadence had said mildly. Ones that didn't require switchbacks because of the extreme elevation gain.

He wanted to walk down, but she and Tom agreed that was a nonstarter even though the steep descent meant carrying the fellow more than they could wheel him.

At the best of times, this wasn't one of her favorite hikes. The difficulty wasn't justified by the mostly limited views, although Wagonwheel Lake, a deep aquamarine color, was beautiful. This was one man who'd never see that particular lake, however.

Thankfully, both his sons—fit men—a daughter-in-law and two sons-in-law in their twenties had accompanied him. They had enough muscle-on-the-hoof to be able to take turns with hefting the gurney and preventing it taking off at a precipitous speed downhill.

Her attention wasn't 100 percent on doing her job. Nope, she was riveted by the radio traffic. During the shoot-out, she let one of the sons-in-law take her place so she could drop back and listen. Her body jerked involuntarily at the sound of shots. She could picture what was happening frighteningly well.

She stopped, letting the rest go on, as she absorbed the snapped orders and comments. Neither deputy had been seriously injured, but both were shaken. She'd encountered occasional Mason County sheriff's deputies on the job, but didn't recognize either of these names. She had the impression that one was young; his voice had been high and panicky at a moment experienced police officers maintained an unnatural calm.

The roadblock had accomplished one thing, however; the fleeing Tahoe had sped onto the offshoot, Highway 119, that ultimately met the graded gravel road that followed the shore of Lake Cushman…then entered the national park where it came to an end. At the Staircase campground. Where Cadence and her party would be appearing once they managed the steep descent, and where she hoped an ambulance would be waiting.

Surely to God the two killers would realize their mistake long before they reached the primitive campground, and turn around or try to find a way to go to ground. The tight band around her chest was a good reminder that they hadn't used any common sense yet, however, not from the very beginning when they chose an isolated gun shop in a rural county without many options to flee, when they thought gunning down a law enforcement officer would help their cause, or when they kept speeding down a narrow, scenic, too-busy highway even though they had seen or been briefly seen by a number of cops.

They had to be desperate by this time, grappling wildly for any way at all they might escape the disaster they had created.

Their most logical, if terrifying, option was to grab some hostages at Lake Cushman. Use those hostages to persuade law enforcement to let them drive on toward a city where they might still hope they could vanish—or, at the very least, to surrender safely.

She gazed after the party she needed to rejoin without really seeing them.

No, men still willing to shoot themselves out of trouble weren't thinking about surrender.

WHEN GARRETT AND another experienced deputy from Jefferson County paused briefly at the scene of the roadblock, nobody questioned their presence. These men had been listening to his voice for much of the day. No matter what, the manhunt had become multijurisdictional. Garrett's boss had talked about calling in the FBI in hopes they'd send the equivalent of a SWAT or Hostage Rescue Team to provide assistance. They were fast approaching that level of desperation.

He drove in a convoy with his coworker and two Mason County Sheriff's Department vehicles. Garrett had mostly stayed on paved roads thus far, while Deputy Dawes's vehicle was dust coated. They passed the Lake Cushman Golf Club and the beginnings of rustic businesses, including some that rented boats or offered small cabins for rent. They split up to search parking lots, short lanes leading to resorts or boat launches, the park. Garrett took responsibility for questioning people at the park.

Nothing.

Lake Cushman was magnificent—long and narrow, surrounded by steep, forested foothills. Right now, everything from kayaks to power boats were scattered across the lake. The view from the beach here in the park was impressive, although he barely gave it a passing glance.

Shouldn't somebody have noticed a speeding vehicle spitting gravel behind it as it headed for the park entrance? Garrett asked himself as he got back into his vehicle. Only, what if the Tahoe hadn't been speeding anymore? It was too late in the day for campers to be arriving at Staircase; the limited sites would already be full. But that didn't mean there wasn't still some traffic going that way. Maybe folks who just wanted a look at the river, the rapids, the bridge. Campers who had taken in other sites today. Tourists would have no reason to pay attention to other tourists, and locals? High summer was the equivalent of the biblical plague of locusts.

Damn it. He'd have to drive to the park entrance station and be sure the fugitives hadn't fled to the very end of the road.

"Someone appears to be holed up in an isolated house," came the voice of one of the MCSD deputies. "Landlord came to clean up, because it's supposed to be vacant and he has new renters due tomorrow. Door is barricaded and he heard shouts."

"I'm on my way," he said, and on leaving the parking lot turned back the way he'd come.

STILL DISTRACTED BY the heavy volume of traffic on the radio, Cadence had to jog to catch up with the others. It sounded as if events had descended into chaos. She was ashamed to realize that what she was really listening for was Garrett's voice or call signal. Naturally, he was still in the middle of this.

She assumed she'd be joining the manhunt as soon as she reached the foot of this infernal trail, but there was a ways to go yet. She might not be to keep from worrying about him, but that didn't mean she looked forward to seeing him.

Nearly an hour later, her group had reached a stretch passing through a dry forest of young Douglas fir when she heard a far-off scream.

They all stumbled to a stop, heads turning.

The second scream was thin and high, and moments later was joined by more screams and voices yelling. Unless another group of hikers who were approaching had just had a cataclysmic accident—and she couldn't imagine what that would be—she had to be hearing people at the campground or trailhead. Cadence regretted suddenly the ranger's insistence on accompanying her. If he'd been there to intervene and report on what was happening—

Tom's eyes met hers. "I'll go—"

"No, I should." He didn't carry a gun, but did have the same EMT certification she did, which made him capable of continuing to monitor the health of their patient. "I'll radio you when I find out what's happening."

He looked like a horse straining to bolt, but nodded. "Go!"

One of the sons-in-law had been listening and now

stepped forward to take her place. "We're down the worst part. Dad will be fine. *We'll* be fine."

God, she hoped so. She couldn't remember ever abandoning a person in distress to plunge into another crisis. She wouldn't have felt she *could* had Tom not been here.

She gripped the straps of the small pack and broke into a headlong run. Time seemed to both speed and slow down. What was *happening*? She had a sickening fear that it involved the two men who'd already killed once, but why would they have gotten themselves pinned at the edge of a vast wilderness? No, she realized: at a campground occupied by families.

She hadn't heard a gunshot. That was one blessing. But the closer she got, the more a babel of voices and the sobbing of a woman reached her.

Once she tripped over a root that snaked just beneath the dirt on the trail and had to do a dance to right herself. Under other circumstances, she'd have paused to catch her breath, but she couldn't. It was a huge relief to finally burst out on the paved path that led from the trailhead to the ranger station, then on to the campground where people were gathered. And, oh God, a seemingly empty, dusty black Tahoe sat askew in the middle of the circle road, blocking access to a campsite.

She hurried toward the crowd, raising her voice to make herself heard.

They engulfed her, men, women, teens. A few children peeked from tents or campers or clutched their parents' legs.

"I'm Park Ranger Jones," she said loudly. "Who can tell me what happened?"

They rushed into speech, talking over themselves, so that it was impossible to make out any coherent narrative. One woman kept sobbing like a metronome, in and out, in and out.

Cadence broke in. "Please, one at a time. You." She

pointed to a man who'd been trying without success to get a word in edgewise.

"Two armed men jumped out of this SUV." He jerked his head toward it. "They waved guns. Slammed them into a few heads."

"What?" She looked around. "We have injured?"

"I don't think seriously."

At his nod indicating direction, she saw several men sitting on the dirt right off the road. One held his bent head between his hands. There were bruises, some blood, but nobody was dying.

"Okay." She had to lift her voice again over the din that had resumed. "Then what?"

Someone had started screaming the minute one of the men pointed a rifle at her. He yelled at her to shut up. The two had stood back to back, ordering everyone to stay put. Unfortunately, nobody had thought to try to slip away at the beginning. For what good that would have done, when they'd have found the ranger station empty.

A guy who looked to be about her age stepped forward.

"They wanted backpacks, insisted on meals for several days. The two of us—" he indicated a second man who stood beside him "—had already loaded up for an early morning departure. We intended to climb—" He swallowed. "I guess that doesn't matter. We nabbed a campsite because our wives and kids planned to wait for us here."

Cadence nodded her understanding.

"They took the packs. While one of them kept his gun on us, the other one poked around in both packs to be sure we weren't lying. When he seemed satisfied, we thought they'd take off, although…" He shook his head, his bafflement plain. "Where did they think they could *go*?"

There was the question.

She thought they deserved an answer. "A couple of men

broke into a gun store up in Sequim early this morning. They killed a deputy who responded to the alarm. Every law enforcement agency in the area has been chasing them all day. I suspect it got too hot for them out on the highway, and they think they can slip away somehow in the park."

"Yes, but—" The climber jerked his shoulders. His gaze slid to the still crying woman. "They grabbed a kid and hauled him along."

Oh, dear God.

"Um, that's the boy's grandmother," he added.

"How old is the boy?"

"Eleven," said an older man beside the woman, his own face as blotchy as if he'd been crying earlier. "We brought our grandkids camping. Evan is eleven. Tall for his age, but…"

"All right." She did her best to sound confident, in charge. "Did anyone see which way they went?"

The second climber nodded. "I…followed a little ways. North Fork trail. They were moving fast, yanking the kid along. Man, if I'd been armed…"

"I looked in the back of their SUV," another man in the crowd called. "A tarp is covering the load, but an edge of it slid back enough I could see *piles* of weapons. We could break the windows and arm ourselves…"

Others were nodding, one saying loudly, "Let's do it!"

She backed up against that dusty fender and laid her hand on the butt of her sidearm. "I'll arrest the first person who takes a swing at a window. Do you hear me?"

They didn't like it, but they heard. Her gaze roved over the forty plus adults in the crowd. Probably most wouldn't have joined in forming a vigilante party, but a few were champing at the bit.

"Yeah, you going to take them down by yourself?" one was so bold as to ask.

"No. These are extremely dangerous men. They shot and wounded a store owner, killed a sheriff's deputy and opened fire on two other cops who set up a roadblock. I'll get on the radio and have backup here shortly. Law enforcement officers and *only* law enforcement officers will pursue those men on foot. We'll likely get a helicopter in the air to try to pinpoint where they are, in case they leave the trail. I need you to stay calm and give me any and all information you think might be useful."

Thank God none of these campers *had* been armed. Fortunately, carrying a gun of any kind wasn't allowed in the national parks, and apparently no one in this crowd had tried to slip one by. If so, it wouldn't have been a shock; she'd issued many a citation to would-be hunters who didn't respect park rules, or just men who needed the swagger carrying gave them.

"He wanted a map," a woman said, stepping forward. "I'd just been looking at that one I picked up at the ranger station. It shows trails throughout the park. I…handed them that."

"That's good to know." The map in question didn't have the scope and detail of the larger topographic map put out by *National Geographic*, but she wasn't sure that mattered. "Okay, let me make my call."

Some people shuffled off toward their campsites. Others seemed to need to talk, but she tuned them out, giving her call sign and saying, "The fugitives who burglarized the gun shop and have been pursued all day drove into Staircase campground in the national park. They left behind their black Tahoe." She gave the license plate number. "Heavily armed, they have fled on foot deeper into the park, taking an older child hostage with them. They've now had as much as an hour head start. I need armed searchers carrying what they'll need for potentially two to three days. We all know there's a lot of country out there they can get lost in." She paused. "Please respond."

LISTENING, GARRETT COULD have sworn the hair on his arms stood on end as if he'd been electrified. He'd been apprehensive before—during last week's traffic stop, for example—but scared like this? Not even at the worst moments in foster care.

She's okay, he told himself. It didn't sound as if she'd seen them, much less confronted them. That should have been some comfort, but she would definitely be among the group heading deep into the park to find two men who had nothing to lose at this point.

This intense reaction alarmed him. Where had it come from? Yeah, he'd missed her, but he'd move on eventually. That's what he did. No, this was just his protective instinct, a big part of him. On some level, she'd been *his*, and even if that relationship proved to be temporary, he couldn't turn off this fear for her...or the certainty that his primary goal now was keeping her safe.

He leaped back into his SUV, leaving two deputies to extract what appeared to be squatters from a rental house, and exploded back onto North Lake Cushman Road. He raced past the park entry, noted a couple of ranger vehicles parked by the station as well as an ambulance that had somehow beat him here. Entering the campground circle, he immediately zeroed in on the too-familiar Tahoe. It wasn't so much parked as abandoned where the driver had slammed on his brakes.

Two medics appeared to be looking over a few battered men. Amongst the clusters of agitated people, Garrett didn't immediately see Cadence. She wouldn't have gone in pursuit on her own, would she? He wouldn't believe that. She could be reckless, but—

He was suddenly able to breathe. There she was, crouched with an arm around a distraught older woman who sat in a lawn chair someone had carried almost to the road for her. Garrett had seen compassion on Cadence's fine-boned face before, but he was inexplicably surprised by it anyway. As fit as she was, she'd just loaded herself up with medical supplies and hiked—or jogged—almost to Wagonwheel Lake, an elevation gain of at least 3,000 feet. She'd treated a man with heart trouble, then despite her slight body, helped carry him most of the way down on a gurney—until she'd rushed headlong down to the campground. There, she'd been met by a lot of upset people who still milled around.

And, yeah, he saw sweat circles under her arms, a dirty streak on her face, and her usually smooth dark hair was escaping a braid with one especially long strand that she pushed impatiently back behind her ear. Yet she was still herself, every movement graceful even as she remained composed and yet exuding warmth for a deeply distressed woman.

Cadence's head turned just then, and her dark eyes locked onto his. Whether he liked it or not, his heart gave a hard squeeze. The relief on her face eased his tumult, and he walked toward her. She never looked away.

"Can we talk?" he said.

"Of course." She murmured something to the woman, gave her a hug and then rose to her feet, coming toward him. Her Kevlar vest only emphasized how willowy her build was. She might be delicately made, but she was stronger than anyone first meeting her would suspect. He'd climbed and hiked with her enough to know just how fit and capable she was.

Sounding anxious, she said, "We need to get going as soon as possible. What are you hearing?"

"The license plate was stolen off another vehicle, to no

one's surprise, but once the techs lift some fingerprints from the Tahoe, I'm betting there'll be matches."

She only nodded, and he understood why she wasn't excited. Identifying the men didn't help right now.

"We'll have two other teams besides ourselves ready to go within another hour, hour and a half," Garrett continued. "Everyone had to hustle home to grab their backpacks and supplies. We might still add another team before nightfall. Others will set out in the morning."

"Morning." She sounded almost numb.

"You know we'll be unlikely to catch up to them tonight."

"We're in good shape!" she cried. "They may not be."

"They may not be runners, but from the footage I saw, they have to be weight lifters and maybe use machines in a gym. Or box or—" He stopped. "We can't assume they'll be slow."

"I know, but…"

"Cadence." He made sure she met his eyes. "In the morning, we'll send in searchers from other directions. Up the Duckabush River, for example, and maybe the Dose, since the trails all connect. It's too late in the day to get a helicopter in the air, but I know the air force base is prepared to send one in the morning."

She was breathing harder than he'd seen her yet. He made an involuntary move toward her that she didn't seem to notice, but made himself stop, his hands fisting at his sides. They couldn't be seen wrapped in each other's arms in front of a campground full of frightened tourists—assuming she'd have let him gather her to him.

"It's the boy," she said so softly he just heard her. "He's only eleven. He must be petrified."

"Yeah," he said regretfully. "I know." He'd been trying not think about the poor kid, or what his captors would do with him if he couldn't keep up with them or was foolish enough to try to make a break for it.

He did take her hand and gave it a quick squeeze. To his relief, her fingers tightened on his, if only momentarily. Had she realized from what he said that he fully intended to pair up with her? If so, she wasn't arguing, thank God.

Lucky, because he wasn't taking no for an answer—not about this, not from her. After all the shocks of the day, he had some thinking to do. What he knew right now was that he wouldn't be able to do his job if he couldn't have her as close as possible.

Chapter Six

The brief touch of his hand reignited her wariness. Getting over him meant rebuffing any hint of tenderness. She deliberately raised her chin. "What about you? You surely don't carry your pack around."

He'd know that she did.

"My grandfather is meeting Deputy McCall, who has a young woman deputy with him. I don't know her well. They're both outfitted."

"Alysa Bailey? I've met her. She talked about competing in a triathlon."

"Excellent. Two Mason County deputies are on their way, too—both say they're climbers and know this part of the park well. That'll give us six to start out. I'm told the park ranger is organizing people, but since you're the best informed, he's leaving you in charge for now."

She'd half expected him to argue, not so much because he was male and she was female as because taking charge came naturally to him. But obviously he recognized that they were now in her jurisdiction, and in territory she knew better than he did.

"I had a call from him," she agreed.

"I took the liberty of setting up what I could," Garrett continued. "If you disagree…"

"No." She tried a smile that didn't quite make it. "I'm grateful. I…hadn't gotten that far in my thinking yet. You have no idea how much I wanted to charge after them, but at least I knew better than to do that."

"I was glad to see you," he said abruptly, something odd in his tone.

She raised her eyebrows. "Because you thought I might go ahead on my own."

"No, you said you wouldn't." He cleared his throat. "But waiting isn't always the easiest thing to do."

"No." She sighed and told him that half the men in the crowd would be thrilled to be issued weapons so they could join the manhunt. She was reasonably sure she'd squelched the surge of volunteerism, but was still keeping an eye on the ringleaders. "By the way, as one of them pointed out, it appears there are plenty of weapons in the back of the Tahoe."

"They're not covered?" he asked in surprise.

"There's a tarp, but it may have slipped during their high-speed maneuvering. Either that, or they grabbed some weapons from the back. I hope you have someone coming to secure the vehicle and contents?"

"Yeah, a park special agent is on his way along with a Clallam County detective, since the original crime was theirs and the weapons will eventually be returned to the gun shop owner."

"Oh, right." Her head turned sharply. "Some reinforcements."

The driver was wedging his department vehicle off the road to the best of his ability. Garrett said, "Those are the Mason County guys. You might want to talk to them. I met one of them earlier." He grimaced. "I'll guard the stockpile here."

Oh, yeah. Good idea. She nodded and went to meet the two men who had the back of their official vehicle open and were swinging packs out onto their backs. One had salt-and-pepper hair. She'd guess him to be in his upper forties or even fifties, but he was lean and fit. The second deputy was probably around her age, more powerfully built. That wasn't necessarily an advantage for what lay ahead of them, but she wouldn't judge ahead of his performance.

She introduced herself, and they did the same. The older man was Eric Sutherland, the younger Tyler Murray. She decided their vehicle could stay where it was, then sent them on to join Garrett while she jogged back to the ranger station to update Tom Chaffee.

"Hell of a day," he said, on seeing her. "Ambulance just left. Our patient looked good. I suspect he'll be released this evening. The medics decided to take one of the campers who got slammed with a rifle butt, too. They suspect a concussion."

The one clutching his head, Cadence presumed.

Tom raised his eyebrows. "I assume you're going in pursuit."

She nodded. "I need to grab my pack out of my car."

He asked about the SUV full of stolen weapons and was obviously relieved to hear people were on their way to take charge of it.

"I put a Closed sign at the entrance. There's no space at the campground, anyway, and we don't need any gawkers."

"No." She hesitated. "You stay sharp. It's unlikely those two men can figure out how to loop back here, but they may be thinking they can. Even if they can't recover their Tahoe, hey, point a gun at some campers and steal *their* car."

"I'll have an eye out," he agreed. "Keep us informed."

"Will do." She smiled crookedly. "The kid's grandparents are site number eight. You might stop by and reassure them."

"Had that in mind."

She pawed through her own pack briefly, adding additional medical supplies from the bag she'd carried earlier and discarding a few extras before closing fasteners once she was satisfied. Then she took her M16 rifle from the rack, stuck extra ammunition for it and her handgun in outside pockets of her pack and heaved it experimentally onto her back. Heavier than usual, but fine, she decided, and carried it to rejoin the others.

Unbelievable. Six of them were to plunge into the park to track and eventually attempt to subdue men who were probably better armed than the pursuers. Men who'd already displayed their willingness to kill. She hoped her compatriots were dedicated enough to put in regular time at the range to stay sharp.

Let us recover the boy, she begged, before bullets start flying.

CADENCE WASN'T HIDING her impatience well, although Garrett couldn't blame her. These things always dragged on for a frustrating length of time.

A month ago, Garrett and Cadence had hiked the beginning of this trail but detoured to have lunch at Flapjack Lakes before turning back. He seemed to remember that she'd hiked most of it—maybe cutting over to Enchanted Valley—but Garrett hadn't. Now he carefully studied the map she pinned to the bole of a tree with one hand.

"Unless it looks like someone set out cross-country, we'll stick together until here." With a glance around, she pointed at the trail that wound to Flapjack Lakes and beyond, to Mount Cruiser, a tough rock climb Garrett hadn't yet attempted. Unfortunately, that same trail had at least one other branch leading to a series of lakes as well as a more primitive track that met the main North Fork trail at a campsite called Big Log that he and she would pass in a few hours. "At least one pair should split off there. If we had more people, I'd say two pairs, but once we reach the Big Log spur, which continues along Six Ridge, we'll need to explore that possibility, too."

Garrett agreed with her reasoning, and saw that the others did, too. Since the Six Ridge trail meandered south toward the national park border, it might seem like a good option to men desperate for a way out.

"Remember," she added, "you need to watch for game trails and unmarked trails used by climbers or backpackers wanting to set up camp off the beaten path. Even trails made by animals. You'll see plenty of them."

More nods.

"That brings us to the subject of how we should pair up," she said, as if it had just occurred to her. Her gaze didn't meet Garrett's. "If anyone has a particular strength or weakness—"

He interrupted without apology. "It seems to me we should pair with the person we know best and have worked with before. It's important we can read each other in a tight spot and know how our partner will react."

Her mouth tightened.

The older of the two Mason County deputies said, "I agree. It might be different if we had a larger group to organize, but as it is, we arrived two by two. Why don't we keep it that way?"

He could tell she didn't like that, but nodded curtly. The others—well, except for the Jefferson County duo—couldn't possibly guess that he and Cadence had been sleeping together and recently parted ways, that there were some touchy feelings between them. But he trusted her skill, and thought she did his. They couldn't let those feelings get in the way of rescuing the young hostage.

"What if we spot them?" asked Deputy Bailey.

"That depends on whether they see *you*," Cadence said.

"If possible, radio in the sighting first. Keep in mind that the safety of the hostage has to be our priority. If you find yourself under fire... Backing off might be the best tactic until we can overwhelm them with numbers."

"We're lucky this is Tuesday," Garrett commented. "The weekend running into Monday would have been the most crowded up here, but even so we have to assume they will meet other people out on the trail."

Eric Sutherland pointed out, "There's not much we can do about that. Let's just hope people use their common sense, and that our fugitives aren't too trigger-happy."

Garrett's jaw tightened. He could see any number of possible bad outcomes when a party of climbers, say, came around a bend in the trail to find themselves face-to-face with men toting forbidden automatic rifles.

They threw around a few more thoughts, Cadence all but dancing in place from anxiety and impatience. Understanding, Garrett suggested he and she as well as the two Mason County deputies set out now, while the Jefferson County pair hung around until someone arrived to take responsibility for the Tahoe and its cache of weapons.

Cadence assigned those two, once they were able to get moving, to take the trail to Flapjack Lakes as well as the dogleg to Smith Lake. "It's not much over three miles to reach that turnoff," she said. Given how late it's getting, you might want to set up camp right at the junction." She looked around at all of them. "It probably goes without saying, but use flashlights as little as possible. You won't want to pinpoint your location."

By the time the foursome set out on what had originally been a generously wide road grade, it was with the knowledge that the light would start failing in just a couple of hours. They didn't dare continue in the dark for a number of reasons, but the big one was that they might miss seeing evidence that the men had left the trail.

Ian Sutherland and Tyler Murray fell in behind Garrett and Cadence, both appearing comfortable carrying the heavy packs and weapons, their strides long and relaxed. Garrett saw that Cadence was surreptitiously checking them out, too, her forehead smoothing when she turned her focus onto the trail ahead.

They'd walked for fifteen minutes, the rippling sound of the river accompanying them, before she said, voice low but intense. "I *hate* that we let them get so far ahead of us."

Feeling a stir of the same anger, he said, "I don't blame you. We've had no choice but to react to these SOBs all day long. Not my favorite position to be put into. The one time we got in front of them, we didn't have enough force in place to stop them. In retrospect, I don't know how smart it was to set up that roadblock, given that it took every option away from them but this one."

"Yes, but their chances of disappearing with the stolen weapons would have been greater once they reached urban areas."

He grunted. "There's a lot of miles out here to get lost in."

She gave something like a shudder. "They could get lost with my blessing, if only they hadn't grabbed the boy."

Except they would have had access to other hostages if they needed a replacement. Garrett didn't say that.

"I think we can assume that we'll be able to move faster than they will." He went for calm. "By tomorrow, we'll have a full-blown manhunt in place, including eyes in the sky."

"Which may or may not do any good, considering much of the time anyone out here will be hidden by lush forest."

He shrugged his concession, guessing she'd see him out of the corner of her eye. He thought about bringing up the subject of their pairing, but decided not to. He'd have dug in his heels even if the logic behind the decision hadn't been so compelling, but she didn't know that. If she was angry enough at him to have trouble working cooperatively, he might regret his insistence, but he didn't think so.

"Take it easy," he said, after a minute. "You're all but running." He kept up with his longer stride, but had to push a little. She knew better than to take a chance of injuring herself by starting too hard and fast.

She shot him a dark look, but did slow down to a more natural, steady pace.

The two behind them were chatting, but quietly. He noted places where a tree had fallen over the trail, but crews had sawed through to clear the way. Cadence didn't even pause when they reached a viewpoint above the river. That was fine, but they needed to make sure they weren't walking right by some trampled vegetation or other indication that people ahead of them had set off cross-country. He suggested she be responsible for scanning to the left, him to the right.

She bit her lip. "I doubt they'd leave the trail this soon, but…you're right. That's a good idea."

He started watching more carefully for any small indication that someone had stepped off the trail—broken undergrowth, a boot print, scuffed soil—even as he kept more of an eye on her than she'd like. They'd been equal partners when climbing; he'd never had any doubt that, with her on the other end of the rope, he didn't have to worry. He probably wouldn't be in the profession he was if he didn't have a need to protect, but it wasn't usually so powerful, or so focused on a woman who wasn't actually in danger.

At the moment, he reminded himself, not liking the idea that the two of them could come unexpectedly on those bastards. The tension that squeezed in his chest made him think it was just as well she *had* ditched him. Feeling this way wasn't comfortable. It was part of what he'd been determined to avoid by keeping his friendships and involvement with women shallow.

After a couple of miles, the trail narrowed enough they needed to go single file much of the time, taking a gradual downward trend that led them into the lush forest. Now and again they had to step over horse droppings, this being one of the trails in the park where horses were not only permitted, but accommodated with corrals.

Sunlight became diffused, filtering through the needles and lacy branches of ancient Douglas fir, cedar and hemlock rearing high above them. Any opening in the canopy had been filled by maple trees. Moss draped over vines, ferns and other undergrowth made this a world of dozens of shades of green. The temperate rainforest on the western side of the park might be more spectacular, with lichens draping from branches like tinsel on a Christmas tree, but this section was magnificent in its own right, and all too rare. Thanks to Cadence, Garrett knew that the park sheltered 250,000 acres of old-growth forest, while, thanks to logging and human-caused fires, only a tiny percent remained outside those boundaries. He'd read that Douglas fir this size could be a thousand years old, or more. Planting replacement trees didn't cut it. The land protected by the park wasn't just to be appreciated for its beauty, the diverse forest was a resource for the future.

He was disturbed to realize how dry the forest looked right now. Moss shouldn't be brown. He hadn't noticed at first, but his eye became more discerning. The small streams they crossed ran low enough, there was no danger of anyone getting wet. A good rain would help, but with the driest months of the year coming they'd mostly see drizzle.

The two behind them had quit talking. Garrett would have felt the weight of the silence, except complete silence was rare in the backcountry. A breeze stirred branches in the upper canopy, water burbled in the distance, birds called. An occasional rustle in the underbrush would turn his head until he was certain it had been caused by wildlife and not a crouched human being.

He thought all of them felt the uneasy prickle of awareness that they could be watched through powerful rifle scopes. No, it wasn't likely, given the density of the vegetation and the breadth of the trunks of these old-growth trees, but he couldn't rule out the possibility that armed men might decide to pick off any pursuers.

Garrett was suddenly glad of his Kevlar vest, and that Cadence wore one as well, as did the other deputies and every other individual who would set out to hunt a pair of cop killers.

CADENCE WAS AWARE of every feature along the trail that gave her a good guess at how far they'd come and what lay ahead. The forest changed, and they entered an impressive stand of big-leaf maple. Slate Creek was a warning of what lay ahead: a burned landscape that encompassed more than 1,300 acres. The Beaver Fire had been set many years ago by an illegal campfire, and she always found it shocking to see how far the land still had to go to regenerate. Shrubs had popped up first, then quick-growing deciduous trees from seeds dropped by birds or wafted by winds. Small firs, cedars and hemlock gave hope for a return to the forest that had once covered this land, and would again, even if so long in the future no one living now would see it. The blackened skeletons of forest giants reared above, warning of how easily this could happen anywhere. Cadence always thought about these sad remnants when she cited campers and backpackers for illegal fires. So few people understood how fast a flame could get away from them, how danger-

ous a few cinders glowing against the darkness could be if
they found dry tinder.

"I don't like us being so out in the open," Garrett said
abruptly, the first words he'd spoken in ages. She glanced
at him to see him scanning their surroundings, tension in
his bearing.

"Places like this almost make me a believer in ghosts,"
she heard herself say. "Not necessarily human, but..." She
shrugged.

She felt his gaze touch on her, but he didn't comment,
certainly didn't reason with her by pointing out that massive fires were a part of the ecosystem in any forest. She
wouldn't disagree with that viewpoint, but *this* fire hadn't
had to happen. Humans were so careless.

The two behind them murmured, voices low enough she
couldn't hear what they said.

They all noted without comment the trail that cut away
to the east that the Jefferson County deputies would take.
As they hiked on, she became increasingly conscious of
the deepening light as dusk crept toward them. The valley
pinched, the trail they followed carved on a hillside above
the rivers and streams that flowed at the narrowest point.
Places like this descended into darkness long before the or-
ange orb of the sun sank behind the curve of the earth out
over the ocean.

Maybe unconsciously, she and Garrett stepped up the
pace, the others staying with them. A few times, they paused
to check out signs of a faint trail to one side or the other.
Most led to a riverside spot where hikers had paused for a
snack or to splash water on their faces. Others were clearly
animal trails. Cadence kept a sharp eye out for bears, which
were commonly seen in the area, but didn't see much in
the way of wildlife at all. The call of a grouse was the sum
total. A mile and a half later, give or take, they spotted the

designated campsite called Big Log, presently dotted by a half dozen tents. Funny they hadn't already met hikers on their last leg to the trailhead. Her uneasiness increased now that she'd consciously realized why she'd been so aware her small party was completely alone.

She stopped. "We need to find out if anyone saw who passed."

They split up, each taking one or two of the parties or individuals. Turned out, only one couple had paid any attention to a threesome that passed what might be a couple of hours ago.

"I'd have sworn they were carrying rifles," said the young woman. "But I didn't have any way to report them—" cell phone service was rare in the park "—and I didn't see them that closely."

"Any idea whether they continued north or headed toward Six Ridge?"

"I'm sorry, I wish I had."

"Okay." Cadence raised her voice so that everyone present could hear them. "It should be fine to stay here tonight, and to hike back to Staircase in the morning. If any of you were planning to continue on—"

Two men were.

"This area of the park has been closed because of the men you just heard us talking about," she told them. "I'm afraid I have to ask you to go with everyone else back to Staircase in the morning." She suggested they talk to the ranger there, who might be able to redirect them to another area of the park where they could hike or climb instead.

They didn't look happy, but they'd heard the mention of rifles and could see that Cadence and the three men with her were also armed and wearing police vests.

After thanking them for their cooperation and accepting their promises to pass on the information to any late arrivals, she and the others continued over a pack bridge that crossed the North Fork Skokomish River. Usually she savored the view here of the river passing through what was nearly a gorge, but today she was blind to scenery.

The trail she and Garrett would follow continued north on the eastern bank of the river now. Here was the cutoff for the Six Ridge trail that Ian and Tyler were to take. For the moment, though, they continued together, passing the site of an old mine that had been worked for copper, iron and manganese around the turn of the twentieth century, and on to Camp Pleasant, which turned out to be more occupied. Two horses drowsed in the corral. If the men and boy had been seen continuing north along the river, well, then maybe she wouldn't have to split her forces.

And, oh yes, be alone with Garrett for who knew how many days. The man who deserved to know she was carrying his baby.

Chapter Seven

Cadence had continued monitoring her radio, as she felt sure the others were. She was relieved when Ed McCall, one of Garrett's coworkers, reported that they had passed off custody of the Tahoe and its contents at last and were on their way.

"Should make the junction before dark," Ed added.

She confirmed she'd heard. "Copy."

Cadence knew she might be wasting the time of two members of her small team since she now had confirmation the men had fled with their hostage well past the Flapjack Lakes turnoff, but they could certainly circle back to those lakes from the Big Log campground, and chances were good there'd be other ways for them to cross the North Fork Skokomish River and go cross-country to join the very trail she'd assigned to Alyssa and Ed. No, she couldn't afford to ignore any possibility. Given the popularity of Mount Cruiser and surrounding peaks, she'd be willing to bet there were any number of tracks that might tempt fugitives to think they could evade their pursuers.

While she spoke briefly to Ed, Garrett had stayed close to her, but Ian and Tyler had gathered the campers and begun questioning them.

Cadence joined them just as a man stepped forward. She

was very conscious of Garrett sticking to her side, his upper arm brushing hers.

"Yeah, the four of us—" the man gestured to a couple of other men and a woman "—are planning to climb O'Neil Peak tomorrow. We got a later start than we'd meant to from Seattle, ran into traffic—you know how it is. Anyway, we'd almost reached the bridge back there when these two men and a kid came up from behind us. They seemed to be in an almighty hurry."

"I thought we were going to get run off the trail," one of the men commented.

"We waved them on—" said the first guy.

"I was about to ask if they knew guns weren't allowed in the park when Tony here elbowed me," said the third man.

Tony was apparently the original man who'd spoken up. "Figured we'd report them when we got down," he said. "Uh…even though that wouldn't have been a couple of days from now."

"The boy worried me," the woman said, voice soft. "He looked… I don't know."

Scared, Cadence thought. That's what he'd looked.

"You did the right thing to keep it casual and let them go on," she said. "They're dangerous men."

The woman's dismay was apparent. "The boy?"

"A hostage," Garrett told them bluntly. "That's one of the reasons we've launched a manhunt. I hope you can tell us which way they went."

"Which way? Oh, you mean Six Ridge or north?" That was the original speaker. "We kind of stopped and huddled. You know. Because they gave off such a weird vibe. We didn't want to get near them again." His mouth twisted. "I didn't see what they did once they were over the river."

None of them had. Cadence wanted to scream. Having witnesses that could have narrowed their search area but decided *not* to see was frustrating. And yet, in being cautious they'd made the right call again.

Her hope wasn't entirely dead, but as it turned out, not a single soul who had earlier set up camp had paid any attention to other hikers coming or going on the trail.

A chorus of voices gave perfectly valid excuses. "I mean, I know there were some, but I was trying to figure out how to work my new stove."

"We walked over to look at the mine."

"People were partying at the state campground last night. I napped for a little while once we'd set up here."

Doing her absolute best to mask her frustration, Cadence gave the same instructions to this group, and the party that had intended to climb O'Neil Peak tomorrow didn't argue. She did get some kickback from two young guys who wanted to know if they could cut over on the Flapjack Lakes trail— or cross-country—to Mount Gladys and Mount Cruiser to climb tomorrow instead of continuing north to their original goal.

"No, I'm sorry." She made damn sure they could tell she meant it. "This entire area of the park is closed." Seeing that one was about to open his mouth, she said, "If you can detour that way, so can they. Don't provide them with another hostage."

That seemed to get through to them, possibly reinforced by Garrett's commanding stare. He definitely had the gift of stopping people dead with one hard look.

She, Garrett and the two Mason County deputies retreated.

"We'll split off now," Ian Sutherland said.

If only *someone* had seen which way the two gun-toting men with the frightened boy had gone. Since nobody had, Cadence was left with no choice but to send two of her small search party on the initially steep trail to reach Six Ridge and ultimately leave the park and connect with some forest service roads.

That left her and Garrett to continue the pursuit north.

"I'd hoped we could eliminate that possibility, but since we can't…"

Ian only nodded. "We might spend the night at Big Log."

She didn't even have to glance up to know the color of the sky was deepening. Features were becoming subtly less distinct.

"Good. Stay in touch," she said.

The two swung packs onto their backs again and strode back the way they'd come.

"We could stay here," Garrett said into the silence.

That made sense; of course it did. There were reasons the Park Service normally allowed camping only in designated sites. In this case…there were primitive toilets here, which was a big plus.

Garrett saw something on her face and said gently, "I'm sure we can find a place to set up just off the trail."

She heard herself make a sound even she couldn't have named. "Let me make a pit stop first."

Literally, as it happened. They took turns, the brightness of the day diminishing even in that short time.

"We should stay."

"Your call," he said, with that same careful lack of pressure.

Her shoulders sagged. "Let's grab a spot close to the trail."

He smiled at her. "We wouldn't have gotten much farther."

"I know."

They chose a site sheltered by old conifers that was near to both the trail and the river.

"One tent or two?" he asked, as he set down his pack and undid straps.

Oh, heavens. It was silly to set up both tents when they'd

shared one so often. In the interests of speed and doing as little damage as possible to native vegetation, they probably wouldn't be able to each have their own after this, not unless they were able to conveniently stop each night at other designated campsites. On the other hand…could she sleep inches away from the man she loved, the same man who'd shrugged and made clear he didn't feel anything close to the same for her?

GARRETT WAITED, feeling new tension. He'd sleep better to have her close. He didn't like the idea of tent walls separating them, of him potentially not hearing someone approach or her slipping out of her own tent. But he was painfully aware he had no right to push.

"One's fine," she said finally, "as long as it's clear the tent is *all* we share."

He hid the irritation that spiked and said, "I get it."

Without asking, he set up his slightly roomier tent, then tossed his pad and rolled sleeping bag inside. While he was doing that, she got the stove going and chose a couple of packets of freeze-dried… He couldn't make out the handwritten labels, but trusted her on this. She freeze-dried her own meals instead of buying them from outfitters the way he did.

Seeing what she was doing, he crouched to spread both their pads and sleeping bags with a noticeable gap between them, then lowered himself to sit on an upended log.

"We should start at first light." She mostly had her back to him, but Garrett could tell she was aware of his every move.

Of course they would.

They ate with near silence between them, but other voices and the soft gurgles and splashes of the river prevented some of the awkwardness that they might otherwise have felt. He was aware of regret, though, and what might even have been grief. During their backcountry trips, he had enjoyed their talks, wandering unpredictably from exchanges about their jobs to politics, ethical dilemmas, philosophy...anything and everything except family and how they felt. He flat out loved her voice, coming from the darkness. Faint huskiness had made him think about the night to come, when they'd be tangled together on top of their sleeping bags, Cadence crying out as she clutched him, Garrett pushing into her exquisitely tight body...

Damn it, damn it, damn it. His body had reacted instantly to his vision. Lucky the darkness and lack of a fire would keep her from noticing.

He let his body know it wasn't getting what it wanted and did the minimal cleanup, while she got on the radio and responded to the chief ranger about tomorrow's plans.

When she was done, she asked, "You heard all that?"

"I did. I wish they'd been able to muster a second helicopter, but one may be enough."

She made a frustrated sound. "I just keep thinking...what happens when we do see them? Worse yet, what if it's sudden?"

"I don't love having us spread so thin," he admitted. Major understatement. "It's too much like today's fiasco. As you said, though, we've got to get the boy away from them."

She released a shuddery breath that made him want to reach for her. He actually started to before forcing himself to stay where he was.

"Everyone knows that's their priority." He didn't really need to say that, but knew she needed to hear it anyway.

Stirring, Cadence said after a minute, "I'm not really sleepy, but I know dawn isn't that far away."

Days were exceptionally long in the northwest at this time of year. The longest day of the year was near, in fact, the summer solstice. That gave them more daylight and chance to hunt down these bastards, but the downside was that the men could more easily stay on the move, too.

He grunted his agreement and reached over his head to stretch, hearing a faint crack or two, appreciating the effect on his muscles. "If I have to tell people to shut up, I will."

She gave a choked laugh. "If either of us has to do that, it should be me. And really…nobody is being that loud."

He cocked his head. She was right. In fact, the hum of voices seemed unusually subdued to him. The people camping here must be feeling uncomfortably vulnerable. Yeah, he doubted any of these folks would make a late night of it. Most would be fleeing down the trail as early as they could be ready come morning.

"Maybe we should commandeer those horses," he suggested, not serious.

Instead of laughing, she said thoughtfully, "Maybe we should. Think how fast we could move."

"Uh-huh. One problem: I've never been on a horse in my life."

"You're kidding!"

"Nope. City boy. And problem number two—did you see the couple who got here on horseback?" They looked to be in their fifties, weathered skin, the guy with a belly starting to inch over his belt, the woman tiny and so fine boned, he hoped doctors were checking her bone density. Cowboy boots that would raise blisters in the first half hour of hiking. Backpackers, they weren't.

"Yeah, yeah." She huffed. "I didn't mean it."

"I know." Both were keeping their voices low, creating a sense of intimacy. He'd sounded…he didn't know, just that it made him uneasy. "Let's hit the sack," he said abruptly.

"Sure." She popped to her feet and gestured. "I'm going to use the facilities again."

"Me, too," he agreed, "but I'll wait until you get back." They couldn't leave their rifles and handguns unprotected.

What moon had risen was barely past a crescent and didn't offer enough light for him to watch Cadence for more than a few steps. When she vanished in the darkness, he tensed, eyes fixed on where she'd reappear. *For God's sake*, he thought, but couldn't make himself do anything but listen hard for a sound that was out of place, for her voice, for her footsteps.

Her voice he heard a few minutes later. She obviously stopped to reassure several sets of campers before materializing in front of him.

"Your turn."

As he could have predicted, she must have stripped in record time. By the time he got back, she was already in her sleeping bag, curled up with her back to him. Probably a smart move on her part, he conceded, avoiding the awkwardness of them bumping into each other as they peeled off tops, set boots aside and actually maneuvered into the side-by-side bags.

He wadded up his fleece quarter zip, figuring it was as good as he'd get for a pillow, laid his cargo pants aside and maneuvered into his own sleeping bag, all the while conscious of her so close. Cadence didn't move enough to cause even a faint rustle. Was she breathing? He gritted his teeth, forcing himself to think about what lay ahead of them.

Sunrise would come barely after 5:00 a.m. this time of year. Without cell phone service, they had no way to set an alarm, but he knew he'd have no trouble waking up, and Cadence was probably the same.

After an early start this morning and the stresses of the day, he should have been beat, but tell his brain that. He couldn't turn it off. Mostly, he couldn't prevent himself from remembering all the other times he'd shared a tent with Cadence.

He lay as still as he could, able to tell she was doing the same. Finally, he said aloud, "Hell! Neither of us will get any sleep." He reached for her. When he tugged, she rolled, her head finding his shoulder and his arm closing securely around her.

She fought. "What are you *doing*? You promised."

"I'm trying to get comfortable enough to sleep. That won't happen while we're lying here as rigid as a pair of mummies!"

"Speak for yourself!"

Conscious of other campers, he murmured, "Shhh."

She quit struggling, but said from between her teeth, "I was fine."

"I wasn't. But suit yourself." Closing his eyes, he deliberately relaxed the arm that encircled her and waited to see what she'd do.

The seconds stretched into a minute. Maybe two. Then she sighed and relaxed.

In the darkness, Garrett smiled. Unfortunately, his erection took too damn long to subside enough to let *him* sleep.

MORE COMFORTABLE THAN she would have wanted to admit to Garrett, Cadence knew she had even less chance of sleeping anytime soon. Well, she'd have been unlikely to, anyway. Her thoughts raced as she reran the day's events, her every decision, the decisions *everyone* had made. If only the pair had been stopped before they reached a trailhead. Worse yet, a trailhead near a campground full of people easy to intimidate. The last thing anyone coming to one of the most beautiful national parks expected was violence.

A part of her wished the grandmother hadn't showed her the photo on her phone of her grandson. Being able to picture Evan's face didn't help. Eleven years old, Grandma had said, but he was still skinny in the way of a boy just a few years away from puberty. The only hope Cadence held was that, according to Grandpa, Evan played soccer at a high level. Surely that meant he was in good shape...and fast, if he got the chance to run. The kid had brown hair, brown or hazel eyes and an infectious grin.

Hold on, she thought. *We're coming.*

That circled her back around to her worry about her and Garrett alone confronting men so brutally willing to use violence and even kill.

They could call in help.

But what would happen to Evan if the men knew they were cornered?

Out of the darkness came a husky murmur, "Easy." He squeezed her, just a brief tightening of his arm.

Was her body so stiff he'd been able to tell how tense she was? She made a face. Probably. Okay. Deep breath. Let it out. Another one. She imagined herself in a yoga class, lying on a mat, eyes closed, listening to her instructor.

Except in one way this was better. Her pillow might be firm, but the curve where his chest met his shoulder was shaped just right for her head. And...she could hear, or maybe it was just feel, the rhythm of his heartbeat. Strong and steady. She should have set up her own tent, but then she wouldn't have even begun to relax. In one way, it was torture being so close to Garrett, but his strength, the heat his big body radiated, were also comforting.

More than that, she admitted to herself that there was no one she'd rather have at her side on an operation that filled her with trepidation. He was smart, with lightning quick reactions, able to answer violence with violence in a way she'd never had to do before. And she knew, even though the two of them were done as a couple, that he'd be determined to keep her safe while also having enough respect for her skill on the job to not try to hobble her.

What more could she want?

Astonishingly, her eyelids felt heavy and her body seemed to be relaxing toward sleep.

I have to tell him, was her next-to-last thought, followed by, *Not until this is over. This isn't the right time.* They had plenty of worries without adding one so personal.

Coward, she accused herself, but didn't find an answer for that before she slid into dreams.

Chapter Eight

Cadence's eyes popped open, and she knew immediately why. Stomach roiling, she lay as still as she could. Oh, no! This was the *worst* timing.

Yeah, and what had she expected? She was at least queasy every morning, and quite often so sick to her stomach she had to run for the bathroom. This was a good reason she should have slept in her own tent.

Her head was still pillowed on Garrett's shoulder. He stirred slightly, making her realize light had filtered through the tight weave of the tent walls. Dawn was close enough, he'd be waking up any minute.

Her first movements were slow as she separated herself from him one careful inch at a time. He made a whuffing sound that might become a question. Her shaking hand found the sleeping bag zipper even as she also groped for pants and boots.

By the time she squirmed out of the sleeping bag, she was moving fast. Swallowing back the bile in her throat. Pants on, feet shoved into boots. Snatch up a roll of toilet paper. She parted the tent flap as Garrett said, "Cadence?"

"Gotta go." Run. She hated the idea of puking in the pit toilet, but what else could she do? She wouldn't want to bag her own vomit and stow it in her pack, the way she'd have to if she sprinted for the woods.

Thank God no one else was ahead of her. In fact, she didn't see any other movement around the campground. She had just enough privacy to heave, whimper and do it again. Then she wiped her mouth with a few squares of toilet paper, straightened and read her body.

Yes, she was done. She'd rinse her mouth out quick when she got back, and she knew from recent experience that she'd be fine eating breakfast. Most days, this would be it, while occasionally she had other, unpredictable bouts of nausea, but if that happened... Well, it wouldn't be hard to make an excuse to leave the trail and open enough distance from Garrett that he wouldn't be able to hear her.

Unsurprisingly, he was up, dressed in cargo pants and a T-shirt, and was firing up the stove. He looked up as she approached, though, those blue eyes sharp.

He can't know.

"You okay?" he asked.

"Sure." She shrugged. "I should have gotten up during the night, but I didn't want to. You know what that's like."

His gaze lingered on her face as if he sensed a lie, but at last he said, "Oatmeal?"

"Sure. Did you bring some, too?"

"Always have it in my pack." He rooted around in said pack, a dark green, and produced other sealed packets. "Raisins or cranberries?"

"Um...cranberries. Wait, I have some nuts, too."

She could have started rolling sleeping bags and pads, but gave herself the gift of sitting for a few minutes, watching his quick, sure movements. Once he dished up the oatmeal, he put water on to boil. He carried coffee, as did she. Unfortunately, she'd had to give up coffee for the time being.

Smelling it should be okay, especially outside where any aroma dissipated fast.

When she saw the water close to boiling, she hunted for the box of tea she'd stuffed in the top of her pack and took out one bag.

"I'm in the mood for tea," she said, and handed him her mug.

That earned her another of his thoughtful and too-piercing looks, but he didn't question her. She'd read that some caffeine was all right, so she'd bought a couple different kinds of black tea. She could only imagine what he'd think if she'd produced an herbal tea!

Nobody else had stirred when she rolled up both their bags and pads while he washed their minimal dishes, dried and stowed them in his pack. He took care of the tent, since it was his, and they split up again to use the incredibly primitive facilities.

Then both donned belts with holsters and guns and swung first packs onto their backs and then rifles over their shoulder.

"You don't think they could have slipped by during the night."

"No," Garrett said. "I sleep lightly. As it was, I woke up several times when other campers got up. Somebody snored."

She wrinkled her nose as they reached the trail. "I heard that."

Gradually, they stretched their legs, slowing to use rocks to cross a stream that flowed to join the North Folk River, and plunged into heavy forest. The quiet was more profound this morning, as if even the birds were reluctant to violate it.

"Two hours ahead of us," Cadence said. "That means they could have gotten as far as Eight Stream."

"Unless they turned off."

She'd studied her map last night in minute detail. "I'm thinking Hammer Creek."

"If they can get across the river there. I kind of doubt they'd try."

Hammer Creek flowed from the higher elevation of Smith Lake and Black and White Lakes—which were officially accessible by the Flapjack Lakes trail. Climbers took that route to reach several popular climbs, including one of the park's best known: the daunting spear of rock that was Mount Cruiser. It would be logical for climbers who'd first climbed Mount Duckabush or the like farther north to look for a shortcut to Cruiser.

She could only hope Ed McCall and Alyssa Bailey had gotten an early start up that trail.

The trail was smooth; no issues with fallen branches or the mud or washouts that might have plagued it during the spring. Cadence saw a few places where understory vegetation was trampled enough to suggest someone had stepped off the trail. It was hard to tell how fresh those signs were. After the brief conversation, she and Garrett stayed silent, communicating when they paused with raised eyebrows and hand signals. She didn't really believe they would catch up so soon, but if the men were inexperienced, possibly suffering from blisters... Who knew?

"Bear," Garrett murmured, and she turned her head sharply.

A lone black bear, spattered with water, was making its way up from the river. Beady eyes fixed on them and it stopped, then lumbered across the trail right in front of them and crashed its way into the deep forest. The black bears were rarely a problem, unless a mother felt her cubs were threatened, but an occasional one became aggressive. Those who mooched food at campgrounds from people who didn't know better sometimes had to be trapped and relocated where they were less likely to encounter humans. Most often, the bears ran, just as this one had.

A squawk from her radio startled her. She pulled it from the outside pocket on her pack and adjusted the volume. Behind her, she realized Garrett was doing the same with his. She was reassured by reports from other pairs of law enforcement rangers and law enforcement officers who had started as early as she and Garrett had. Two rangers she knew well had started up the Duckabush River trail, which unfortunately began well outside the park boundaries. *At least five or six miles from a gravel or dirt forest road*, she thought. Not that the park boundary mattered, except that men on the run might see it as a trail that would lead them out of the park and onto forest roads, where they could arrange a pickup if either of their phones worked.

The best news: a helicopter was on its way from the air force base on Whidbey Island and was aiming straight for the trail that lay ahead of Garrett and Cadence.

IN THE FIRST HOURS, they heard the helicopter a few times rather than seeing it, sheltered as they were by the tall hemlock, fir and cedar forest. The pilot and a spotter reported seeing people, both hikers and climbers, but nobody meeting the right description.

Cadence and Garrett came face-to-face with one party of climbers who seemed startled to meet armed law enforcement.

When told about the manhunt, they explained that they'd spent the night at Nine Stream. "Haven't seen any foot traffic this morning at all," one of the men added, "but we did get an earlier start than a lot of people do."

They promised to stop anyone they met coming up the trail who wasn't a cop or a ranger, after which they strode out.

Watching them go, Cadence said, "The Nine Stream

campground is, what, another three miles on? Are they still that far ahead of us?"

"They might have heard someone coming and just stepped off the trail. In the right place, they wouldn't have had to go more than ten feet to avoid being seen."

The lush vegetation in this river valley made that very possible.

Predictably, she argued anyway. "Or they could be somewhere else entirely."

His eyebrows climbed. "But where? In the next hours, we'll have this corner of the park blanketed by searchers. They could hunker down somewhere they won't be seen, but then what's their plan?"

"If they have enough food, they might think they can just outwait us."

"They could have done that more easily before they sped down Highway 101 in full knowledge they'd attracted pursuit," Garrett said dryly. "If they'd used their brains, they would have looked for an empty house, a garage where the Tahoe could be hidden..." He shrugged. "Now they're out of their element."

She wrinkled her nose at him. "We think."

What could he say but, "We'll find them," and hope she didn't resent what might as well be a pat on the back.

If Cadence was annoyed, it didn't show. She simply nodded and turned to continue north.

The going was slow, because they had to divert every time they spotted evidence that people had beaten a path off the trail, paths that didn't appear on the topographical map that Cadence pulled out at intervals. Most often these dwindled, or ended at an obvious wilderness campsite. Really, in this stretch the river had carved its way along the foot of steep ridges and even mountains, rising too steep above the trail to offer any easy access. Dragging a boy along, carrying borrowed packs, wearing boots that, from the description, weren't hiking or climbing boots with the needed deep-cut tread, would this pair really part from a well-trodden path to take what would be a perilous climb? Garrett couldn't see it.

Eight Stream came and went, the trail rising above the riverbank. Given the steep terrain, Garrett wasn't surprised to have to cross several avalanche slopes, covered by the usual brush and new growth. Once again, he disliked feeling so exposed, even if his uneasiness was unwarranted. The fugitives weren't going to hang around to take potshots at anyone pursuing them.

It was all he could do to get Cadence to stop to have lunch once they'd reached a sun-dappled forest. She was 100 percent focused on that kid, ready to push herself until she broke. Once he succeeded in persuading her to set her pack aside and sit on a rock on the riverbank, Garrett studied her. He wished she weren't carrying as much weight as he was. Yes, she always did when they'd hiked or climbed, but today they'd been moving faster than they would have if this outing had been recreational. She looked tired, although she'd claim he was imagining things if he said anything. After cutting ties between them, she was unlikely to appreciate any remark she saw as disparaging her capabilities. He was well aware that to this day women in law enforcement with any jurisdiction faced discrimination, and he wouldn't blame her for being prickly.

Accordingly, he made himself dig in his pack, seeing out of the corner of his eye that she was doing the same. He also caught a glimpse of some of the contents of her pack, and realized that she'd brought medical supplies beyond the basics he always had and therefore was carrying *more* than he was.

He found a packaged nut and dried fruit mix first, even as he wondered whether he could talk her into stowing her tent under a bush to be picked up later. Or letting him carry some of those extra supplies that helped make her pack bulge.

She handed him her water bottle. He took a swig and gave it back.

"You have to hunt for lost kids on a regular basis," he observed. "They're often in as much danger as Evan is, if for different reasons."

"But that's it," she said. "It's the…the malevolence of grabbing a child, using their vulnerability."

Yeah, a child hostage raised the emotional quotient for anyone mounting an attack, but Garrett guessed that it was the ease of controlling a kid versus an adult that had motivated this particular choice. But he knew what she meant.

"You just saved a little girl," he pointed out.

"It happened so fast."

He shrugged to concede the point.

She produced some packaged cheese and crackers probably meant for school lunches, which made him smile. He enjoyed his, even if the cheese presumably wasn't the real thing.

Before she could get too antsy, he closed up his pack and said, "Ready?"

"Yes." Even after hefting her pack onto her back, she all but bounced to her feet.

Yeah, she was tougher than he'd been giving her credit for. He always found her strength surprising, given how slim she was. Self-preservation had kept him from ever saying that he thought her well-worn boots were cute in what she'd admitted was a size six.

The footbridge crossing Nine Stream was solid, leading them to the camp. He was relieved to see it empty but for two tents that had been left, any possessions zipped inside them. Cadence scribbled notes that they managed to attach to the tent flaps, informing their owners that the park was closed and they needed to proceed south to Staircase.

Then she and Garrett moved on. Shortly thereafter, the river swung to the east, while they crossed a stream and continued north. They began to gain elevation here, the trail consisting of short switchbacks. As nonrunners/hikers, he'd expect the men to founder here. Feathery hemlock trees shaded them as they ascended—and hid them from above, as it would have hidden their quarry.

The forest seemed unnaturally quiet again. Garrett was in the lead, and he realized neither of them had said anything in a while. Yeah, sure, the climb here was steep enough he felt it in his thighs and was probably breathing a little harder than he had been. He stole a look back.

Damn it, Cadence had a talent for hiding what she thought and felt that he hadn't known she possessed. He'd liked the openness of her expressions, the glow of happiness when she first saw him, the subtle displays of humor, her laughter. He'd been so sure she couldn't lie to him. Now he had to wonder if she'd been lying to him all along, and this was the real her.

Or whether she'd retreated deep inside, hiding behind a pleasant, professional facade.

She was sweating, but not breathing any harder than he was. Her head turned constantly as she searched the forest. You'd think she would stumble on the sometimes rocky trail, but she stayed sure-footed.

He glanced at his watch and discovered it was later than he had realized. They'd come on a camp pretty soon. Two Bear lacked any sanitary facilities. After that, a push to First Divide, and another camp. He guessed Cadence would expect to get that far, and even push on to a meeting with the upper Duckabush River. That's where they'd have to start making some serious decisions.

Had they been wrong in assuming these bastards weren't experienced backwoodsmen? Garrett had to wonder. Despite the various brief detours, he and Cadence had made pretty good time. They and the other pairs advancing this direction wouldn't quite come to anything resembling a hub of a wheel, but as they approached, they'd constrict the area to be searched, closing in on the threesome no matter which way they turned.

Unless, a quiet voice in the back of his head murmured, they really had holed up, maybe even watching as their pursuers strode blindly past.

Yeah, but that didn't mean they could stroll back the way they'd come. He'd followed radio traffic well enough to know the numbers of searchers continued to climb. The Tahoe had long since been towed away, and the campground should have emptied by now. With a little luck, two or three days in, there shouldn't be any vehicles left at the trailheads, either, except those left by searchers from one jurisdiction or another. Sooner or later, the men would be spotted. *Just, please, God, don't let them come face-to-face.* A shoot-out at a roadblock was one thing, standing fifty feet apart with no engine block to hide behind, another.

The designated campsite at Two Bear was laid out by a rushing creek and shaded by a thick canopy of mixed evergreen trees. *Nice*, he thought, saw it was empty and kept going.

As he and Cadence pushed on toward the pass at First Divide, following the stream, they left behind the forest for subalpine meadows filled with berry bushes and what would be a blaze of wildflowers a little later in the summer. He stopped to use his binoculars frequently.

A rustle ahead brought him to a stop. He lifted those binoculars again. He thought Cadence came close enough to walking into him that she braced a hand on his pack.

"What…?"

"Bear," he said, seeing the bushes shaking. On its own, or… No. Fifteen or twenty feet to the left, he spotted a cub. No, two—one on each side of the trail.

"Damn," he said.

"We could try to scare them."

"I don't want to face down a mama bear who thinks we've gotten too close to her cubs. It won't kill us to wait for a while."

She glared past him at the fluttering bushes heavy with ripe berries.

Garrett looked around and saw a reasonably flat rock. Cadence sighed and nodded.

He, for one, was just as glad to take off his pack for a few minutes. The back of his shirt was soaked with sweat. He sat, stretched out his legs and was able to pluck a handful of purple-blue berries.

He offered them to Cadence, who was stretching her neck and shoulders after dumping her own pack. That was as much admission as she'd ever make about the stress on her body.

"Oh, thanks, but I'm not hungry."

His body had long since forgotten their relatively scanty lunch and was ready for a snack, at least. He shrugged and popped the berries into his mouth, the taste a burst of sweet and tart at the same time. No wonder the bear family was so happily occupied. He swiveled to pick more.

Cadence did take out her water bottle, drank from it and offered it to him. He did the same and handed it back, grimacing at the purple stain on his fingers.

"What if they don't move on?"

"You know they will sooner or later. I'd say I'm sorry our targets didn't stumble over mama bear, except I'm guessing they'd have shot her."

"Yeah, most people don't realize a bullet or two won't stop a full-grown bear, but given the kind of armaments they're probably carrying..."

They might well have killed the mother bear, orphaning two cubs too young to survive on their own.

"Are you planning to stay around for a while?" she asked, her tone casual, something not as casual beneath.

Stay around *here*?

He flicked a glance at her. *Oh.* She meant on the Olympic peninsula, working his current job. She was staring straight ahead, as she'd been prone to do yesterday and today. God forbid she meet his eyes.

"I'm not setting a date to go," he said after a minute. Feeling his forehead crease, he thought again that maybe he should, now that Cadence and he weren't seeing each other. But he continued, "Living with someone can be difficult when you're not used to it, but...it's been good getting to know my grandfather."

At last, her head turned and she had a recognizable expression on her face: startlement. "What do you mean, *getting to know*?"

Why had he told her that? There was a reason he just didn't talk about family. He rolled his suddenly tight shoulders.

"I didn't know my grandparents when I was a kid," he said, voice clipped. Something he didn't understand compelled him to continue. "I didn't even know I had them. My mother—" wow, those two words felt strange in his mouth "—hated them. She was, uh, pretty disturbed. She never talked about being a kid."

"Did she...run away or something?"

"Yeah, when she was fifteen or sixteen, I think."

"Do you know what was going on?"

Why had he opened his damn mouth? But now that he

had, he reluctantly said, "No. She was…classic. I used to think she was screwed up by an abusive childhood." He jerked one shoulder. "I guess she did butt heads with my grandmother, but Grandma… What can I say? She was a good woman. She…really broke down when I showed up on their doorstep." He'd grieved her death from cancer only a couple of years after he located them. Shaking that off, he said, "Looking back, I think my mother had to be mentally ill. If doctors ever prescribed pills, she didn't stay on them. Fortunately, except for the early years, she only appeared in my life once in a great while."

"Oh, Garrett." Cadence's voice was as soft as a touch. He'd rather have had the touch, except he couldn't let himself be that vulnerable.

He shrugged. "Long time ago."

"Is she dead?" she asked hesitantly.

His jaw clenched, and he had to let a minute pass before he was able to speak without emotion. "Once I became a cop, I checked. She OD'd…four or five years before that. So fifteen years or more ago. Can't even picture her face." Which was a lie.

This time, she laid her hand on his bare forearm. He looked down, feeling a lurch at the sight of her long, graceful fingers and fine-boned hand and wrist. All he could do was clench his teeth and wait until she withdrew it.

Neither said another word until the rustles just north of them subsided, and he hefted his pack onto his back and rose. "Probably safe to go on."

He was grateful that Cadence followed suit without remark.

Chapter Nine

"I haven't heard the helicopter in a while," Cadence said, as soon as the realization crossed her mind.

"They're losing the light and need to get on the ground. They promise to be back come morning."

Oh, wonderful. She should have paid more attention to radio traffic, but the steep ascent to First Divide, a high ridge that offered a sweeping view of the mountains rearing to each side, had a monotony despite the views that allowed her brain to sink into a form of apathy. Wow, she didn't like to think how unobservant she'd been!

Really, what thinking she'd done had to do with the man who was a mostly silent presence behind her. She was bothered to have to keep reminding herself that there was nothing personal between her and Garrett anymore. She winced. Well, except for the baby he didn't know about yet.

So why had he told her about his mother and at least sketched in the childhood that explained so much about him? Oh, maybe he'd had a kind, steady father, but she would bet anything that wasn't the case. Commitment to a woman might truly be beyond his imagining if he'd spent his life in foster care or group homes. A lifetime of temporary relationships. Did the fact that he'd told her as much as he did, and so out of the blue, suggest he was showing a willingness to open up to her?

Right. All she had to do was remember the expression on his face when she'd asked if he had any interest in the possibility that their relationship could become more. Shock, followed by an implacable mask.

Yeah, no.

She forced her thoughts to focus on the here and now. They'd almost have to stop at the designated campsite at First Divide. Or... For the first time, she noticed how quickly the sky was dimming. She had a faint memory of climbing Mount Hopper with a fellow ranger when she first started at the park. A faint but obvious trail turned off just before First Divide. She vaguely remembered it opening eventually into a beautiful alpine meadow that lay at the foot of a steep boulder field.

"You okay?" Garrett asked from behind her.

She must have slowed down. "Yes, but I remembered that access to Mount Hopper should be coming up on the right anytime. It wouldn't make *sense* for them to go that way, but..."

"Nothing they're doing makes sense," he growled. "Especially if they have binoculars, they could have caught sight of us coming up behind them and wanted to get out of sight."

"We almost have to look," she said, without enthusiasm. One more wasted detour.

"Anyplace we could set up camp?" Garrett asked.

"It's only a few hundred yards before Home Sweet Home." Personally, she thought the name of the designated campsite atop First Divide was nauseatingly sweet, but it did have restroom facilities of a sort. "We can sleep there and turn back in the morning. Unless the helicopter gets here in time to do a sweep of that track and the side of the mountain."

"Makes sense," he agreed, without commenting on her wishful thinking.

Lord, she hoped the campground was empty...except being utterly alone with Garrett would increase her tension. And decrease the chance she could avoid notice if she woke up with her usual morning upset stomach.

When they arrived, the meadow was entirely empty.

"Pick your spot," Garrett said wryly, looking around.

She wanted to say, *You set up your tent over there, and I'll put up mine on the exact opposite side of the meadow.* Unfortunately, she had too much pride to give away any hurt feelings.

"Let's make it by that clump of trees," she suggested. "Not quite so...open."

Her chosen spot wasn't far from the toilet, either, just in case. Or the trees would give her another option.

"Works for me."

Once they'd dropped their packs and begun unfastening straps, she said casually, "I might set up my own tent tonight. There's plenty of room."

He stopped what he was doing to scowl at her. "I make you that uncomfortable?"

She hated seeing how still he held himself. "It's not that," she said weakly.

"Then what?"

"You wouldn't like more room to stretch out?"

"No." His jaws worked. "I want to be able to see you. I don't like the idea someone could sneak up, slit the tent and grab you without me having any idea what was happening."

Her body might have given a betraying jerk. Damn. Now, if she insisted, she wouldn't be able to sleep a wink. *Thank you, Garrett.*

"You win," she conceded.

"I'm not trying to—" He hesitated.

Given the awkwardness, Cadence didn't look at him. "No, you're right. It could work the opposite way, too. You could be killed without me even knowing."

He still hadn't moved. "It won't happen. I just... Call me paranoid."

She made a face. "No, it's okay. You're right. I'll sleep better."

After a moment, he nodded and went back to spreading a tarp on the ground and setting up his tent.

Given her aching back and shoulders, she kind of wished she'd left hers behind. It just hadn't occurred to her... No, the surprise had been his insistence on pairing with her. He'd made it next to impossible for her to say, *No, that's not happening.*

And how would she feel if she had rearranged the pairings? Behind Garrett's back, Cadence grimaced. She wouldn't have trusted any of the other deputies the way she did Garrett. She would have thought about him, worried he and his partner might be the ones to come unexpectedly on their quarry. If he'd been gunned down...

Had she really convinced herself she wasn't in love with him anymore? Like that happened practically overnight. He'd hurt her, she *needed* to move past these feelings, but she hadn't yet. And wouldn't be able to until this was over, she'd told him about her pregnancy and they'd parted ways. It might be best if he did go back to Seattle, she thought. *Out of sight, out of mind.*

Or so she wanted to believe.

Maybe *she* should start looking into a transfer. Except she didn't have a clue what kind of future she'd have in the park service. And...what if Garrett wanted some contact with his child?

CADENCE HAD FALLEN quiet after they settled whether they'd share a tent or not.

They parted to use the facilities and briefly discussed

which of their limited menu options they'd have for dinner. Garrett had gotten on the radio and identified their location and plan for morning, listening as other teams did the same.

The pair assigned to the Duckabush River trail had made good time, but after starting out a day later than Garrett and Cadence, were overnighting at the Ten Mile encampment on One Too Many Creek.

Too many what? Garrett wondered, but didn't linger on the question.

Jefferson County deputies Ed McCall and Alyssa Bailey had explored every trail, any hint of a spur leaving it, and nook and cranny of the cluster of lakes they'd been assigned to investigate. They'd scrambled to Smith Lake, the headwaters for Hammer Creek, and finally backtracked to set off behind Garrett and Cadence. They were likely too far behind to be helpful, but Garrett had stayed uneasily conscious all day that their quarry could have hidden and now be hustling down the trail and thinking they were home free.

Ian Sutherland and Tyler Murray had reached Sundown Lake, and since there'd been sightings of the men and boy so far north, were to be picked up by the helicopter in the morning and set down on the Quinault River Trail, potentially to connect with a pair of rangers who were already in the Enchanted Valley, a favorite destination of backpackers that lay along the Quinault River. A pair of deputies from Clallam County were heading southwest along the west fork of the Dosewallips River.

All well and good, but too few of them were spread over a vast stretch of the national park, separated by sharp-toothed mountain peaks, rivers, long ridges and in places, dense forests.

Brooding as he ate the meal Cadence had prepared, he said finally, "We need another helicopter."

"Yeah. I wonder if there's been a crisis elsewhere?"

He grunted. "You'd think they'd tell us. Having to close so much of the park with the height of summer coming up so soon can't be good for the National Park Service image."

She made a face. "I can only imagine the press. I mean, there have been other manhunts in the park, but none that started with dynamite, a cop being shot and killed, a dangerous pursuit on Highway 101 and the abduction of a child from a campground."

"Never mind the heads they bashed at said campground." He paused. "And the number of witnesses who are no doubt eagerly talking to reporters."

"The head ranger must be having conniptions."

He laughed. "Maybe we should count our blessings. Here we are, alone in beautiful country, stars coming out overhead…"

"And having no idea how close those killers are."

Mildly chagrined, he said, "You're right."

"But you are, too. It *is* a beautiful night." She sounded faintly surprised.

Romantic, even. With an intensity that shook him, Garrett wished nothing had changed. That despite the seriousness of their purpose, they would make love once they bedded down for the night.

His body responded to the mere thought, leaving him grateful for the darkness. No fires were allowed in the backcountry, which encouraged early to bed, early to rise. Which was fine, but days were long in the Pacific Northwest at this time of year. Fortunately, not quite as long, given the mountains rising to the west of them, especially Mount Olympus. The sun dropped below those considerably sooner than when it painted magnificent colors over the curve of the earth seen when you sat on a bluff above the Pacific Ocean.

He knew that, because he and Cadence had rented a cabin for a couple of nights at Kalaloch Resort on the ocean. Holding hands, they'd walked on the beach, rolling up their pants and letting the foam from waves wash over their feet despite brisk spring temperatures. He remembered seagulls crying, piles of driftwood at the foot of the bluff. Those had been a couple of the best days of his life.

Tension gripped him. In response, he rolled his shoulders. It had been a good place to take a woman, that's all. Once he started up something with someone else— His mind hit a wall.

What was wrong with him?

"I'm ready to go to sleep," Cadence said, reaching into her pack. "At least, I'm ready to try."

"You're right. The sooner the better, so we can be up at first light again."

They shared the cool water in a pan to brush their teeth, then parted ways briefly before returning to the tent. He let her crawl in first and gave her a few minutes to strip down before he knelt and followed. Not like he could have seen her, but he didn't have the right anymore to savor the sound of her squirming to get a shirt over her head, or pants down those long legs.

When he thought about it, she'd either moved really fast, or had remained partially dressed. Yeah, he'd do that, too, he decided. Just in case they heard something, he wanted to be ready to go. He laid his rifle to one side, but set his handgun within easy reach as he had last night and suspected she'd done the same.

Then he balled a fleece quarter-zip to serve as a pillow and stretched out on his back, very aware that she lay curled away from him, her knees and face all but pressed against the tent wall.

"Good night."

"Sleep tight," she murmured, just as she had on other occasions when they'd been together.

The ensuing silence wasn't an easy one. He was willing to bet she regretted reminding him in any way of their time together.

And, damn, he couldn't imagine dropping peacefully off to sleep at any time in the foreseeable future. Reaching for her as he had last night... She couldn't have made her wishes clearer.

Brooding held sleep off long enough to make him tense with the knowledge he'd be tired tomorrow. He must have finally dropped off, though, because he surfaced to find that he and Cadence were plastered together, her back to his front, and he'd taken his arm out of the sleeping bag so he could wrap it around her. His hand had found its way to her breast. Still half-asleep, he gently squeezed her breast and rubbed his palm over her nipple, already firm and ripe. For just a moment, he'd have sworn her back arched to push her breast more fully into his hand, but when he went still and held his breath, nothing happened. Temptation tore at him, but if he coaxed her, half-asleep, into making love with him, she'd regret it in the morning. He'd hate that. What's more, it wouldn't help his cause with her. Whether she really was asleep or only pretending, he couldn't violate her decision.

He forced himself to release her and pull his arm back into his own sleeping bag.

CADENCE'S FIRST THOUGHT on waking was that she wanted to roll over and go back to sleep. Despite her exhaustion, she hadn't slept well. There'd been an interlude she might have dreamed when Garrett was touching her the way she loved. What's more, her right hip ached and—

Her second full awareness was powerful: she needed to upchuck, and she needed to do it *now*.

On an involuntary moan, she scrambled out of her sleeping bag, pushed aside the tent flap and lurched out onto her hands and knees. Her stomach was already heaving. Oh, God, oh God, she had to get away.

But she knew too well that Garrett had reared up and gotten far enough forward for his head and shoulders to poke from the tent.

"Cadence?"

She tried to speak but made a retching sound. She crawled away but was too sick to rise to her feet. Suddenly, an aluminum pan appeared in front of her and she gave up, snatching it from Garrett's hands and puking. *Please let it be big enough*, she begged. *Don't let me make this even worse than it already is.*

A big hand smoothed hair from her face. He was crouching beside her, she realized. When she was finally done and started to sag, he supported her until she managed to get into a sitting position, albeit swaying.

She couldn't look at him. Despite the gentleness of his hands, he hadn't said a word, not even a soothing, *You'll be fine*.

He set the pan out of her sight and magically produced a water bottle. She rinsed, spat into another dish and did it again. Gradually, her muscles unwound. This nausea had hit harder than usual.

Of course it had, given that this was the worst of all possible times.

"Better?" His first word was almost kind, if she couldn't hear an undertone.

"I think so," she mumbled. "Wow."

"Yeah. Wow."

"I need to—" She gestured vaguely.

"You need to talk to me," he said in a hard voice. "You were sick yesterday morning, too, weren't you?"

She could lie, but would he believe her? And…even if this

timing sucked, she had to tell him sooner or later. It looked like it would be sooner.

She bobbed her head.

He cursed. "Were you ever going to tell me?"

For the first time, she let herself look up, seeing anger in his eyes and thinning his mouth. "Of course I was." Feeling like a rag that had just been wrung out, she couldn't summon any vehemence. "This—" she waved a hand "just all blew up so suddenly. I wasn't ready."

Garrett swore again. "Did it ever occur to you that you had no business throwing an overloaded pack on your back and storming off into the wilderness after a pair of killers *when you're pregnant*?"

"No. This is my job! Women don't sit around twiddling their thumbs because they're pregnant! I'm *fine*—"

"Except for needing to puke your guts out on a regular basis?" He was furious, and not hiding it.

"It's mostly mornings. Not that big a deal. Now, if you'll let me brush my teeth, we should get ready."

His "Not a chance," was soft and ominous. "This makes me wonder if you ever would have told me. How long have you known you were pregnant?"

"Does it matter? I'm not very far along." Six weeks? No. "Maybe two months now. Women often miscarry in the first three months. That's why it's common not to share the news so early."

"With their partners?"

"We're not partners!" she flared, pain mixing with white-hot anger. Her stomach lurched again.

"You're denying I'm the father?"

"Of course I'm not!"

"Then we're partners whether you like it or not."

Oh, that made her mad and stiffened her spine. Glaring at him, she snapped, "You've made plain how uninterested you are in any ties at all! I would have told you, and if you want to be involved in the baby's life—"

His stare blistered her. "You thought I *wouldn't* be?"

"I…" Cadence closed her eyes. "Can we dial this back? I feel lousy. I'd like to clean up and get dressed."

Muscles knotted in his stubbled jaw. "Yeah," he said tightly. "Go ahead."

Radiating tension, he turned his back on her and reached inside the tent for clothes, dragging his pack out. "Go ahead," he said shortly, nodding at the tent.

More than getting dressed, what she really wanted was to scrub her mouth out and have something to eat or drink that would improve the taste and settle any lingering queasiness, but it did make sense to put on some clothes first. It was a way of armoring herself, and she'd feel a little less pathetic.

In the dimness of the tent, she contorted to pull up her pants before digging a clean bra and shirt out of her pack. Socks, boots. And she could only imagine how awful her hair was. She took the time to brush it smooth and braid it as she did most mornings.

She composed herself.

He'd calm down. Garrett wasn't an unreasonable man. He'd been the one to lay out his terms, the one to close any door to altering those terms. The pregnancy had taken her by surprise as much as it had him. They'd used birth control without fail. Usually, two versions, since he had always insisted on donning a condom even though she'd worn a patch. Which, yes, had gone missing a while ago, but she hadn't worried because of the condoms.

No method of birth control was 100 percent, condoms least of all.

What she didn't dare tell him was that, however unexpected and unplanned this pregnancy was, shock hadn't been her only emotion when that test had come up positive. She wanted this baby.

And if he knew that, he'd accuse her of getting pregnant on purpose, which would sour any possibility of civility going forward.

She was having this baby, whether he liked it or not.

Chapter Ten

Squatting on an upended log, Garrett bent over the stove. Water in the pan boiled by the time Cadence crawled out of the tent. "Coffee?" he asked. "Or tea?"

"Tea, please. I'll get it out of my pack." She disappeared again briefly, dragging her pack when she reappeared. A moment later she handed over a tea bag.

He was trying to stomp down on the anger, but all that did was make him aware of how much else he felt. Too much, a lot of it unfamiliar. His chest was about to explode from the pressure.

Expecting his hands to be shaking, he was surprised by their steadiness when he poured the hot water into the two cups and set the pan back down. He'd need to refill it to heat water for their oatmeal, but that could wait. Garrett just wished he knew what to say.

No, he knew the first thing he had to ask.

"You planning to have this baby?"

Her head shot up. "Yes!"

"Pregnancy will torpedo your career."

Outrage remaining on her fine-boned face, she opened her mouth…then closed it. "I've…been putting off finding out what park service policy is."

He clenched his teeth, the better to keep his mouth shut.

Cadence bent her head and gazed into the steeping tea as if it could offer her a prophecy. "I know I'll have to take time off," she said softly. "Maybe...try to get shifted from the law enforcement focus."

He had to say this. "We need to get married."

"What?" She lifted her head to stare at him. "Don't be ridiculous! This isn't the fifties!"

"It's still the right thing to do. I can get you and the baby on my health insurance, take care of you when you can't work."

"If I can't keep working, I'll go home."

He'd been afraid she would say that. He needed her here, where he could see her daily, with much the same intensity as he'd needed to share a tent with her.

"That's my baby," he ground out.

Hot color blazed on her cheeks. "No, it's *my* baby."

His gaze lowered from her face, and when she looked down she blinked at the sight of her hand splayed over her abdomen in instinctive protection.

He took a deep breath and let it out. "Ours."

Their eyes met.

"Why are you so worked up?" She sounded genuinely puzzled. "You were really blunt when you told me this isn't anything you want. Marriage, children... Maybe you just weren't interested in anything lasting with me, but you will be eventually with someone else."

There wouldn't be anybody else.

"I don't know," she went on. "But... It doesn't matter. I'm not trying to trap you into this, if that's what you're thinking. If you'll pay child support, I'll be grateful, but I won't even hold you to that. I can cope."

He felt sick with the knowledge that this was what she thought of him, that he was a man who could shrug off the knowledge he had a kid out there somewhere, not willing to make any effort to stay in contact or pay his share of expenses.

Countering her perception meant baring himself in ways he never had before, but he didn't see a choice. "I...don't know who my father is. Whether he knew my mother was pregnant or not. From what I remember about her...he was unlikely to be any prize." His throat tried to close. He pushed past it, voice hoarse. "I will never allow any child of mine to grow up feeling unwanted."

Seeing her expression soften, Garrett had to look away. He hated pity.

"I...won't try to keep you from being a father," Cadence said softly. "I promise."

"Then marry me."

She shook her head. "No. I won't marry a man who doesn't love *me*. First and foremost. That's...a recipe for disaster." Her mouth twisted. "I should say, for a quick divorce. You *know* that's not what you want."

"You're wrong. I want us to raise this child together. All of us living in the same house." This certainty was only one of the tangled feelings he hardly understood.

Her head shook again, hard enough that her braid flopped over her shoulder. "That's what your grandfather would have said in this situation. People have children out of wedlock all the time these days. We can share custody without the bitterness and anger that an eventual divorce would brew. Wouldn't that be better?"

"No." He let her see and hear that he wouldn't change his mind. "You said yourself, we were good together. We have what it takes to..." He stumbled over how to finish the sentence. Be happy together? For a lifetime? Something he'd never imagined being possible, but Cadence had shaken some of his preconceptions, he couldn't deny that. Why else had he been so stunned when she'd shrugged and said *See you around*?

"I saw the expression on your face that day in the café," she said quietly. "You're not in love with me, or even close. You were shocked that I'd imagine for a minute that our relationship might be going anywhere besides bed when we can both get off work at the same time. Say what you will, but you were clear from the beginning."

"This is why you confronted me, isn't it?" The realization had just jumped into his head. "You already knew you were pregnant."

"No." She hesitated. "I guess I'd begun to suspect. And… before I found out, I did need to know how you felt about me, whether you'd changed your mind about the future."

"If you'd explained—"

Her dark eyes sparked with anger. "You're not hearing me. I needed the truth. And no, I won't marry you because of the baby."

He opened his mouth without any idea what he was going to say, but she shook him off.

"Garrett, we have more important things to do right now. There's a scared boy out there depending on us. I'm not having the baby tomorrow. Even assuming all goes well, we have seven months to talk about how we'll handle things in the future. Okay?"

No, it wasn't okay. Garrett wanted everything nailed down. Too much of his life had been a walk along the sharp edge of a knife blade. A teeter, and he'd go down. It had happened too often. But she was right to remind him of priorities. Her refusal to even consider marrying him was so adamant, it was clear he wasn't going to crack it in the immediate future.

"Have you seen a doctor?"

"No. I…did two separate pregnancy tests, and they were both positive. That's all I know right now."

God. How was he supposed to throw on his pack and march up the trail hunting killers, when his backup was a woman carrying his baby? When he knew that, if things blew up on them, he was at risk of losing both of them?

The baby was a few cells, he told himself. A fantasy. And he wasn't in love with Cadence—she was right about that. He felt more than he had let himself admit, but love? No. He felt…responsible, sure, but he had to stop himself from getting carried away.

So he forced himself to give a clipped nod and said, "I'll make the oatmeal if you want to roll up our sleeping bags."

Her eyes lingered on him, but he didn't let himself try to read anything in them. She said, "Sure," nothing special in her agreement.

They ate in complete silence. Afterward, he took down the tent and stuffed it in its bag, rolled the tarp with his pad and stowed everything back in his pack. He looked around, seeing that Cadence was doing the same. A few dusty prints, some flattened grass, was all they'd leave behind. That seemed wrong, given how momentous the past hour had been.

CADENCE STUMBLED TWICE in the first five minutes because she wasn't paying attention to where she was putting her feet. She had to hope he was being more observant in other ways than she could claim to be, too.

They quickly retraced their way to the spur trail she might not have noticed had she not been looking for it yesterday— and if she hadn't been here before, last summer. The trail curved around a slope, and she could faintly hear the stream that they would encounter ahead. There was still enough snowmelt, it must be running higher than it would later in the summer.

They reached the meadow, as pretty as she'd remembered it. Steep boulder field and stark rock of the mountain. She looked up toward the summit.

Garrett startled her when he spoke. "They wouldn't want to climb a mountain."

"Unless they thought that trail goes somewhere else?"

He cocked a brow.

"You're right. They wouldn't be able to hide above the tree line, and they must have heard the helicopter yesterday and guessed it'll be back today."

"I agree. Let's get back to First Divide."

Fortunately, they hadn't lost more than half an hour, if that. Garrett strode in the lead, his long legs making the pace effortless for him. She didn't quite have to jog, but close. Truly, she didn't mind; she shared his sense of urgency.

They passed the still-empty campsite they'd left so recently without slowing and almost immediately began the descent. And, ugh. Downhill was harder on the legs than uphill. She didn't usually notice, but after sleeping so poorly last night—

Garrett stopped suddenly, frowning. "Do you hear—?"

The crack of a gunshot made her jerk and spin around. Was someone shooting at *them*?

As if she'd spoken aloud, Garrett said tersely, "Too far away." He edged past her and broke into a bounding run down the trail. Thinking she heard shouts, she did the same, seeing he'd already pulled the Glock he carried on his hip. She groped for the snap on her holster and managed to get her hand on the butt of her gun without tripping and face-planting.

Crack.

Another shot. Handgun, she thought. A bellow. Thuds

that made her think someone was running away? Climbing toward them, or dropping downslope?

She was mostly looking at Garrett's back, and what glimpses she had ahead were limited by bends in the trail and forest.

Abruptly he slowed, as if somehow he'd been able to pinpoint how far away those gunshots had been. She didn't like the prickling feeling that a watcher could be hiding among the trees.

Garrett signaled for her to stop and remain silent with a flattened hand, then eased forward. Now he gripped his pistol in a two-handed firing position. Cadence hastily imitated him. She was a heck of a shot at the range, but had so little experience actually firing it in action.

She'd fired when she had to a couple of weeks ago. The reminder gave her confidence. Still, goose bumps pricked her skin and she listened with everything in her.

The trail dropped sharply, a switchback turn ahead keeping them from seeing anything beyond it. Garrett moved carefully, tension in every line of his body.

A moan drifted to them, the only sound she could hear. Even birds had gone silent.

Ahead of her, Garrett said suddenly, "Oh, hell." He didn't relax his stance, but he moved faster. She couldn't see past him... Then she did.

Two people sprawled across the trail, their body positions so *wrong* that it took her a moment to realize why. One lay ominously still, the other whimpered and tried to push himself up. He failed, groaned and then managed to turn his head. He'd seen Garrett, she realized.

The injured were both men, she saw. The eleven-year-old boy hadn't been dropped here like a discarded rag doll.

Garrett rushed to the two, looked down, then paused and

glanced back at her. He took one hand from his weapon long enough to point ahead, waited for her nod and kept going.

With complete irrationality, she wanted to beg him not to risk himself advancing close behind men who'd just gunned down two more victims.

It was immediately obvious that the bulk of the packs explained in part why these men's sprawl was so awkward. The moaning guy had been able to roll to his side, but the second man, unconscious or dead, lay bowed backward over his, the position painful to see.

The coils of rope strapped to their packs told her these were climbers.

Cadence blocked her fear from her mind, set down her pack and laid her own gun down where she could grab it quickly. Then she knelt beside the conscious man. "You were shot."

"Yeah," he pushed out between gritted teeth. "What the—?"

"You must not have gotten word that the park is closed."

She doubted he'd taken in what she said. Blood soaked his pant leg. He clutched that leg in agony. Cadence pulled his pack off his shoulders and set it down so that she could use it to elevate his leg. If the bullet had opened an artery... She tore open her pack and took out gauze pads, ripping the packaging, pressing several against his thigh even as she scanned his body for other wounds without seeing any.

Sweat dripped from his face, and his eyes were wild. "Not me. Take care of Jeff."

"Can you hold this?"

He nodded with difficulty and pushed himself up on one elbow. When she placed his hand over the thick pad, his tendons strained on the back of his hand. Even then, she paused for an instant, watching to see how fast blood soaked those pads.

Not as much as she'd feared.

A part of her didn't forget for a second that Garrett was putting himself out there, and alone. But she was where she needed to be.

Accordingly, she swiveled on her knees to examine the man she'd suspected was dead from first sight. Seeing glazed eyes fixed on the sky and utter stillness, she knew she'd been right. Nonetheless, she quickly checked for a pulse in his throat and felt nothing. She yanked up his shirt and took a look at the obvious bullet wound in his immobile chest. There wasn't very much blood. It was the living who gushed blood, not the dead. The force had driven him backward. She thought the bullet had gone through his heart, and he'd been dead in an instant. Certainly before he hit the ground.

A part of her wanted to move him so that he didn't look so horribly uncomfortable, but she couldn't. Investigators would photograph and examine this scene. She'd do enough damage saving one life. She had no excuse for rearranging this man.

From behind her came a gasped, "Is he—?"

She struggled to compose her face before she swiveled again. "I'm sorry. There's nothing I can do."

His eyes squeezed shut. "God."

GARRETT DIDN'T DARE move as fast as he'd have liked. This was like clearing a building. Slow and careful. As cool as the early morning was, sweat stung his eyes. In the back of his mind, he couldn't help thinking how close by these bastards had been last night. Not so close they'd heard him and Cadence talking, or they'd be dead, but why hadn't he gone on enough to be sure they were truly alone?

A flash of red caught his eye. Was that the boy? The men wore black. Backpacks…green and navy blue. If the boy lagged behind…would a few carefully placed shots give him a chance to run?

They couldn't be moving fast, or he'd surely hear them, Garrett thought. Had they caught a glimpse of him? If so, were they lying in wait?

A crackly voice came from his radio and he winced, freeing a hand to turn down the volume. A branch cracked ahead, followed by a muttered curse. Was there any chance they'd understand that they were screwed, that escape was no longer possible?

Sure, that's why they'd just shot two unarmed mountain climbers who were no real threat to them. Men who likely wouldn't even have been able to report the encounter until they had cell phone service two days from now.

Garrett's foot slid a little on a slanted face of a boulder that formed part of the descent. He regained his balance quickly. Eased toward the next bend in the trail. And, hell, didn't see in time a loose rock that tumbled away from his booted foot.

Gunfire erupted. He felt a hard punch in his chest as he flung himself to one side. Bullets ripped shreds from the bark of trees all around him and pinged off rock. He hit the ground hard and rolled until he slammed to a stop against one of those trees. Damn, his arm stung and he wondered if he'd just broken a few ribs. He managed to get his Glock out in firing position and yelled, "Police! Put those guns down! We have your Tahoe and the weapons, and we know who you are!" *He* didn't, but someone would by now. "You have nowhere to go!"

At the next barrage of shots, he scrambled farther from the trail and pressed his back to the largest tree he saw. They weren't even bothering to aim, just spraying bullets everywhere. Thank god Cadence hadn't come with him. He'd give a lot to return fire…but without an adequate sightline, the risk of killing the boy was too high.

Of course, that's why those two slugs had snatched him.

When quiet descended, Garrett pushed himself to his knees, and risked stealing a look around the rough-barked tree trunk blocking his body. He saw absolutely nothing except fresh wood chips and small, feathery branches on the ground. He heard something, though: a snarled voice that came to him so faintly he knew they were running again.

He let loose of some language he rarely used, and let his head fall back and bump the tree trunk. He wouldn't accomplish anything continuing the pursuit right now. At least he knew exactly where his quarry was, if not which direction they'd choose when they reached the intersection with the Duckabush trail, not much over a mile ahead. But others were closing in. Garrett would feel more confident, if not for the boy meant to be their shield.

Chapter Eleven

Cadence heard Garrett before she saw him. Of course he'd know she was guarding her patient in case Garrett was dead and the gunmen had turned around, thinking they could retrace their steps to escape.

"It's me," he called, and she whimpered in relief. She'd never been so scared in her life as she had been when she heard that fuselage of gunshots. At that instant, she'd been acutely aware that she loved him, whether she wanted to or not. No matter what, he was the father of the baby she carried. Thinking he'd been killed…

Hands shaking now, she lowered her gun.

Maybe because she was already rattled, she was instantly aware that he looked different. A livid scratch crossed his cheek. And…that was blood on his upper arm. Mostly, though, it was his eyes. His usual calm was nowhere to be seen. Instead, she saw a wildness that might be desperation.

"You're hurt."

"Nothing serious." Not even blinking, he crossed the distance separating them before he once lowered his gaze to take in the injured man—and the dead one. "Help on its way?"

"Yes, the helicopter shouldn't be more than fifteen minutes out. Ryan needs a hospital." She swallowed. "His friend is dead."

"Yeah." He'd pulled gruff sympathy from somewhere. He nodded at the man she'd doctored to the best of her ability, but who she suspected would need surgery. No exit wound, so somebody would have to extract the bullet as well as patching up the damage.

Garrett lowered his pack to the ground beside her and crouched to meet Ryan's eyes. "I'm sorry we didn't have any way to issue a general warning to people who weren't carrying a SAT radio."

Ryan Lavosky still lay flat on the ground, his leg elevated, but he'd mastered the pain well enough to talk. "We were climbing," he said in a near monotone. "Mount Duckabush first, then O'Neil Peak. Thought about doing Mount Hopper, but our supplies were running low." He grimaced. "We didn't get that far, anyway, as it turned out."

Garrett rested a hand on the injured man's shoulder and squeezed lightly. "I imagine Cadence has told you what triggered the manhunt."

"Yeah." He seemed to take a minute just to breathe before he said, "I don't know if they'd have let us by, but Jeff—my friend." Seeing Garrett's nod, Ryan said, "He's a cop." His flinch was obvious. "I mean, was. Ah, King County Sheriff's Department. He started to give them hell for carrying guns in the park, and then he asked that boy if he was all right."

A nerve jerked beneath Garrett's eye.

"If he'd just kept his mouth shut—"

"They might have let you by," Garrett said. "But they just as well might not have. They're volatile, and incredibly violent. No hesitation, as you saw."

Tears glazed the guy's eyes, but he blinked them away. "You're bleeding," he said, noticing Garrett's arm.

"Just grazed."

Cadence said, "Let me see it."

He didn't argue, and she found he was right. Which didn't

mean he didn't hurt. The groove was deep enough to guarantee a scar. Trying to hide how bothered she was to see him injured, she cleaned up the ugly gash and bandaged it. When she was done, he lifted his arm and rotated it a few times before seeming satisfied.

In the meantime, she'd been inspecting him. Her gaze settled in horror on a tear—or was it a hole?—in his shirt. Right smack in the middle of his chest.

Fingering it, she said, "What's this?" Her voice came out a little bit too high.

"You know I'm wearing my vest."

She wore hers, too, but—Oh, god. "A few inches lower, and that wouldn't have helped."

He grimaced. "Now, *that* hurts like a—" He cut off what he'd been about to say. "I might have cracked my sternum. Or ribs."

Cadence sank back on her heels. *"Might?"*

"I've been shot a couple of times before. The vest probably saved my life. Some pain for a month or so, that's nothing."

If she wasn't mistaken, he was admitting to having taken bullets at least three times, counting today. He'd talked some about his years with Seattle PD, but being shot hadn't been included in any of those stories.

Her teeth wanted to chatter, but she wouldn't let them. "I have cold packs."

"I'm…not real comfortable taking off the vest while we're exposed like this."

Her head turned sharply toward the trail behind him. "You think—?"

"No, I don't." He caught her hand in his. "But we can't rule anything out."

"No." Foolishly, she had ceased being watchful the minute she heard his voice.

"Company coming," Garrett said, and she realized she'd been hearing the helicopter for a few minutes. "It won't be able to land here. We may need to carry Ryan up to First Divide."

As it turned out, the hovering monster above them lowered a Stokes basket, essentially a backboard in a cage, and they strapped Ryan in.

He held out a hand and mouthed the words, "Thank you."

Cadence had been thinking earlier while she waited for Garrett, and now, once the injured man had been lifted on high and disappeared into the open door of the helicopter, she used the radio to request they take the friend's body, too.

Garrett seemed to understand that the pilot or medic would be answering to orders from the park ranger. He used the delay to take detailed photos of the body with his phone. Cadence hadn't wanted to do that earlier—it might have seemed sort of cold-blooded to Ryan—but Garrett was using his head.

Eventually permission came in. Leaving the body of a visitor to the park where it might be dragged away and dismembered by bears or other wildlife wasn't a good option, but neither would be asking Cadence and Garrett to stay put for what might be hours to protect the remains. Eventually the body—Jeff Yonker—was also lifted to disappear into the helicopter, both men's packs accompanying him.

The helicopter pilot told her that their intention was to fly low and look for the men and boy before taking Ryan to the hospital.

"Should be back in a couple of hours," he said. "Faster if we can connect with an ambulance."

Probably she should have told somebody about Garrett's injuries, but she'd left that decision to him. If he thought he could go on, that was his business.

And when they were so close behind…

NOW THAT THE adrenaline had ebbed, Garrett felt worse than he had admitted to Cadence. That didn't mean he needed to be hauled off to the hospital. Not like doctors could do a thing for cracked or broken ribs or breastbone except for wrapping them, and he could have her do that later if necessary.

Neither of them moved as the roar of the helicopter gradually diminished. Finally, he said, "This isn't a great place to stop."

"Are you sure you're okay to go on?"

"Yeah. We won't be catching up in the near future, though, and I wouldn't mind a chance to sit along the way for a few minutes."

"Did you, um—" she pressed her lips together "—well, shoot back?"

"No." Damn, he wanted to wrap her in his arms, both to soothe the anxiety on her face and because holding her would comfort him. Her stiff posture suggested she wouldn't be receptive, however. So he nodded at their packs. "Let's clean up and get moving until we find a good place to stop. We can talk while we walk."

Her gaze followed his to the scattered wrappings she'd discarded along with blood-soaked gauze pads. "Sure. You're right."

"You know how often you say that?" he joked.

She gave him a weak smile before picking up after herself. He didn't offer to help. Bending over wouldn't feel great at the moment.

Five minutes later, she insisted on lifting Garrett's pack so he could shrug into it as easily as possible, then held out his rifle for him to slide his arm inside the strap. She helped position the thing before picking up her own pack. It felt heavier than it had when they started the day.

"The other people who crossed paths with these guys were even luckier than we knew."

"If this Jeff Yonker was more than a rookie, he should have known better than to confront two men carrying the kind of weapons they are."

"From what the friend said, it might have been Evan that worried him," Cadence said.

He grunted, resettled the pack on his back and said, "You ready?"

"Anytime."

As they started out, she wanted to know if he'd seen Evan, and he told her about the flash of red he'd guessed was the boy's sweatshirt. "We already know he's still with them."

"Yes." Cadence sounded subdued. She stayed quiet for quite a while after that, despite earlier seeming to want to talk. In truth, unless they were to talk about themselves, what was there to say?

They did find a sawed-off part of a log that appeared to have been positioned to provide a bench of sorts at the crook of one of the switchbacks. Reluctant to take off his pack, Garrett asked if she had ibuprofen handy and swallowed three tablets when she produced them. He wasn't hungry, but she insisted he eat something, so he downed a couple of handfuls of peanuts.

He was finding the trek down to the narrow valley floor tougher than the climb to First Divide had been. No surprise there, given to the pain wrapping his torso and the burn and ache in his bicep. If Cadence noticed that he was moving noticeably slower than usual, she didn't comment. These had been a stressful couple of days; she probably wasn't feeling at her peak, either.

Garrett briefly pointed out where he'd encountered the men. She stopped to stare in shock at the raw slices on the trunks of old trees, the chips and broken branches and even a place that a bullet had scraped rock.

After a minute, she wrinkled her nose. "A good ranger would hunt for any cartridges and bullets. Not the kind of thing we want littering this country."

"No, but figuring out where all those bullets went…" He shook his head. "The head ranger can send someone out here later if he feels inclined."

She made a face, but walked on without argument. It had to be five minutes before she said, "I can't imagine how you survived that." So her mind had stayed on the scene behind them. Any chance she'd been scared for him?

"Quick reflexes. I dived for the ground, rolled, got behind some trees."

"And you were wearing a vest."

He glanced at her. "They can be miserable, but when you need it, you need it."

Mostly, they quit talking as they neared the intersection with the Duckabush River. That seemed like a good place for a break…but he stayed uneasily aware of how close he and she followed the men who hadn't hesitated to gun down more people who probably couldn't have done more than annoy them.

As they reached the tumbling river, he speculated on whether *they* stopped here, too. He eyed the ford that consisted of scattered rocks, guessing nobody crossed the river without getting wet to their ankles. The steep flanks of Mount Anderson rose right across the river. Glaciers weren't far above them. A stream that was more a series of waterfalls tumbled down to join the river. It was probably one of countless similar streams created from melting snow that fed these headwaters of the Duckabush River.

Now came time to decide which way to turn, although he knew the decision probably wouldn't be theirs to make.

Cadence might be keeping track in her head of where other searchers would be about now, but the picture had grown fuzzy for him. The incident commander—the head ranger, last Garrett knew—would have a map in front of him and might even be moving tacks along the trails for a clear picture. Once they let him know where they were, the call would be his.

If they turned west, they wouldn't have to ford the river. East, they would have to. If anybody asked for preferences, his would be west, on a trail that climbed to O'Neil Pass and led to a series of lakes that were supposed to be beautiful. Ultimately, both choices were part of a kind of loop that encompassed Mount La Crosse and White Mountain.

He had a brief vision of camping tonight at Marmot or Hart Lake, and maybe stripping to immerse himself in cold, astonishingly clear water. The day wasn't hot, but, man, that would feel good.

Yeah, assuming he and Cadence had been here for recreational reasons. Garrett reluctantly banished the fantasy.

"Nobody in their right mind would take the route heading up to La Crosse Pass," Cadence said suddenly. "I mean, we've agreed they're probably not backwoodsmen. A scramble like that… Wearing boots with inadequate tread…"

"Would they know it's a scramble?" Garrett had been thinking about this. "On the topo map, you can see the elevation gain and the little zigzags that make up the trail. I haven't looked at the less detailed one given out to tourists by rangers, but if that's all they have, does it even hint at what they'd be facing?"

"I…don't remember." She promptly dug in her pack, and had to keep digging until she came up with the much skimpier map. "No," she said immediately. "It just looks like a trail. And a short one to cut over to their choice of the Quinault River trail going southwest or the West Fork Dosewallips going northeast. They surely couldn't be imagining they could make it all the way to Hurricane Ridge and become lost in the sea of tourists."

For many visitors to the area, a drive up to Hurricane Ridge and a few minutes appreciating the spectacular view was the closest they'd ever come to the glorious mountains, deep valleys, countless rivers and even a glacier or two that made up the Olympic National Park.

"Hell," Garrett said aloud. "I don't suppose that part of the park has been closed."

"No, doing that would have been premature. Still would be. I mean, Hurricane Ridge is a super long hike away from here."

"True." He let out a breath, grimaced at the sharp pain that lanced his chest. "You ever taken the trail over La Crosse Pass?"

She shook her head. "I hear it's awful from this side. Calling it a 'trail' is kind. Really, it's a climb gaining nearly three thousand feet in elevation, if I remember right. It's so steep, it can't exactly be groomed, and last I heard, there were so many blowdowns, hikers had to duck under downed trees or climb over them, plus it's pretty shrubby. Maybe somebody has gotten out there to saw downed trees to clear the way, but this is only June, so I wouldn't count on it." She paused. "It might look like a good place to get off the radar to those guys, though."

"We've agreed they wouldn't know that unless it turns out one of those stolen packs had a better map in it."

"Which is possible."

He groaned. "I'm going to ford the river and see if there's any indication someone else crossed here not very long ago."

"Oh. That's a good idea." She frowned at him. "Why don't you let me do that?"

He shook his head. "I have longer legs than you. I should be able to make it without getting wet."

Her mouth opened, then closed as she decided not to argue. She found a suitable boulder to sit on and eased her pack from her back, setting her rifle near at hand. "Go for it."

What Garrett feared was that these slugs *would* choose the toughest route, because where better to hole up?

Inevitably, one of the already slick rocks midriver wobbled, his foot slipped, and he found himself ankle-deep in water that felt like it should have a skim of ice on it.

He allowed himself the luxury of some serious swearing since Cadence wouldn't be able to hear him, pulled his foot out and shook it before gingerly setting it down on a broader and, he hoped, more solid rock.

Once he reached the other side, he looked carefully for wet tracks. There were some damp places, but he also saw bear tracks. It went without saying that a black bear wouldn't bother tiptoeing from one rock to another to cross.

He yelled back to Cadence, "Undecided!"

Didn't it make sense for the pair of rangers advancing up the Duckabush River Trail to get assigned to the La Crosse Pass route? Their hike thus far hadn't been nearly as arduous as his and Cadence's. They hadn't been shot at, or had to load the body of a young man in a helicopter.

Garrett didn't like feeling like a pawn someone else was moving around a board, but he'd knowingly accepted a job where he wouldn't have the same relative autonomy he had as a detective with Seattle PD. Being there for Granddad had an importance that made the tedium of routine patrols and the occasional requirement for him to swallow his pride nothing he couldn't handle.

He *shouldn't* be directing his and Cadence's movement now. He knew that—but he was also the only person who knew about her pregnancy. Hurting more than he wanted her to know, he made the river crossing in reverse, slipping again and, of course, getting his dry foot wet.

At least Cadence appeared sympathetic rather than amused. He carefully sat on the rock beside her and told her his observations. "Bear tracks looked fresh. It could have tromped right on top of any other sign."

"Yes." She bounced the radio in her hand. "My gut says they'd go that way, but I don't really know why."

"Maybe because the part of the loop that includes the lakes is meandering and pointless for someone who just wants to get the hell out of the wilderness?"

"That might be it." Her really dark eyes held his. "What do you think?"

"Whoever is approaching on the Duckabush trail should turn there. That makes more sense than sending us."

"Unless they're still too far away."

He grunted his displeasure.

"Grumpy." The corners of her mouth quivered this time.

"Yeah, yeah."

After scrutinizing Garrett, she announced her intention to get out her stove and cook a real meal—or as real as freeze-dried food got. He must look like hell, he thought ruefully.

"Why don't you check in first?" he suggested. He'd have preferred making the call himself, but she was the law enforcement park ranger, having started out in charge. "I'll fire up the stove."

She agreed, and moments later he heard her giving her call sign and location. Garrett could only hear her side of the conversation, but that was enough for him to know he wouldn't be setting eyes on the idyllic lakes, not this trip.

Chapter Twelve

"What happened to the pair who should be getting close?" he asked, the minute she set down the radio.

"Nothing bad. They should be behind us once we start the ascent. The thing is, the two rangers who were already in Enchanted Valley are taking the loop toward Marmot Lake."

"The helicopter?"

She'd been wondering herself why she hadn't heard it. "Had to fly to the hospital, then refuel. They'll be back soon, which may or may not do any good. I know there are meadows up near the pass, but we'll be closed in by forest for a good part of the ascent."

The lines in Garrett's forehead deepened, but she wasn't sure how much of that had to do with facing what would be a strenuous hike slash climb, and how much because of pain he was keeping quiet about.

"About the time they'd be useful, they'll need to head back to base to beat nightfall."

"Oh, come on! It's only lunchtime." She looked down to see that she'd chosen the menu and put water on to boil. Fine time to realize she wasn't the slightest bit hungry. In fact, her stomach did a roll at the idea of eating the chili she'd picked without thought. Garrett would have been less likely to notice she wasn't eating if they'd grazed on nuts and dried fruit, the way they had other days. On the other hand, he didn't look his sharpest, so maybe he wouldn't pay attention.

Sure.

He seemed to be gazing fixedly at the water, which wasn't in any hurry to boil. *A watched pot*, she thought facetiously.

"You carry a picture of your family?" he asked, out of the blue.

She had no trouble understanding why he was interested, when he'd never been before. Without a word, she took her phone from an outside pocket of her pack and called up photos and then favorites. For a moment, she studied the picture of the four of them that she especially treasured. Her father had his arm around her mother, while each had laid their free hand on one of their children's shoulders. It felt like a circle of love, however sappy that sounded. Simon didn't often like being touched, but he was smiling at her in this photo, looking completely happy.

Along with the squeeze of love, Cadence felt faint apprehension. They'd support her. Of course they would. That didn't mean her plan to raise a baby on her own wouldn't… not disappoint them, just make them feel sad.

A little apprehensive, she handed the phone to Garrett and watched him study it. What he'd see was a plump, blue-eyed, blonde mom; a stocky brown-haired man; Cadence, who didn't look anything like either of them; and her brother, who was mixed race but identified as black. He'd also see that Simon appeared to be in his mid-to-late-twenties.

Garrett blinked a couple of times. "You're adopted."

"Yes. So is Simon, obviously."

"He still lives at home?"

"He's autistic."

His too-perceptive blue eyes now inspected *her*.

"He's on the functional end of the spectrum," she babbled on. "He has an AA degree, a job and friends, but he's happy living at home, and Mom and Dad are happy having one of us still home."

"Huh." Garrett went back to studying the photo as if he could see more than a picture of four smiling people could possibly reveal.

Or maybe it revealed even more than she'd realized.

"You make me see what a coward I've been," he said so quietly she wasn't sure he'd meant for her to hear.

What did he mean? What could she possibly say?

Startled to realize that the water was boiling—of course it was, because both had quit watching it—she held out her hand. Without further comment, he laid the phone in it, the touch of his fingers making her shiver. She closed out photos and dropped the phone in the same pocket before concentrating on pouring the two mixes of freeze-dried chili into the water. She busied herself stirring, then dished it up, hoping he didn't notice what a disproportionate share she served him.

"You made this?" he asked, his pleasant tone reinforcing her impression that, as far as he was concerned, any talk about their childhoods was finished.

"Yes. It's a favorite of mine."

He accepted the pan and a spoon, but hadn't taken a bite when he lifted his head and his gaze speared her.

"Do you know anything about your birth mother?" he asked after a few bites.

She looked away, although not really taking in the view of the river, a deer and a fawn drinking from it and a fish jumping. "My mom left a note when she signed away her parental rights. Said she couldn't take care of me. Whoever was doing intake asked some questions about health concerns that might be passed on, and she claimed there was nothing like that. She wouldn't—or couldn't—answer questions about my father."

"You ever think about looking for her?"

She bent her head over her bowl and swallowed bile. Usually, she loved the spicy aroma, but not now—and especially not when talking about the woman who had given her up with no more than a quick note saying she was sorry. Having a baby couldn't help but open the door to worries about her unknown genetic heritage.

But she said strongly, "No. Why would I? I have the best parents in the world. I didn't miss a thing."

Feeling a sudden misgiving, Cadence sneaked a sidelong glance to see that Garrett was eating with a single-mindedness that suggested he really wasn't thinking about anything else. She didn't believe that for a minute.

"I'm sorry," she said softly. "I imagine you wish your mother *had* surrendered her rights."

He was quiet longer than she liked before saying, "By the time I was old enough to think anything like that, it was too late. Nobody adopts ten-year-olds who are in trouble all the time, or thirteen-year-olds who already top six feet. Once I had to start shaving…" He shrugged. "Not quite what adoptive parents are looking for."

There were people out there who saw deeper than he implied—her parents hadn't hesitated to adopt and love a mixed-race child whose father hadn't been able to deal with a son who recoiled from his touch. Of course, Simon had been only four, but look at Garrett now. Tall, athletic, incredibly handsome, smart, determined…oh, she could go on and on. Surely people should have been able to see behind his youthful, angry facade!

Not that he'd had a chance, when his mother insisted on reappearing in his life just often enough to keep it unsettled.

"It was all a long time ago." Whether he was as indifferent as he sounded, Cadence couldn't tell. He glanced at her untouched bowl and raised his eyebrows.

She almost went with, *I'm not hungry*, but why bother? He already knew about her queasiness. She hadn't admitted that it struck throughout the day when she least expected it, but how could she hide it when they were together 24/7?

"Seconds?" she offered, holding out the bowl.

"You sure?"

"Yes. I'll nibble as we walk. I wasn't thinking when I decided on chili."

He took the bowl, downed her share without commenting on the state of her stomach, thank goodness, and said, "You cooked, I'll clean."

Grateful for the offer, she prepared to get back on the trail. Garrett handed her the stove and dishes to stow in her pack.

"We shouldn't have taken so long," she said.

"I think we both needed a break. Plus, with luck it gives our various backup teams a chance to get in position to do some good."

She smiled at his acid tone. "You know, these guys might be charging on down the Duckabush Trail, and it's Don Phillips and Erik Sorensen who'd come face-to-face with them."

"They know that's a possibility?" He sounded sharp.

Cadence said, "All of us are supposed to be prepared. It just happens you're the one who came the closest."

He made one of his noncommittal noises and swung his pack onto his back without waiting for help. If it hurt, you'd never know from his expression. She handed over his rifle, slung her own over a shoulder, and they walked the short distance to the ford.

GARRETT WOULD HAVE liked to extend a hand to Cadence so she'd have some support as she made her way gingerly from rock to rock, but was well aware how surprised she'd be. She had considerably more backcountry experience than he did. Without making it obvious, she'd led their previous expeditions into the heart of the park. Unless he'd seen her falling, it wouldn't have occurred to him back then to play the gentleman. Of course, in part this wave of protectiveness came from knowing she was pregnant.

That was *his* baby she carried.

He heard her say, *No, it's* mine, and winced.

Mostly, though, he worried because she wasn't eating enough, because she was too pale, because she wasn't hiding the stress she felt as well as she probably thought she was. Garrett didn't like seeing Cadence as anything but the confident, capable, serene woman he knew her to be. If he could lessen that stress…but he couldn't, and the last thing he wanted to do was undermine her.

She wobbled, held both arms out as she teetered…and found her balance. He wasn't paying enough attention to where he was putting his own foot and slipped.

"Damn," he muttered. This water was *cold*.

Just ahead of him, Cadence played leapfrog and made it to the far bank of the river, boots and feet dry.

He stopped long enough to check to be sure his socks weren't soaked enough to cause discomfort and even blisters, then grinned at her. "You're a ballerina."

She chuckled, her expression easing for a moment. "Your feet are too big."

"That's it. How could I help myself?" Since he wore a size twelve, she had a point.

They moved in concert along the well-groomed trail that followed the Duckabush River. Garrett had guesstimated that it would be three miles, give or take a little, before they reached the La Crosse Pass cutoff. He also knew the La Crosse trail was an additional six and a half miles, a figure that was deceptive, given the extreme elevation gain and loss. Plus… He did a little adding. They'd started with a three–mile round trip from the campsite back to the spur leading to Mount Hopper and then retracing their steps. Two and a half to three miles from First Divide down to the river where they'd just eaten lunch. Never mind the shuddering on the way that included a dead man and bullets flying. The mileage alone added up to... Eight and a half miles, approximately, before they turned off this pleasant, level trail to begin what sounded like a grueling ascent unless the park had gotten some workers out here with chain saws to cut up all the fallen trees and clear the way. Not far for either of them on a usual hike, but...

Given the delays, the sun was still high but noticeably on its way down. Yeah, the day was long, but he'd also noticed some thin clouds he didn't like the looks of. Given the dry winter, rain would be welcome. Not so welcome for a pair of tired hikers trying to catch up with two killers and their hostage.

They were well on their way when he drew Cadence's attention to the clouds. "Those look like rain to you?"

She studied the sky. "Maybe. It's hard to say. If so, it might not come until tomorrow."

"Okay." He waved her ahead, wanting to evaluate her condition. "Next time you're on the radio, why don't you ask about the weather report?"

"Will do." Her strides were long; he didn't see any sign she was flagging. He also hadn't seen, or heard, any indication she'd had so much as a bite to eat.

He maintained his awareness but felt sure the gunmen weren't hiding along here. The densely forested land to one side climbed at a pitch that made him wonder who had decided a trail heading straight up it was a good idea. The river to their right created a pleasant ripple, and from time to time they saw deer, including a doe with two fawns having a drink. A black bear who stood in the river—fortunately, closest to the other bank—appeared to be fishing, but lifted its massive head to watch them pass. Birds aplenty sang and occasionally spread wings and darted within their sight. Cadence had tried to teach him which birds were which, but he hadn't been an A student. There were so many, and a quick glimpse of outstretched wings didn't tell him if it was a Townsend's warbler versus another kind of warbler, a thrush, a northern flicker or a brown creeper. In another mood, at another time, he'd have asked.

His mood darkened further at the reminder of their purpose and awareness of how soon they'd turn off the trail and begin the scramble that would take them up nearly three thousand feet in elevation in not much over two miles. The abused muscles in his torso spasmed at the mere thought.

When they reached the cutoff, he was encouraged to see that the sign appeared to have been recently replaced. With luck, that meant some real work had been done this spring and early summer on the route.

The initial stretch once he and Cadence turned their backs on the Duckabush River was flat enough, he'd call it a terrace. Old-growth hemlocks towered over them, shutting off sunshine. Now Garrett swept his gaze from side to side, his uneasiness like an itch he couldn't quite reach. As a cop, he knew that feeling too well.

Whether Cadence's unease had increased, Garrett didn't know, only that she wasn't talking. They began the climb, the forest around them changing to a lush mix of silver fir and hemlock, with an understory of ferns, vine maples and devil's club, appropriately named. He'd had an encounter with the spiny leaves one of his first times hiking in the park, and took care now not to brush against one.

Evidence that a chain saw had been used to clear the trail was immediately evident. Large trees had fallen, ripping their roots out of the ground. With the trunks cut to create openings, the scent of evergreen needles and sawdust was sharp in Garrett's nose. Salal had been crushed by the fallen trees. Branches, cut from the trees, had been tossed carelessly into piles. The trail would have been damn near impassible if this much work hadn't been done.

Even Garrett's legs began to burn from the steep climb, but Cadence continued to move with seeming effortlessness. He took a moment to savor her long, slim legs from behind, wishing her bulky pack didn't prevent him from seeing her sleek, dark hair bundled at her nape, as she so often wore it when working. The feel of that hair slipping between his fingers made them tingle now.

She made an exclamation that broke into his thoughts, which she wouldn't have appreciated.

"What…?" He didn't have to complete the question. It appeared the trail work hadn't progressed far at all. A massive tree lay right in front of them, blocking their way. Torn branches might have been planned as an obstacle.

"Damn."

She gave him a sidelong eye roll. "I think we can get under if we take our packs off."

With his larger body, he'd have to squirm like a snake, and he didn't like the possibility of being gashed by the sharp end of one of those broken branches hidden in the dirt. "I think I'd rather go over."

Cadence said, "Hold my pack?"

He took her rifle first, rested it against the trunk, then accepted the weight as she shrugged out of her pack. He couldn't prevent himself saying, "Be careful," as she dropped to her knees.

She was able to mostly crawl beneath the fallen tree, lowering herself at one point to press forward. He saw her butt waggle, then her booted feet, and she was through. Her head just reappeared above the trunk of the tree.

"Ready for your pack?" he asked, and she nodded.

He pushed it, and she pulled. It met resistance, then suddenly popped from his hand. He sent the rifle after it, then eyed the tree. He calculated a route to climb, using stubs where branches had broken off as well as intact ones, and began to climb. He grimaced at the feel of sticky pitch on his hand, but kept going, glad when Cadence came fully into his sight.

He was able to stand upright atop the tree trunk, but any hope of a decent view ahead died a quick death. The zigzagging line on the map perfectly described the route ahead of them. He couldn't see past the next turn.

Normally, he'd have considered jumping, but with his torso already complaining about the scramble, he didn't dare. Just as well—it wouldn't be safe, anyway, given that he could land on a hidden rock or ground soft enough to throw him off-balance. A broken ankle would be a disaster.

He chose to lower his pack and rifle to her, then clamber carefully down. Reclaiming the pack, Garrett knew one thing: he didn't like Cadence in the lead. If there were any surprises facing them, *he* intended to be the one to bear the brunt.

Chapter Thirteen

That first fallen tree was only a foretaste of what was ahead.

A couple of vicious storms had struck the Olympic Peninsula this past winter, near—hurricane force winds sending ocean waves slamming into cliffs along the coast, spray rising frighteningly high. Cadence had stayed in a cabin at Kalaloch once during a storm and enjoyed watching the turbulent ocean throwing new drift logs high up onto the beach. The following morning, she and the other guests at the rustic resort had been able to find all kinds of treasures strewn on the beach, including, in her case, an increasingly rare glass Japanese float that now sat in her closet, for lack of space. That storm, she knew, had been nothing to the later battering that had done this much damage inland. She knew what could happen even in forests that had stood for a thousand years. She just hadn't been able to picture it.

Looking at a couple of trees in front of them that had tumbled one atop the other with so many scattered branches, she thought of the game Pick Up Sticks.

Hands on his hips, Garrett glared at the mess as if it was a personal affront.

"Do you really think they'd keep going once they see what a mess this is?" Cadence asked. He'd know what she meant by "they."

His chest rose and fell with a deep breath. "Yeah, I think it's ideal for their purposes. Nobody can see them from above—"

"Or from twenty feet away," she muttered.

"If they need to stop, they could crawl under a tangle of branches, burrow into the salal and ferns, and who would notice them?"

"Evan—" She bit her lip.

She felt his gaze resting on her face, but didn't let herself look to see what he was thinking.

"A scrawny kid like that, and an athlete, can squirm through a mess like this, no problem. It sucks for us bigger guys who never did gymnastics and don't want to."

She felt a tiny bubble of humor. "Really? I can see you on the rings. You're strong enough for that. Twisting and flipping in the floor exercise, though…"

"It definitely wasn't my sport."

She knew he'd played football both in high school and for the University of Washington, a top program, but hadn't been drafted into the pros. When he'd told her about it, on one of the rare occasions he'd talked about his younger self, he'd said he hadn't been interested, big money or not. He had gone straight to the police academy, as he'd intended since he'd been fifteen or sixteen.

What he hadn't told her was what had happened to him to light the fire of his determination to go into law enforcement. In her case, it had been all but accidental. For him, it was something else altogether, maybe having to do with the time he'd spent with his mother, maybe even living on the street.

She shook off her curiosity. He hadn't talked about it to her because he didn't want her to get to know him well, any more than he'd wanted to plumb her depths. Except…she had a feeling that now, if she asked him, he'd answer. He seemed determined to lower barricades, even if they creaked as if rusty. She wanted to feel hope.

Now was not the time. What she needed to do was focus on how to make her way under, over and between the current obstacles.

As before, she mostly squirmed through gaps, while Garrett climbed over the top. Of course that made sense, given the breadth of his shoulders and his height, but she also wondered how much his decisions were made by his pain level—the one he implied was next to nonexistent.

Typical man.

She wrinkled her nose. Not like she appreciated whiners.

Impeding both of them were the Kevlar vests that added bulk to their torsos. Evan wouldn't have that handicap, either.

They toiled through several more obstacles before taking a short break. Garrett dug out some snack foods from his pack and handed them to her with an expression that said she'd better eat or else. He got on the radio, only to have to wait in increasing frustration as other talk dominated. Apparently a nasty domestic dispute had erupted at the Elwha RV campground, which was momentarily at the forefront of the dispatcher's attention. Another ranger was behind a speeder on Highway 101 along the coast and wanting more information on a license plate number.

Cadence nibbled while Garrett swigged water and listened until he heard at least some of what he wanted to know, it seemed.

"Did you get that?" he said finally. "Phillips and Sorensen—I assume you know them?—aren't far from us, and the rangers that were in the Enchanted Valley are approaching the other end of the trail.

"Oh. That's Nathan Ryback and Davis Bourke. They're good."

"Maybe we should wait."

"No!" she cried. "We're quieter on our own."

His mouth tightened, but he nodded.

"All right. I'll concede as much. We'd better silence our radios from here on out and keep conversation to a minimum."

"They've got to be quite a way ahead of us."

"Do they? They're not woodsmen, remember? And who knows what they're thinking at this point?"

He was right, of course. Would Evan seize an opportunity and try to escape? She didn't know if she hoped he did or not. What she felt certain of was that those men wouldn't shrug and let him go. They'd shoot him. They sure hadn't hesitated when the two climbers dared question them, or when they realized Garrett was pursuing them. Evan's youth wouldn't deter them, she felt sure.

Cadence wanted this all to be over with. To restore Evan to his family, watch the two men get hauled off in handcuffs and wave goodbye to Garrett in the Staircase parking lot.

Well, maybe not the goodbye part even if it would surely be the reality, despite the effort he was making.

Anyway, she thought ruefully, they wouldn't be able to hike out today. Whether they accomplished an arrest or not, there would be another night together. A chance for a chivalrous Garrett to press her to do what she longed for, deep inside: to marry him, to lull herself into believing he was capable of loving her and their child, of never regretting a commitment.

Accepting less than she needed and deserved would surely be a terrible mistake.

She wrapped the dried banana chips she hadn't finished and dropped the packet into a pocket. "We'd better get going."

"Yeah." He inspected her with those unnervingly sharp eyes. "You've acquired some scratches."

"I'm aware. They do sting. You have some, too."

He lifted a finger to a scrape on his forehead that was beaded with droplets of blood, touched it and came away with a bloody fingertip. "Not worth cleaning up until we get past this section. I may have words with your boss when we get back."

She shook her head. "You know how underfunded all the parks are, right? It's getting worse all the time."

He let out a long breath. "I do know that. Under normal circumstances, we could call this an adventure. But today…"

She didn't say anything. He groaned, leaned back to shrug on his pack and waited to pick up his rifle until she was ready to go. Then he set out, leaving her to follow.

IT WAS ALL very well to start in the lead, but several times Cadence slipped through the downed hemlocks or firs ahead of him and emerged on her own. Garrett hated every minute he lost sight of her.

As tedious as all this was, he found his mind occasionally wandering. If he'd brought a handsaw, he could have at least lopped off some of the limbs to make it easier for the next hiker without slowing himself down much.

He couldn't believe she had flat out refused to marry him, now that she was pregnant. Just because he hadn't been able to say the words, *I love you*, did she believe he'd walk out on her? Or cheat on her? Didn't she know what the changes he'd made in his life to support the grandfather he hadn't known all that well meant about who he was? And hadn't she noticed how cheap the easily spoken words, *I love you*, too often were? She'd said herself, the two of them were solid together. If he was able to love a woman, Cadence would have been the one. He'd already acknowledged that much to himself. He'd hated losing her. Even before he knew she was pregnant, the idea of never seeing her again had shaken him. He tried to be honest with himself, but it had taken days before he admitted as much.

Once this operation was over, he'd press her on the subject. He could be stubborn. She'd see that marrying made sense. No way was he willing to be an occasional father!

The sound of a branch snapping ahead sharpened his focus. Cadence was already in the act of wedging herself under the latest blowdown, but had miscalculated. It hadn't been a real big branch, though, he saw; nothing that would have injured her.

"Hold up," he said, suddenly in the moment. "Don't get ahead of me."

Her response was a breathless, "There isn't room for both of us."

"Then let me go ahead."

"Don't be silly. I'm almost through. You should be able to make it under this time, too."

He thought so, too. Laid his rifle on the forest floor and pushed it through behind her, then lowered himself to his hands and knees. When he started, he could see her legs from this perspective, but she took a few steps and he lost sight of her.

With sudden urgency, he called, "Cadence!"

A cry came from her.

The alarm made him careless. His pack snagged on a sharp stub of a snapped-off branch.

The next muffled cry from her sounded like she was trying to say his name—or to warn him.

That rumble had to be a man's voice. Feeling as if he was moving in slow motion, Garrett tore himself from his pack and grabbed at the rifle even as he threw himself forward. What he saw was his worst fear.

A brawny man was wrenching Cadence up a gritty slab of rock to the side of the trail. She fought him, literally tooth and nail. The boy was struggling against a second man waiting higher up.

Garrett yanked hard at the rifle, but resistance meant that strap was snagged, too.

After her teeth sank into the creep's bicep, he slugged her. Her head snapped to one side. Somehow, she still reached high and took hold of the young boy's arm, tearing him free from his captor at the top of the slab. Face contorted with fear, the boy slid uncontrollably on his butt. Cadence got out a "*Run*, Evan!" before a meaty hand covered her mouth and wrenched her head back.

Sweating, filled with rage, Garrett gave up on the rifle, unsnapped the holster and pulled his Glock. Still on his stomach, he reached out to brace his grip with both hands.

The delay was enough to let the vicious guy all but throw her up into the arms of the second man crouched at the top of the slab. Then he got a hand on Evan as he slid past, pulling him up as a shield. Garrett's shot was riskier than he liked, but...

Free the boy. That's what Cadence would want, what she'd fought for rather than trying to get away herself.

Flung into the cold space that was his norm when he had to make quick decisions and fire his weapon, Garrett's hands stayed steady as he aimed for the shoulder that was too broad to hide behind the lanky kid. He pulled the trigger once. Blood blossoming on his upper arm, the man recoiled. Garrett pulled the trigger again.

Evan fell free and rolled down almost to Garrett's feet. The son of a bitch above barely hesitated before lunging over the lip and disappearing. Garrett's last sight of him he'd clapped a hand to his gory arm. His shooting arm, Garrett sincerely hoped.

They had Cadence. He couldn't let himself think of everything they might do to her.

"Let's get out of sight." He pushed the kid ahead to squeeze past his pack and get behind the one fallen tree. Unsnagging rifle and pack on the way, he followed, standing on the other side. His voice was harsh. "Are you hurt, Evan?"

"I…don't know." Confusion and fear showed in hazel eyes. "Who was she?"

Was. Past tense. Garrett shut down the snarl that wanted to form.

"Cadence Jones. Park ranger and—" *My partner. My lover. The mother of my baby.* He couldn't say any of that. "We've been following you since they kidnapped you at the Staircase campground. I'm Jefferson County Deputy Garrett Wycoff. Sit down here and let me take a look at you."

His skin felt too tight as his instincts screamed for him to go after her. Now. He felt a pull that was hard to resist. The kid would be all right waiting for the others, he tried to convince himself.

No, he had to make sure.

The boy's teeth chattered. "Who *are* they?"

Garrett summarized everything that had occurred since the gun shop robbery. "They knew a hostage might be all that would save them."

Eyes watery, Evan whispered, "But…now they have *her.*"

"Yeah."

He put the boy through a basic set of motions, and determined his skinned back from the uncontrolled slide down the rough rock slab was his worst injury. Garrett eased that red sweatshirt over Evan's head, sprayed his back with some painkiller, gently laid on salve and covered it all with a clean T-shirt he dug out of the bottom of his pack. Best he could do. Cadence would have had better supplies, but at his last sight she still had her pack with her. Then, seeing the boy shaking, he added one of his flannel shirts, rolling the sleeves until the kid's hands actually poked out.

"They been feeding you?" he asked.

"Um…sort of."

Garrett handed over water first, then snack foods and watched the kid eat like there was no tomorrow. He remembered too well those years when he was growing like Jack's beanstalk and was starved all the time.

Then, reluctant, he took out the radio. He hoped like hell the pair hadn't yet investigated Cadence's pack and discovered *her* radio. But he couldn't send an eleven-year-old boy down the trail or leave him sitting here alone, without rangers Phillips and Sorensen knowing they'd be coming upon him. Garrett couldn't take a chance that one of them would get trigger-happy when they saw movement. Also, he couldn't justify leaving Evan's grandparents and other family in agonizing suspense.

But he had no intention of hanging around for long, not when it meant letting those bastards get more lead than they already had.

CADENCE TASTED BLOOD in her mouth and gritted her teeth against the pain as one of her kidnappers threw her forward on rocky ground. She made the mistake of trying to control the fall. She knew better; she should have twisted instead of catching her weight on the heels of her hands. Her wrists felt as if she'd broken them, and a shock wave rolled up her arms to her shoulders. Her palms stung.

The man who was bleeding lifted her handgun from her holster, glanced at it and dropped it into one of their packs. Standing above her, his expression ugly, he snapped, "Don't think you can slow us down, bitch!"

The buddy grabbed her arm and yanked her to her feet, hard enough that she couldn't prevent a pained sound from escaping. On top of everything else, she felt as if he might have dislocated her shoulder.

They were big guys, somewhere around Garrett's height of six foot three. Over her head, they had an angry, obscenity-laden exchange. From it she determined that their names were Cole and Mason. Teeth showing in a snarl, Cole clutched the bloody wound at the top of his arm. Along with being mad at the world, they were furious with each other. Both seemed to feel the need to blame the other for their predicament, and why not? It took some maturity to say, *Yeah, we screwed up.* And even more to say, I *made a bad decision. It was* my *fault we took that last disastrous turn.*

If the packs they'd stolen had contained any toiletries like razors or soap and water, there was no sign they'd used them. Those had to be the clothes they'd started in days ago. Both had stubble turning to ragged beards, sweat stains under their arms and filthy cargo pants. Boots...she'd call them work boots, probably with a decent sole but not the kind needed for hiking tough terrain. A picture flashed through her head of the two men whose backpacks these were. They'd been lean and athletic, but not big. No, their clothing wouldn't fit either of these two.

Both these men looked like dedicated weight lifters. Mason, the larger of the two, had hair that might be blond if he ever washed it again. He aggressively demanded to know how his partner could have lost that scrawny kid.

Cole, the one who'd chosen to hold on to her instead of Evan, gave a one-shoulder shrug. "She's better than the boy." Teeth bared, he looked her over in a way that made her skin crawl. "Nice piece of ass."

The buddy shrugged. "Kinda skinny."

"All the more for me."

Oh, God. Please, please, Cole was trying to scare her, versus being serious. Surely he wouldn't take time to—

She didn't get past the image of his thick fingers ripping her shirt off.

She didn't kid herself. He was already wanted for at least two murders. Whatever brakes he'd once had on his behavior would be nonexistent now. *Pedal to the metal*. Her father had used that term.

She could only try to hold out. Hold on to her memory of the way Garrett had called her name, the agony in his eyes before they turned ice-cold when he fired his gun. He might not know how to love, but she believed he would do anything, die in her place if that was the only choice, to save her. This certainty, her trust in him, felt bone-deep, and she had the fleeting thought that maybe she'd misjudged him. Maybe his commitment *would* be powerful enough to make up for the lack of romance.

The thought came and went, lost in the fear as Cole demanded she put on *his* pack while he took hers, and shoved her ahead on the poor excuse for a trail.

Of course, they almost immediately came to the largest fallen tree yet, an ancient giant she'd have mourned under other circumstances. Mason kicked it and berated her. She was a park ranger, and her *job* was to clear the goddamn trails. What did she do instead, wander around at campgrounds and tell stories to the kiddies by firelight?

Not a good idea to inform them that, actually, her role in the park was law enforcement. Or that, as the courts would see it, they had kidnapped a federal agent. FBI, DEA, National Park Service, it didn't matter.

She tried very hard to hide the shudder that wracked her. No, as she'd already reminded herself, it *wouldn't* matter to these men who she was. What was one more crime? Nonetheless, she for damn sure wasn't going to mention that the latest kidnappings would mean two trials: one in a federal courtroom, one in a Washington state court.

Mason swung himself over the massive trunk, picking his way and pushing between the unbroken limbs, and disappeared to the other side. Cole shoved her beneath the trunk and waited until his buddy called, "I've got her," before also climbing over. His right hand left bloody smears behind. Holding his injured arm against himself, he mumbled to himself the entire time. He had the foulest mouth she'd ever heard, and that was saying something.

The broken branches as well as the ones still attached were as difficult as the downed trees themselves. They trampled through, whips of fir and cedar branches wrapping around their ankles as if they'd been set as snares. A hard shove from behind sent her crashing down onto something sharp. She didn't see what ripped through her shirt and into her flesh until she whimpered and pushed herself to her hands and knees. The end of a shattered piece of branch, half-driven into the soil, was as sharp as if it had been meant to be a spear.

"Up, up! We don't have time to lie around!" Cole snarled. For all the rage and fear on his broad face, the fact that he still had the control to keep his voice low scared her as much as anything.

As she climbed shakily to her feet, she bent her head to see a long rent in her shirt, blood soaking it and the bra visible through the tear.

Cole pushed her again, and she wheeled to snap, "Stop that unless you want me to keep falling down!"

He leaned in until his face was inches from hers, and then grabbed her left breast. "If you get too mouthy, we won't bother hauling you along. Get that? *This*—" he squeezed her breast painfully hard "—is the only reason I'm being so *patient*."

It was all she could do to hold his stare without cowering. A flash of emotion in his eyes told her he didn't like her lack of reaction.

And wasn't that too bad.

She looked him up and down. "You know, I'm an EMT. I can probably patch you up, if I'm not injured too bad to help anyone else." Without another word, she turned and struggled on behind Mason, who had paused a distance ahead to watch them.

She had no clue which of these men had actually shot the Clallam County deputy or the climbers. Right this second, Mason scared her a little less than the buddy who followed her so closely, his horrible breath all but tickling her neck.

Her stomach turned.

How far behind was Garrett? Or was he still taking care of Evan? *Please hurry*, she begged silently. *Please*.

Because she had to wonder what these two had in mind, given that they had to know a noose was closing around them.

If she saw even the smallest chance to run, she'd have to take her chance.

Chapter Fourteen

Head hanging, Evan mumbled, "It would have been better if they'd kept me."

"What?" Garrett turned his head. "Why would you say that?"

"'Cause they didn't really hurt me." Exhaling, he looked up. "But she's a girl. A woman," he corrected himself. "She'll be easier to hurt."

This was the last conversation in the world that Garrett wanted to be having. But he couldn't let this poor kid get stuck with a major guilt complex because Cadence had essentially traded herself for him. And if the boy hadn't considered the possibility of rape, Garrett wasn't going to raise it.

"No," he said. "They don't know it, but she's a trained law enforcement officer, not just the kind of ranger who gives nature talks. She arrests people regularly. A couple of weeks ago, she brought down a really bad guy who had kidnapped a little girl. I know she looks…" *Delicate*, was how he always thought of her, but said, "Slender. It's deceptive. I've mountain climbed with her. She's strong. Plus, if she can get her hands on a gun, I'm betting she's a better shot than either of those two." He tried for a grin that had to be crooked. "They look like they're better at lifting weights than they are at using their heads."

"Yeah! I mean, how do they think they're going to get away from *here*?"

"I suspect they keep thinking a hostage is all they need, but they're wrong," Garrett said grimly.

Evan's eyes widened. "You mean, like, if they threaten to kill her, the cops would say, do it? We're still not letting you go?"

Nobody had better say anything resembling that in Garrett's hearing range. He breathed deeply. "If we say it, we won't mean it. Really, what will probably happen is that we'll make promises to those men that we won't keep. We'll convince them to believe they can still pull this off, when really they don't have a chance. And I suspect we won't even have to do that. I'm betting Ranger Jones either escapes, or brings them down on her own."

The hope on the boy's face hurt to see. Garrett wished he believed his own words.

"Wow! She must be really something."

"Yeah." He cleared his throat. "She is."

"Deputy? That you?" a man called from a short distance down the trail.

Garrett stood. "It is. You Phillips or Sorensen?"

"We're both here."

Within moments the men came into sight, their appearances more reassuring than Garrett had anticipated. Both were, like Cadence, law enforcement rangers. Neither seemed as if the maddening obstacles on the trail had hampered them in any meaningful way. Garrett felt sure he was a lot scruffier at this point. One of the two had significant gray in his hair, but looked strong despite carrying a hefty pack and a rifle. The other guy was younger but had the same air of confidence.

Of course, it was easy to be confident when the woman in such peril wasn't everything to *them*.

Garrett felt the ground beneath his feet shift, but he couldn't acknowledge it. Not here and now.

He held out his hand. "Garrett Wycoff."

They shook hands all around, Evan watching warily.

Garrett told them what had happened in more detail than he'd shared over the radio, then said bluntly, "I'd like one of you to take Evan back down. I know it's late in the afternoon, but once you're on an open trail, you might want to call in and see if a helicopter can pick him up." He squeezed the boy's shoulder. "I suspect his family would like to have him back as soon as possible."

Don Phillips smiled at the boy. "I hear your mom and dad drove over and are waiting at the campground with your grandparents. There might have been something about two sisters, too."

Evan scrunched up his nose, but said, "A helicopter? Really? That might be cool."

Phillips raised his eyebrows at Garrett. "You've been on this a lot longer than we have. I gather you were shot."

"Nothing significant." It was obvious where the guy was going with this, and it wasn't happening.

"Maybe you should take Evan and let us step up now."

"No. Cadence is my partner. We were—" he hesitated and settled for "—friends. We've done some climbing together. I can't walk away."

The younger ranger spoke up. "We're both pretty well acquainted with her, too."

"She has her radio with her. I'm assuming they'll use it to get in touch. I'm former Seattle PD. I've had training as a negotiator. Along with that, I also know Cadence well enough to read between the lines if she's able to tell us what she thinks we need to know."

The two men glanced at each other, Phillips finally nodding. "I've attended workshops on negotiating, but I can't call that real training. I gather that some rangers have started up this trail from the West Fork Dosewallips River end already. Unless the men we're pursuing pull a rabbit out of a hat, we have to be heading toward a standoff. They've got to be tired. If you can drag things out while keeping Ranger Jones as safe as possible, she might have a chance to make a move—or we can when one of them is asleep."

Garrett nodded. "That's what I'm thinking."

He didn't like envisioning the situation she was in, but it was unavoidable. He had to get into the heads of those two pieces of scum…and read Cadence's mind, too. Until this week, he'd have said avoidance wasn't one of his weaknesses, but he was learning better. What else could he call his refusal to acknowledge what he felt for her?

The two rangers consulted briefly. Without paying a lot of attention, Garrett had the impression that they made the decision to leave Eric Sorensen to partner with him because he was the better shot. *Army trained as a sniper*, he told Garrett. If he was good enough to pick one or both of these scumbags off, Garrett was fine with that. He'd arrested plenty of men or women who he could acknowledge had a core of decency, had had some hard knocks that led to bad decisions, or who deserved sympathy or at least pity from him. The decisions these two had made told him they were bad, plain and simple. Their readiness to shoot and kill anyone at all so they could get out of trouble said enough, but adding on their decision to grab a kid as hostage…?

His molars ground together. And now Cadence. What she might be enduring…

He *couldn't* let himself imagine too much, or he'd lose it. He had to stay clearheaded for her sake. And right this minute, not much else mattered but Cadence.

After hearing Garrett had fired his handgun, Phillips gave him a spare magazine.

"I'll rejoin you two if I can get a pickup for Evan." He smiled at the boy. "I hope I can, instead of making you walk all the way out. *And* spending another night on the way."

Evan looked close to tears that he didn't want to embarrass himself by sharing. Garrett cuffed him lightly on the back.

"Remember, Ranger Jones made her choice. You were her biggest worry. Knowing you're safe and on your way back to your family will be a weight off her mind. I promise."

The boy's Adam's apple bobbed. "You'll let me know? I mean, what happens?"

"Yeah. Here." He took out his mostly useless phone, relieved it had enough juice left to allow him to pull up contacts. "Give me your number, and I'll call you myself when I can."

He entered the number and saved it, then turned off the phone and pocketed it again. "You're a gutsy kid," he said with a nod.

Evan astonished him by giving him a hard hug before sniffing, wiping his nose on the hem of his shirt and starting down the trail. Phillips lifted a hand and followed.

"That's nice, what you said," Sorensen commented after a minute.

Garrett grimaced and told him about Evan's guilt that his safety had come at the expense of Cadence's.

"You're right," the ranger said. "Good heart, too."

Garrett cleared his throat. "Yeah." He felt a hard tug on the line that pulled him toward Cadence. "You ready?"

"When you are."

He'd been ready since that last desperate look he'd shared with Cadence. Without another word, he heaved his pack onto his back, then slung both Cadence's rifle and his own over his shoulder.

CADENCE PRESSED A hand to her torso just beneath her right breast. She hadn't bled copiously enough to worry her, but she had at the least bruised her torso severely, and conceivably cracked or broken a rib.

Garrett and she made a fine pair.

She'd asked to take a minute to clean and bandage the wound, but Cole had, predictably, sneered. *He* was tough enough to handle a bullet wound and didn't give a damn what her problem was.

"Don't think we'll let you drag your feet."

That hadn't been her intent then, but she set out after that to slow them down. Once, she snagged her pack as she scooted under a fallen cedar and required Cole's irritated assistance to free her; the other time, she tripped and went down, groaning and pretending greater difficulty than she felt as she pushed herself back to her feet.

The trail was as steep as guide books warned. Bringing up the rear, Cole breathed like a winded horse. His face was beet red, partly from sunburn, if she had to guess, but otherwise from exertion. The color did not look healthy. If only he'd drop dead from a heart attack, she thought vengefully. Unfortunately, although he'd bled plenty, he wasn't gushing.

Despite *not* being injured, Mason wasn't doing much better, although he had the sense to save his breath for hiking instead of complaining and swearing constantly. Garrett had been right, Cadence decided; they'd gained those impressive muscles in a gym, not doing an aerobic activity that might have helped them now. Still, they were scared enough to keep moving. If it hadn't already occurred to them, she wasn't going to mention that sometime in the next hour or two, they'd come face-to-face with yet more armed pursuers.

And Garrett… Garrett would be right behind, moving a lot faster than these two did.

The landscape around them changed subtly as they gained elevation. Undergrowth diminished because the trees were closer together. A denser stand meant fewer of them had fallen in the storms, leaving the trail clear for longer stretches. That would have allowed them to move faster, except that the steep climb slowed the pace instead. She was practically walking on Mason's heels, although some of that had to do with the creepy-crawly feelings she had, knowing how close Cole was behind her. Wondering if he was assessing her, imagining what he could do to a helpless woman. She hated knowing that, sooner or later, she'd have to clean up his shoulder and bandage it.

In scattered places that were open enough for the sun to reach the forest floor, she spotted huckleberries...and bears. Cadence kept her mouth shut, wondering if either man had noticed. Apparently not, because it took a roaring, grumbling sound before Mason jerked as if he'd gotten an electrical shock.

"What the...?"

Guarding two cubs, Mama bear was still far enough away, Cadence suspected she was only posturing. Swearing, Mason grabbed his rifle and started to lift it.

"Don't!" Cadence leaped forward and gripped his arm. "If you kill her, the cubs will starve to death."

"Looks like she wants to eat us," he growled.

"No, she's just putting on a show to keep us from approaching. Besides...she's big enough, she'd be hard to bring down. A few bullets would just make her mad."

"Then what does Miss-Know-It-All suggest?" Cole asked, his sarcasm not hiding his fear.

She stepped forward, waved her arms and yelled, "Shoo!"

Mama shuffled back a few feet.

Cadence lowered her voice. "Just keep moving."

They did, the men watching the bear as closely as she watched them. Cadence took satisfaction in seeing the whites of their eyes. She was surprised that they hadn't had previous standoffs with bears. Unless they'd been way farther ahead of her and Garrett than she thought they'd been, she'd have heard the gunfire if they strafed some poor black bear with automatic weapon fire out of ignorance as much as malice.

"Don't want to make the noise anyway," Cole snapped, earning a glare from his friend, who then turned and marched on.

The pause had regulated Cole's breathing, but that didn't last long. As the trail took another switchback, he began puffing again. Likely neither of them appreciated the sight of wild rhododendrons in full bloom, the pink flowers a beautiful contrast to the dark green backdrop.

"Isn't there a pass up here, somewhere?" Mason grumbled.

"You don't know where you're going?" She knew she sounded incredulous.

He clearly didn't like it, wheeling around, his expression dark. "Watch it."

She resisted the desire to shrink back. "Um, La Crosse Pass. It's known for spectacular views."

"Views?" Now he scowled. "Like, we'll be in the open?"

"It's almost high enough to be a mountain summit. I think Mount La Crosse isn't that much higher."

He looked past her. "We've got to find a place to get off the trail and stop. We ought to be able to hide in the trees."

"I wouldn't mind shooting down a helicopter." Despite the heavy breathing, Cole sounded like he meant it.

Could they shoot one down? Even though she'd vaguely thought it would take a rocket grenade or something like that, Cadence had a bad feeling. If fully automatic rifles...

Pretend you're a tour guide, she told herself. *Calm, sharing interesting information.*

"If you did that, you could set off a forest fire. This is... early in the year, but the winter was dry." A serious fire was still unlikely in June, but she wouldn't tell *them* that. "You're not feeling much wind, but if you look up, you'll see the tops of the trees bending."

Both of them tipped their heads back.

"A forest fire leaps from treetop to treetop. It's terrifying. We couldn't outrun it."

"Light's going," Mason observed. "We can hole up for the night."

Wonderful. Why had she opened her big mouth about the glorious view from the highest point this trail reached?

Mason was right, though; in her brief glimpses of the sky, it was shading to violet that would deepen to purple before nightfall. The sun would make an early descent behind the dozen peaks to the west, from Mount Christie to the much nearer White Mountain and Mount La Crosse. If she and Garrett had been hiking for pleasure—her heart compressed at her choice of word—she'd have suggested the same. The hard part would be scrambling across the steep, heavily wooded slope and finding a large enough spot that was flat.

"Left or right?" Cole snapped.

"You're asking me?"

"Who else?"

"I...really don't know. My topographic map shows it equally steep either way. I mean, until you get closer to the top."

"To the pass."

"We'd be almost there once the trail levels out."

"Hell with it." He nodded to the daunting forest to their left, where trees grew at a sharp angle from the ridge.

This might be her chance. A few steps, and she could put some trees between them. She could also break an ankle with the slightest misstep, she thought ruefully.

The two men looked over her head again and came to an apparent, wordless agreement. Looking sullen, Mason started picking his way into the trees, feet skidding. He had to grab for feathery evergreen limbs or rocky outcrops, even wrap his arms around the trunks of smaller trees. Within a few steps, his feet went out from under him and he came down on his knees, swearing viciously.

Hey, they might comprehend the benefit of switchback trails carved laboriously out of the side of a ridge this steep.

Trying to appear casual, Cadence crossed her arms and watched. In reality, she groped with the hand Cole couldn't see to find something, a scrap left from a food packet, an empty evidence bag, *anything*, to drop as a signal to Garrett.

My ring. The thin ring banded from two colors of gold she'd worn on her right hand since her mother gave it to her on her sixteenth birthday. Garrett would recognize it. As long as he spotted it…

Cole shoved her. "Go."

She'd almost worked the ring off her finger. *Drop it in front of herself where he wouldn't see.* What if he did?

She had to take a chance.

Cadence lowered her hand and let the ring fall. It was too obvious there on the trail. Cole would see it. He'd—

She made a production of starting after Mason, tension running up her neck. Was Cole right behind her, or still standing on the trail?

Given experience approaching mountains where no trail had ever been even unofficially established, she moved with more ease at first than the big guy in front of her did. Her better traction helped, as did her much smaller feet. Still, it was really hard going.

A grunt from behind let her know Cole wasn't letting her get far ahead of him. He'd have said something if he'd seen the ring, wouldn't he?

Eventually, she got careless because too much of her brain had turned to plotting. If this happened, what would she do? If that happened instead, how could she take advantage?

What if Mason really fell? If she whirled and rammed Cole, could she knock him down, too? If only she still had her handgun. Waiting until they stopped might give her the chance to get her hands on one of their rifles...

The left toe of her boot hooked on a rock or exposed tree root, and she plunged down, hard. Before she could stop herself, she'd rolled over a six-or eight-foot drop-off and slammed to a stop against a really sizable tree trunk. Her ribs screamed, and she started retching even as she drew her knees up under her.

Idiot! she castigated herself, clutching at her belly and torso, dry heaving.

"What the—?" Venting his usual obscenities, Cole the creep used those overblown muscles to lower himself to her. "You're not that good an actor!"

"I'm not..." she got out between heaves of her stomach.

"You're like a deer," he said in obvious disgust. "If you break a leg and slow us down too much, we'll put you out of your misery."

Gritting her teeth against the agony and the bile that soured her mouth, Cadence felt sure he meant what he was saying. He'd have no compunction about putting his barrel to her head and pulling the trigger. She *had* to get up, keep moving. Garrett couldn't save her, if she didn't save herself first.

Anyway...it wasn't just her anymore. *Baby, I'm sorry*, she thought. *I'll get us out of this. I will.*

Aside from everything else, even if Garrett didn't, couldn't, love her, she knew what finding her dead body and all possibility of their child having a life would do to him.

Groaning, she pushed herself to her hands and knees. "I hit that tree hard. I think my rib might be broken." If it hadn't already been. "But don't worry, I can keep going."

"You'd better." He nudged her with a booted foot, almost

knocking her over again. "You're my ace in the hole, so don't do anything stupid."

She bobbed her head. "I won't."

"Then get your butt moving."

Pain increasing tenfold, her stomach somewhere between queasy and outright rebellion, she did what he asked. At least he wouldn't question further nausea when it hit her for a completely different reason.

Chapter Fifteen

Garrett and Eric, now on first name terms, moved more slowly than Garrett would have liked, but he didn't want to miss anything. With daylight beginning to wane, he had trouble believing the pair would march on to the pass. They wouldn't risk being caught out in the open. On the other hand, this steep sidehill didn't suggest a comfy campsite might lie just out of sight.

If they had a topographical map, they'd be able to tell when the elevation gain began to ease and maybe start looking then for a place to stop. If they didn't...

Damn, he hated having to second-guess these bastards at a time when every decision meant so much. What if he and Eric hiked right past the threesome, huddled a mere twenty feet away?

If they did part ways from the trail, would Cadence be able to post a sign for him? Might be easier said than done. She couldn't be obvious, and that was assuming she had anything at all small enough for her to get away with dropping it.

"I think that's the helicopter," Eric said.

Garrett paused and heard the muffled roar. "About damn time."

"Won't be able to see them anyway. Or us, for that matter."

All true, but the presence of the helicopter, which began

making regular passes overhead, put pressure on the two men who didn't dare be glimpsed. How they'd use Cadence in that situation, he didn't like to think, but didn't let himself off the hook.

Don Phillips would be here in his place if anyone running this operation had a clue that Garrett and Cadence had been lovers. If one of his fellow deputies involved had a suspicion, he or she must have kept their mouths shut. Cadence's roommates must have known she was seeing someone, gone overnight or even for two nights a few times, and why wouldn't Cadence have identified him? Yeah, but both were seasonal employees, and from what she'd said, liked to party and had a different social circle than Cadence did. He was lucky, because he couldn't have handled being banned from this hunt.

God, if anyone knew that she carried his baby? He wouldn't so much as be allowed an opinion, much less essentially being in charge of on-scene operations now that Cadence had been snatched.

He had to be more careful what he said.

The light was failing. It was growing harder to pick out details. He'd been determined to pinpoint the exact location where Cadence was being held before stopping for the night. If they were far off the trail, it wouldn't be easy to bring in reinforcements to surround them, though. This was the worst possible terrain for an ambush.

"Damn it," he muttered, just as the younger ranger behind him said, "We'd better start thinking—"

He opened his mouth to agree, but saw a glint on the trail ahead. He lifted his hand in a "wait" gesture and continued, not taking his eyes off whatever he was seeing for an instant. He stopped to crouch, desperately hoping Cadence had left a message and this wasn't nothing but a shred of trash a hiker had dropped without noticing.

The moment he reached his finger out, he knew. It was gold, a ring, and an unusual one at that. He'd never seen anything else like it. Rose gold interrupted the more common gold. Cadence said it had belonged to a great-grandmother. An adoptive great-grandmother, but Cadence had the security of owning her family, of knowing she was *theirs*. That still bemused him.

"What is it?" Eric asked softly, crouching to join him.

"A ring." He picked it up, holding it in his palm. "It's Cadence's. I noticed it and asked about it earlier." Months ago, but he left the implication it had been in the past day or two. "She had to have dropped it here on purpose."

Eric lifted his head and frowned as he looked around. "Which way?"

"It's at the very edge of the trail. I'm going to say that's part of the message."

"Makes sense. So now what do *we* do?"

"They can't have gone far."

Eric didn't say anything.

"Stop right here." And, damn, were those words hard to say.

Hand closing on the ring, he imagined it still held some warmth from her hand. He surveyed the trail. Not anyplace meant for two men to stretch out in comfort, but he suspected no such thing existed until closer to the pass. The sense of an unseen strand connecting him to Cadence seemed to quiver, giving a tug. *This way*, it whispered. No, he didn't intend to lengthen the distance between them by even a few strides if he could help it.

"This is as good as it's going to get." She'd been relieved to see a place where several trees appeared to have sprouted from a nurse log, their trunks now all but grazing each other to form a near wall. The result was soil dammed up above them. "Do either of you have an ice axe?" she asked.

"A *what*?"

She lowered the pack she carried and leaned it against a tree, immediately seeing what she sought. "This," she said. An ice axe was strapped to Cole's pack, the one he'd lifted from the climber. She'd avoided looking at him as much as possible. She was surprised he hadn't discarded the axe, but maybe he'd envisioned it's possibilities as a weapon. It would have made a good walking stick, besides, but the head had a sharp point designed for stabbing into a crack in the rocks or ice to arrest a fall, while the other side widened into a blunt tool for scraping.

After leaning her pack against a tree, Cadence demonstrated how this ground could be leveled, then continued since neither man volunteered to take over the task. *She* couldn't help envisioning what she could do with that sharp steel point. She imagined herself turning fast, already swinging. That steel point would easily crack open a head. She made herself picture the moment of impact, the sound of a skull splitting, and her queasiness increased. She'd never actually killed anyone before, and had hoped never to have to do so. Especially in such a gruesome way. But if that was the only way she could save herself and her unborn child, she couldn't let herself be squeamish.

Her muscles tightened.

How fast would the men react when she started swinging? Would she die before she could get her hand on a gun or lift the axe for a second swing?

Calming herself with an effort, she thought, *Not now. If I get desperate...*

Or was she hesitating out of cowardice?

No. She pictured Garrett's face, outwardly calm even

when his eyes were sharp with intensity. He wouldn't be far away. She *felt* him. As long as she was alive...

Right this minute, no one was threatening her. In fact, she had the impression that the men felt some wariness toward her. Maybe it stemmed from the usual male dislike of needing to depend on a woman for knowledge or skills they lacked. Did they see her as both their ace in the hole, as Cole put it, and a threat, too? Really, it was surprising when they listened, as they had when she hustled them by the mama bear.

Garrett was among the few men she'd known who bowed to her expertise without question, as he had when they climbed. Despite the background that left him unable to trust on an emotional level, his confidence in himself was solid enough that he could admire and take advantage of someone else's skills without feeling diminished himself.

Cole and Mason had let her take charge a couple of times, but she'd seen the anger simmering in their eyes.

Unfortunately, what confidence she'd been summoning dissipated in a slow trickle with the darkening sky. She decided reluctantly that she had scratched out as large a semilevel spot as was possible.

She leaned the ice axe casually against one of the tree trunks, within easy reach. "I think this works. There should be room for the three of us." And Cole wouldn't be able to drag her off into the darkness to rape her. Even he had to be smarter than that. Of course, this nice, wide spot would do fine if the two were into gang rape...

Mason hadn't given off that vibe, though. She felt sure that Cole was dominant; Mason had followed orders a number of times. Even so, would he just turn his back if—

Cadence cut herself off. Worry about it when the time comes. When she *had* to fight. Remember, Cole was wounded.

Mason looked more thoughtfully than she liked at the ice

axe, then at her, but all he said was, "Let's spread that tarp and our pads. I'm hungry."

"Hungry? To hell with that!" Cole snapped. "You're not the one bleeding like a stuck pig!"

He pulled her own pack over to her, then hung over her like a vulture, thinking his meal was going to up and walk away while she dug in it. Mason stepped closer, too. Cadence reminded herself that they were bound to suspect she had a second handgun stowed away.

If only.

As Cole, grunting and complaining, pulled his shirt over his head and she used antiseptic wipes to cleanse his bloody upper arm, shoulder and chest, she tried really hard not to look closely, and especially not to breathe. She'd sweated all day, too, but he *stunk*. She did her best not to study his tattoos, crude compared to what she was used to seeing. Prison tattoos? she couldn't help wondering. Oh, and pretending his head wasn't *right there*, too, as he watched every move she made, was a challenge.

She had quite a pile of wipes by the time she had him clean enough to press a gauze pad to the hole that sullenly seeped more blood. "Can you hold this?" she asked.

He did without comment while she uncapped the antibiotic ointment and stacked a few gauze pads and readied the tape.

"There's no exit wound," she told him. "You'll need to have the bullet surgically removed as soon as possible." *If you're not dead.*

He grunted.

She went back to work, doing her best while blocking out the fact that she loathed this man. It was hard not to picture the frozen shock on the face of the dead climber as she worked to save Cole Whatever His Name Was.

Because the wound was high on the shoulder, it was hard

to wrap. She ended up winding tape around his upper torso to help anchor the bandages.

"Do you have a clean shirt that will fit?" she asked finally. "This one—" she lifted it between thumb and forefinger "—is disgusting."

"No. I should dump most of what's in here." He lashed out with his booted foot and knocked over the pack she'd been hauling.

He was likely right, she realized. The surprise was that he and Mason hadn't already gone through their packs and discarded most clothing, if only to lighten their loads.

"Let me look," she said.

He removed her handgun from the outside pocket and pointed it at her. "Go for it."

More pretense. A big, square hand, fingernails filthy, wasn't holding a gun on her.

She worked fast, tossing most of the clothing aside. She could cut up that T-shirt to make a sling, if he'd be willing to wear one. Probably not, but she set it aside anyway. She finally found a Seattle Mariners sweatshirt that would certainly have been oversize on its owner and held it out. "Let's try this."

Mason made an irritated sound. "About time. We could have eaten first."

Cole lunged toward his friend, his good hand with the gun lifted as if he'd use it like a baton to beat Mason.

Mason managed to scramble back just in time. "What the—?"

Well, he said more than that. Cadence tried to unhear it. And it wasn't as if she didn't hear foul language on a regular basis and even, in extremity, used it.

Cole answered in kind. Both of them seemed to puff up like those creatures in nature that made themselves look larger than they really were to repel predators—and these men were already massive.

She froze, doing her best to be invisible as they glared at each other.

Seemingly satisfied, Cole turned his attention to her. Not invisible.

"Why aren't you setting up the stove and cooking?"

Because that's what she'd been thinking. Let the two friends chat while she assumed her role as chef. Once she got her hands as clean as she could under the circumstances. Ugh. She didn't like the idea of his blood on her, but it had been unavoidable.

Her voice came out on a squeak. "I…was afraid the stove might get knocked over and set something on fire."

"Well, get on with it."

She hesitated. "I have Tylenol in that kit. Do you want some?"

His eyebrows drew together. "Of course I want some! Why didn't you give it to me before?"

"I'm sorry. It didn't occur to me."

He had more to say about that, of course. She tuned him out while she shook several pills into his hand and offered the water bottle.

Then she located the stove in his "borrowed" pack and set it up. When she pulled out packets of freeze-dried meals to see what they had, he snapped, "That stuff's crap." He eyed the packets in disgust. "It looks like dog food."

"That's what happens a lot of the time when you freeze-dry meals." These were a commercial brand undoubtedly bought at an outfitter's. "They usually taste fine. You just don't want to look at your food."

His eyes narrowed. "Bet you have something better."

Actually, she did, because she freeze-dried her own meals. Cadence used to love cooking. Lately, by the time she got home she was too tired to bother. Either that, or one or both roommates were already doing something in the cramped kitchen. She did occasionally, on a day off, make big batches of a couple of her favorites because they were superior to the commercial options.

Maybe better food would soften them a little, she thought ruefully. Her common sense muttered, *Right*. If Cole-the-creep's heart had a soft spot, she didn't want to find herself in it. She already hated the way he eyed her.

"I know I have a chicken marsala," she said, pulling her pack closer to her again.

"Is that some kind of foreign food?"

"Indian."

"Don't you have anything decent?"

She bit back what she'd like to say and dug to the bottom of her pack where the food often settled. "Beef stew."

"Now you're talking."

She took that for assent, asking if either had a full water bottle. If they hadn't used the purifying tablets, she thought boiling the water would kill any bacteria. She'd save what remained in her bottle for drinking.

She'd point out the tablets and suggest refilling bottles, except she hadn't heard the sound of a stream recently. There'd been one close to the trail early on, tumbling down the slope to join the Duckabush River. She had a feeling they wouldn't see another stream or river until they had descended from the pass tomorrow—if any of them ever made it so far.

She wondered if that was even Mason and Cole's real goal. What *did* they think would happen? They couldn't possibly be deluding themselves that holding her hostage would protect them while they strolled the many miles out to a road, where a friend would be waiting to pick them up in a car or truck that, of course, authorities would permit to drive away in peace. After all, a promise to release her once they were safely away was as good as gold, right?

An ache that felt more like a hollow seemed to expand. *Oh, baby.*

AFTER ERIC HANDED him a dish, Garrett nodded his thanks and ate mechanically. He had no idea what he was eating and didn't care.

Why hadn't those bastards contacted someone on Cadence's radio? Or were they waiting for morning, under the belief they had just cleverly vanished and could slumber unworried?

If the light had held up better, Garrett wouldn't have been able to prevent himself from attempting to follow. Probably that was just as well; with the terrain so difficult, he'd be bound to make some noise.

But waiting… It was killing him.

Aware Eric was watching him, he walled off any visible emotion.

"What if you try calling her?" the other man asked.

"She had it silent." He was sure he'd explained before. "We both did."

"What if they found it, and have been listening to everything said since?"

"They'd have had to do so almost immediately, and I can't see that happening." Explaining what felt obvious to him made him realize that even his jaw muscles were stiff. This took an effort. "They wouldn't have dared make a racket close to the trail. They knew how close behind I was."

Garrett had updated incident command—currently a deputy chief ranger—as soon as he discovered Cadence's ring and made assumptions he felt sure were accurate. In turn, he'd been put in the loop with the pair that had gone over the pass and were now looking for a place to bed down that put them close. Early morning, a helicopter was to return, drop another pair of law enforcement rangers on the slopes of Mount La Crosse, placing the prey—and Cadence—in the midst of a triangle. Where could they go? Especially since the helicopter had been charged to hover right overhead. That should pin the fugitives down and scare the you-know-what out of them. So far in their trek through the Olympic National Park, they hadn't felt seriously pressured. Why would they, with so many trails and so much wilderness to get lost in?

But taking this route, they'd made a mistake. He guessed they'd discovered quickly that their cell phones didn't work, and therefore they saw no way to negotiate until a park ranger offered herself as their hostage in place of the boy they'd taken originally.

Now it was a waiting game.

Garrett couldn't see himself sleeping, even if he and Eric took shifts. God. He felt as if fire ants were crawling all over him as it was, and at least for the moment, he had to make desultory, low-voiced conversation, help clean up after the meal he hadn't tasted and go through the motions of laying out pads and sleeping bags.

What if he hadn't screwed up so terribly with Cadence after that lunch when she confronted him about his feelings? Would anything have changed? If they'd taken a couple of days off to talk out emotions—he winced—and future plans, might she have been working a different shift when all this started? No matter what, she'd have been summoned to join the pursuit, but she might have taken Don Phillips's place advancing up the Duckabush. If that had been the case, Garrett sure as hell would have chosen Eric to keep moving with him while sending Cadence back with the poor kid.

Lying back on his sleeping bag, staring up at what stars he could see between dense evergreen growth, he pictured that. No, he wouldn't have been in a position to send Cadence anywhere, because this was *her* jurisdiction, not his. She and Eric would have discussed it, and she might well have won that battle and be lying next to him now.

Still safe, he thought.

And...he wouldn't have let her win, even if he had to tell the other man she was pregnant. She'd be mad as hell, but alive and *really* safe.

Instead, he closed his eyes, knowing he'd give anything to hear her voice, soft in the darkness. To be able to roll toward her, gather her into his arms, feel the trust that he'd thrown away.

Chapter Sixteen

Cole held her radio, his blistering stare finding her. "Why didn't you tell us you had this?"

"It doesn't work like a phone, you know." Cadence could not afford to lose her composure. If she cowered from them, they'd start terrorizing and hurting her. She knew it. "You can't call some friend."

She could tell he didn't like her answer, but bought it.

"Who can we call?"

"Olympic Park Dispatch, who'd put you through to whoever is coordinating the search for you—" *hunt* didn't seem like a wise choice of words "—and eventually, if necessary, a ranger or sheriff's deputy who is closest."

Garrett. Please, Garrett.

Cole looked as close to thoughtful as he was probably capable, bouncing the radio in his big, filthy hand.

Cadence had had to bed down compressed between the two men. Fear had all but electrified her. Cole had squeezed between her thighs, laughed when she stiffened and said, "Maybe tomorrow." If he'd gone for her breast, he'd have come up against the stiff bulletproof vest. She had to wonder if they had forgotten she wore it. She couldn't imagine they hadn't noticed it at all.

Cole, at least, snored, so she'd been able to tell when he

slept. Mason must have slept, but quietly. She'd never had a single chance to slip out from between the two of them and get her hands on one of their rifles or the oh-so-tempting ice axe.

The result was, sleep for her had been snatched in what felt like ten-or fifteen-minute increments. Naturally, she'd been awakened by a rough shake and ordered to make them something to eat. She hadn't even had that realization, *Oh, God, I'm a hostage.* No, the powerful need to throw up even what little she had in her stomach had driven her.

She'd gurgled something, crawled out of her sleeping bag and a few feet away so she could heave. Since she'd actually eaten her share of the stew, enough came up for whichever man had stepped aggressively toward her to retreat.

When she finished, she closed her eyes and let her head hang.

There was a moment of silence.

"What the hell?" Cole growled. "That's disgusting. You're not sick, are you?"

Oh, that was something for them to worry about: catching a stomach virus.

Mason, who tended to keep his mouth shut, said, "Hey, you're not...?"

No, no, no. Don't let that *idea enter their heads.*

"It's the ribs," she mumbled. "When I started to sit up... I don't know. I hurt and had to puke, too. It's like my body thinks I can expel whatever's wrong."

Mason never did finish his thought, thank goodness.

Cole, charming as ever, snapped, "Well, cover up that disgusting mess and get your butt over here to make breakfast."

Dear God. If she'd really been sick, she couldn't imagine how she would have complied. As usual, her stomach felt better, at least. The rest of her would feel fine once she rinsed her mouth out.

Neither remarked on her brushing her teeth before breakfast.

They weren't happy to learn their options were oatmeal with raisins, or oatmeal with dried apricot chips.

"It's quick, it's hot, it tastes good and it's filling," she informed them. "If you hate oatmeal, you can snack on granola and nuts instead."

Oatmeal it was.

She had just finished cleaning up when Cole started digging through her pack, tossing out the contents as he went. He'd gotten about halfway when it occurred to him to check the outer pockets, which was when he'd come up first with her phone, which he tossed, too, then with the radio.

She stacked the last few dishes together, then sank down cross-legged on the thin pad she had yet to roll and stow away.

Cole kept glaring at her. She raised her eyebrows.

"If I want to talk to someone, who should I ask for?"

"I'd suggest the man I was with when you grabbed me. I assume he's in immediate charge, and you know he isn't far away."

"What's his name?"

"Garrett Wycoff. He's a sheriff's deputy rather than a park ranger. A lot of the people looking for you are."

His lip curled. "Cops."

Gee, maybe because you committed multiple crimes?

"Park law enforcement are cops, too, you know." Not a good time to remind him that, even worse, they were *federal* law enforcement.

"Let's get moving," he said suddenly. "Pack everything up, in case we have to spend another night out here."

Mason looked at him with open incredulity, which Cadence shared.

She was careful to limit her response to nodding at the heap in front of her pack. "Are you done with all that?"

As if reminded, he stuck his arm in the pack and rooted around, coming up with a few hard objects: a pack of batteries for the flashlight, an extra fuel canister for the stove and her electronic reader, which was undoubtedly drained of battery power. In each case, he glanced, dropped them back in and then rose to his feet.

"Do it."

Their packs were scarcely disturbed from the night before, since she'd done the cooking using food she'd packed, and the stolen clothes they still carried didn't fit anyway. Mason did roll up Cadence's mat and hand it to her while she folded clothes and had to stuff it all back where it had come from. What almost might be consideration startled her.

She'd used quite a few meals by now, but they weren't space intensive, and Cole's arm had worked like a mixer in pancake batter. Now, with him standing above her, radiating impatience and the never entirely buried anger and hint of violence, she didn't dare take time to do a good job.

She stuffed, shoved her feet in her boots and tied them, then rose, too. And, oh, she ached, but that was nothing compared to the stab of pain in her torso. She pressed a hand to the exact spot. Why hadn't she thought to take some ibuprofen with the oatmeal? Only, was ibuprofen safe to take when she was pregnant? She probably should know, but either didn't or was too stressed to summon even common knowledge.

She glanced around, just as she always would when packing up to move on, and saw that the ice axe still leaned exactly where she'd left it.

With two sets of eyes on her, she didn't just snatch it. Instead, she gestured. "We should take that. It's a useful tool and makes a good walking stick besides. Especially in rough conditions. That's why mountain climbers carry them."

Nope—mountain climbers rarely paused to envision kill-

ing someone with their ice axe. She congratulated herself
for calling the tool "that," instead of by name. "Axe" had a
whole different connotation.

Cole said impatiently, "Fine. Stick it back on my pack
where it was."

He turned so she could do just that. Unfortunately, Mason
continued to watch carefully.

Mason, she was beginning to think, was the brains of the
pair, Cole the weapon he loosed when necessary. Cadence
wondered if Cole realized his place. Clearly, he thought *he*
was the alpha. Or was it possible they hadn't been long-term
partners, and Mason was discovering that Cole was more
than a little off?

"Ready?" Cole tipped his chin. "Up."

GARRETT WAS RELUCTANT to advance up the trail until he'd
been assured Don Phillips and a couple of deputies from Jefferson County had started to the pass behind him and Eric.
He thought it unlikely in the extreme that Cole and Mason
would think they could safely rejoin the trail to climb to the
pass…or to head back down the way they had come, thinking that would be a surprise to their pursuers.

That said…did they have any idea how tough it would be
to scramble up a ridge so steep without a trail? And one that
was thickly overgrown with everything from low-growing
salal and Oregon grape to devil's club and huckleberries?
Such evergreens as grew here weren't the friendly kind that
held out branches to be convenient handholds, either. In fact,
their lowest branches tended to be high above human reach.

Or, hey, to scramble *down*? That, he suspected, would be
even tougher. Sooner or later, someone's feet would go out
from under them, and the fall could be long and painful.

Just sitting here rubbed at Garrett, and he decided to gam-
ble that the men would head up, thinking the pass wasn't

far above them. Difficult, though, to see how they thought they'd be able to negotiate a way out of here, but that had to be what they were thinking by this time. Cadence wouldn't be much use to them otherwise.

And, man, he hated thinking of her as a pawn.

Even though the crackle and voices would permit anyone nearby to pinpoint his and Eric's location, Garrett now monitored radio traffic. He needed to know who was where… and to be available if those murderous slugs decided it was time to talk their way out of the trap they'd gotten themselves into after their poorly planned spree.

He kept an eye on his watch. They wouldn't have slept in, any more than he'd been able to. He had to assume they were on the move, and not far from him and Eric…or the twosome who had started down from La Crosse Pass half an hour or so ago.

The sun was rising higher than he'd expected, making him begin doubting himself by the time Dispatch connected to him, asked for confirmation of his call-in and informed him that Ranger Jones wanted to speak to him on behalf of Cole Souza.

Late yesterday, Garrett had learned both men's last names. They'd surely understood that fingerprints from their truck would open a book on both of them for law enforcement.

Souza had served a ten-year term in the Monroe Correctional Complex northeast of Seattle for second-degree murder. Mason Fitch was on record because of several traffic violations and an accident for which he'd been charged, but got off with a hand slap. Garrett wanted to think that knowing their criminal histories wouldn't make any difference in how Cadence responded to them. If Cole was the more volatile of the two, she'd have noticed by now. She had a gift for easing tempers, he'd noticed before, and relating to most people he and she had encountered.

"Standing by," he said into the radio.

"Garrett?"

Cadence's voice cracked. Or was the effect from being on the airways? He hoped so.

"It is," he said, going for calm. "Are you all right? Have you been hurt—"

He heard something muffled, then a man came on. "Cut the BS. We have things to talk over."

"I agree," Garrett said. "But I'm not prepared to discuss your situation until I hear Ranger Jones herself tell me that she hasn't been injured. This is nonnegotiable."

"You heard him," the voice snapped, and Cadence came back. "I'm injured, but not—" A man's voice burst out in the background. "Give me a second!" she snapped, her fiery response soothing Garrett's suppressed fear and fury. "I was *about* to say, I fell yesterday after we left the trail. You know how steep the ridge is. Neither Mason nor Cole has hurt me."

"All right," he said. "How badly—"

"I think a rib or two," she said hastily, but Cole was back. Or was it Mason?

"She was clumsy. Now can we talk?"

"We can."

Eric hovered close, his gaze on Garrett's face. Garrett didn't meet his eyes, afraid of how much he might give away.

"You in charge of where that helicopter goes?"

Garrett had been aware that it had been flying a slow pattern over the ridge this morning.

"I am the person you need to speak to," he agreed, which was far from the truth, but he'd seized the authority to negotiate, and he'd use any resources necessary to accomplish his goals: get Cadence safely back in his arms and nail these two bastards. "I'll have to clear any demands to use the helicopter with other people."

"Then you're not in charge."

"Neither the park service nor either county where you committed crimes owns a helicopter. We have arrangements to borrow one. As I said, I'm here to listen to what you want, and I'll get back to you once I have questions or answers."

Silence followed. Since these two were trapped like a calf in a chute, he didn't worry that they'd decide they didn't need him.

"We'll need a lift," the voice said. "Pilot only, unarmed. If I see a gun, I'll shoot him, and you can find a different one."

"Shooting a pilot will dig you deeper in a hole. You can't afford that."

"One body, two bodies..." He was undoubtedly shrugging.

"That would make three," he said flatly.

"Don't matter."

Oh, it mattered, as he would soon discover.

"You planning to fly far?" he asked.

"You think I'll tell you that?"

"The 'copter has been in the air quite a while this morning already. Unless you're thinking about a real short haul, it will need to refuel before it's any use to you."

"Do it."

Garrett nodded at Eric, who moved a distance away to open a communication on his own radio—assuming there was an effort this morning to prioritize their needs.

"What's the rest of the plan?" he asked.

"Like I'm going to tell you?" he sneered. "Not like you can't track us in the air anyway."

Garrett pictured a fighter jet screaming right above, keeping a *very* close eye on that helicopter and its occupants.

"Somebody will be able to," he agreed. No point in pretending.

Damn, even his experience as a negotiator wasn't helping him maintain the composure and dispassion he needed.

Envisioning Cadence's face, her smile, helped in one way and not at all in another. "I meant that you'll have to tell me where you want the helicopter to set down to pick you up."

"Pass, but not right on the trail. Maybe we'll lay out stuff from the packs to make a circle."

"Noted. In exchange for the helicopter and the pilot's willingness to offer himself up as a hostage, we need you to show some good faith by releasing the woman."

The rude laugh was about what he'd expected, but he had to try.

"You're asking for a lot," he said mildly. "It's not unreasonable of us to expect you to give a little."

A snort. "Yeah, you can't tell me the pilot won't be a cop of some kind."

A US Navy airman, actually.

"If he goes into this unarmed…"

"How am I supposed to know he really is until I'm in the copilot seat with the barrel of my gun shoved against his temple? No, as long as we have this pretty lady, we have you by the short hairs. I don't think you have the balls to come in with bullets flying when she's in the middle of it."

Garrett ground his teeth together. That was putting it succinctly. He didn't know, though, how he could handle seeing her shoved into the helicopter, maybe looking for him over her shoulder, and then it lifting off. Would she become less necessary to them then, or would they still deem her their best safeguard for the few minutes after the helicopter set them down for another attempt at a getaway? And even then. From their point of view, why not haul her along? The kid would have worked as well, but they hadn't lost anything with the exchange.

The only difference, Garrett believed, was that she was an experienced law enforcement officer. She'd be calculating at all times, looking for an opportunity to take them off-balance.

He just hoped she wasn't too reckless when she thought she saw an opening. If she was killed—

The taste of bile rose in his throat.

"Let me talk to her again."

"HE WANTS TO say his bye-byes." Cole shoved the radio at her.

Cadence accepted the radio. If only she could think of a single thing she could tell him that would help him find them. She couldn't imagine she'd have any hope of doing anything but what they told her to when the terrifying moment came to walk into the open to the waiting helicopter.

She turned her head to see nothing distinctive. They had scrabbled upward for what she estimated to be three hours already, but the going was so slow she had no idea how close they might be to mounting the ridge. One tree looked much like the next...except she could tell they'd entered a band of what was called montane forest, high enough in elevation that the trees grew slowly and any understory—the plant tangle that had tripped them up easily—diminished. She was able to spot some silver fir as well as the Douglas fir and western hemlock. None were huge even if they were old, given their precarious grip on the steep sidehill.

"Hey," he said, calm but...gentle. "You heard that?"

"Yes." They planned to use her until the bitter end. These were exactly the circumstances that led to a hostage being killed, as likely by friendly fire as by the bad guys. "Evan is okay?"

"Yep. The helicopter took him back to the campground, where he was reunited with his grandparents *and* his parents. He...had some things to pass on to you, but this probably isn't the time."

"No." A numbness seemed to be creeping over her. "Is the helicopter going to make it back today?"

"So far as I know."

"Okay." Why Cole in particular hadn't cut her off, she didn't know, but she wanted to get this out. "Some of what you said…you were right. It's not just for my sake I wish—"

Cole wrenched the radio from her hand. "That's it."

Garrett was trying to say something, but Cole shut him off. His narrowed eyes zeroed in on her face. "You and that guy. You got something going?"

"Don't be ridiculous," she said coolly. "We talked a bunch the past couple of days, that's all."

"Well, damn. This might've been even more fun if you did."

Mason intervened. "Let's move. We need to get in position while there's still plenty of daylight."

Cadence wondered what they would do if she crumpled and said, *I can't go any farther.*

Shoot her, the way Cole had suggested? Take turns using a fireman's carry to haul her carcass along whether she wanted to go or not?

Imagining her belly and rib cage crushed against one of those shoulders was all she needed to give her a second wind. There was pain…and then there was agony.

Chapter Seventeen

Nobody Garrett consulted with was surprised by the demands. What other options could there be? *Beam me up, Scotty?* From the minute the men had been pushed into turning onto a dead-end road, the possibilities diminished to near zero.

Unfortunately, they had a strong ace in their hands: Cadence.

Garrett might have lost it if anyone, including the chief ranger or county sheriff had so much as implied that she was any less than number one on their priority lists. If they'd been able to hold on to the boy, too, even Cadence would have put him first. Garrett tried to clutch onto that one positive: Evan was safe.

The pair that had been descending to meet him and Eric turned around. His reasonable assumption was that Cole and Mason would stop just before the tree line, when they lost their cover. That left only the mystery about where they'd pop out. Not expecting to hear from them any sooner, he and Eric hauled ass to reach that same tree line.

He briefly conferred with the others that he was now directing, but not a one of them knew this pass well. Alyssa Bailey, the triathlete, had hiked it, but had been wrapped up in the magnificent sweep of mountains, with no reason to study the immediate terrain for places flat enough for a helicopter to set down. A skilled pilot could load with just one skid on the ground if necessary, but that would be less than ideal for a lot of reasons.

What he was set on was taking the two down *before* they reached the helicopter. That would involve finding them, while remaining unseen. Maybe once they reached the ridgetop, Cadence would be able to offer a hint that would permit him to move into position.

Assuming he was allowed to speak to her again, he thought wryly.

And what could she possibly say? *I estimate we're three to four hundred yards west.* Sure. And west of the trail near the pass would involve more climbing, as Mount La Crosse reared directly west, the trail cutting across the slope.

This was magnificent country, he was reminded when the view opened ahead of them. Mountains everywhere, snow clinging in shadowed hollows, the rock gray and intimidating. Wildflowers and the small, windswept alpine fir in clusters. He'd forgotten there was a small lake and few puddles in the basin east of the pass. Better ground for a helicopter to land over there. Would Cadence suggest it to them? Would they listen to anything she did suggest?

The distance from the pass to the lake was too open for them to be willing to trot to it—unless they'd crossed the trail behind Garrett and Eric to edge that direction.

Now, that *was* the kind of thing she might have suggested.

The radio remained silent. He and Eric would have made better time, Garrett reminded himself.

Two rangers sat in plain sight right at the pass, but they stood and trotted toward Garrett and Eric when they appeared.

He'd not met them before. They were the two men who had already been in the so-called Enchanted Valley area tucked beneath Mount Anderson. One had white-blond hair, wasn't over five foot eight or nine, and was almost slender. Garrett had a feeling the unprepossessing appearance was deceptive, however. The guy could well be a distance runner, like Alyssa Bailey. The other was closer to Garrett's height, solidly built, face at least two days from a shave, eyes steady.

They moved to a clump of silver fir and a few small western hemlocks to be out of sight, then shook hands all around. Garrett answered questions, filling them in on what they hadn't heard and telling them his best guesses.

"I know Cadence," said the thin one, who'd introduced himself as Nathan Ryback. "We did some cross-country skiing not long after she was hired."

"I've met her, too," Davis Bourke agreed.

Garrett felt a surge that was painfully close to jealousy. He'd felt an instant rapport with Bourke, a sense that they'd understand each other…and that they had enough in common physically, Cadence might be drawn to him.

He shook off the personal pang that had no place here, and said, "I'd like to know about your backgrounds. For example, have either of you had sniper training?"

Bourke bent his head in acknowledgment. "I have. I was army for ten years. Decided to go into law enforcement when I got out, thought I'd like a lot of open space and ended up at the Grand Canyon."

"I hear it's busier than Times Square in New York City."

"Yeah, not quite what I had in mind."

"Have you kept up at the range?"

"Not usually at the distances I once could do, but enough."

"Good. I don't know how you feel about it, but—"

Bourke's face hardened. "I feel fine. After they gunned down a sheriff's deputy and then some poor sucker who was here in the mountains for fun? And then there's Cadence." He was clearly done.

Garrett nodded acknowledgment. With Eric, that made two decent sharpshooters. That was pure luck, given how few of them were here.

"All right. I'm hoping we can get close, but until we know where they're going to emerge and expect the helicopter to land, we can't make any solid plans. Oh, we should have three more people with us shortly. Eric's partner, Don Phillips, and two Mason County deputies, if I remember right."

Eric nodded.

"You've talked to Cadence." That was Ryback.

"I have. As I told you, she apparently took a fall hard enough that she thinks she has broken ribs. It's…causing some nausea, too." He assumed she'd hidden the real reason for her on-again, off-again nausea from Cole and Mason, as he would now. "Far as I know, she's still on her feet, and we know what tough conditions they're in. She's quick thinking, and if she's strong enough to make it up here, we shouldn't count her out as help."

There were nods all around.

He hated waiting.

WHEN THEY REACHED the trail, Mason and Cole had both settled their rifles in firing position, one looking downhill, the other up. Cadence tried to remember who was supposed to be where and couldn't put the pieces together. She'd lost any reliable sense of how much time had passed. She just thought intensely, *Whoever was supposed to be on their way up…don't. Not now.*

Nobody appeared. She and the two men actually half jogged up a brief stretch of the trail before reluctantly—on her part—returning to the cover of the trees and the steep rock and soil she kept skidding on. Any patience either man had felt for her had eroded. She didn't dare hold them up. It was surprising enough that they'd taken her advice to risk showing themselves by crossing and climbing what quickly felt like even more difficult terrain to the east side of the trail. Still, it was her job to make sure they saw a realistic rendezvous point atop the pass once they reached it. She convinced herself that Garrett would prefer that, too. He'd need someplace that he could conceivably surround them for an assault.

When her stomach turned over this time, she couldn't blame pregnancy. No, it was the picture of her in the middle of an assault team. There had to be a way she could take herself out of the picture. There had to be. Because otherwise…

No. She paused long enough to wipe sweat off her brow and breathe deeply. Sacrificing herself wasn't on the agenda, and she felt sure Garrett would never consider that as a plan or even a possibility. He'd throw himself over her first. What did matter was stopping Mason and Cole before they got in that helicopter and pressed a gun barrel to another hapless hostage's head, this one who'd volunteered himself.

Like she hadn't?

That hadn't been her intention. Only freeing Evan. As awful as this was, better her than an eleven-year-old boy. And…there was the vest. If she could avoid literally being held upright as a shield, if she could drop flat…

She kept reverting to what she could do if this or that happened. Somehow, she also paid attention to her next handhold, if there was one, to making sure each step was solid before committing to it.

"WHERE'S THE GODDAMN HELICOPTER?"

Garrett crouched behind a rock and the feathery branch of a stunted fir, hoping his tan cargo pants and long-sleeve, faded green shirt were adequate camouflage.

He pressed his thumb to reply. "I'm told it's not far out. I don't hear it, either."

"I want it to land as close to the tree line as possible. I see some puddles out there. I expect it to be south of those."

"I'll let them know. I can't guarantee a particular landing zone. I'm not a pilot."

"You can see a flat place as well as anyone else. No excuses."

"I need to talk to Ranger Jones," he said in a hard voice. "This deal is entirely dependent on her well-being."

After a momentary silence, he heard her hesitant, "Garrett?"

"That's me."

"I don't think my thigh muscles will ever recover."

He chuckled. That had been one hell of a steep climb. "At least there weren't any more trees down across the trail the last ways."

"No? Well, the ones up here are built to bend before wind and snow. Except—"

"What are you telling him?" a man asked roughly in the background.

"I'm not telling him anything!" she snapped. "We're just talking. I like to hear a friendly voice."

"Do what you're told and you'll hear one again."

"Sure." Her sadness and disbelief leaked through.

Garrett shared that fear. "You still hurting?"

"Of course I am." Now she was more subdued. Cole's hand probably hovered inches away, ready to snatch the radio. "I'm trying not to, um—"

"That's enough!" one of the men growled, and the connection was severed.

Kneeling beside him, Eric raised his eyebrows. "Get anything from that?"

Garrett bent his head for a moment. *Get a grip.* Then he said roughly, "Yeah. Couple of things." He surveyed the land in their vicinity. Whether it had been their idea or Cadence's, the pair must have done as Garrett had guessed they might: they'd crossed the trail at some point to place them near the shallow basin here. And…yeah. There it was.

He pointed toward one of the thicker clusters of the stunted evergreens that were about all that survived at this elevation, and as exposed to the elements as they were. "Top of the tree's snapped off."

Eric's gaze followed his. "How did you get that?"

"She commented on how the trees are flexible enough to bow before any strong winds. And then she said, 'Except…' That's the only tree I see with the top broken off."

"Well, damn." Eric pondered. "Do we try to move on them?"

They were close; so close, Garrett cautioned the other man not to make sudden movements that would draw the eye. "It's too risky. They're watching for us. We'd be crossing open ground. If we can coordinate with Don it would be one thing, but right now I think it's best if we stay off the radio except for touching base with the helicopter pilot and Souza and Fitch."

Eric sighed. "What if the damn thing lands *between* us and them, and blocks us?"

"We suggest a different place to set down." Should he say anything about Cadence's last suggestion, as abortive as it had been? He grunted. He had to prepare his partner as well as he could. "There at the end," he said. "I think she was letting us know that she'll use her nausea, real or pretend, to delay or drop to the ground when she thinks the moment is right."

"How's that going to protect her? Or is it her idea of a signal?"

He stretched his neck to one side until it cracked, then to the other side. "Don't know. If they think she's just diving for cover, they might shoot her then and there. They might hesitate if she's puking. Keeping her as a hostage is essential to their plan to somehow disappear when their ride ends."

Eric studied him quizzically. "You think that's what she was talking about when she said she's trying not to do something?"

"I do think. She wasn't finished with what she was trying to say."

They lapsed into silence. The sun continued moving across the sky, the delay excruciating. Garrett began to feel chilled. Would they let Cadence add another layer? He didn't want her to be cold.

Had someone higher up blocked the use of a helicopter to transport a pair of killers, given that their expressed intention had been to hold a gun on the pilot? Were no pilots willing? But Garrett didn't believe it, given that machine and pilots both were US military.

Usually a patient man, Garrett stayed rigid, his skin prickling. He hated not being in complete control. Maintaining readiness for an operation that could happen anytime—ten minutes or two hours—always felt this way. Life and death decisions weren't new to him…but they'd never before involved the woman he loved.

By this time, using the word didn't even surprise him.

A QUIVER RAN over Cadence when she first heard the helicopter. It was definitely approaching.

"That's it!" Cole snapped. "Everyone on their feet and ready."

"What?" Mason said. "We're just going to run out there and wave, 'Here we are! Shoot us?'"

This argument hadn't changed, and they were still at it. Personally, she gave thumbs-up to Mason's side. Partly because authorities in the form of park law enforcement and deputies weren't going to let two men who'd already killed stroll out and hop into the helicopter just because they were ushering her along with them. They'd try not to shoot her, but that was no guarantee. She even understood. Garrett might be fighting on her side, but likely someone with park law enforcement was in charge by this time.

She had the fleeting thought, *If he let them be.*

Cole glowered. "I should have thrown something out to tell that pilot where to land, like I said."

"And that wouldn't have given away where we are?" Mason said in disbelief.

Please, Garrett, be nearby.

Here the 'copter came, the rotors whipping overhead so that the trees shook as if in a storm, the noise almost deafening. It passed almost overhead, but not quite; head back, she didn't see the pilot looking down, as she'd hoped she might.

At least one thing was on her side: her stomach was plenty ready to play its part. In fact, she'd been at least queasy for most of the day, more than usual. Because of stress? Or thanks to the sharp pain in her side? Either, or both?

Usually as soon as she was done puking, she could eat. This morning, she hadn't wanted to, but made herself. And during their brief stop to eat midday, she'd forced more down.

The helicopter settled slowly down on a piece of rocky ground closer than she had wanted, farther away than Cole and Mason had in mind.

"Get on the radio!" Cole screamed. "That's not good enough!" He added invectives that had Mason flushed and angry, too. Mason tried to connect with the radio, but static and voices didn't let him. He finally threw it down and lifted a big, booted foot with the clear intention of stomping on it.

Because that would do so much good.

Cole swung a fist at him, knocking him back. Cadence

cowered from the outburst of violence, using what was surely a natural reaction to also open a few feet of separation.

Her pack? Leave it on? Take it off so she could move faster?

Wear it, she decided, as she had already done earlier. Along with her vest, it would give her some protection from gunfire.

A door in the helicopter opened and she saw a man in a helmet wearing headphones lean over to look at them. Apparently he *had* spotted them as he settled down. He waved his hand.

"The pilot," she said. "He's...he's signaling for us."

Mason and Cole snarled at each other again, then turned to look. The distance wasn't great. Maybe thirty yards?

Where was Garrett?

Had he understood her hint? Did he have his eye on them right now?

She wanted, quite fiercely, to believe he did.

She knew what she had to do, although this would surely go down in the annals of law enforcement as the most embarrassing way to self-protect ever.

Ruthless hands grabbed at her, pulled her roughly to place her to one side. She would have guessed that direction was their greatest vulnerability, too—unless the pilot was armed and started shooting. It was Mason who had her upper arm in a tight grip.

"Let's move." Cole was still giving the orders, although she intercepted a dirty look from his partner.

He held his rifle in firing position. Mason's remained slung over his shoulder, but he had his pistol in his free hand. Just before they stepped out of cover, he pushed the barrel against her temple.

She hadn't expected that, and it scared her more than anything else about the situation. She tried to tell herself to ignore the gun. He wouldn't keep pressing it to her head, would he? Cadence fixed her gaze on a slanted boulder ten or fifteen feet away. If she could throw herself behind it...

As if reading her mind, Mason's fingers dug hard into her flesh. "Don't screw this up," he murmured in her ear.

"I'm sick to my stomach," she whispered. "Can we wait? I think I need to—"

Not hearing her, Cole had stepped into the open, starting to move and rotating his rifle from side to side as he watched for any movement. Mason kept pace, Cadence stumbling. She gasped for breath, her heart racing. God, don't let *him* stumble, or his gun could go off.

They were close to the long, low ridge the slab of rock made.

She swallowed. "I *have* to—" So much for real heroism.

He glanced at her in some alarm. "Don't even think about it."

She pressed a hand to her belly beneath her rib cage, pushed as hard as she could bear and vomited.

"What the—?" Mason's hand jerked, the barrel lifting.

Cadence managed to turn her head far enough to send a stream of bile at him. He started swearing savagely even as she let herself fall as if to her knees. For a moment she hung from his hand, but in her peripheral vision, she saw movement, heard shouts.

"Drop your weapons! *Now!*"

Mason tried to lift her, but even for someone as powerfully built as him, deadweight was hard to control with one hand. The instant she felt the pain in her knees as they hit hard ground, she wrenched to free her arm. She had to roll.

Cole began shooting, spraying bullets far and wide. There'd be answering gunfire any second.

Chapter Eighteen

Despite their inability to communicate, Garrett saw out of the corner of his eye that Don Phillips and two other men had appeared to the far side of the fugitives. Too exposed, he knew, but like him they were all thinking about Cadence and her vulnerability.

Everything was happening too fast. He saw her seemingly trip and start to fall, and the instant of revulsion that distracted the man holding her. He kept his grip even as she started to go down, but at the first shouted order looked up.

Cadence hit the ground, flung herself full length and tried to roll. Not happening with that damn pack sticking out of her back, but she kept scrambling.

The SOB with the rifle hadn't taken his finger off the trigger, firing a fusillade covering nearly a hundred-and-eighty-degree arc. Bullets pinged off the helicopter, the door of which had closed. Garrett saw somebody go down—one of the men with Phillips. He himself had yet to fire, but now he did, close enough to have decided to rely on his handgun. Lifting the Glock with both hands, he didn't allow himself any distraction. Giving himself over to tunnel vision, he aimed for the thigh of the man shooting the rifle. Pulled the trigger. Once, twice. Again as his knees buckled, this time aiming for the upper arm or shoulder.

The rifle fell even as the man did. The others were running forward, bullets flying. Dangerous when the assault teams were on nearly opposite sides of the people they were trying to bring down. His own arm stung, but he kept closing in.

The second guy leaped toward Cadence, but Garrett thought it was Bourke who fired a warning shot right in front of his boots. The man lurched back, let his own gun fall to the ground and raised his hands.

Please, God, don't let her have taken a bullet.

Someone was cuffing the man who had now fallen to his knees, while Eric and Don Phillips stood over the man Garrett had shot. A wound in Phillips's thigh soaked his pants with blood. The one Garrett didn't recognize wasn't moving at all.

Garrett ran for Cadence, found her at the edge of a rock slab that protruded a few feet above the rest of the ground, the face she turned to him shocked, too pale, scratched and dirty. Her finely cut cheekbones were more prominent than they should be. She whimpered, scaring the crap out of him, and dry heaved a couple of times.

He all but fell next to her. "Are you hurt? Tell me you're not hurt."

"I'm…not hurt," she whispered. "Just…" She waved a hand.

He let a prayerful word escape and sank to his butt beside her. "I didn't know I could be that scared."

"Me, either. Ugh."

Garrett laughed. He'd have sworn he'd forgotten how, but damned if he didn't do it. Her expression was indignant, until he said, "Morning sickness as a tactical move. Never seen it employed before."

Her lips twitched. "I'm an original."

"Yeah." He swallowed and helped her slip out of the pack

and push herself to her hands and knees. Then he decided he didn't care what anyone thought about them and gathered her into his arms. Thankful. So thankful.

"Do they all know?" she asked.

"Know what?"

"That I'm pregnant?"

"Oh. No. I let them think the nausea is because of your ribs."

She bit her already cracking lower lip, then tried to peer past him. "Are...are they dead?" she asked.

He must be blocking her sightline to the others. Garrett turned his head. "Not sure about the one. No, he's moving. I shot him several times myself. The guy who was dragging you along looks okay. He's got his hands in the air."

"Mason." She said the name so quietly he had to tilt his head to hear her. "He... I don't think he wanted to hurt me."

"Yeah? Didn't look that way to me."

"He's the more stable of the two. I suspect Cole is the one who did the shooting and probably killed the two men. Mason was...pretty frustrated with him."

"Shouldn't have gotten in the truck in the first place then, should he?" He knew how hard his voice was. "Given their planned activities."

"No." She tried for a smile that twisted. "I'm not nominating him for citizen of the year. Just...saying I don't think he's the killer."

"Okay." It was taking some time, but holding her allowed his heart to reset so it wouldn't pound through his chest wall, and his muscles to begin to relax after some belated twitches. "You know he'll be charged anyway."

Her head bobbed, bumping his scratchy chin. God, he wanted to kiss her, but—

He jerked when a voice spoke from right above him.

"Ranger Jones? You okay?"

This smile was weak but present. "More or less. Just taking a minute to get myself together."

It was Eric looking down at them. "Understandable."

Garrett pulled himself together. "Cadence says the one who is down is Cole Souza, the other Mason Fitch. Souza in bad shape?"

"Not good. The Clallam County deputy is badly injured, too. I don't like having them share a ride, but we don't have a lot of choice but to load him and Souza both onto this helicopter. Your...injuries don't look life-threatening, Cadence. If I'm wrong—"

"I can wait. I do think I have broken ribs, but I've hiked halfway up a mountain since I injured myself, and nothing has punctured my lungs yet."

That was upbeat. Garrett wanted to see her given priority, but she was right; her injuries weren't urgent. And that would give them some time to talk.

"Fitch will have to wait," Eric added. "We've got some other people hurt, too."

Cadence was looking at him. "You're bleeding," she said suddenly.

Both he and Eric glanced down at themselves. Garrett saw that the sleeve of his shirt was blood soaked and... Yeah, he found the tear, remembering the sting he'd felt.

"Nothing serious," he said.

"You've been shot in *both* arms now!" she exclaimed. "Don't tell me that isn't serious!"

Eric looked mildly surprised at her vehemence, but did glance at Garrett as if reminding himself that, yeah, his right upper arm was thickly bandaged.

Reluctantly Garrett decided he'd better check out the wounded man and oversee the scene. He gently set Cadence aside, but she made motions as if she intended to stand, too.

He opened his mouth to tell her to stay put, but had the

brains to understand that this was one of those moments that could make or break their relationship. So instead, he held out a hand and applied enough pull to get her back on her feet.

They left her pack where it was and picked their way toward the cluster of men around the one who was being edged onto a backboard.

At first sight, he'd have said their small force had multiplied, but that wasn't true. He counted: him and Eric, Don Phillips and the two he'd brought with him, and Bourke and Ryback. Then there was the guy in a flight suit who seemed to be overseeing the arrangements to load the deputy ahead of Souza. Garrett did wonder whether he'd come unarmed or not. Not, was his best guess.

Mason, on his knees, didn't raise his head. His hands were cuffed behind him. He was as filthy as the rest of them, visible skin scratched, but Garrett didn't see any blood.

Cadence took a step away from Garrett and laid a hand on the guy's shoulder. She said quietly, "You could have shot me."

Mason grimaced, still not looking up. "Lousy plan," he mumbled. "I don't do shit like that."

"Thank you," she said. "I'll speak for you to investigators."

The guy didn't say anything else, and Cadence walked to the helicopter to say a few words to the seriously injured man and to the pilot.

Then she looked around for her pack and called, "Anybody who is bleeding, come see me." She raised her eyebrows at Garrett. "Starting with you."

"I'll get the pack."

She opened her mouth, he quirked an eyebrow himself, and she shrugged acquiescence. He brought the pack to her.

The important stuff he had to say would have to wait.

A SECOND HELICOPTER carried everyone who was injured to the community hospital in Port Angeles on the north shore of the Olympic peninsula. Cadence felt a little guilty, looking out the window at the scene receding as they rose from the ground. The few people who were completely uninjured would be hiking out. She was intensely glad Garrett wasn't among them. Right this minute, she needed to be within touching distance of him, even though she was still confused about how to answer him.

The racket was too great to allow for conversation, but he sat right beside her, their shoulders pressed together. She couldn't care less if his blood was soaking into her uniform shirt. That shirt was destined for the trash, anyway.

She felt very strange. So much had happened. Examining her tangle of emotions, she realized she hadn't really believed she would survive. Garrett's determination and sheer competence couldn't have saved her if Mason had pulled that trigger...or if any of the other bullets flying around had struck her. Fear left her shaky, but a sense of weightlessness, as if she wasn't belted into a seat at all, was way more than relief. Hope was buoying her, she finally decided.

No one else seemed to be paying much attention to her, so she risked laying her hand on her abdomen. *We made it, baby. I'm so sorry I took any chances with you.*

When she glanced at Garrett, it was to see his gaze had followed her hand. When he lifted that gaze to meet hers, his expression was raw and she knew he had read her mind. Or maybe he'd been thinking the same thing anyway.

The next second, determination hardened his face. "You know what I want to say."

"Not the time."

He turned his head, grimaced and said, "Soon."

Would she be able to resist him? Should she?

She gazed out the window, then closed her eyes, tipped

her head to touch his shoulder briefly, smiled and didn't meet his eyes until medical personnel met them at the hospital and steered them separate directions. Looking perturbed, his gaze didn't leave her until a curtain closed her into a cubicle.

A young woman doctor arrived almost immediately and examined her. "We need X-rays, of course."

Cadence lowered her voice to be sure she couldn't be heard on the other side of the curtain. "I'm pregnant."

"Ah. You're certain."

"I've done a couple of home tests. And I have morning sickness."

The doctor decided she needed to pee in a cup. The results of the urine test didn't take long.

The doctor smiled. "You're definitely pregnant. I assume you're happy about it?"

"Very."

"Do you have a partner who will be able to help?"

Probably not her business, but Cadence nodded.

With extra precautions being taken, she had the X-ray, which revealed two cracked ribs. Actually, the doctor's words were, *Only* cracked.

Thank you. Cadence rolled her eyes behind the woman's back.

In the end, she was wrapped a few inches below her breasts in a mummy-like fashion, and prescribed a painkiller the doctor assured her was safe. The doctor encouraged her to see an obstetrician soon, start on prenatal vitamins and consider not throwing herself off cliffs for the next seven months or so.

After filling the prescription, Cadence decided she needed to wait for Garrett. An aide carried her pack to the waiting room for her, where she sat. The next step—transportation—didn't seem very important right now, with so much going through her head. One certainty rose to the top: she had to resign from her job—or be transferred to a non–law enforcement capacity, if that was available.

From past experience, she doubted it was. If not…could she find another job locally? Or should she go home to Idaho?

But…what about Garrett?

Other people came and went, but sitting alone in her corner she knew the moment he came out of the back. His presence was that dominating. Even though his injuries were worse than hers, nobody carried his pack. He walked straight to her, those blue eyes never leaving her face. Truthfully, he looked as bad as she suspected she did: dirty, tired and moving carefully. His stubble was turning into a beard. He carried a paper bag with the pharmacy logo on it that matched hers.

"Hey," he said, stopping in front of her. "All patched up?"

She wrinkled her nose. "Literally." When she mentioned her mummy comparison, he chuckled.

"You and me both. Cracked sternum." He gingerly sat in the chair beside her.

"Two ribs."

"And your bullet wounds?"

"Wrapped anew. I don't think they did any better job than you did. I have prescriptions for antibiotics and painkillers."

"I already got mine. Um…maybe we can share a taxi home?"

"I called my grandfather. He's on the way to pick us up." *Us.*

Cadence shifted uneasily. "Does he even know I exist?"

"Of course he does." His mouth twisted ruefully. "He's been giving me hell for not fighting for you."

She blinked at that. "You're serious?" And, "Is he okay to drive this far?"

"Yeah. He's doing great." Something shifted in his expression. "Let's go wait outside. I think there are benches."

After a moment, she nodded. Even with the advent of evening, the air was warm. She inhaled it and let Garrett steer her to the farthest bench from the entrance. Nobody would notice them here.

"You asked if I'm serious," he said after a moment. "Damn straight I am."

Cadence took a deep breath. "Just because you feel responsible—"

"I *am* responsible. But that's not the point."

"Of course it is."

He shook his head, sadness momentarily showing. "No, Cadence. I didn't want to admit it, but I'm in love with you. I want to marry you. I swear."

She straightened, winced but squared her shoulders. "When did you decide you were in love with me? When you thought I might die? That's sort of classic, isn't it? Pretty sure emotion born out of fear isn't lasting."

"No." He took her hand this time. "I ignored what I was feeling until you issued your ultimatum and I panicked."

"So I saw," she said tartly.

"When you drove away, I felt like I'd just been in a head-on crash. Dazed, disbelieving. Unsteady on my feet. I'd have been calling and knocking on your door any day. I just… had to come to terms with feeling something for you that I'd sworn I'd never let myself feel."

"I do understand," she said softly. "It's just…"

"Just what?"

"I couldn't bear it if you started to pull away." She had an awful lump in her throat. "If I could tell you were sorry for making a commitment like this."

"I will never be sorry." There was steel in his voice she'd heard when he was on the job, but never with her. "I knew you were different from the beginning. I was a coward, that's all. I want you to marry me. I *need* you to marry me. The idea of having a family—"

Had his voice thickened?

"I...want that, too," she admitted. "But I'm still scared. I can't decide if it would be worth having everything and then losing it, or starting off strong and on my own in the first place."

"You will never be on your own." He swallowed. "I love you, Cadence. I want to be a father. Please, will you marry me?"

She made herself just breathe for a minute, then said, "Maybe?"

"Maybe?"

"We don't have to decide today."

"And when do you decide?"

"Well, before the baby is born?"

He gusted out a breath. "You want to waddle down the aisle?"

Suddenly, she was smiling. "I won't wait that long. It's just...you should have time to be sure."

That's when his head tipped and his gaze sharpened, if such a thing was possible. "But you? You don't need time to be sure?"

"I've been in love with you for months," she admitted. "I let myself hope for longer than I should have."

He unexpectedly grinned, looking rakish. "I'll tell you what. Give me overnight, and we'll have this talk again."

"Overnight?"

"Sounds like plenty long to me." The smile had died, and he had the intent look on his face that she recognized. "Can I kiss you?"

Her eyes burned, but she reached for him even as she nodded. The feel of him, the taste, was so familiar, and she knew she hadn't imagined the tenderness she'd always felt from him. Or the passion. His jaw was scratchy, but she didn't care as he claimed her mouth. She *wanted* him. His hand slipped around her nape, kneading, kneading, and she wanted to crawl onto his lap, but they *were* in public. And both injured.

He broke off the kiss to murmur against her lips, "By the way. I told Granddad we'd stop at your place and pick up some clean clothes and whatever else you need, and then you'd come home with us."

Her mouth opened and closed a few times, guppy-like, before she laughed. "You might try *asking*."

"Yeah, the asking wasn't going so well, but I figured you wouldn't hurt my grandfather's feelings by refusing. I think that's his truck I hear."

Part of her wanted to hold out, to demonstrate her stubbornness and independence, but really, she couldn't think of anything she'd like better than going home with Garrett. And, hey, it wasn't as if her current digs were all that great.

Plus…by including his grandfather—his only family—he was showing that he was all in. How could she resist that?

So she said, "Well, if you have better water pressure than mine."

With a hand on his chest, she felt the rumble of his laugh as much as heard it. "I'm sure we do."

She'd complained before about the pathetic drizzle that she called a shower.

"Do you have a bathtub?" she thought to ask.

"Umm-hmm. Claw-footed. Deep enough to swim in. If we could get Granddad out of the house, we could share it."

The rusty creak of a door slamming came to her ears.

"You win."

The gleam in his eyes joined with his grin. "What do I win?"

And she laughed. "You'll have to wait and see." Her gaze

went past him to the tall, only slightly stooped, white-haired man who approached. Somehow he'd spotted them with no trouble. She'd have known he was related to Garrett if she'd happened on him at the grocery store anytime these past few months.

He raised a white eyebrow at her, and she stood, smiling, to meet him.

It only got better when Garrett rose, pulled her close and said, "Granddad, meet your soon to be granddaughter, Cadence Jones."

Really? She was going to surrender this easily? Of course she was, she admitted. How could she say no when the man she loved offered her everything she'd ever wanted?

And all she had to do was remember the desperation she'd seen in his eyes several times the past few days to know he wanted it all, too.

* * * * *

HOSTAGE SECURITY

LISA CHILDS

With great appreciation for my wonderful readers and a special shout-out to the ones who post the most wonderful reviews that make writing so rewarding: Vicki Watts, Elaine Sapp, Bea Followill and Tammy Morse. I'm very sorry if I missed your name and you've been posting reviews. I very much appreciate all my readers!

Prologue

"Have you changed your mind?" Garek Kozminski asked his brother-in-law Logan Payne during the opening celebration of the most recent franchise of the Payne Protection Agency in River City, Michigan.

Logan was also Garek's boss and one of his best friends. It hadn't always been that way; they'd once been enemies. Logan had believed Garek's dad had killed his dad, while Garek and his siblings had believed their father had been framed for the police officer's murder. Eventually they'd been proven right, but by then it had been too late for their dad—he'd been murdered, too, in prison.

"Changed my mind?" Logan asked, raising his voice so that Garek could hear him above all the other people at the party. "About what?"

Garek gestured around the warehouse space that had been sectioned off into rooms with glass walls and high-tech equipment. On the exterior brick walls hung vivid artwork; most of the partygoers were looking at that more than anything else. "Have you reconsidered agreeing to this franchise of the Payne Protection Agency, the Kozminski branch?" Garek was opening it with his wife and his brother Milek.

Logan snorted. "It's a little late now. While I regret losing some of my best bodyguards, I don't dare back out of our agreement. My wife and yours would kill me."

Stacy and Candace were standing together, their arms around each other as they watched nieces and nephews putting a puzzle together in the middle of the concrete floor. Stacy was petite with long wavy titian hair while Candace was tall with short black hair.

His heart swelling with love, Garek chuckled. "Yeah, I don't know which one I'm more afraid of. My sister would come up with some clever, creative way to kill you."

Stacy was a world-renowned jewelry designer.

"While Candace will just make it hurt. Badly," Logan said with a chuckle.

Candace, Garek's beautiful wife, was one of the toughest Payne Protection bodyguards. And after Logan's younger brother, Cooper, and Logan's twin brother, Parker, started their own branches, there were a lot of bodyguards. Except for the ones who were off on assignment, all of those bodyguards had showed up to celebrate the opening of this branch.

Logan sighed and began, "I'm going to regret losing you and Candace and—"

"No mention of me?" Milek Kozminski interrupted as he joined them. While Logan with his black hair and blue eyes looked exactly like his twin, Parker, and their younger brother, Cooper, and half brother, Nick, Milek and Garek could have been twins, too. They both had blond hair that they probably wore too long, and their eyes were the same weird silvery gray color.

"He's happy to get rid of you," Garek teased his younger brother. "You're always slacking off on the job. So easily distracted. I'm not sure how Amber puts up with you."

Milek was as renowned as their sister for all the vivid art that hung from the walls in the new agency. It also hung in galleries, museums and personal collections around the world.

Totally unoffended, Milek grinned. "I'm not sure how my lovely wife puts up with me, either. She could do so much better. She's brilliant and beautiful." And as devoted to Milek as he was to her.

Garek, Milek and Stacy hadn't had an easy start to life with a father who was a thief who had spent so many years in prison, not for theft but for a murder he hadn't committed. They'd had to rely on each other after he went away, doing whatever they'd had to in order to support and protect themselves. But their lives eventually changed for the better.

And that was mostly because of the Paynes.

Penny Payne-Lynch rushed up and hugged first Milek and then Garek. "I'm so proud of you two," she said, tears sparkling in her coppery brown eyes. Her hair was the same coppery brown with only a few fine silver strands wound through it. She was the most amazing woman. Even when everyone else had thought the Kozminskis' father had killed her husband, she had tried to help them, tried to take care of them just like she took care of not only the four kids she'd raised on her own after her husband's death, but everyone else.

"Thank you, Mrs. P," Garek said. "Couldn't have done it without you." And he really couldn't have.

"None of us could have," Logan agreed, and when his mom stepped back from the Kozminskis, he hugged her, too.

"You all give me too much credit," she said. "It's your hard work that has reaped all the rewards you so richly deserve."

"The work is just starting here," Garek said.

Someone called out to Penny and Milek, and the two walked off arm in arm to greet whoever had called out. Probably the chief of police, who was also Penny's second husband, Woodrow Lynch. Not that he would be the chief much longer, if he had his way. He'd expressed his desire to retire soon, no doubt to spend more time with his beautiful wife.

Milek's wife, Amber, walked up seconds after her spouse left with Penny.

"You just missed him," Garek said, pointing after his brother.

"You're the one I wanted to talk to," the River City district attorney said. "We both know my darling husband isn't going to be doing the administrative work. You and Candace are."

Garek chuckled at how well his sister-in-law knew her husband and him and his spouse. The woman was brilliant.

"And they both have my support," Logan said.

"They're going to need it," Amber said. "I'm working to get some of the gun rights restored to your new bodyguards, but it's not going to be easy."

Garek shrugged. "I didn't hire them to shoot people," he said. "I hired them to protect them but mostly to protect their things. Our branch is focusing on special security."

Logan chuckled. "That whole *it takes a thief to catch a thief*?"

"We're more focused on stopping the thieves," Garek said. "We're hired to prevent thefts."

And he'd just taken on a big client that morning: an insurance company that was concerned about the recent spate of theft claims they'd paid out, because all their clients were getting robbed around the same time, and the new CEO wasn't comfortable with coincidences.

Neither was Garek.

"How are they going to do that without weapons?" Logan asked.

"Speak softly and carry a big stick."

Garek wasn't the one who'd repeated the old quote. It was the chief of police who'd walked up with Penny and

Milek. The tall man with the iron gray hair reminded Garek of the character Tom Selleck played on one of his favorite TV shows. Looks weren't the only thing Chief Woodrow Lynch shared with the character; he also had the same idol. President Teddy Roosevelt was who had said the quote first.

Speak softly and carry a big stick...

"A stick isn't much protection when the other people are armed," Logan pointed out.

"Hopefully nobody will need a gun or a stick," Garek said. "Just our high-tech security systems." While he was happy to emulate his brother-in-law and start up his own branch of the security business, he didn't want to suffer the losses that Logan had. In addition to losing his dad when he was a kid, Logan had also lost some of the bodyguards who'd worked for him. While some of them had left to start or work at the other two franchises, a couple of them had died.

Garek looked around the warehouse, his gaze resting on each of the new guards he'd hired.

Ivan Chekov and Viktor Lagransky had the same Oliver Twist upbringing that Garek and his siblings had, and they'd even had the same Fagin, a greedy crime boss who'd forced his own nephew and the kids of his former employees to commit crimes.

Blade Sparks was even bigger than Ivan and Viktor and had had to use his size to support himself. Dark-haired, dark-eyed Josh Stafford wasn't as big as the other new employees, but he was tough. He'd had to be in order to survive his five-year prison sentence.

Milek had hired him based on Amber's recommendation. Or maybe her insistence. She'd once accepted Josh's plea deal for a crime she didn't think he committed. But she didn't know why he would take the blame for something he hadn't done.

Garek did. He'd done the same to protect someone he loved.

So he understood all of his new employees very well. They had already suffered enough in their lives. Some of them had lost people they'd cared about, and some had lost their freedom for a while.

He had to make sure that he kept them all safe now, so that they didn't lose their lives, too.

Chapter One

Five years behind bars for something he hadn't done could have made Josh Stafford incredibly bitter. But he was the one who'd turned the proverbial key in his own cell door and thrown it away, along with everything else from his old life. Everything that had mattered to him.

But he was out now, for the past few months, with a second chance and a new career in security with the Payne Protection Agency. The picture on his security badge, which was clipped to his pocket, didn't look that different than his prison ID. Same dark hair worn a little too long, same scruff on his face, same dark eyes that had seen too much over the past five years but hadn't seen enough before that. While the Kozminski brothers, who ran the branch of the agency Josh worked for, had given him a second chance to prove that he was trustworthy and honorable, he didn't expect anyone else to give him one.

And so he'd opted to keep his distance from the new client the agency had just taken on.

The work he did to protect Croft Custom Jewelry, he did at night when nobody would see him guarding the perimeter, but he would see if anyone tried to break into the building to steal anything. While at first he'd been apprehensive to be anywhere around *her* again, he was glad he'd been assigned to her family business because all he'd ever wanted to do was keep her safe.

All he'd ever wanted to do was keep everyone he cared about safe. That was why he'd taken the blame all those years ago even though he hadn't committed the crime.

But that was all in the past, and there was no sense looking back. He could only look forward. At the moment, though, he was looking down as he climbed the stairs to his apartment on the fourth floor. The building, which had once been a school in downtown River City, Michigan, had no elevator. Ordinarily Josh didn't mind having to walk up all those flights. The stairwell was wide with terrazzo flooring and steps and concrete block walls. Because he was so damned tired, he had to watch where he was going to make sure he didn't trip and fall.

But as tired as he was, he wasn't eager to go to sleep because he always saw her then...in his dreams. That was the only way he'd seen her for the past five years. And it was the only way he intended to see her now because he couldn't meet up with her in person, not after how badly he'd hurt her. The nicest thing he could probably do for her was to never see her again.

Which was not going to be a problem since she had tried only once over the past five years to visit him. And that had been at the very beginning of his sentence.

He released a ragged sigh that echoed off the concrete walls of the empty stairwell. Since it was daytime, most of the other tenants were probably at work or school. Finally, he reached his floor and opened the steel door to the hall, and that silence stretched like a cocoon around him. Until he stepped into the hall, and the door slammed shut behind him, the sound jarring and unexpected, like a gunshot.

Nobody had been in the stairwell besides him, so there must have been some kind of air flow issue that made it slam, like a door opening on another floor or maybe one on this floor.

Definitely this floor.

As he approached his door, he noticed that it was open and swinging slightly in the splintered frame, the dead bolt banging against the damaged wood trim. Someone had broken into his place.

A laugh bubbled up the back of his throat. Why the hell would someone break into his apartment? He had nothing to steal. The only piece of furniture he owned so far was a bed. Actually, it was just the king-size mattress and box springs sitting on the floor of the one bedroom. And if the thieves had managed to carry that thing down four flights of stairs, they'd just about earned it.

But what if they weren't after something to steal?

What if they were after him?

He reached for his weapon. It wasn't a gun. Not yet. But a lawyer, actually the River City district attorney, was working on getting his gun rights restored. In the meantime, he carried a can of pepper spray, which had also required special approval for an exemption.

Maybe if he'd considered some of the consequences of taking the blame…but there would have been more consequences if he hadn't. So he wouldn't have done anything differently.

But he might not be able to say the same this time as he edged closer to his damaged door. Because his can of mace wouldn't be much protection against a gun.

He pushed open the door, and a piece of the splintered frame dropped onto the floor in front of him. Had someone kicked it open or pried it with a crowbar? And why had none of his neighbors reported the break-in?

He glanced around the hall, checking to see if any of the other doors along it were in the same condition as his. But they were all tightly closed and probably locked as well. Nobody else's place had been broken into but his.

Why his?

And had none of his neighbors heard anything? Or were they like the neighbors he'd had the past five years, and they ignored what they heard and saw because they didn't want to get involved?

He could hardly blame them for that, though, since he'd done the same thing himself. Even before prison, he'd ignored a situation until it was too late.

He should probably ignore this broken door, too, and call the police to deal with it instead. But...

He passed through the broken doorjamb into the hallway of his apartment. The foyer closet was partially open, clothes jammed in the crack. With the pepper spray canister in one hand, he used the other to open the door. He glanced inside, but there was nothing in it but empty hangers and the coats lying on the floor.

He continued down the hall to the galley kitchen on one side with the bathroom on the other. The cabinets in both were open, drawers upended on the floor. Someone had been looking for something.

The living room was untouched, probably because it was empty of anything to search. But his bedroom was a mess, clothes tossed out of the dresser and the closet, pockets turned out of his jeans. And the mattress hadn't been stolen, but it had been slashed, and so were the pillows. The breeze blowing through the open window sent the stuffing tumbling across the hardwood floor.

What the hell had someone been looking for?

The only thing he'd had that cost any significant amount of money was the mattress. Hopefully it wasn't ruined because he was too damn tired to go out and buy another one. He was too tired to deal with the police right now, too. The burglar was gone, and nothing had been stolen. So what could they do?

Check for fingerprints while keeping him awake asking questions he couldn't answer?

He had no idea why someone would break into his place. Clearly they'd been looking for something, but he didn't have anything anybody would want.

Maybe the previous tenant had, and the burglar just hadn't realized they had moved.

But then Josh noticed a slip of paper sitting atop the old thrift-shop dresser. An ink pen held it in place even as the wind blowing through the open window lifted the corners of it. The pen was heavy, made of metal not plastic. And the logo on it and the company name had every muscle in Josh's body tensing.

Croft Custom Jewelry. That was the new client Josh hadn't wanted to go anywhere near and reluctantly had but only after business hours.

So he wouldn't see her.

Had she been *here*, in his apartment? Was she the one who'd been looking for something?

But why?

Five years ago, she'd taken back the only thing he'd ever had of value: her heart.

His hand trembled a bit as he reached for the note, unfolded it and read the words spelled out in block letters:

Hand over the diamonds, or you'll never see your son again.

"What the hell?" he muttered.

He didn't have any damn diamonds. He didn't have a son, either, at least as far as he knew.

Unless…

The last time he'd seen her, she'd wanted to tell him something, but he hadn't given her the chance. He hadn't wanted to put her through anything more than he already had, and so he'd insisted on a clean break.

But she hadn't protested. She hadn't tried again to see him. And wouldn't she have if she'd been pregnant with his child?

No. It wasn't possible. This whole thing was a mistake. But he needed to find out for certain, and he needed to make sure that there wasn't some child out there in trouble.

ALONG WITH HER SISTER, Dena, Natalie Croft had grown up in the family business, sleeping in a crib in the backroom during the day while her mom and dad worked. Her dad was in sales, out front, running things while her mom had been the talent behind the scenes, making the jewelry until rheumatoid arthritis ended her career. They'd found other designers to work with, other people to create the engagement rings, necklaces and heirloom pieces for which the store was known. Croft Custom Jewelry was a well-respected establishment in River City, Michigan.

Natalie sat in the backroom of the store now, but she wasn't designing jewelry like her mother had. Despite all the years she'd watched her mother make the custom pieces, she hadn't learned or inherited that talent from her. She wasn't artistic like her mother; instead her talent was numbers. As a child, she'd been able to figure out the taxes and add up the invoices for her dad's sales.

Unlike her sister who hadn't wanted to spend any more time in the store after she grew up, Natalie was now the accountant for the family business, responsible for the payroll and taxes as well as all day-to-day expenses and receivables. Usually her job was pretty easy, and it didn't take much time, so she could spend the majority of her days where she really wanted.

But lately…

Inventory had been disappearing, leading to an issue with their insurance company which had threatened cancellation of their policy or denial of their next claim if they didn't upgrade their security. So right now, Natalie was staring at the monitors that played back the security footage from the night before.

At the insurance company's recommendation, they had hired the Payne Protection Agency to install a new security system for them. It was so much better and more high-tech than their old one that the images were vivid on the screen now, not blurred. So there was no doubt in her mind who stood outside the store night after night, staring at it.

The sharp nose, the granite jaw, the dark, deep-set eyes were all unmistakably his. And the way her heart pounded so fast and frantically at the sight of him confirmed it.

He was out. When had he been released? And why was he hanging around her family business night after night?

"It's him, isn't it?"

She jumped at the sound of her brother-in-law Timothy Hutchinson's voice. She'd forgotten he was standing behind her in the backroom because she'd been so fixated on that screen, on *him*, just like she'd been in college. She'd had no idea then who and what he really was. She'd found out too late…too late to save her heart from breaking.

"What was his name?" Timothy persisted. "You brought him over to my and Dena's house a few times for dinner and games, but that was years ago. I'm not even sure why you stopped seeing him."

Dena knew, but Natalie, horrified and embarrassed, had sworn her older sister to secrecy. Because of their some-times-tumultuous sibling relationship, Natalie was a bit surprised that Dena had kept the secret. But then her older and more socially conscious sister had been horrified and embarrassed, too. That was about the only thing Natalie had in common with her sibling.

They didn't even look that much alike.

With her weekly trips to the salon, Dena kept her hair a pale blond with nary a split end while Natalie kept her hair its natural dark blond in a clip on the back of her head. She wore glasses instead of the contacts that Dena wore—a shade paler than her dark blue—while Natalie's eyes were a mossy green instead. She also dressed for comfort whereas Dena dressed in the latest fashion whatever it was and however much it cost. Dena had always cared more about appearances and status than Natalie ever had. Growing up, Dena hadn't had time for the family business because she'd been too busy with cheerleading and student council, with anything that made her popular.

While growing up, Natalie had been focused on the jewelry store, school and then later college. And when she'd met a certain young man in college, on him.

But all Natalie cared about now was...

"Who is he?" Timothy prodded her.

Her throat thick with emotion, Natalie could only whisper the name, "Josh Stafford."

Timothy released a sudden gasp and pointed to one of the monitors, the one with the live feed from the camera that covered the front of the store. Josh's handsome face filled that screen now as he pulled open the door.

Natalie gasped at the sight of him and at the realization that he was so close to her. All she had to do to see him in person, to talk to him, to touch him, was just step out of the backroom and walk through the showroom. It wasn't at all like the last time she'd seen him, when he had been behind security glass like the expensive pieces they kept locked in the cases in the store.

He hadn't always been untouchable to her, though. She remembered all too well and all too often how much she'd touched him and he had touched her. How they'd kissed with such passion and intensity, how they'd…

What was he doing here?

What did he want? Or maybe more importantly, what did he *know*?

MILEK KOZMINSKI WAS well-aware that there had been a lot of truth behind Logan and Garek's teasing at the party for the launch of the newest franchise of the Payne Protection Agency. Logan probably wouldn't miss having Milek on his team, and Garek and Candace probably weren't super thrilled about including him in their new branch.

Milek was always more focused on his art than the bodyguard business. But painting was such a solitary and sometimes all-consuming experience that he felt isolated while working on his latest project. So he enjoyed taking breaks from his art to work with his extended family when he wasn't with his wife and his son and their toddler daughter.

This franchise that he, Garek and Candace had started was also near and dear to his heart because it focused on protecting beautiful things, like art. But he knew that Garek and Candace did the majority of the work, so he'd urged them to get away for a few days for a romantic retreat. With them gone, he was in charge. But maybe that was fate since he, more than anyone else, could understand what Josh Stafford was feeling.

He followed the man into Croft Custom Jewelry, catching the door just as it was about to swing shut on him. Unlike the door at Josh's apartment that wasn't going to shut tightly anymore, not until the entire jamb was replaced. The police were there now, processing the scene, but the break-in had Josh too unnerved to stay and wait for someone else to find the answers he needed. The police had taken the original of the note left for him and had promised to assign a detective to investigate as soon as possible.

But Josh had been too impatient to wait for answers and had decided to seek them out himself. Milek hadn't wanted the younger man to be alone. Most of their new staff were loners, though. They didn't have the family and relationships that Milek had always been so lucky to have. Josh seemed even more alone than the others, but maybe that was due to his choosing as much as circumstances.

After the break-in at his place and that mysterious note, circumstances had changed. And Milek knew all too well how that felt, to have that inkling, that suspicion.

Of course Josh had to find out what the truth was, he had to know what was going on.

If there was any truth to the note...

They would find out here.

At least that was what Josh believed, but he'd seemed almost reluctant to admit it, as if he didn't want to even consider the possibility that he had a child. Maybe that was why he called Milek about the break-in, why he waited for him and the police to arrive at his apartment before he charged off here. He'd wanted to believe what he kept insisting to Milek, that it was all a big mistake.

Someone had picked the wrong apartment.

He didn't have any diamonds, and he definitely didn't have a kid.

But despite how often Josh had repeated that to Milek, to the police and to himself, he must have had a niggling doubt, something that compelled him to come here. Croft Custom Jewelry wasn't the only one of their new clients who had diamonds, so there had to be another reason that Josh wanted to check them out first.

Because the note had mentioned his son? A son Josh claimed he didn't have.

A dark-haired young woman stood behind one of the jewelry counters and looked up with a smile when they entered. But there was no sign of recognition on her face at the sight of Josh. An older man stood behind another counter, and he looked past Josh to focus on Milek instead. His gaze was a bit blurry, like he might have cataracts, but then he blinked and tried to focus or maybe tried to place him.

"I'm Milek Kozminski with the Payne Protection Agency," he introduced himself to the man. "You met with my brother, Garek, over security." Garek and Candace met with all their clients. But the guy probably thought Milek was Garek.

The older man's head bobbed. "Yes, of course. The insurance company and my daughter insisted on having the new system installed. I hate it. No matter what I do, I keep setting off the damn alarm."

The younger woman laughed and then smiled at Milek and Josh. "Mr. C is not great with technology."

That was something that he and Garek heard often. Garek more than Milek since his older brother handled most of the complaints. Garek was the charmer, or so Candace claimed, but she hadn't fallen for him because of that but despite it. She was too no-nonsense to tolerate charmers or complainers. And Milek was usually just too distracted.

"Is that why you're here?" Mr. Croft asked. "Did my daughter, Natalie, ask you to come by to show me how it works again?"

"I didn't ask them here," a female voice said, and it was so cold that Milek nearly shivered while Josh's long body stiffened and his jaw clenched.

"Why are you here?" another male asked. This one was

younger than Mr. Croft, probably in his late thirties to early forties since his hair was thinning and fine wrinkles fanned out from the corners of his eyes.

"We have a concern that the security might have been breached," Milek admitted even though he shared Josh's hope that the note left for him was a mistake. Verifying if the diamonds were still here would prove that it was. "We want you to check to make sure that nothing is missing."

"And nobody..." Josh muttered beneath his breath.

The others probably didn't hear him, but Milek did. If a child had been taken, his safety was their main concern, more so than any material possession.

"We've been checking the security footage," the younger man said. "And he's been here every night." He pointed at Josh. "Casing the place."

Milek tensed now. He'd been judged because of who and what his father had been, because of who and what he had been. That was why he and Garek had wanted to hire staff who needed someone to give them another chance. And Amber had insisted that no one deserved that second chance more than Josh Stafford.

"He hasn't been casing the place. He's been protecting it," Milek corrected. "Josh is one of our security specialists. And please, we need you to check your inventory. Now."

Because he had a feeling...

He wasn't like Penny Payne-Lynch, with her infamous sixth sense for knowing when someone she cared about was in danger, but maybe he'd spent enough time around her that he was picking up on the same cues she probably did.

The undercurrents.

They were in this room, in the looks between Josh and Mr. Croft's daughter. And Milek got swept up in those undercurrents as did Mr. Croft and the other man. While the dark-haired woman remained where she was standing, the five of them headed toward the backroom, where some monitors played back the footage of Josh standing outside in the dark.

Milek felt like he was the one in the dark now, unaware of the history between Josh and their client's daughter. "We need to know if any diamonds are missing," he said. "If I remember right…" from his brother's notes "…loose ones are kept in a safe."

But the safe was more like a bank vault, the door to it nearly as big as a regular door.

"In there," Mr. Croft confirmed as he pointed at the door. Then he gestured at his daughter. "Please, you open it, Natalie. I can't remember how with this new system."

She touched his forearm briefly, as if comforting him. Then she approached the door and punched in a long series of numbers. Obviously she'd had no problem remembering it. Who else had memorized it?

And why? The code was supposed to change frequently. The Crofts had chosen this system over the one that required fingerprint access, probably because this system was cheaper. But in the end, would it wind up costing them more?

Once the lock clicked, she pulled open the door and stepped back. "I need to find the inventory list."

Her father shook his head. "I remember what should be here…" And when he stepped inside, he gasped. "They're missing!"

"What, Daddy?" she asked with alarm making her voice sharp. "What's missing?"

"The diamonds," Mr. Croft said. "The ones we just bought to be used for the custom engagement rings. They're gone!"

Milek probably should have been concerned about how his and his brother's new business had apparently failed one of their first clients. Garek and Candace would be upset about that, especially since they'd set up the security system themselves. But Milek wasn't worried about the missing diamonds.

He was worried about the other part of the note that had been left in Josh's apartment. Because that note had been right about the diamonds, it could be right about the other part.

About Josh's son…

Chapter Two

The diamonds were gone.

Natalie's brother-in-law stepped inside the vault and confirmed it while she stood next to her father who'd gone pale and shaky.

In the five years that Josh had been in prison, Claus Croft had aged, but Natalie hadn't. She looked exactly the same as she had when Josh first met her in college, naturally beautiful with her golden hair and deep green eyes. There were no lines on her smooth skin, no hardness in her face or her curvy body. Until she looked at him, then she tensed, and her gaze hardened.

"You were outside here," she said. "Night after night. If you were really guarding the place, you would have seen someone get in and steal them."

"I would have," he confirmed. "If someone from outside had come in and taken them."

She gasped. "You're saying this is an inside job?"

"I couldn't care less about the diamonds right now…" Josh began.

"What the hell!" the brother-in-law exclaimed. Timothy something.

Josh had met him a couple of times, but the guy was so

average that nothing much stuck out about him or was at all memorable.

"They're worth hundreds of thousands," Timothy continued. Then he turned toward Milek. "We hired your agency to protect them, not to steal them."

"I didn't steal them," Josh said. But clearly the note writer wasn't the only one who suspected that he had. "What I really want to know is about the kid."

Natalie's face grew as pale as her father's, and the older man had to steady her now with a hand on her elbow. "What?" she asked so softly that her voice was just a raspy whisper.

"Someone broke into my place," Josh said. "And left me a note. 'Hand over the diamonds, or you'll never see your son again.'"

She shook her head so vehemently that her glasses slipped down her nose, and her hair spilled out of the clip, which dropped to the floor. "No…"

Despite her denial, panic and something else, something warm, gripped Josh's heart, and he knew it was true. Not just about the diamonds but about his son. He had a son. But unlike the note writer had implied, Josh had never seen him before. He needed to see him now, to make sure that he was safe.

"Where is he, Natalie?" he asked. "We have to make sure he's all right."

Josh wasn't. He hadn't been this scared since those prison bars had closed, locking him up for something he hadn't done. But now he wasn't scared for himself. He was scared for someone he hadn't even met: his son.

NATALIE FELT HOW her father, with his early onset Alzheimer's, must sometimes feel, like she didn't know what was going on.

Seeing Josh on that security footage had been shocking

enough, but now he was here, crammed into the backroom with her and her father and Timothy and one of the Kozminski brothers. She wasn't sure which one because the two of them looked so much alike.

She wasn't even sure what the men were saying now because the only thing she could hear was a sudden buzzing in her ears.

Then Josh touched her, his fingers sliding under her chin like he used to do just before he tipped her face up to his. So he could kiss her like he had so many times before. But when he lowered his head, it wasn't to kiss her, because there was no passion or desire on his handsome face. There was only impatience and fear.

"Natalie!" he nearly shouted at her now. "You need to tell me. Do we have a son?"

"We? Natalie, who is this?" her father asked, sounding as befuddled as he usually did lately. But this time he had reason to be since she was, too.

Josh pulled something from his pocket and unfolded it. "This isn't the original note. The police have that—"

"The police?" she squeaked.

This was real. This was happening. It wasn't all some strange dream she'd had after having two too many glasses of wine at book club.

"Read the note," he told her.

She could barely focus, but she pushed her glasses up her nose and read the words, in crude block letters, that he'd already recited:

Hand over the diamonds, or you'll never see your son again.

Then she shook her head, like she had just moments ago. "This makes no sense." So few people knew the truth…

"You don't have a son?" Josh asked.

She couldn't deny him, not her sweet little boy. "Yes, *I* have a son." But Henry was all hers, nobody else's, even though she could remember, and often did in pulse-tingling detail, the night that they had probably made him. The night Josh had asked her to marry him and make him the happiest man alive. And she'd been so happy, too, so foolishly happy.

"Where is he?" Josh asked with such urgency that her heart started pounding even faster and harder than it had since the instant she'd seen him on that video surveillance.

"He's probably still in school," she said. But then she noticed the time. The morning had already slipped away from her while she'd been studying the footage on the security cameras, while she'd been studying Josh. "No. He'd be done already."

"So where is he now?" he asked.

"He…he's with my mom," she said.

"You need to make sure that he's actually there. Now!" he demanded.

Even before the words were out of his mouth, she reached for her cell and pressed the contact for her mother. One ring pealed out of the speaker and then the voicemail began to play.

"This is Marilyn, please leave a message. I prefer that to texts so I don't have to put on my glasses and let everyone know that I'm old."

Usually that voicemail brought a smile to Natalie's face but not now, not this time. After the beep, she said, "Mom, call me right back." But she didn't wait for a response before dialing again. And again…

Each time it went to voicemail after that lone first ring.

"Where could they be?" Josh asked.

"I… I don't know," she said. "He would have just gotten off the bus, so they should be home."

Josh said, "Let's go—"

"We need to call the police first," Mr. Kozminski interjected, and he was pulling out his cell phone. "A detective is being assigned to handle the case. They're going to need to talk to you and they'll look for the boy."

But Natalie grabbed her purse from the desk. She didn't care about the diamonds. She didn't care about anything but making sure that Henry was safe, that he and her mother were all right. Digging in her bag for her key fob, she rushed out the back door to the alley where there were a few employee parking spots.

Before the door could swing shut behind her, someone caught it. Then a big hand closed over hers, taking the keys from her. He clicked the button, flashing the lights of her little SUV.

"I'll drive," he said as he slid beneath the steering wheel on the driver side.

Sparing them both an argument, she took the passenger seat. She was shaking so badly now that she wasn't sure she could drive herself safely to her parents' house. And with Josh in the vehicle as well, she probably would have crashed for certain.

"Do you remember where my parents' house is?" she asked him.

"They haven't moved?" he asked.

"No." Neither had she. She lived there, too. The old Tudor house was big, in a safe neighborhood, and she and her mom helped each other—her mother with Henry, and lately Natalie had to help her mom with her dad. Fortunately, he was just in the early stages, and on a medication that seemed to be helping him remember more.

Josh turned the SUV to head just east of downtown. He glanced across the console at her and said, "You should keep trying to call your mom."

The cell phone was still in her hand, but every call kept going directly to voicemail. "She could have just put it down and forgotten about it," Natalie said, which was what she hoped. "She does that a lot, especially when Henry gets home from pre-kindergart—"

"Henry?" Josh interrupted, his voice gruff. He cleared his throat and asked, "That's his name?"

"Yes." She'd named him after her maternal grandfather, who'd been such a sweet man.

"Is he my son, Natalie?" Josh asked, his voice cracking now with emotion.

She could only whisper, "He's mine."

"Natalie—"

"You chose," she reminded him. "You chose when you committed those crimes. That was what you told me when I went to see you that last time..." Tears rushed up to clog her throat and sting her eyes, but she blinked them away. "You said you chose that life over me. And you wanted me to leave and never look back. You didn't want to ever see me again."

After that day, she hadn't wanted to ever see him again, either. But she had, and she did, every time she looked at their son. Henry had his dark hair and his dark eyes and his impish little grin. She needed to see her sweet son now, needed to hold him and make sure he was okay.

"Hurry," she urged as yet another call went to her mother's voicemail.

Marilyn Croft hated her cell phone, but with her husband's recent diagnosis, she never went too long before she checked it for messages. So why hadn't she called back yet? Or at least picked up?

"None of this makes sense," Josh muttered beneath his breath. "How could someone know what I didn't even know myself? Who did you tell?"

"Not many people know," she admitted. "Just my sister and my mom." They hadn't even told her father. He just knew that it was some boy from college who hadn't wanted anything to do with being a father.

And it had been. She'd met Josh in college, his senior year, her junior. He'd been going for criminal justice, which was incredibly ironic now, while she'd been going for accounting and business management. Then after graduating, he'd stayed on for his master's degree while she finished up her senior year. Once she graduated, they'd planned to get married. Although he hadn't been able to afford a ring yet, he'd proposed. And she, who'd been raised in a jewelry store, hadn't cared about the ring, just him.

She'd been so excited to spend her life with him. And the night they'd celebrated their engagement had been so full of passion and excitement. Every kiss, every caress had been like a surge of electricity going through her body, making her feel more alive than she'd ever felt. More hopeful. More loved. More in love.

Then everything had gone so wrong.

Just like today.

"This has to be a mistake," she said. Henry and her mother had to be safe.

But that note had been right about the diamonds. They were gone.

Was Henry gone as well?

When Josh turned onto the tree-lined street where she lived, she started reaching for the handle. And once he steered her SUV into the brick-cobbled driveway, she threw open the door and jumped out before he'd even fully braked.

"Natalie!" he called out.

She ignored him and ran for the side door of the two-story Tudor house, but before she could reach for the handle, the door blew open. It hadn't been closed. Henry wasn't always good with closing doors. That had to be what happened.

And that meant he was here, surely. Or maybe…

"Henry!" she called out as she stepped into the mud-room. "Mom?"

His backpack wasn't hanging from the hook in the little cubby where he usually hung it once he got off the bus from morning kindergarten. It should have been there. But the hook was empty.

She glanced at her watch, the one her mother had personally designed, with the diamonds around the mother-of-pearl face, for Natalie's graduation. Henry should have been home nearly an hour ago.

"Mom!" she yelled, and she stepped onto the first stair of the three leading up to the kitchen. Before she could go up another, a strong hand caught her elbow.

"Wait," Josh whispered, his voice low and deep.

His breath was warm against her ear, but instead of heating her, it made her shiver.

"Stay here," he said as he brushed past her. His hand was in one of his pockets. Was he carrying a gun?

Was he armed?

He was a security guard or something, so maybe he was. But instead of making her feel safer, a chill rushed over her. She didn't want weapons around her son or her mom. She didn't want them to see that ugliness, to be any part of what Josh Stafford had been part of.

Maybe that was why she'd taken the easy way out the only day she'd visited him in prison. When he'd told her that their life, their love, hadn't been real and that he didn't want to see her again, he'd given her an out. An excuse.

To not tell him that she was pregnant.

That life they'd lived together might not have been real, but the life they'd created was. And her baby, even in those early stages of her pregnancy, meant everything to her. She'd chosen to put her child first, and she'd never wanted Henry to be part of Josh Stafford's sordid world of stealing and prison sentences.

But Josh was here now, probably out on probation. And the diamonds were stolen.

And where was their son?

She had to know, so she ignored what Josh said and started up the steps after him. He tensed, but he didn't turn back. He just kept walking, through the kitchen, which was empty.

The coffeemaker was still on, though the coffee had burned down to sludge in the bottom of the pot. Usually, her mother tossed it out shortly after Natalie and her dad left for the store. The breakfast dishes also sat in the sink, the toast crumbs and bits of egg still stuck to them. And there was a bowl on the table that was more than half full of oatmeal. Henry's barely touched breakfast.

She opened her mouth to call out again, but the way Josh was moving, so stealthily, kept her silent, too. Was someone else here with her mom and son, keeping them quiet like Josh's presence was keeping her silent?

But she wasn't scared of him; she was just scared, scared of what they might find…if anything. Or maybe that was what scared her most, that they wouldn't find anything or anyone.

As they went from room to room, they found each empty of all but personal possessions. There were no people in the house but the two of them. They even checked the backyard but found that empty as well. The swing was swaying gently in the breeze as if an invisible hand was pushing it.

"Where are they?" she asked herself aloud, her heart beating so hard that she barely heard her own voice.

"Does your mother have a vehicle?" Josh asked.

She nodded.

"Is it here?" He was already walking toward the detached

garage that sat farther down the driveway than the house, near the swing set in the backyard.

Natalie hurried after him. The side door was unlocked, as always, and he opened it and stepped inside. "There's a car here," he said.

"That's my dad's," Natalie said of the late model Cadillac. They'd talked him out of driving although he sometimes forgot that he wasn't supposed to, so they also hid his keys. "My mom has a small SUV like mine." But it was gone like her mother, like her son.

That had to be a good thing, though.

"This means they have to be somewhere together," she said, and she started to back out of the open door. "That they're fine."

"Then why isn't she answering her phone?" he asked. He remained inside the garage, staring at the concrete floor.

"If she's driving, she won't answer it," she said. Her mother had to be driving, which meant she was okay, that they were okay.

"Wouldn't she have told you if she was taking him somewhere?" Josh asked.

The hope she'd momentarily felt dropped to the bottom of her stomach. "Yes, she would have." She mostly definitely would have.

Her mother didn't take Henry anywhere without running it past Natalie first. Even though she often spent more time with Henry than Natalie was able to because of work, Marilyn was very respectful that Natalie was Henry's mother and should always have the final say on where he went and what he did.

"Unless it was just a quick trip somewhere," she said. Natalie had told her mom that she didn't need her approval if they were sticking close to home.

"Would they have gone to your sister's?" Josh asked. "Should you call her?"

Natalie tensed. "No. My sister doesn't like kids. She says they're too loud and sticky even though Henry is neither of those things." Well, maybe sticky sometimes, but that was just if his grandpa made his PB&J sandwich instead of her or her mom.

But maybe she should check with Dena. Not wanting to talk to her, though, especially if Timothy already had, she sent a text:

Have you seen Mom and Henry?

An automatic message came back:

In an appointment until four pm.

What was Dena doing now? Haircut? Manicure? Or maybe some type of exercise class? Or she could be volunteering somewhere. She did occasionally do that, but Natalie wasn't sure where and how often. And sometimes she wondered if she really did or if she just used the volunteerism as an excuse to stay away from the store and away from Dad now.

"Dena's phone is on do-not-disturb," Natalie said, which probably meant that Timothy hadn't talked to her yet, either. That was good, though. The last thing she needed to hear was Dena gloat about the poor choices Natalie had made. "She wouldn't have it on that if she was with Mom and Henry." Dena would probably welcome a distraction if she was with them. She and Mom had never had much in common, and Dena barely paid attention to Henry.

Josh was curiously quiet.

"Maybe they just went to the store or to grab some fast

food," she said. It was lunchtime, and despite having breakfast and a snack at school, Henry was usually ravenous when he got off the bus. "Or maybe she took him to the park to play." Natalie took another step toward the side door of the garage. "We should go look for them."

But Josh was squatting down now. He continued to stare at the concrete floor as if he was intently studying the cracks in it or the finish of it. "No," he said. "We need to call the police and make sure that they're on their way here."

"But why?" she asked, her heart beating fast and hard again at the gruffness and seriousness of his voice. "My mom and Henry are gone somewhere together. It's not just Henry who's missing, so that note was a hoax. I'm sure that they're fine."

But the diamonds were gone. Why lie about one thing but not the other?

"We need to call the police and make sure they're on their way," Josh said again, his voice even gruffer as if he was struggling to get out the words. "There's blood here, Natalie. This is blood." And he pointed to a small puddle on the concrete that, if she'd noticed earlier, she would have thought was oil. But it was red; she could see that now when he stepped away from it.

The brightness and wetness of it indicated that it was fresh. Someone was hurt so badly that they were bleeding. Her mother or her son or both?

Fear overwhelmed her, making her knees weak and her head light. Her legs shook so much that she started to crumple to the concrete, but Josh caught her, pulling her against his chest into his strong arms. But he was shaking, too.

She wasn't sure if it was with fear or with rage. He was entitled to both. A kidnapper had told him he had a son before she had.

"We'll find them," he said. "We will find them."

But she couldn't believe him. She couldn't believe anything he told her. He'd lied to her before. He'd broken promises to her before. He'd broken her heart.

And if he didn't keep this promise, if they couldn't find them…

She couldn't let her mind or her heart go down that dark route. She couldn't consider any possibility other than finding them.

And when they found them, they had to be all right. They *had* to be.

"MIMI," HENRY WHISPERED.

It was dark, wherever they were, and Henry hated the dark, especially this kind of dark where he couldn't see anything at all.

Or anyone.

But Mimi was here somewhere, too.

She was sleeping. At least that was what the person in the mask had said.

Why were they wearing a mask? It wasn't Halloween for a long time yet.

And this wasn't a fun game of hide-and-seek like that person said they were playing.

Just playing…

Who was that person?

They talked so funny that Henry couldn't tell if it was girl or a boy. With the hood of their big puffy coat up over their head and the mask on their face, Henry hadn't been able to see if they had long hair or short or anything else about them.

Then they'd put something over his head, too, so he couldn't see where they were going for this dumb game.

Tears burned in his eyes. He hated this game.

"Mimi," he called out again.

"Ummm." The sound, more like a moan, came out of the darkness.

"Mimi!" On his hands and knees, Henry crawled around on what felt like a concrete floor. It was cold and hard, like the floor in the garage where Mimi had fallen. She'd been so sleepy even before she fell. But he hadn't seen her fall. He wasn't even sure that she had...on accident.

"Mimi?" He reached out, trying to find his grandmother in the darkness, and his hand touched something warm and soft. "Mimi..."

She didn't answer him, though; she just moaned again. Sometimes Mommy groaned when he hopped into bed with her in the morning and tried to wake her up to play with him. But this was different than that.

"Mimi?" He patted her soft hair. It was so white that he could see some of it in the darkness. But it wasn't all white, like it usually was, there was something in her hair, something sticky.

Not like the gum that he accidentally spat out in Chelsea Oliver's hair or like the peanut butter and jelly that oozed out of the sandwiches that Grandpa made. He put a lot of both on the bread. Too much, Mimi said. But Henry liked them like that, and Grandpa knew that. He remembered that. He remembered a lot of stuff. He wasn't losing his memory like everybody kept saying, usually when they thought Henry was asleep or not around.

Thinking about those sandwiches had Henry's stomach growling. It felt hollow and empty. He was hungry. All he'd had to eat today was breakfast because he hadn't gone to school. So he hadn't had his snack.

Or lunch.

They'd missed the bus this morning. He wasn't sure why, but something had been wrong with Mimi. She'd been acting like Grandpa, a little confused and really tired, too. And when the bus passed the house, she'd promised to drive him to school. But when they got to the garage…

That person had been in it, waiting for them in the mask. And somehow Mimi fell down.

Henry wasn't sure if the person pushed her or if she just slipped. But before Henry could scream or do anything, the person had put their gloved hand over his mouth.

"There is no school today," they told him. But that was a lie.

Henry knew it. He'd seen the bus go by.

"Today we're playing a game of hide-and-seek. I'm going to hide you and see if someone can find you." The person took their hand away then.

And all Henry had been able to say was, "Mimi…"

"She's going to be okay. She's just sleepy today."

That was true. She had seemed sleepy all morning even though she'd had a lot of coffee. She hadn't even noticed that Henry didn't finish all of his oatmeal. He wished he had now because his stomach growled again.

But he wasn't just hungry. He was scared. And not the fun kind of Halloween scared or watching-a-scary-movie scared. He was really scared.

"Mimi," he whispered this time. Because it just occurred to him that he didn't know where that person with the mask had gone. Where were they?

It had been a while since they brought him and Mimi here, to this hiding place. But someone was supposed to be looking for him.

Just before the person had closed the door and locked them into this place, they'd told Henry who was supposed to find him.

"Your daddy."

Henry didn't even know that he had a daddy. Mommy said it was just them, like that was all it ever was. Just him and Mommy and Mimi and Grandpa and Aunt Dena and Uncle Timothy.

If Henry had a daddy, he must have been hiding this whole time. So he had to be good at this game. Hopefully he would find them.

Soon.

Chapter Three

In that moment when he first pointed out the blood and Natalie nearly collapsed, Josh had caught her and closed his arms around her. But touching her evoked so many overwhelming emotions, it had nearly been his undoing, like seeing that blood had been hers.

Whose was it?

Her mother's? Or their child's?

Their son. The son Josh hadn't even known he had. And his name was Henry.

Now, as Josh and Natalie stood on the cobblestone driveway outside the garage where crime-scene techs were collecting evidence, he was torn between wanting to comfort her and wanting to confront her with his anger over keeping his son's existence from him. But could he really be angry with her after what he'd done?

After how he'd lied to her?

And he hadn't lied to her just about the thefts he hadn't really committed. He'd also lied to her when he'd told her their relationship wasn't real. Because it had been all too real to him.

The first time he met her, in the campus bookstore, he'd been attracted to her realness. As well as being naturally beautiful, Natalie was straightforward and honest. When he asked her out, she told him upfront that she was an old-fashioned girl. She didn't sleep around and was looking for the kind of commitment and devotion that her parents had.

She'd told him about the jewelry store they had started and how they worked hard to make it a success, spending so much of their time there. And even though they spent all that time together, they never got irritated with or sick of each other. How they enjoyed every minute they were together, laughing and joking and loving. Then she'd laughed and said that she'd probably scared him off.

He hadn't been scared; he'd been impressed.

Almost immediately his attraction to her grew from interest to love as he got to know her better, her kindness, her cleverness and her sense of humor and her passion.

When she first told him about her parents, he wasn't able to understand how they could spend every moment together and never get sick of each other. His parents hadn't been like that and had divorced shortly after he was born. But after spending time with Natalie, he understood because that was the way he'd loved her—completely, passionately. Even now, all these years later, he could feel the silkiness of her lips against his; he could taste the sweetness of her.

No, despite what he'd told her that day she'd visited him in prison, his love and their relationship had been very real. And he'd imagined their love lasting a lifetime.

But he'd been sentenced to eight years in prison—though he'd served only five with good behavior—Josh hadn't wanted her to make the sacrifices he'd chosen to make. And so he'd done what he'd thought was magnanimous and selfless in the moment—he drove her away from him for her safety and for her happiness.

He'd driven her away too well. She'd only visited the prison that one time to see him, and she never returned.

After that, she hadn't even sent him a letter or a card during his incarceration. Definitely not a birth announcement for their child.

She wasn't the only one who'd never visited him, though. His father had disowned him, and his sister…

He couldn't think about Sylvie right now. He couldn't think about anything but his son. And he had to put aside his anger at Natalie for not telling him about Henry, especially since that was definitely more his fault than hers.

He had to focus on what mattered most: finding Henry and the little boy's grandmother as well.

After Josh called the police about finding the blood, it hadn't taken them long to show up at the scene. Some of the techs had even been pulled away from the jewelry store, but a missing child took priority over all else.

The head detective and heir apparent to the current chief's throne, Spencer Dubridge, was leading the investigation. But the chief was here, too, along with his wife who also volunteered with victim services. At least, that was what she'd told him and Natalie when she'd introduced herself.

But Josh wasn't the victim. An innocent child and his grandmother potentially were. God, he wanted to believe what Natalie kept muttering to herself.

"This is all a mistake. They're fine," she whispered. "They have to be fine."

But her face was still as pale as it had gone when she'd seen the blood, and her body was trembling slightly. He ached to hold her again, to comfort her.

But he'd already made her a promise that he might not be able to keep. That, depending on who was wounded and how badly, he might have already broken. He might not be able to get her mother and their son safely back home.

But he intended to do everything within his power to try.

NATALIE HAD NEVER felt as helpless as she did now. Not even the day that she'd gone to see Josh in prison had she felt as out of control of her own life as she did now.

Crime-scene technicians, officers and detectives walked in and out of her family home and the garage and the yard. They even canvassed the neighborhood, going from door to door, interviewing the neighbors to find out what they'd seen and heard that morning.

"You didn't know that Henry didn't go to school?" the dark-haired detective asked Natalie.

She shook her head. "No. I thought he went." Henry hated missing school. He liked learning as much as he liked socializing with other kids.

"The school didn't call you to question his absence?" the detective asked. "They claim they talked to someone."

She held out the cell phone she'd been grasping in one hand because she really believed, or at least hoped, that her mother was going to call and tell her that this was all a misunderstanding. That they were both fine.

She unlocked the phone before the detective took it from her hand. He scrolled through her call log and then moved onto her texts and then her settings.

"I don't have any missed calls," she said. "They probably called my mother." Because the school knew that Marilyn was the one responsible for getting him on and off the bus. She also volunteered at the school, sometimes with Natalie and sometimes in Natalie's place as a room parent.

"They claim they spoke to someone—"

"My mother then. So they must be fine." Or maybe Henry was the one who'd been hurt. But if her mother had talked to the school, she would have called Natalie, too. Why hadn't she called? Or was she not who'd spoken to the school?

The detective handed back her cell. "I sent a link from

your phone to one of the crime-scene techs. We'll put a trace on this and on your mother's phone, too."

"Can't you ping it now and find her location?" Josh asked. He stood next to Natalie, but he wasn't touching her like he had earlier, like how he'd held her when she initially fell apart.

Maybe that was why she could think clearly now, because he wasn't touching her. He wasn't reminding her of the past, so she could focus on the present.

"Oh, my god!" Natalie exclaimed. "I can do that. We put that app on all of our phones so we can track each other." That was because of her father, though. Natalie had never used it to find out where her mother was. Usually, she knew; Natalie had never had to look for her until now. She fumbled with her cell, trying to find the app.

"I checked it," the detective interjected. "Her phone is not showing up, and according to our techs, it's because it's turned off. That's why we can't ping it."

"Maybe it's broken. Maybe that's what happened in the garage," Natalie mused, her mind flitting from scenario to scenario. "Maybe Mom fell onto the floor or something, and her phone broke. And she's bleeding and she drove herself to the ER with Henry." Natalie reached out and grasped Josh's arm, which tensed beneath her fingertips. "We should go to the ER."

She wasn't sure why she was including him now when she hadn't for all these years. Despite how they ended things, she could have sent him pictures of their son or some of his artwork from school. She could have made both Josh and Henry aware of each other. She could have told them about the other. But it had been easier, for her, to pretend that Joshua Stafford had never existed. Then she didn't have to remember how badly he'd disappointed and hurt her.

But he had also given her the most precious part of her life: Henry.

"We've already checked the hospitals," Detective Dubridge assured her.

Which meant that her mom and Henry weren't there, or Dubridge would have told her already. She wished not finding them at the hospital meant nobody was hurt. But it could also mean they were hurt but hadn't been able to seek medical treatment.

"What else are you doing to find them?" Josh asked the question that was burning the back of her throat.

Because it seemed to Natalie that they were all just standing around.

She knew that wasn't true. She was the only one who was just standing around, helpless to help her son. Josh had been walking around, talking to his boss and the techs and to the detective. He'd even gone to a few of the neighbors' houses, too, before coming back to her.

"Using those photos you gave me, we have an Amber alert out on Henry with his description, as well as a description of Marilyn Croft and her vehicle, too," the detective said.

Josh just grunted like he wasn't impressed or maybe he just didn't think it was enough. She definitely didn't. But she had no idea what else to do, how else to find them.

"I know how you must feel," the detective said.

Josh snorted now, as if he didn't believe him.

"Nine months ago, shortly before we got married, my wife was abducted," the detective said. "A dangerous criminal, Luther Mills, took her hostage as he escaped from the courthouse during his trial."

Josh gasped then, and Natalie turned to find that the color had drained from his face. "Luther Mills," he murmured beneath his breath.

"I remember hearing about that," she said. "It had a positive outcome." But then she remembered why. "She was a Payne Protection bodyguard and former police officer, so of course *she* was able to protect herself."

Not like Henry or her mother who, thankfully, had no experience with violence or even with violent people. Despite how confused Natalie's father sometimes got, he was always kind and gentle. Everyone in Natalie's world was kind and gentle and law-abiding, except for Henry's father. Josh was the only person close to Henry who'd actually committed a crime.

"When Keeli was taken hostage, she'd just discovered she was pregnant with our baby, a little girl who's now eight weeks old," the detective said. "And the hell I went through thinking about them..." His voice, gruff with emotion, trailed off.

"Hell," Josh muttered, his voice gruff as well with emotion.

Hell.

That was exactly what this was.

Natalie could only hope that she was able to navigate her way through it to find her son and her mother safe and well.

PENNY WASN'T SURE what to do. She'd only just recently volunteered to work for the River City Police Department's victim services. She needed something to do since her full-service wedding planning and venue business hadn't been very busy lately, not since her son Parker's bodyguards had all gotten married. The last couple wedded six months ago. Every member of Parker's team had found love while protecting the people associated with the high-profile murder trial of a dangerous drug-dealing gang leader. For a while, it had seemed like some of the bodyguards and the people they'd been assigned to protect might not survive, but it was the perpetrator who'd died.

Luther Mills.

And the man who'd killed him walked up to her now. "I just blew it," Spencer Dubridge said with a heavy sigh, and he shoved one of his hands through his dark hair.

"What?" she asked with alarm. Was it already too late? "Did you find the little boy? Is he not all right?"

"I don't know," he said. "I was trying to comfort and re-late to the parents, and I blew it. It's a good thing the chief brought you here, Mrs. Lynch."

"Penny," she reminded him. "And there is no way to com-fort parents whose child is missing." It didn't matter how old that child was, either. But to have one as young as this little boy, who wasn't quite five yet, missing had to be an absolute nightmare.

He nodded. "True. It was bad enough when Keeli was missing, and finding out she was pregnant with Barbie at the time. And now that Barbie's here, I can't imagine ever not knowing where she is."

At Woodrow's request and with his wife's urging, Spen-cer had agreed to come back early from his family leave to help find the missing boy.

"So I really can't relate to what they're going through," he said.

But Penny figured he could, and so did Woodrow; which was why he'd asked Spencer to cut his leave short to lead the case. They both remembered all too well how upset he'd been when Luther Mills had been holding Keeli Abbott hostage.

"Since my wife agreed that I needed to do whatever I could to help out if there's a little boy hostage, I was happy to come back early for this case, but the chief can't really believe that I'm the person who should take over for him," Spencer said. He gestured back to where Woodrow was talk-ing to the parents now.

Penny followed his gaze, and her heart skipped a beat

as it always did when she looked at Woodrow Lynch. With his silver hair and blue eyes, he was so good-looking, but it was more than his appearance that had attracted her. It was his very soul. Hers had recognized a kindred spirit in his.

They were meant to be together, and they just *fit*.

While the couple with whom her husband was talking didn't look very comfortable with each other at all. When the man reached for her, the woman stepped back and walked away from him.

Not that people had to be in love with each other to have a child.

Penny wasn't naive enough to think that, not when her own late husband had surprised her with a son she hadn't known he had with another woman. She hadn't learned of Nicholas's existence until several years after her husband Nick Payne's death.

Apparently, from what Milek had shared with her, Josh Stafford hadn't known about his child's existence, either, until whoever had broken into his apartment had left a note claiming they'd abducted his son.

She couldn't imagine the fear that they were all feeling, Josh and Natalie and most of all that little boy. But somehow, it was almost as if she could *feel* it.

Some people thought she had psychic powers because she had an uncanny ability to sense when people were in danger. But she didn't think she was psychic as much as she was empathetic, and sometimes she could just feel what other people were feeling no matter where they were.

Like now, as she studied the couple who stood so far apart, she could feel the fear both parents were feeling for their little boy. She was also feeling something else, the tension between them, the betrayal, the pain...

They had left a lot unsaid and unfinished between them.

But she wasn't feeling just the parents' fear now; she was

also feeling a child's fear. The little boy was alive, she believed that. She just prayed that he stayed that way until he could be found.

Chapter Four

"That's the detective you have leading this investigation?" Josh asked, gesturing toward where Dubridge stood next to the chief's wife. He wasn't just skeptical of the detective's abilities, he was furious with him.

For the first time since this whole nightmare began, Natalie hadn't been able to stop her tears from falling. And this time, unlike the times before when she'd been scared and upset, she hadn't allowed him to comfort her. She'd stepped back before he could even reach for her, and now she stood alone by the swing set, her back toward them, but her shoulders were shaking as she obviously sobbed alone.

Her loneliness echoed hollowly inside Josh. He'd felt alone like that for five long years.

Would it have made a difference if he'd known about his son? Would he have told the truth all those years ago? Amber Talsma, now Kozminski, would have believed him. She'd always thought he was taking the blame for something he hadn't done.

But he had his reasons for doing that, life and death reasons for other people. Even for Natalie. Because if he'd told her the truth, her life would have been in danger.

There had been so many threats. Amber had suspected as much and had promised to protect him if he told the truth. But he hadn't been able to trust her with other people's lives, too. And in the end, she'd had no choice but to accept his plea.

That was also why she'd recommended Josh to her husband for this job.

But Josh wasn't the only employee of the new branch of the Payne Protection Agency who had a criminal record. Could it be one of them? They would have known how to disarm the security system. But if they'd stolen the diamonds, why would they take his son, too? They already had what they really wanted.

His head pounded with confusion and exhaustion. And he felt unsteady now, so unsteady that Milek gripped his shoulder as if he'd noticed it, too. "Spencer is one of the best," Josh's boss assured him.

"Since so many of River City PD's finest went into private security, he's definitely the best we have left," the chief said. "And I hope he agrees to become chief soon, once his family leave is over."

So he came back early for this case, for Henry. Josh couldn't summon any gratitude, not with his skepticism and his exhaustion weighing so heavily on him.

"You look like you're ready to drop," Milek said as he tightened his grip on his shoulder. "You were awake and working all night. You need to get some rest, Josh."

Josh shook his head. There was no way he could sleep, not until he knew where his son was, which was ironic since until just a few hours ago he hadn't even known he had a son. He had to make sure that the little boy and Marilyn Croft were both okay. "I have to find Henry."

But he had no idea where to look. He had no idea why anyone would have taken the little boy, let alone where they might have taken him. Josh didn't have the damn diamonds. So did that mean there were two separate situations going on? Someone had stolen the diamonds, and someone else had taken Henry and his grandmother?

"You need to let Dubridge do his job," Chief Lynch said. "He'll find him."

Josh's stomach knotted with dread. He couldn't leave it to him. And it wasn't just Dubridge he didn't trust. He really didn't trust any police officer, not after what happened to him.

Amber had figured out he hadn't done what he'd taken the blame for, so shouldn't some of the police have figured it out, too? Maybe some of them had been paid to not look into it any further, or maybe they'd just been more eager to close a case than to find out the truth.

Not that he'd really wanted them to find out the truth back then. He'd felt guilty and protective of the real perpetrator and had been convinced he was doing the right thing, that it was the only way to keep the people he cared about safe.

And it had been.

But he'd hurt Natalie. And he'd hurt himself. And he'd lost out on years with his son. Yet if he hadn't done what he had, he might not have a son at all because Natalie might have been hurt physically as well as emotionally.

But Luther Mills was dead now. He wasn't the threat he'd once been to Josh, to Natalie and to the person for whom Josh had taken the blame five years ago. But after he'd taken the blame, that person hadn't come to visit him any more than Natalie had.

Even though he'd urged her to go somewhere else and start her life over, he had still expected her to send him cards. Or call...

He'd made a huge sacrifice for someone who hadn't really seemed to appreciate it. Hurt and a bit resentful, he hadn't reached out to her, either, during his time in prison or since

his release. He'd made even more sacrifices than he'd realized, like fatherhood.

And the person for whom he'd taken the blame...

Had she turned her life around? Or was she still stealing? Could she have been the one who'd taken either the
diamonds or his son?

BECAUSE NATALIE COULDN'T listen to the men any longer, she
stood far enough away in the yard that their voices were just
low rumbles, like thunder way off in the distance. They had
no idea how she felt, no matter what they claimed. She was
Henry's mother. She was the one who was supposed to protect him and keep him safe and always know where he was.

And she had no idea.

And she was so damn scared. Not just for him but for
her mother, too. Because if someone had truly kidnapped
her son, they wouldn't have gotten Henry away from his
grandmother without one hell of a fight. She remembered
the blood on the garage floor.

Maybe it wasn't Henry's or her mother's, though. Maybe
Henry's *Mimi*, as he'd always called her, had hurt whoever
tried to grab him, and they were hiding somewhere. Maybe
they were safe and unharmed.

That was why they hadn't turned up at the hospital ER or
anywhere else. They weren't hurt. They were hiding until
it was safe to come out. That had to be the case. So maybe
Natalie should try to call her again. Or send a text that the
police were here, and that it was safe to come home.

Natalie had been clasping the phone so hard in one hand
that she had to unlock her fingers from around it to touch
the screen. But just as she reached out to start a text, her
mother's specific ringtone rang out: "Mama Said" by The
Shirelles.

Mama couldn't have known that there would be days like

this, though. That on the very same day an old love would come back into Natalie's life, she might have also lost her most important love: her son.

Her finger shook as she swiped to accept the call. "Mom!" she exclaimed. Either her excitement or the ringing of her cell had Josh and the detective both rushing toward her.

"Give the phone to Josh Stafford," a voice rasped out of the speaker of her cell.

That was not her mother's voice. She'd never heard a voice like this before. It didn't even sound human.

"What? Who is this?" she asked, her voice cracking with fear. "Why do you have my mother's phone? Where is she? Where is Henry?"

"Give the phone to Josh Stafford," the person repeated.

How did they know Josh, and how did they know that they were together? That he was here?

She glanced around the area, checking to see who was watching her. Everyone in the nearby vicinity was staring at her, but she was the only one on a call. But the detective was furiously texting on his, hopefully trying to find her mother's location.

Josh plucked her cell from her hand. "This is Stafford," he said.

"You know what you have to do—"

"I don't have the damn diamonds," he interjected. "And you have to know that."

"I don't care," that weird raspy voice replied. "If you don't have them, you need to find them if you want to see your son again."

"I haven't *ever* seen my son, and you've given me no proof that you actually have him," Josh said.

Natalie's breath caught. What was Josh doing? Was he trying to make the person angry?

Despite what she'd hoped just moments ago, Natalie knew

she was wrong. Her mom and Henry weren't hiding some-where until it was safe to come out. This person calling from her mother's phone was proof enough that they'd taken them hostage. Her mom and Henry were gone, the only thing left behind a small pool of blood. Despite her earlier doubts, or maybe hopes, that was proof enough for Natalie.

Her hand shaking, she reached to grab her cell back from Josh, but he held it away from her.

"Call back on FaceTime," Josh demanded. "Show me my son, prove that he and his grandmother are both unharmed, or you won't get anything out of me." Then he swiped to disconnect the call.

"That wasn't enough time," the detective said.

Fury bubbled up inside Natalie. Fury at the person who'd taken her son, but mostly fury at Josh. She swung out, slap-ping his shoulder so hard that he staggered back a step. "No! No! How dare you! How dare you hang up! How dare you!"

Josh reached out and grasped her shoulders. "We have to have proof, Natalie. We have to know…"

That he was still alive.

He didn't finish saying it, but she knew what he meant. "This is all your fault!" she yelled at him. "This is all your fault!"

"I don't have the diamonds," he said.

"Then how the hell are you going to get him back?" she asked. "How the hell are you going to save Henry and my mother?"

"I don't know," he said softly. "But first we need to know if they're alive."

The horror of that struck her so hard that her knees nearly gave way. But he was already holding onto her. Then his arms closed around her.

She wanted to hit him again. To slap him away, but she found herself hanging onto him as her world spun out of control. Just a short while ago she'd been hopeful that her son and her mom were all right, that they were safe.

But now she knew the nightmare was really happening. Someone had taken her mother and her son. What if it was too late to save them?

HENRY MUST HAVE fallen asleep because a noise jerked him awake. But when he opened his eyes, it was still dark. Like night.

But he didn't think he'd been asleep for very long. He and Mimi were still wherever that person had taken them, and they were lying on the cold hard floor. Mimi was next to him, her body soft and warm against his back.

She wasn't moving, though. She was still asleep.

"Mimi?" he whispered.

Then he heard the rumble of an engine, and a little while later, there was an echo of footsteps on something metal or hard. He must have woken up because of that vehicle. And it was still outside running.

Mimi's car? That was what the person had driven here, with Henry in the booster seat in the back and Mimi lying on the seat next to him. But the person had put that hood over his head then, so Henry wasn't sure where and how that person had been driving.

With their mask on?

"Mimi," he whispered, as those footsteps got louder. "Somebody's coming!" Maybe it was his daddy. Maybe he'd found them.

He had to be really good at hide-and-seek since Henry hadn't seen him his whole life.

Metal rattled, and then a garage door slid up. The person who ducked under it was still wearing that weird mask. It wasn't his daddy who'd found them. It was the person who brought them here coming back. Why?

This game wasn't fun. Henry didn't want to play it anymore. He wanted to leave. And he knew he should get up and run, try to get to that car and get help for Mimi.

But he was just a little boy. He didn't know how to drive. And Mimi...

She couldn't run.

She couldn't even wake up.

"Mimi?" He shook her shoulder, trying harder to get her to answer him.

With the light streaming in through that big open door, he could see that she wasn't just sleeping. She was hurt. Blood was sticky in her hair. It had matted it down and turned the white to a dark red. There was a cut and a bump on her forehead, but it looked like the blood had dried on it. She wasn't bleeding anymore.

But why wouldn't she wake up?

"Mimi?"

"Ummm..." she muttered.

"Mimi needs help," Henry said, his voice so squeaky it hurt his ears. He was scared, but he was getting mad, too.

"She's just tired," the person said.

But that person was lying. Henry could see the blood now. He knew she was hurt. "She's got a cut," he said. "She needs to go to the doctor."

He hated going to the doctor because of the shots they kept giving him. But maybe the doctor wouldn't give Mimi any shots. Maybe he would just do something to make her wake up.

"I'm tired, too," the person said in that weird, whispering voice. "Your daddy isn't playing the game like he's supposed to."

That was why Daddy wasn't here yet. He wasn't playing. Henry didn't blame him; he didn't want to play this dumb game, either.

"I need you to make him play," the person said.

But Henry didn't know how he was supposed to do that when he didn't even know who his daddy was.

Chapter Five

Oh my God.

Josh's stomach churned with nerves and fear. "What if I just screwed up?" he whispered to Milek. He didn't dare say it any louder. He didn't want Natalie to hear him.

She was with Penny now, but they were just a short distance from where he and Milek stood by the swings. Natalie and Penny were on the cobblestone driveway, sitting in some folding chairs that Penny had taken out of the back of her vehicle. They weren't allowed inside because the house and garage were still being processed as crime scenes.

"What if I pushed the kidnapper too far when I hung up?" Josh asked. "I know I'm supposed to try to keep them on the phone so it can be traced."

"I doubt they would have stayed on the line long enough for us to trace the call," Dubridge said as he and the chief joined them. "They already knew to turn off the Find My Phone app because we weren't able to pull up the location, either."

"You handled that exactly right," Chief Lynch assured him. "You need to have proof of life."

Especially after seeing that blood. Josh had to find out if his son and the boy's grandmother were okay or if one of them had been hurt. Josh wanted so badly to see his son in person, too. For the first time.

He'd seen the pictures Natalie had shared with Dubridge, of the little boy with brown hair and heavily lashed eyes. His smile had a gap where his two front baby teeth had fallen out and his adult ones had yet to come in.

"And getting to see the boy might give us clues as to where he's being held," the detective added. "It was definitely the right move."

"Guess my criminal justice degree didn't entirely go to waste," Josh muttered.

The chief and the detective exchanged a look. "You have a background in criminal justice?"

He sighed over their obvious surprise. "You thought I was just a criminal?"

"Amber doesn't and didn't ever believe that he was guilty of the charges," Milek spoke up in his defense.

"But yet she and a judge accepted his guilty plea," Dubridge pointed out. "And that judge sentenced him to eight years in prison."

"So instead of trying to find my son, you've been wasting time checking me out," Josh surmised.

Dubridge narrowed his dark eyes and stared hard at Josh. "You have a criminal justice background. You don't think I should have checked you out? Your place was broken into and tossed because someone was looking for diamonds they think you stole."

"I didn't take them," Josh insisted. "Until today I hadn't stepped foot into Croft Custom Jewelry in more than five years." And then he'd only been there once, when Natalie had showed him the place after hours. They'd made love in that backroom where earlier today they'd discovered the diamonds were missing from the safe.

"But obviously, since you share a son, you have a history with the owner's daughter," Dubridge said.

"I didn't know I had a son," Josh said. "I had no idea she was pregnant when I pled guilty…" To something he hadn't done. "I had no idea."

Dubridge flinched as if he could commiserate. From what he'd told them earlier about his wife and his baby, he probably could.

"Natalie said that only her mom and her sister knew," Josh told them. He didn't believe Marilyn Croft had left him that note and abducted his son. Natalie and her mother had always been so close, and from what Natalie had shared, they seemed even closer now that Marilyn was helping raise Natalie's son, *their* son.

"And her mom is gone," he murmured. With Henry. Or so he hoped. He hoped the little boy wasn't alone with a kidnapper, and he hoped that nothing had happened to Natalie's mother. But he'd found that blood in the garage, and Marilyn hadn't been offered in exchange for those diamonds. Only the little boy.

Did that mean the boy's grandmother was already dead?

And what about Henry?

Impatience and fear churning inside Josh, he snapped, "Why the hell aren't they calling back?"

"Maybe they weren't with your son when they made the call," Milek suggested. "Maybe they called from somewhere else."

"And where is her sister? The officer cordoning off this area said that nobody has tried coming to this house," Dubridge said. "Why isn't her sister here with her?"

"Dena Hutchinson's phone is on do-not-disturb," Josh said. "Natalie thinks she's getting a spa treatment or something."

"It's the *or something* we need to check," Dubridge muttered. "We'll track her down and confirm what her involvement might be in this situation."

Natalie didn't have the relationship with her sister that she had with her mom. She and Dena didn't even have one as good as the one he had with his sister. Dena had always made it clear to Natalie that she would have preferred to be an only child. They weren't close. While his sister...

Josh couldn't think about her now. He hadn't even talked about her much to Natalie when they'd been dating, and the two women had never met. It hadn't been that he was ashamed of her, but maybe he'd been ashamed of himself. And then...

None of that mattered now. All that mattered was finding Henry and his grandmother.

"From what Natalie said about her sister, Dena doesn't like kids," Josh told the detective. "She says that they're sticky and loud." So why would she kidnap one? And her father owned the jewelry store, so it wasn't as if she'd had to steal to get her hands on some diamonds.

Dubridge chuckled. "I can confirm the loud part already. Barbie is tiny but has one hell of a set of lungs."

Josh felt a pang of envy that he'd missed that, that he'd missed seeing Henry born, seeing him as a baby. Hell, with every minute that passed without the kidnapper calling him back, Josh was getting more and more afraid that he might have missed seeing his little boy ever.

But he couldn't let himself consider that as an option. He had to focus on finding him instead.

"Well, given how Dena feels about kids, I hardly think she would kidnap one," Josh pointed out.

If only he could be as certain that his sister wasn't involved in this...

But he hadn't seen or talked to her in so long. Maybe she'd done what he'd told her to, maybe she'd made a new, better, *safer* life for herself. But…he hadn't wanted to know if she hadn't.

That was why he hadn't tried to find her while he'd been in prison or even since his release. He considered asking Dubridge to track down his sister now, too, but Josh wanted to talk to Sylvie himself first. He wasn't sure he would be able to trust what she told him, though.

He wasn't sure that he could trust anyone anymore. Sylvie hadn't been honest with him all those years ago until it was too late.

And then his dad had turned his back on him.

And Natalie…

Even Natalie, whom he'd loved for being so straightforward and honest, hadn't told him about his son.

But before Josh talked to Sylvie, he wanted to talk to his son, wanted to make sure that he was still alive. "Why aren't they calling back?" he asked again.

Nobody answered him. Probably because everyone else was scared to say out loud what they were thinking. What he was beginning to think…

That it was too late for proof of life.

NATALIE COULDN'T STOP shaking, and it wasn't just with anger now. She was so damn scared. For Henry and for her mom.

Where were they?

What were they going through?

Which one of them was hurt? Were they both hurt now? Or worse?

Why hadn't the person called back yet?

She stared at the phone lying in the palm of her right hand. The detective had a trace on her cell, but he'd said the last call hadn't been long enough to ping more than the main tower in River City.

River City was the biggest city on the west side of Michigan. It was even bigger than Detroit. So that didn't narrow down the location of her mother's phone or of her mother and Henry.

She'd cursed Josh for hanging up that call too soon, for not giving them enough time to trace it and for not giving them a chance to get Henry on the line before he hung up. But the detective had assured her that Josh did the right thing.

Mrs. Lynch sat next to her, holding her left hand while in her right, Natalie held her cell, willing it to ring. "They will call back," the older woman said as if she could read Natalie's mind.

But then she was a mother, too. She had to know that Henry was all that was on Natalie's mind, making sure that he was all right, that she got him back. She was worried about her mother, too, and having Mrs. Lynch here holding her hand did give her some comfort. But it was bittersweet because it made her think even more of her mother.

Marilyn Croft wasn't just her mother, though. She was Natalie's best friend. They were so close. Marilyn was always there for her and for Henry and for everyone else that she loved.

Where was she now?

Was she all right?

"Ms. Croft," Detective Dubridge said as he returned to where she and Mrs. Lynch were sitting. "We should get in contact with your sister."

"I think she's at a salon or maybe a doctor's appointment." Guilt jabbed Natalie. She'd forgotten all about Dena and her father and Timothy. They had a right to know what was going on. She should have called them already. "I better tell her and my dad."

"What salon?" the detective asked. "And do you know what doctor she sees? We'll check them both."

She furrowed her brow, trying to recall the names. "I don't know…"

"You've never gone with her?"

She shook her head. "No." She nearly smiled as she reached up to touch her messy hair. "I haven't been to any salon in a while." Let alone one with her sister. Dena was six years older than Natalie and had never wanted to do anything with her. Natalie was probably the first child that Dena thought was sticky and messy and loud.

"You're beautiful," a deep voice murmured.

It wasn't the detective, but Josh who'd walked up beside him. And the way he looked at her made her feel beautiful. But then his face flushed as if the admission had embarrassed him. She flushed, too.

Then she focused on the detective again. "I don't know where she goes. Did you ask her husband?" Hadn't the detective been at the jewelry store investigating the missing diamonds before she and Josh discovered that Henry and her mother were missing, too?

"Or I can…" She should have already called Timothy. Her dad and Timothy and Dena all had a right to know what was going on with the people they cared about. They were going to be so upset that Mom and Henry were missing.

The detective glanced around the area. "Where is your brother-in-law?"

She hoped he was still with her father, but before she could reply, Josh answered for her, "Dena's husband, Timothy, was at the store earlier when we discovered that the diamonds were stolen, like the note claimed."

"The note claimed you took them," Natalie reminded him and herself.

Had he taken them? She wanted to believe that he hadn't, but after what had happened in their past, how he'd lied to her…she couldn't trust him. She would never make that mistake again.

"I didn't," he insisted.

"That's not what the person who took our son believes," she said as the anger and frustration bubbled up inside her again. She wasn't as mad at him as she was at whoever had taken their son, but she was still angry that Josh was part of this, that he might even be the cause. "And if you don't produce the diamonds, how are we going to get our son back?"

That was the real question. While the others didn't think Josh had blown it, she was worried that he had. Why would the person call back if they believed Josh didn't have what they wanted?

And what would the kidnapper do with her mother and her son then if they couldn't use them to get what they wanted? Or what might they have already done to them?

Was that why they hadn't called back yet?

MILEK'S CELL RANG, startling him and everyone else standing around outside the Crofts' home. The crime scene. There had definitely been a crime here. And at least one person was injured, two missing.

He pulled out his phone and glanced at the screen. "It's Garek calling," he said aloud and apologetically to the tense people staring at him.

They were all waiting for a call but not this one. Someone in the office had probably told Garek or Candace what was going on since Milek had already called in all the bodyguards for backup. He'd put out an all-hands-on-deck request for everyone to work on finding Josh's son. But despite his efforts to lead the search from the Payne Protection side, he wouldn't have put it past someone to call his brother or sister-in-law because they didn't think he could handle this situation.

Despite issuing orders on what everyone should do, like searching through video surveillance in the area of the Crofts' house and the store for anyone suspicious, he wasn't sure what other steps to take that the River City PD wasn't already taking.

But he wasn't handling it all alone. Logan, Parker and Cooper were pulling in their crews to help, too, and their sister, Nikki Payne-Ecklund, was coordinating with the police, too. They all had more experience than he did or even Garek and Candace.

Milek hadn't called his brother and sister-in-law because he suspected that after all the stress of getting the business up and running, they really needed to get away and have some alone time. Also, he didn't know what more they could do other than what he, Logan, Parker and Cooper already had their crews doing.

He wasn't sure what more anyone could do until they knew for certain that the little boy was alive. The difference between a rescue and a recovery was huge. He knew that.

So maybe he could use Garek and Candace's help. But he hesitated before swiping to accept his brother's call. Detective Dubridge was damn good at his job as well as every other Payne Protection bodyguard in town already doing everything they could to help.

"Call him back later," Josh said. "We don't need any distractions right now."

But he was clearly distracted and distraught, alternating between cursing himself and cursing the kidnapper. And the way he kept looking at Natalie Croft…

It reminded Milek of all his conflicted feelings when he'd found out Amber had had his son. Like Josh, Milek hadn't learned about his little boy until he'd thought it was already too late. He thought then that he'd lost them both.

He hadn't, though. They had found their way back to

each other. And they had made a life together, a home. They were happy.

Milek hadn't known Josh for very long, but he wanted that for him, too. From what Amber told him about the younger man, Josh deserved happiness for the sacrifice he'd made.

Why was the kidnapper taking so long to call back?

Milek declined his brother's call. Like Josh said, he could call him back later. If he needed his help.

Otherwise, he intended to leave Garek and Candace out of the loop, at least for now. They'd probably just arrived at their romantic destination, so they wouldn't be able to return quickly anyhow.

Penny stood up from where she'd been sitting next to Natalie. "You got this, Milek," she assured him as she squeezed his forearm. "We're all working together."

He wasn't worried about how he was going to handle this, though. He was worried about Josh. And that little boy, who was out there somewhere, possibly bleeding, probably totally afraid…if he was even still alive.

But the more time that passed since Josh's demand for proof of life, the more Milek feared that they weren't going to get it.

Chapter Six

Josh felt just like he had five years ago when he'd had to make some tough decisions and choices. He felt like he was being torn apart between guilt and love and fear.

"I can't do this anymore," he muttered to Milek. He couldn't just stand around and wait for the kidnapper to call back. "I can't just do nothing like the police are doing."

"The police are doing something," Dubridge said defensively. Yet all he seemed to be doing was eavesdropping on conversations.

Josh threw up his hands. "What? Have you found my son?" My son. The words would have felt foreign to him just hours ago, but now they came from his heart. He hadn't seen the little boy before, but he'd claimed him.

Dubridge just stared at him.

"What about the diamonds?" Josh asked. They would need to find them in order to negotiate for Henry and hopefully his grandmother's return as well.

"With Nikki Payne-Ecklund's assistance, we're going over all the security footage from the jewelry store," Dubridge said. "We'll figure out who took them."

"Nikki is good," Milek assured Josh. "And she isn't looking just at that security footage from the store but all the doorbell camera coverage in the area of the Crofts' home.

She's a computer genius. She'll be able to blow up the footage and see things that other people might have missed."

Had Josh missed it? Had those diamonds been stolen during his night surveillance? Taken right out from under his nose, just like other things had happened that he'd had no idea about until it was too late?

"And we also know that Mrs. Croft might have been drugged," Dubridge added, his voice pitched low. "The techs discovered a high dose of sleeping pills dissolved in the pot of coffee."

"My mother was drugged?" Natalie asked. She was standing now, pacing like Josh while she stared at the cell she clutched.

"We don't know that she actually drank the coffee, or if she did and had enough of it to affect her," Dubridge clarified.

"But how?" Natalie asked. "My dad and I were here this morning. We both had the coffee, and we're fine."

"It must have been put in the pot after you left then," Dubridge said.

"Did anyone show up to the house as you were leaving?" Josh asked. The detective had already taken a timeline from her, but Josh had been so distracted and tired that he couldn't remember exactly what she'd said. He needed to focus now for his son.

Natalie shook her head. "No."

"We're checking with the neighbors and have requested all the video footage off their video doorbells or other surveillance cameras," Dubridge said. "So far, we haven't seen another vehicle pull into the driveway after yours left with you and your father inside. But someone could have come through the alley that runs behind all the houses on this street and the ones to the east of it. We haven't found any cameras that point into that alley yet."

"So whoever it was must have walked through the alley and the backyard and then driven off with them in Mrs. Croft's vehicle," Josh said. "Wouldn't they have to know her for her to let them into the house so they could slip pills in the coffeepot?"

"Someone could have gotten inside when she was upstairs with Henry, helping him get ready for school," Natalie said.

"Would she have left the door unlocked?" Josh asked. Because then anyone could have slipped inside.

Natalie shook her head. "No. Dad always locks it behind us when we leave. It's something he never forgets to do."

"Then if she didn't let them in, whoever got those pills in the coffee had a key," Josh said.

It had to be someone she knew. Or maybe Natalie was wrong about her dad. Maybe he had forgotten. Josh's paternal grandmother had had Alzheimer's. It was an insidious disease. It didn't make people forget just things, but people, too. Some even forgot who they were. So it wouldn't surprise him if her dad had forgotten to lock it.

But Natalie bristled with defensiveness. "You're blaming my family. While Dena isn't a fan of kids, she would never hurt Henry, and she would definitely never hurt our mother."

"What about your dad? Your brother-in-law?" Josh asked.

"My dad... He has early onset Alzheimer's," she said.

"So you don't know what he would do," Josh pointed out. He knew all too well. Grandma had done some wildly out of character things.

"My dad was with me," Natalie said. "The entire time. There's no way he had anything to do with this. And his medication is helping. He really remembers better now than he has for some time."

"What about your brother-in-law?" Josh asked. "Was he at the store when you got there?"

Natalie tensed now, her brow furrowed. "I don't know. I don't remember…"

Josh wasn't sure that he believed her. "Don't remember, or you don't want to consider it?" he challenged. "It's easier to blame me."

"I wasn't the one who blamed you," Natalie said. "Whoever wrote that note blamed you."

He didn't understand that, either. Why him? Just because he was the ex-con? The easy scapegoat? But why take his son if they didn't really believe he'd taken the diamonds? For some reason they must think that he had.

"None of this makes sense," he said with a groan of frustration.

"We were hired to improve the security in the store because you were already having an issue with theft," Milek reminded Natalie. "Your insurance company was going to cancel your policy over it."

Natalie's face flushed.

"This sounds more and more like an inside job," Josh said. And he hoped like hell that it was. If it was someone from her family, they were less likely to hurt her mother and her son than a stranger would.

"Those could have been customer theft. They went missing from the showroom, not the vault, and nothing was as valuable as those diamonds," Natalie said. "And those were not taken until after we hired the Payne Protection Agency at the request of the insurance company."

The theft of the diamonds could still have been an inside job, but inside the Payne Protection Agency or the insurance company as well as Croft Custom Jewelry. Everyone inside the agency knew about the system and could probably get access to the codes. And the insurance company had insisted on knowing the security system and the measures taken to protect the inventory they insured. Someone from either one of those companies could have figured out how to bypass the system and steal those diamonds.

But why take his son?

His cell rang. It was probably Garek calling him since Milek hadn't picked up moments ago. But when Josh pulled his phone from his pocket, the screen was lit up with a blocked number requesting a video call. And a sudden chill gripped him.

Telemarketers didn't make video calls. This wasn't spam.

"I'm going to take this," he said.

Milek began, "If it's Garek…"

Josh swiped the screen to accept and immediately hit the record button. The screen of his phone went dark. Had they hung up on him? Had they realized he was recording the call?

"Hello?" he said into the speaker. "Is anyone there?"

His screen got a little lighter, light enough for him to see the pale face of a child. The boy blinked long, dark lashes and focused on the phone. "Daddy? Is that you?"

Josh froze, like his vocal cords were paralyzed. He didn't know what to say, what to think… He could only feel the emotions that overwhelmed him.

Relief. The boy was alive.

Fear that he was being held somewhere and for something that Josh didn't have.

And love…

"Daddy?"

That was a word Natalie had never heard her son say before. She always told him that it was just the two of them, that some kids didn't have daddies and that was okay. They had Grandpa and Mimi and Auntie Dena and Uncle Timothy instead. And they made up for it.

Henry never argued with her, but she suspected he never

totally accepted what she said and that he wanted a father like his friends had. And she could hear that in his voice, the hopefulness in that one word.

And the fear...

Josh just stood there, staring at the screen he held, while he was struck mute for some reason. From shock? Or the same fear that was coursing through her?

"Hey, honey," Natalie said. "Mommy's here." She pressed up against Josh's side so that she could see her little boy. His face took up the entire screen, but it was like shining a flashlight on it in the dark. He looked ghostly and pale. "Are you all right?"

He nodded. "Just hungry."

She would have been alarmed if he wasn't always hungry. But she still hated the fact that he was, that he was wanting for anything, and she wasn't able to give it to him.

"Mommy, I want to come home," Henry said, and there was a slight whine in his voice now, "but Daddy has to find me. Is that man my daddy?"

Josh cleared his throat as if he was trying to find the words. But they didn't come out.

So Natalie answered, "Yes, honey. This is your daddy. He's been gone for a long time. That's why you didn't meet him before this."

"He was hiding," Henry said. "So he knows how to play this game."

"I... I do know how to play," Josh said, his voice gruff.

"This person has different rules, though," Henry said.

"What are the rules, honey?" Natalie asked. She didn't know if the detective had put a tracker on Josh's phone, but she wanted to keep her son talking no matter what.

"Daddy needs to get something first to the person in the mask. And then they'll give Daddy a clue to where me and Mimi are, so he can find us."

"Is Mimi okay?" Natalie asked, her heart aching with fear for her mother and her son.

Henry's head bobbed. "She's sleeping."

Was that because of the drugs in the coffee? Her mother usually drank a couple cups in the morning. How high had the dosage been?

Or was she not sleeping at all?

"She's not hurt?" Natalie asked him.

"She fell and hit her head," Henry said, his voice shaking as a tear streaked down his cheek.

A moan coming out of the darkness reached the speaker on the phone that someone held in front of Natalie's little boy. And then she heard her mother's voice calling to him, "Henry? Henry?"

"I'm here, Mimi," he said. "We're going to be okay. Daddy will find us."

"Daddy has to find something else first," that weird raspy voice spoke from the darkness. "And when he has the diamonds that I want, we will make sure he finds you."

Then the screen went entirely black, the call ended.

She reached for the cell, to grab it out of Josh's hand, to somehow call Henry back, to keep him on the line, to keep watch over him to make sure he was safe.

But Josh held it out of her reach as he turned around and handed it to the detective. "I recorded it," he said. "But I want Nikki to go over the video."

The detective didn't argue. "She's already working with our crime-scene techs. She's had clearance for years. I'll get this to her."

"Can you use the video to find him?" Natalie asked hopefully.

The detective didn't quite meet her gaze. "We'll try. But the video was really dark. Hard to see anything but your son. And I didn't hear any background noise, either."

"So you don't think you'll find him from it," she concluded.

And again, the detective didn't argue with her.

"Then *you* have to find him," she told Josh. "You have to give back those damn diamonds!"

"I didn't take those damn diamonds," Josh said. "I didn't take anything now or…" He shook his head. "That doesn't matter. All that matters is getting Henry and your mother safely back home."

She waited for him to promise that he would do that, like he had earlier. But he didn't make that promise again.

And she suspected that he was telling the truth. He didn't have those diamonds. She actually wished that he did. Because if he didn't have the diamonds and couldn't find them, they might never get their son back. She should have been happy that she'd seen Henry, that he was alive and her mother was alive.

But for some reason she was even more afraid. Maybe because now it was all so real. Before she'd been able to hang onto her hope that this was just a mistake and that her mother and son were somewhere safe.

But they weren't safe. And her mother was hurt.

Natalie was hurting now, so much so that she couldn't stop the tears from coming. But just as he hadn't made her any promises, Josh didn't try to comfort her, either.

He was gone.

PENNY'S HEART ACHED for Natalie, for her pain and fear. She closed her arms around the young woman and hugged her tightly. "Your son and your mother will be all right," she said. At least she hoped that was the case. "With River City PD and the Payne Protection Agency working on this together, they will find them." She'd personally witnessed the miracles they'd managed to pull off so many times, all the lives they'd saved.

But lives had also been lost.

Natalie drew in a deep breath and pulled back, her face tearstained and flushed. "I just don't understand."

Penny shrugged. "People do a lot of horrible things to each other for a lot of senseless reasons."

"Greed," Natalie said, her voice sharp. "This is about money, about diamonds."

"They'll find those, too," Penny said.

"You don't think Josh has them?" Natalie asked.

Penny shook her head. "I don't know Josh very well. But Amber Talsma, Milek's wife, is a dear friend and like a daughter-in-law to me just as Milek and Garek and Stacy are like children to me."

"What does Amber have to do with anything?" Natalie asked, and she pushed up her glasses to peer through her lenses at Penny, probably wondering if she'd lost her mind.

"She's the district attorney," Penny explained, and she felt a surge of pride in the young woman who truly was like another one of her children. "She met Josh when she was the assistant district attorney who reluctantly accepted his guilty plea."

"Reluctantly?" Natalie asked. "Why?"

"Because she didn't believe he did it," Penny said. "She always thought he was taking the blame for someone else, that he was sacrificing himself for whoever was really guilty. And a man who would do that, he will do anything to get his son back safe and well."

Anything.

Like sacrificing himself again…

Chapter Seven

Josh had the confirmation he'd been waiting for, that he'd needed so he could figure out his next move. His son was alive. Mrs. Croft was alive, too, but injured. He didn't have much time to find them, especially if he used any of that time to find the diamonds first. As exhausted as he was, he couldn't work out which was the right avenue to pursue.

The diamonds or his son.

The police and the Payne Protection Agencies were working both angles as well. They were already going over all the security footage from the jewelry store to try to find out when the diamonds disappeared. Dubridge had sent himself the recording of the video call from Josh's phone. Nikki and the crime-scene techs would work together to discover what they could from the video of his son.

But Josh had something else he needed to find out about that cell phone, the one that the Payne Protection Agency had issued to him.

Nobody else had that phone number. He had no friends left from before he'd gone to prison. His own father had stopped talking to him once he'd taken that plea bargain. Josh hadn't reached out to him or his only other remaining family since his release.

So how the hell had the kidnapper gotten the number?

Josh damn well intended to find out. He slipped away from the Croft house in the long black SUV that Milek had left the keys in and drove straight to the old warehouse that had been converted into offices for the newest branch of the Payne Protection Agency.

There weren't people milling around the place like there had been at the opening celebration several weeks ago.

Josh believed Milek when he said that he'd rallied all of the Payne Protection Agencies to help find his son. So they must have been working out of the other branches. Nikki and her husband worked for Cooper Payne's franchise, so maybe they'd all gathered there.

Because it didn't look like anyone was here.

The main offices for Garek and Candace were empty and dark behind their glass walls. Milek had a desk, but it was out in the open area, like Josh's and the desks belonging to the other security agents. That was what Garek and Candace called them. They weren't bodyguards like the other Payne Protection Agencies. They were security specialists.

Josh snorted, and the sound echoed off the concrete floor and metal ceiling. Some security. One of their first jobs, and a bag of diamonds had been stolen and two people abducted.

What a freakin' mess...

A chair creaked, and then a blond head appeared above one of the cubicle walls. "Hey, Josh."

"Ivan."

The man wasn't an ex-con like Josh and some of the others, but that might have just been because he'd never been caught. His uncle, Viktor Chekov, had nearly gotten away with all his crimes until Garek and Candace finally got him where he belonged, behind bars for the rest of his miserable life. Or maybe Ivan's crimes had been committed in his youth, like the Kozminski brothers, and so his juvenile records had been sealed or expunged.

"Did they get ahold of you?" Ivan asked.

Josh tensed. "Who?"

"The person who called for you," he said. "I couldn't tell if it was a man or a woman. And the number was blocked, but they said it was urgent and that you would want the call."

"So you gave them my number?" Josh asked.

Ivan nodded. "What? Shouldn't I have done that?"

In his mind, Josh could see his little boy's pale face, tears trailing down his cheeks. His long lashes blinking furiously as he fought the tears, as he tried so hard to be brave. And he could hear the echo of that little voice calling him Daddy.

"No, I'm glad you did," Josh said, his own voice gruff with the emotion rushing up to choke him.

Ivan came around the low glass walls of the cubicle. He was a big man, bigger than Josh, with broad shoulders and the arms of a boxer. He had the slightly crooked nose of one, too, but not as crooked as one of the other specialists, Blade Sparks, who had actually been a boxer.

"I also contacted Nikki Payne, so she'd be ready to do her magic with your phone to hopefully track down the caller," Ivan assured him. "Milek gave us all the heads-up, so I know about the break-in at your place and about the diamonds and the kid. I had a feeling that was *the* call."

"It was," Josh said, emotion choking him. It might have been the most important call he'd ever taken, especially if Nikki was able to track down the caller. And if she wasn't, maybe she and the River City PD could get something off his recording of the call to lead them to where the little boy and his grandmother were being held.

"Are *you* all right?" Ivan asked. He was a giant of man, but until this moment of kindness, Josh hadn't considered that he might be a gentle giant.

Josh had come to the office to question his coworkers because he wanted someone to blame, someone to have stolen those diamonds or taken his son, so that he could get the little boy back. "Are you the only one here?" he asked.

Ivan nodded. "A few of the others have been in and out. We're all working."

While the agency was new, it was already busy with new clients. Many of which were due to that insurance company that had urged its clients to increase security given the recent spate of losses.

"We're working with the other branches of Payne Protection, doing everything we can to try to find the kid and the diamonds," Ivan assured him. "I have the shift at this office in case something comes through here again, like that call, or something else."

Like what? Another note? More ransom demands? Or something worse… Like a finger or an ear? Wasn't that what kidnappers sometimes sent to whoever they were trying to get ransom from?

"We got this, so you don't have to worry," Ivan said. "You can get some rest. You had the night shift. If you need someplace to stay because yours is a crime scene, you're welcome to crash at my house." He reached into his pocket as if reaching for his keys.

"No," Josh said. "I'm not going to be able to sleep until…" Until he found his son.

"You want to find who broke into your place and left that weird note," Ivan finished for him. "I get that. But it sounds like it was a mistake. You didn't take the diamonds."

"No, I didn't," Josh said. But why was Ivan so certain of that? "How do you know that?" Had Ivan taken them? Josh didn't know his coworkers very well yet, mostly because he wasn't sure he wanted to get to know them. He'd spent the last five years trying to stay uninvolved and away from the fray.

The taller man shrugged those broad shoulders. "I grew

up around good men and bad men. I got pretty good at being able to tell the difference."

If only Natalie could tell the difference...

If only she believed that Josh was a good man.

But she still suspected he might have taken those damn diamonds, that he was to blame for their son being abducted.

"You think I'm a good man. What do you think about the others?" Josh asked. "Because all of this feels like an inside job..."

"The diamonds?"

"And my son," Josh said. "Someone took my son."

Ivan reached out then and grasped his shoulder like Milek had earlier today. "I'm sorry, man. I heard there was mention of him in the note, but I didn't even know you had a son."

"I didn't, either," Josh admitted. "I had no idea my fian-cée was pregnant when I went to prison. So I don't understand how someone else did."

"The mother," Ivan said.

Natalie might have told someone besides her mom and sister. But she hadn't taken their son. She clearly loved the little boy too much to put him through the fear he was feeling now. And the boy was hungry.

Josh's own empty stomach clenched at the thought. He should have taken over that call, he should have made more demands when he had the chance. But he'd been so struck over seeing his son for the first time that it was like he'd been paralyzed.

"She didn't have anything to do with taking him," Josh said with certainty.

"What about the diamonds?" Ivan asked.

Josh tensed. He would have automatically said no if not for Sylvie. Since his judgment of his sister had been so off, maybe it was off about Natalie, too, because he certainly had never suspected that Sylvie was a thief.

But he hadn't really known his younger half sister at all or what was going on in her life. He was only four years older than her, but his father had been granted full custody of him, so he hadn't often seen Sylvie while they were growing up. They hadn't talked much while he'd been in college, and they hadn't talked at all when he'd been in prison.

He had no idea what she was doing now. Despite her promise to him to get away and start a new life, she could have been lying to him. She could still be stealing.

The office door opened, and Milek walked in, but he wasn't alone. The other security experts from this franchise were with him. Blade Sparks and Viktor Lagransky. Like Ivan, they were big and burly with scars and tattoos. They looked more like henchmen than employees.

Were they also suspects?

"We're here," Milek said. He must have called one of them to pick him up from the Croft house where Josh had left him. But he didn't sound angry with Josh at all. He sounded supportive when he added, "And we're going to do everything we can to get your son back."

But would it be enough?

And were they all working to help him? Or had one of them taken the diamonds? Blade, Viktor and Ivan were all like Josh; they had a past they were trying to leave behind them. But what if that wasn't possible?

What if one of them wasn't able to escape from their former life? What if that was what happened with Sylvie, too?

Josh needed to find his younger sister.

But the person he wanted more than anything to find was his son.

JOSH WAS GONE. Natalie wasn't even sure how he'd left her house since her SUV was still there. Currently, she was rid-ing with Chief Lynch in a River City PD SUV back to Croft Custom Jewelry.

"The techs processing the jewelry store said your father is very upset," the chief said, as if warning her as he pulled his vehicle into the alley behind the place.

Guilt weighed heavily on her. Concern for Henry had taken over earlier, and she hadn't thought about how her father would feel about all of this, how confused and perhaps terrified he would be.

And Timothy didn't handle him as well as she did. Even before her dad had gotten Alzheimer's, he hadn't had the best relationship with his only son-in-law. She wasn't sure why because she thought they were quite a bit alike. They handled their clients with charm and their wives the same way. Maybe that was the problem, though; they were too much alike.

While Dena had found a man to marry who was like their dad, Natalie had gone in the opposite direction. Even before she learned Josh was a liar and a thief, she'd known he was different from her dad. Back then, she'd thought he was straightforward and honest, like she was. She'd believed he would always tell her the truth, no matter what it was. Like if she overcooked the chicken or if he hated a movie she loved or if an outfit was unflattering...

But those things were so petty and unimportant compared to the big things, the things that had sent him to prison.

But was Mrs. Payne-Lynch right? Was Josh really innocent? But why plead guilty? Why go to prison for something he hadn't done? Who could he have been trying to protect?

Certainly not Natalie. He'd nearly destroyed her. If not for Henry, she wasn't sure how she would have ever found happiness again.

"What do you know about Josh Stafford?" she asked the chief.

"I know he's determined to find your son," he said.

"What about the diamonds?" she asked. "Do you think he took them?"

The chief sighed. "I don't know, Ms. Croft. I don't know him personally. I haven't even lived in River City all that long. I was a bureau chief in Chicago."

With the FBI.

She knew Woodrow Lynch's history. And that should have made her feel better, confident that he would find her child, but she'd learned to trust no one after Josh broke her heart. So she really couldn't trust Josh, especially now that he'd disappeared.

Apparently, he wasn't the only one. When she glanced around the alley, she noticed that Timothy's car was gone, too. "My brother-in-law isn't here?" she asked.

"We had to close down the store to check the inventory and process the scene," the chief said. "He may have left because of that. He could be on the way to your house or at his. I know Detective Dubridge spoke to him before he left."

Their salesperson, Hannah, was gone as well. Her moped wasn't here. But that made sense. If the store wasn't open to the public, she had no reason to stay. No sales to make.

But Timothy would have had to help with the inventory. Despite her father realizing that the diamonds were missing earlier today, he wouldn't have been able to remember everything else that they had and didn't have since so many things had disappeared before those diamonds.

"I think Dubridge let him leave because he was trying to find your sister," the chief remarked.

"That's good," Natalie said.

While Dena wasn't as close to them as Natalie and her mother would like, she did love them and Henry. So she would want to know what was going on. Even though they weren't much alike, they were still sisters, so Natalie should have tried harder to find her before now, to tell her what was going on.

If only she knew herself what that was... Why the diamonds, her son and her mother were all gone. And now Josh, too.

MILEK HAD BROUGHT in the others to help, but at the moment, Josh was just interrogating all of them, asking them where they'd been, what they knew about the jewelry store and the diamonds and about him.

"We're here to find your kid," Viktor Lagransky said. "Not be interrogated, Stafford."

"Yeah, man," Blade Sparks said.

He was big, like Ivan Chekov, and had once been a professional boxer. While Ivan had a juvenile record for things he'd had to do as a kid in order to survive, much like Milek, the crime Blade had committed and been imprisoned for had been more of an accident. The guy hadn't realized his own strength until it was too late.

"This isn't an interrogation," Milek assured them all.

Blade snorted. "Yeah, right."

"Why shouldn't it be?" Josh asked. "Who else knew that security system well enough to get into the vault and steal those diamonds?"

"Everybody who works at Croft Custom Jewelry," Ivan replied.

The others nodded.

"The CEO of the insurance company figures that recent spate of thefts were inside jobs," Milek said. "But he isn't sure if it's the inside of his company or of the ones he insures. That's what we're supposed to find out—who's responsible, while also protecting the assets."

But the diamonds had been stolen along with a child and

his grandmother. So Josh was justified in questioning his coworkers. Milek needed to question them, too.

He also needed to call Garek and Candace since they'd handled the initial interactions with the insurance company CEO and the owners of the businesses they were protecting. Garek and Candace would have to return early from their trip. But until they were back, he was in charge.

"We all need to provide our whereabouts for today," Milek said.

"Today?" Ivan asked. "But how do you know when the diamonds were stolen?"

"I don't," Milek said. "But we know when the boy was taken, and he is our priority."

"We need to find the diamonds, too," Josh said.

Milek sucked in a breath, surprised that the boy's father didn't agree with him.

"The kidnapper wants them," Josh said. "Exchanging them for my son might be my only way to get him and his grandmother away from whoever is holding them hostage."

Hostage security was their top priority then.

"We'll figure this out," Milek said. They had to. Lives were at stake. He bypassed his desk and headed toward Garek's office. He had to call his brother, and he didn't want everyone else to hear him. He already suspected they didn't respect him like they did Garek and Candace.

But Josh followed him through the door. "Thank you."

"For what?" Milek hadn't done nearly enough, not yet, because the boy was still missing.

"For making them provide their alibis and for helping me," Josh said.

"I will personally check all those alibis, too," Milek assured him. "You can get some rest."

With dark circles rimming his eyes, Josh looked like he

was about to drop. But he shook his head. "I won't be able to sleep or eat or do anything until Henry is found."

Milek sighed. "I know what you're feeling. I missed years of my son's life. I didn't learn about him until I thought he and Amber were dead."

Josh sucked in a breath. "Oh my God."

"It worked out for me," Milek reminded him. "Their deaths were faked, and they were put into witness protection. Eventually we found out who was after her, and she was able to come back to life with our child."

Josh just stared at him.

"It all worked out," Milek said. "And it will all work out for you, too." It had to. He couldn't consider anything else. It was bad enough they'd lost those damn diamonds. They couldn't lose the child and his grandmother, too.

"This isn't a cover or a ruse," Josh said. "That little boy and his grandmother are in danger. Because of me."

"You didn't take the diamonds," Milek said. Unless Josh had been lying. Unless Amber was wrong about him. But she was rarely, if ever, wrong. "So this isn't your fault."

As if refusing to be absolved, Josh shook his head. "I made a big mistake."

"Everybody makes mistakes," Milek said. He'd made more than his own share. "It's never too late to fix them or at least make up for them."

"It will be too late if something happens to my son."

Milek couldn't argue with him about that. All he could do was try to help him rescue the boy. No matter what he had to do, just as little Henry's father was no doubt prepared to do anything to protect him and get him safely back.

Chapter Eight

Five years ago, Josh had accepted the blame for a crime he hadn't committed in order to protect the people he loved. His sister. Natalie. Even his mother…

Even though he would do the same thing all over again, he also realized there were consequences because of what he'd done. Everyone believed now that he was a criminal. That was why the person who'd taken his son believed that he had those damn diamonds. That was why they'd kidnapped his son and Marilyn Croft.

Was one of Josh's coworkers responsible for the kidnapping or for the theft?

They had all provided alibis for around the time his son must have been abducted, but Josh didn't know if they were actually telling the truth about where they'd been. Milek promised he would verify all of them. While Josh didn't trust his coworkers, he did trust his boss. Well, not all of his bosses, since the timing of Garek and Candace's getaway seemed suspicious to him.

But Josh trusted Milek. Milek really could relate to the hell that he was going through, that Natalie was going through right now, not knowing where their son was.

Natalie…

Josh needed to see her again, to make sure that she was

all right. With Milek's permission this time, he borrowed another vehicle, one of the long black SUVs the Payne Protection Agency leased, and drove toward Croft Custom Jewelry. Milek had told Josh that Chief Lynch had dropped her off at the jewelry store where her father had been left alone with the crime-scene techs processing the place. Lynch had been about to have one of his officers drop her SUV at the store, but Josh had said he would take care of her and her father.

He'd thought he was taking care of her five years ago when he'd accepted the plea bargain, when he'd lied to her. He'd been trying to keep her safe. But he hadn't known then that she was pregnant with their son. Knowing that wouldn't have made any difference, though. He probably would have been even more determined to protect her. She'd had her family and her friends and her career and her strength.

While Sylvie...

She hadn't had anyone. She'd never had anyone but him. But protecting her and Natalie had cost him so much. It had cost him Natalie. And his son. And his freedom.

And now...

All of this.

Like Josh told Milek, it was his fault. If only he'd known what was going on with Sylvie, if only he'd been less self-involved, he might have been able to help her before it got too bad. Before it put her and him and Natalie all in danger. Now Natalie and their son had once again become collateral damage of their relationship with him. He wouldn't blame her for hating him.

He hated himself for putting his son in danger. The only way he could make it up to Natalie for everything he'd put her through was to find their son. He needed her help to do that, though, because he needed to figure out when the damn diamonds went missing. Even if none of his coworkers had taken Henry and Marilyn Croft, that didn't mean they hadn't taken the diamonds. In fact, he would sooner believe one of them had committed theft than a kidnapping.

But was he being as unfair to them as whoever had taken Henry was being to him? Was he assuming just because someone had once been a thief that they still were?

Thinking of thieves made him think of Sylvie.

What if it was true of her? What if she was still a thief? He had to find her. He had to know.

But first he had to make sure that Natalie was okay. And her dad. And he had to try to pinpoint when the diamonds were stolen.

He drove into the alley where there were no vehicles. With only one light burning dimly in the shadows between the buildings that lined it, the alley was dark and empty. Josh wasn't sure anyone was still at the store. Maybe she'd called a cab for her and her dad.

He could totally understand her not wanting to stay here, for wanting to get out and look for their son like Josh wanted to look for him. But first he had to figure out where to look.

He parked near the back door. He'd walked this alley so many times over the past few weeks, just like he'd walked around out front. His presence was meant to deter late-night robbers, and it must have worked because he had never seen anyone lingering anywhere around the building after hours.

He doubted the theft had happened then, that he'd missed the thief. But if the theft had happened in broad daylight and while the store was open, then this thief was bold.

Daylight was beginning to slip away now as the afternoon turned into evening, and that came early here in spring in western Michigan.

He jumped out of the SUV and headed toward the back door. Before he could even knock, it opened to Natalie's anxious face. She must have seen him on the surveillance camera.

"Did you find him?" she asked, her voice a low whisper. "Did you find Henry and my mother?"

God, he wished he could say yes. But guilt and regret choked him, and he could only shake his head.

"The diamonds?" she asked.

A short while ago, she accused him of taking them. Did she have her doubts now? Did she believe him?

"Who is that, Natalie?" a voice called out. "Is that your mother?"

"No, Dad, it's not Mom."

Josh lowered his voice now. "Did you tell him that they've been taken?"

Tears shimmered in her green eyes. "I don't know how to…"

He could relate to that. He hadn't been sure how or even what to tell Natalie all those years ago. If he'd told her the truth, he knew there was no way she would have let him go to prison for something he hadn't done. She would have gone to the assistant district attorney, the judge, even the press. But he'd already been threatened into pleading guilty or people would be hurt. And if anyone had messed up that plea deal, they would be hurt, too.

He couldn't have handled being responsible for Natalie getting hurt. But then he'd hurt her himself. It was the only way he'd known how to keep her safe, though. Because she would have done whatever necessary to protect him. She'd loved him back then. He had no doubt about that.

Natalie loved loyally and completely and fiercely.

He'd never had anyone love him the way she had…except his sister.

Sylvie.

And having to choose between them had nearly destroyed him. But in the end, he'd done what he'd had to in order to protect them both. If doing what he had cost him his son, he would be destroyed for certain.

THE LOOK ON Josh's handsome face drew Natlie toward him. He looked so…shattered. She stepped closer to him and started reaching out her hand toward his face, to touch it, to comfort him. Because he clearly needed it as much as she did.

"Natalie!"

Her father's shout startled her, making her jump. She was torn between wanting to comfort Josh and wanting to comfort her dad.

He'd been so upset since the chief had dropped her off earlier, and she'd found him alone except for one of the crime-scene techs that had remained. The red-haired woman, named Wendy, had been concerned that Claus might hurt himself.

He would never do that. Natalie had no doubts about that. Sometimes he got frustrated when he couldn't remember something, but he never got violent.

The doctor had warned them that it could happen, though. That he'd seen the sweetest, most loving grandmothers become physically combative. And maybe that would happen one day with her father, too.

But it hadn't happened yet.

He'd been doing so well until today, until all of the upheaval. She rushed back inside, though, just to make certain that he was all right.

"Natalie, what is this mess?" her father asked, pointing at the fingerprint dust that was all over the backroom. "Your mother is going to be so angry when she sees this in her workroom." It hadn't been her workroom for years, though. "We have to clean it up. Who made this mess? Your sister? She doesn't love the store like we do."

Natalie suspected her sister was jealous of the store or at least the time and attention their parents had given it, just like she seemed to be jealous of the time and attention they gave Natalie and Henry. Natalie had been trying to call Dena and Timothy both since she'd returned to the store, but neither of them was picking up.

Hopefully Timothy had found his wife by now, and Dena knew that their mother and Henry were missing. Maybe that was why she wasn't accepting Natalie's calls because she blamed her for this, because Natalie was the one who'd brought Josh into their lives. However briefly and however long ago, he still had an effect on them.

"We'll clean it up tomorrow, Daddy," Natalie assured him. "Mom will understand. She won't want us to stay late."

He nodded. "Yes. Yes. Marilyn is an angel. My angel. But my angel has a temper," he said with a chuckle. And he glanced at the Rolex watch on his wrist. "It's getting close to dinnertime. We better hurry home, or she might throw our supper out."

Tears burned Natalie's eyes, and she closed them to hold them in. She couldn't cry in front of him, she couldn't let him see how upset she was.

She couldn't tell him about Mom.

Not now.

Wasn't it getting close to what the doctor called *sundowners*? When the sun went down, Dad was the most confused. It was when he struggled to remember things and people. He hadn't forgotten any of them yet, though. He knew his family, and he knew how much he loved and appreciated them all.

Especially her mother.

"Daddy, I don't know how to tell you…" She had no idea how to broach this horror with him.

"Who is this?" he asked, staring over her shoulder.

She'd nearly forgotten Josh. But he was here, in the back-room with them now.

"Did you make this mess?" Claus asked him sternly.

"I didn't do this, sir," Josh replied, gesturing at that dust all over, at all the markings the techs had left behind. "But I do feel responsible."

Her heart jerked. Had he taken the diamonds? She'd been so hopeful that he hadn't, that he was innocent. Not just now but all those years ago like Penny Payne-Lynch had tried to convince her. But would anyone willingly go to prison for something they hadn't done? And if he'd done it to protect someone, who was it?

"How do you mean you're responsible, son?" Claus asked, and his brow furrowed. "You look so familiar to me. Henry?"

Their son all grown up would look exactly like his fa-ther. "Henry is still a little boy, Daddy," Natalie said. "But this is his father."

Her father's brow creased more, and he rubbed his tem-ples. "I… I'm sorry. Sometimes I get so confused…" He gazed around the backroom. "Like now… I just want to go home. Natalie, please take me home."

Her heart lurched. God, she wanted so badly to take him home. But like the store, it was a crime scene, too. Unlike the store, she wasn't sure it had been cleared yet. Only a theft had happened at the store, while no one was certain what had happened at the house. An abduction but there had been blood, too. "Daddy, I don't know how to tell you…"

"Your wife and Henry are on that overnight trip with the school," Josh said.

Natalie turned toward him, shocked that he'd come up with a lie so quickly. Because of how easily he had, she wondered if she would ever be able to trust him. But then she remembered that he'd once lived with a grandmother who'd had dementia. Maybe he'd had reason to lie like this before. Maybe it was how he'd dealt with her. Regardless, she asked, "Wh-what are you doing?"

"Just reminding your dad that Mrs. Croft isn't home tonight, and the house is being fumigated," Josh continued his string of lies. "So we need to bring you to your daughter Dena's house, Mr. Croft."

Her father focused on Natalie, as if he wasn't sure he should believe Josh, either. But she realized that this was probably for the best. That, in fact, it was kinder to lie to her father than to tell him the truth, which would undoubtedly devastate him.

Was that what Josh had thought he'd been doing all those years ago? Being kind when he actually broke her heart?

She drew a breath, forcing down that old pain and resentment. Then she smiled and nodded at her father. "Remember, Daddy?"

Probably because he was too proud to admit he didn't have any idea what they were talking about, her father nodded, but his forehead was still all deep furrows. "What about you, honey? Where are you staying?"

She smiled with amusement and appreciation that he was sharp enough to remember that she wouldn't feel comfortable in Dena's house, that she would rather stay with one of her friends instead of feeling like the inconvenience Dena had made her feel since they were kids.

"She's staying with me," Josh said, "until Henry comes back."

Natalie's pulse quickened. Did he mean that? Not that she would actually agree to stay with him. She wasn't sure where she was going to go. Maybe she would just hang out at the police department until they found her son. Maybe her constant presence would compel them to work around the clock until her little boy and her mother were rescued.

"And who are you?" her father asked again.

"Josh Stafford." He held out his hand. "Henry's father."

Her dad extended his hand to shake, then he saw the fingerprint dust on his skin. "Oh my. I'm sorry. I need to clean up." Still fastidious about his appearance, he rushed off toward the bathroom.

She stared after him, concerned but also grateful for the reprieve. The tears that had been stinging her eyes slipped free now, sliding down her face beneath her glasses.

"Oh, Natalie," Josh said, and he reached for her.

She stepped back, though, knowing that if he touched her, she would lose it. She would dissolve into helpless sobs. And she didn't want to feel any more helpless than she already felt right now. "I'm okay."

"Bullshit."

"Yes," she admitted. "But you would know. You spew lies like they're easier to tell than the truth."

"To a person with dementia, it's sometimes better to lie than to upset them, especially in a situation like this," Josh said, confirming that he'd lied to her father out of kindness. "My dad and I always met my grandmother where she was instead of trying to correct her or make her remember because that just upset her more. As Dad said…" there was a strange wistfulness to his voice "…we had to meet her in her world wherever it was at the time. Her childhood, her adolescence or some dream she'd had that seemed so real to her."

Natalie remembered him telling her that in the past, too, and his patience with his grandmother was another reason she'd fallen for him. She'd thought he was such a good man then. And part of her, her heart, was beginning to believe that he still was.

"My dad is usually better than this," she said. "It's just been a confusing day for him."

Josh sighed and touched his own head, mussing up his thick brown hair. "Not just for him."

She couldn't imagine how shocked he'd been when he found that note in his apartment. But she couldn't bring herself to apologize to him, not after what he'd put her through. No matter what his reason was or his guilt, he'd hurt her more than anyone else ever had. Until now…until someone had taken her son and her mother.

"We should get your dad out of here," Josh said. "And we can't bring him back to your house."

She nodded. "I know."

"Call your sister and let her know we're bringing him to her," he said.

"She wasn't picking up earlier when I tried calling." But she pulled out her cell phone and gasped when she saw that the screen was dark. The battery had completely run down. "I—I can't…"

"Call her from the store phone," he suggested.

"I tried that earlier, too. I called Dena and Timothy both from my cell and from this phone."

"And neither of them picked up?" he asked, his dark eyes narrowing slightly.

She nodded. "I don't know what's going on with her and Timothy," she said in a whisper. "When the chief dropped me off, Dad was alone with a crime tech. Timothy just left him here. Even Hannah was gone."

Josh flinched. "I'm sorry. That must have been so hard for him to have no one here that he recognized."

Again Natalie's heart reacted to his kindness and understanding, warming. Josh had only been around her father a short while, but he understood more than her brother-in-law did about how leaving her father alone would affect him. But then Josh had experience dealing with a loved one with dementia.

She would rather deal with that, though, than the suspicions plaguing her now. Not about Josh this time, but about her own family.

"I don't know where they are or what they're really capable of," she whispered. "My sister or Timothy…" Or even Hannah.

But the saleswoman was inconsequential. She didn't have access to the vault. She couldn't have taken the diamonds. But Timothy…

"I'm afraid to find out what's really going on around here," Natalie admitted. "More than those diamonds have gone missing."

"That was why your insurance company wanted you to hire us," Josh said.

Of course he knew about that. And he probably knew that those thefts had been happening for a while.

"When were you released?" she asked.

"Eight weeks ago," he said.

The thefts and losses had happened before then. So he couldn't have taken those things and really hadn't taken the diamonds.

Instead of being relieved that he wasn't the thief she'd thought he was, she was scared. Since he didn't have the diamonds, how the hell were they going to get their son back?

AFTER THAT PHONE call with his daddy, the person in the mask had given Henry and Mimi food. So Henry wasn't hungry anymore. He'd eaten a bunch of the pizza. It was all meat and no veggie, just like he liked. Whoever was wearing that mask knew what he liked.

It had to be someone he knew who was playing a game with him and his daddy and mommy.

They'd brought pop, too. His favorite flavor, grape soda. And a lamp so it wasn't so dark anymore.

And they had an air mattress and blankets now, too. So

they had somewhere to lie down that wasn't so cold and hard anymore. Mimi was lying on the bed, but she wasn't sleeping. She looked a little confused, though, like Grandpa looked when it got dark out.

Henry scooted closer to her and snuggled up against her. She was shaking a little. But she shouldn't have been cold. He wasn't cold anymore. And he wasn't even as scared as he'd been before. He'd seen his daddy and talked to Mommy.

"We'll be okay, Mimi," he told her, petting her hair that was still a little sticky. "My daddy is going to find us. He just has to find something else first for the person in the mask."

"What?" she asked in a whisper, like she was afraid that person was out there listening to them.

But Henry knew they were gone. He'd heard the footsteps walking away and then that engine had faded away again. "They're not here anymore," he assured her. "They drove off. I heard the car."

"What do they want?" Mimi asked.

"Diamonds," he reminded her of what the person said, like sometimes he had to remind Grandpa. And then he doubted himself for a second.

Diamonds was the word that the person had used, wasn't it? He'd heard it before when Mommy and Grandpa and Mimi talked about work. They talked about diamonds and rubies and emeralds and different colors of gold. He knew it was all worth a lot of money, but diamonds were worth the most.

He and Mimi must be worth the most, too, if somebody wanted diamonds for them. And if they were worth the most, that person wouldn't hurt them. Not if they wanted the diamonds...

"Henry, we have to figure out how to get out of here," Mimi said, but she sounded a little sleepy again. And she didn't move.

"Don't worry, Mimi," he said. "Daddy will find us."

He'd seen him. For the first time in his life. And he could see how much he looked like him. They had the same brown eyes and hair.

But Daddy had looked worried.

And Mommy...

She had sounded scared, like Mimi did. And now that pizza and pop flipped around a little bit inside his tummy as Henry felt scared again, too.

Wasn't this just all a game? It was a stupid game, though. Because even the air mattress and the lamp didn't make this place anywhere near as nice as his bedroom.

And Mommy and Daddy weren't here, either. He wanted Mommy, but now he wanted Daddy, too. He wanted him to play the game and win.

Henry was really good at games. Mommy wasn't because she always lost. So maybe being good at games was something he got from his daddy, like his eyes and his hair.

Daddy had to be good at games because he had to win. He had to find them.

Chapter Nine

Josh glanced into the rearview mirror, checking on Natalie who sat in the back seat next to her father. She held his hand, but Josh didn't know if she was comforting her dad or seeking comfort. Or maybe both. Because they both needed to be comforted right now.

Josh did as well, but he'd learned five years ago to stop looking for it. All he could do now was focus on finding Henry and the diamonds.

Before her dad returned from the bathroom, Natalie had shared with Josh when the diamonds must have gone missing. She hadn't checked for them the day before, but she remembered them being in the vault the day before that, on Wednesday. So sometime between Wednesday afternoon and Friday morning, they'd gone missing.

And, albeit reluctantly, she'd admitted that she was beginning to share his suspicions about it being an inside job. But which job? Stealing the diamonds? Or abducting their son? Or both?

The kidnapper had to be someone close to Natalie in order for them to know that her son was Josh's, because he doubted anyone he knew was aware of Henry. Josh hadn't even been aware that he had a son. But for some reason the kidnapper must have believed he knew.

"Here," Natalie said, her voice a little sharp but it sounded more like nerves than irritation with him. "Turn right here. This is their street."

"Whose?" Claus asked. "Where are we, Natalie? And who is our driver?"

"Josh, Mr. Croft," Josh reminded the older man, and he glanced in the rearview to see Claus's gray-haired head bob in acknowledgment.

"Yes, yes, Henry's father," the older man said. "Where is Henry?"

"With Mom," Natalie said. "On that overnight trip for school, remember?" Despite rebuking Josh for lying, she must have decided that it was the better alternative to upsetting her father.

Claus nodded again, like he remembered, but there was clearly confusion in his blue eyes. Josh flashed back to his grandmother, to that cloudy look of confusion that had so often been in her dark eyes.

"Timothy and Dena's house is at the end of the street," Natalie said, pointing toward a modern house that was all windows and concrete.

Josh pulled into the wide driveway and studied the structure. He didn't like it, but given the neighborhood and the design, the thing must have cost a lot. "This wasn't where they lived before." He remembered them living in a modest house five years ago.

Natalie sighed. "No. Timothy's parents passed away, and they inherited some money."

"That's what they told you?" he asked. "I should have Milek check on that." Just before he'd left the Payne Protection Agency, Josh had asked his boss to check on something else for him besides those alibis.

Sylvie.

"I went to his parents' funerals," Natalie said.

"I meant the inheritance," Josh explained.

She shook her head as if trying to clear it of confusion. "Oh, I understand what you mean…" Had her brother-in-law really inherited money, or had they stolen it? "I just can't believe they would do that to our family," she murmured.

"Do what?" Claus asked. "What are the two of you talking about?"

"Nothing, Dad," she said. "We're at Dena and Timothy's."

"Why?"

"You're staying here tonight, remember?"

He glanced around. "Where's my bag? Your mother would have packed me an overnight bag."

Behind the lenses of her glasses, tears sparkled in Natalie's eyes, but she smiled. "I'm sure your things are already here."

Claus was the same size as his son-in-law, so he would be able to wear his clothes. But what he was going to wear was the least of Josh and Natalie's concerns about her father. Claus was clearly very dependent on his wife. If he learned she was missing…

And hurt…

Josh's stomach churned with concern for her. Mrs. Croft had to be okay. Because just as she clearly took care of her husband, she was hopefully taking care of her grandson right now. Comforting Henry like Natalie was comforting her father. Although during that video call, it had seemed the other way around, like Henry was comforting his Mimi.

He was a sweet little boy.

Josh had to close his eyes against a sudden rush of tears of his own as yearning overwhelmed him. He wanted his son to be safe and sound. He wanted to meet the little boy, to hold him…

"Are you okay?" Claus asked, and his hand settled on Josh's shoulder.

He smiled. "Yes."

"We better get you inside, Dad," Natalie said. "Dena will be cross if you're late for dinner."

The older man snorted. "Your sister doesn't cook." He chuckled. "But she will be mad if her takeout dinner got cold waiting for me." He opened the back door.

And Josh opened the front.

Natalie hopped out on his side and asked, "What are you doing?"

"I'm going inside with you," he said.

She shook her head. "No. That's a bad idea."

He shook his head now. "Nothing's a bad idea if it gets us closer to the truth."

She narrowed her eyes and stared at him. "What do you know about the truth?" she asked in a soft whisper.

He knew then that no matter what, she would never forgive him and never trust him again.

Part of him had already known that, which was why he'd never reached out to her during those years in prison. As well as keeping her safe, he had also wanted her to move on and be happy. And after he was out, he purposely hadn't looked her up. He really hadn't wanted to know what he'd lost.

But now that he knew...

HE HAD THAT look again, the one he'd had in the alley behind the store. That shattered look that made Natalie want to reach out to him.

But just like then, her father called out, "Are you two coming?"

He hadn't rung the bell yet. Maybe he couldn't find it. The place was so stark and modern that it didn't have anything like a regular doorbell. It just had a camera style one, so Dena should have already opened the door.

If she was home...

Natalie had tried once again to call Dena and Timothy from the store, but nobody had accepted her calls. Her stomach pitched with the dread and doubts she'd already been feeling. They intensified now.

But the door finally opened behind her father, startling him. "Claus," Timothy greeted his father-in-law. He'd never called him Dad. "What are you doing here?"

"What do you mean?" Natalie asked. "Don't you know what's happened?" Surely the detective had tracked down her sister and brother-in-law by now and told them that Henry and her mother had been kidnapped.

"Of course I know about the theft at the store," Timothy said. He pointed over her father's shoulder to Josh. "The one he pulled off. Why would you bring him here, Nat?"

She hated when he called her Nat, just like he hated if anyone called him Tim. But she ignored it. "Where's my sister?"

He sighed. "I just got home and heard the shower running. I assume it was her since we're the only ones who live here."

"You haven't talked to her? She doesn't know?" Natalie asked. "And why the hell weren't either of you picking up your phones?"

He pulled his cell from his pocket, and his face flushed. "I must've turned it off."

"I tried calling Dena, too, and she wasn't picking up. Where was she?" Natalie asked. "And what does she know? What did you tell her?"

He shook his head. "I didn't tell her anything. I haven't talked to her. I don't know what she knows. Like I said, she must be in the shower, and I just got home."

"You just got home from where?" Josh asked the question. "You weren't at the store."

"There was no reason for me to stay after I gave the police the inventory of things that we're supposed to have," Timothy said, his tone condescending.

"You heard about that note that was left at my apartment," Josh said. "You knew that…" He glanced at her father, who was looking from one to another of them like he was watching a television show.

Josh had more consideration for her father than his son-in-law was currently showing, than Timothy had probably ever showed.

"I knew that was bullshit," Timothy finished for him. "Some sick game you're playing to cover up the theft."

"Theft?" her father said. "What's going on?"

"Nothing, Dad," Natalie said. Then she turned on Timothy. "Go get Dena. That note wasn't a lie. The diamonds aren't the only things that were taken."

Timothy stumbled back, inside the open door. Natalie followed him inside. She had to reach back to pull her father through the door, though. He might have resisted if not for Josh helping guide him into the foyer which was concrete and marble. The house looked more like a gallery than a home.

All the color had drained from Timothy's usually flushed face. "What…what do you mean?"

"She means that him getting out of prison is already destroying this family!" Dena said as she came down the stairs. She was dressed in some kind of silky jumpsuit that had deep wrinkles in it. Her pale blond hair was bone-dry and her makeup was a little smeared as if she'd been wearing it for a while. Had Timothy lied about the shower?

"You know then?" Natalie asked her sister.

Dena nodded, and her throat moved as if she was struggling to swallow. "A police car pulled me over, and I was taken in for questioning like a common criminal." She pointed at Josh. "Like him. You brought this on yourself, Natalie, getting involved with him. I knew you were still hung up on him."

Heat rushed to Natalie's face. Just because she hadn't dated after her broken engagement and her broken heart didn't mean that she'd never gotten over Josh. But she wasn't going to argue with her sister right now. "I brought Dad here because he can't go ho—"

"Of course he can't!" Dena interjected. "And that's your fault, just like you're the reason your son and our mother are in danger."

"What…what are you all talking about?" Claus asked, his voice gruff.

"Daddy—" Natalie began.

"Daddy," Dena said as she ran down the rest of the marble steps to hug him. "I'm here for you. Let's get you upstairs to the guest room now."

But Claus planted his feet and looked back at Natalie and Josh, as if they were the ones he trusted for answers. But they'd been lying to him.

"It's all right, sir," Josh told him. "You should go with Dena."

Natalie hugged him, though. "I'll be back in the morning," she said.

"Where are you going?" Dena asked as if surprised that Natalie wouldn't feel welcome staying. "You can't go back to the house, either."

The only place Natalie wanted to be was with her son and her mother. So maybe she would park herself at the police station until she knew where they were.

"Where were you all day?" Josh asked her sister.

Dena's nose wrinkled as she sniffed. "Who are you to ask me my whereabouts?"

"The police must have already asked you where you were when Henry and your mother went missing," he said. "What did you tell them?"

"Whatever I told them is none of your business," she replied.

"Henry is my son," Josh said.

"You've never been a father to him," Dena said. "You were just a horrible mistake my sister made that's come back to haunt us all. Now get the hell out of my house before I call the police to arrest you for trespassing."

Anger coursed through Natalie. But she wasn't sure why she was so angry with her sister. Because she was telling the truth, that this was Josh's fault? Or because Dena had threatened the man that Natalie had once loved, the man who, like her, had a son being held hostage? Or was Natalie mad because her sister didn't seem to care that Henry was missing, and their mother...

Or maybe Dena did care and that was why she was lashing out, because she was feeling as scared and helpless as Natalie was feeling?

Natalie had never been able to figure out her older sister. They'd never had any common ground where they could meet, not even their old childhood home or the store, since Natalie loved them both and Dena hated them.

"It's all going to come out," Josh said, his voice almost chilling in its intensity. "Whatever secrets you two have, they're all going to come out in this investigation."

"You're a criminal, not a cop," Dena said. "You're not investigating anything. You're just trying to cover up your crimes."

"I'm trying to find my son," he said. "And if you cared about anyone but yourself, you would do everything you could to help."

Dena gasped. "How dare you come in my home and talk to me that way!" She turned toward Natalie. "What are you doing here with him? You swore you were done with him when he went to prison, but I suspected it wasn't over." She glanced at her husband. "I even told you that she wasn't over—"

"I want answers, too," Natalie said. "No. I want my son. I don't care about anything else. I want my son and our mother safely back."

"Marilyn?" Claus said. "Where's Marilyn?"

"With Henry," Josh said. "Remember? She's with Henry. They'll be home soon."

He was lying again so her father wouldn't get upset. Natalie had to remind herself of that because she wanted so badly to believe Josh. But they were no closer to finding Henry and her mother. And she doubted they were going to get any answers here.

"Get out of my house!" Dena said. "Now!"

"Why are you yelling at Henry's dad?" her father asked.

Dena shook her head. "You don't know, Daddy. You don't remember what he put her through, how he nearly destroyed her. How can *you* forget, Natalie?"

She hadn't forgotten. And she certainly hadn't forgiven, either. But right now, he seemed like the only other one as determined to find their child as she was. And if Penny Payne-Lynch was right, and Josh had taken the blame to protect someone else...

He might still be the man she'd thought he was. A good man.

"Let's go," Natalie said to him. And she turned and headed back out the door he'd left open behind him.

Still in the foyer, Dena screamed, "Don't be an idiot again, Natalie! Don't go anywhere with him!"

But Natalie ignored her sister, as she often had to, and kept walking toward that SUV.

Josh closed the door to the house and rushed back to the driver side while Natalie climbed into the passenger seat. He pulled his cell phone out of his pocket and sucked in a breath. Then he punched in an address.

"Where are we going?" she asked, not that she really

cared. She just had to get away from here, from her sister's accusations and her father's confusion and Timothy's dumb denials. She couldn't handle anyone else betraying her. She'd already dealt with Josh's betrayal all those years ago.

But what if he hadn't betrayed her? What if he'd been protecting someone, like his lie to her father was to protect him from fear and upset?

But even if hadn't committed the crime for which he'd gone to prison, like Mrs. Lynch believed, that didn't mean Josh hadn't betrayed Natalie. In fact, if he'd gone to prison for something he hadn't done, he might have betrayed her even more than she'd thought he had. Because who had he been covering for?

Natalie knew about his grandmother and his dad. She knew that he had a sister, too, like her, and like her and Dena, they hadn't been close. They hadn't even grown up in the same households since they had different fathers and his had had full custody of Josh.

So would he have lied for his sister? Or for his mother, even though he'd talked less about her than he had his sister?

At the moment Natalie wasn't worried about the past, though. She was worried about the present and the future, if her son and her mother would have one…

PENNY SHOULD HAVE gone with Natalie to take care of her father. Or better yet, she should have taken care of him for Natalie. The last thing that young woman needed was more stress, but Penny had had to help out with a couple of her own grandchildren.

And so she'd left that poor girl alone.

But seeing her grandkids just reinforced her fear for the missing child.

For Henry…

By the time Penny had been able to get away again, the

jewelry store was dark and empty. So now she was at the Payne Protection Agency office, where just a couple of months ago they'd had that party to celebrate its opening.

"Do you know where they are?" she asked Milek, who looked nearly as exhausted and overwhelmed as Henry's father had earlier today.

"Garek and Candace are on their way back," he said. He sat at his brother's desk now. "I should have called him right away."

"You're handling this," she said. "But I was asking about Josh and Natalie." Her heart ached for them as if it could feel their pain.

Milek sighed and nodded. "I have a pretty good idea where he's heading. I'm not sure that they're together, though. But he did text me an approximate time frame for when the diamonds got stolen."

"From Natalie?" Penny assumed.

Milek nodded, and a lock of pale blond hair fell over his forehead into his silvery eyes.

So Josh and Natalie were together. For some reason that made her feel a little bit better. "They need to be there for each other." Josh had lost too many years with the woman he'd clearly loved and with their son. "Nobody else can understand what they're going through..." Penny murmured.

"I can," Milek said. "That's why we need to pull out all the stops to find that little boy and his grandmother, especially since it sounds like she's already hurt. With Garek and Candace on their way back, everyone in all the Payne Protection offices will be working on this."

Like they had when Milek's child and the woman he loved had gone missing.

At least, if Josh and Natalie were still together, they didn't have to worry about each other. Not like Milek had had to worry about Amber.

"You know how it feels, too," Milek said. "There were all too many times that you didn't know where one of your children was."

Including the children Penny's heart had adopted. She had experienced that horror of not knowing where your child was and if they were alive or dead.

She wouldn't wish that horror on her worst enemy, let alone a young couple who'd already suffered too much.

Chapter Ten

"This is a mistake," Josh murmured as he pulled along the curb outside one of the old, downtown River City Queen Anne Victorians that had been converted to a multifamily property. It wasn't a mistake like the wrong address or that his sister wasn't living here—though she probably was. It had been a mistake to bring Natalie with him.

"This is the address you put in the directions for," she pointed out. "Whose is it? Why are we here?"

"You're not the only one having doubts about family," he admitted.

"Family? What are you talking about?"

He shook his head. "It doesn't matter. This shouldn't take long. Just wait for me here." But once he stepped out on the driver side and walked around the front of the SUV, Natalie was already waiting on the sidewalk.

"No. If you think this is a lead to our son, I'm going with you," she said. "Wherever you go."

That was why Josh had lied to her all those years ago. He knew his plea deal was sending him to hell, and he hadn't wanted to bring her with him. Just like he didn't want to bring her here to talk to Sylvie. But he didn't want to waste time arguing with her, either, especially if he was already wasting his time.

"This might lead nowhere," he warned her.

Natalie shrugged. "Where do you think this person or these people might lead us? To Henry or to the diamonds?"

"I don't know," he said.

And he really had no idea. He'd lost touch with his sister like he'd lost touch with Natalie. He hadn't even known that Sylvie still lived in River City. He'd wanted her to leave, to start over again somewhere else, somewhere safe. But Milek had found her here.

He headed toward the porch that wrapped around the side of the enormous house. Next to the door was an intercom panel with a list of names. He found the button for *S. Combs* and pressed it.

He half hoped that nobody answered. That Milek was wrong and Sylvie didn't live here.

That she wasn't in River City anymore.

That she hadn't lived here in years. That she'd kept her promise to start her life over somewhere else, somewhere safe.

The door buzzed and unlocked. And he wasn't sure why. Had she just buzzed him in, or had someone else heard the intercom and unlocked the door?

"Who is S. Combs?" Natalie asked, her face tense.

"Sylvie."

"Sylvie?" she repeated the name. "You already have a girlfriend?"

He snorted. "Sylvie is my sister."

While he'd mentioned his younger sister to her a time or two, he'd made it clear that they weren't close, and he had never introduced the two. And even now he wasn't sure why. Despite his denial, had he realized something was going on with his younger sister?

Or maybe he'd just been worried that Natalie would feel the same way Sylvie did, that he should have tried to spend more time with her growing up, or to get his dad to take her in instead of leaving her where he had, with their narcissistic mother. But he'd been just a kid himself then.

"Combs? Is she married?"

"We have different fathers," he reminded her. Though Sylvie wasn't sure who hers was. Their mother hadn't always been truthful.

"Oh," Natalie said. "I remember you saying that and that you hadn't grown up together..."

While he hadn't introduced them and he'd spared her a lot of the details, he had mentioned Sylvie to her before. That he had a kid sister he didn't get to see often because of his dad having full custody of him.

Because Josh hadn't wanted Natalie to know how messed up his mother was, he hadn't told her why his dad had it or that he and his mother didn't get along, just that his dad had gotten full custody of him after the divorce. And Josh had lived with him and his grandmother while Sylvie lived with their mom and whoever Monica Combs had been involved with at the time. None of them had lasted even as long as Josh's father had.

"Her apartment number starts with a two, it must be upstairs," Natalie said, and she walked across the foyer, with its scarred hardwood floor, to the double staircase. She walked up one half of it, toward the landing that wrapped around the two-story foyer.

Josh sucked in a breath and rushed up to join her just as she reached out to knock on the door of unit 2C.

The door must not have been closed tightly because it creaked open. And his heart started pounding fast and hard as it reminded him momentarily of his place that morning, of finding it broken into. But the doorjamb wasn't splintered. Nobody had forced their way inside this apartment.

Light spilled out along with the smell of cinnamon and

nutmeg. "Come on in. I've got the coffee brewing, so we can study all night," a female voice said.

Studying.

She was in school. At twenty-four. Maybe she'd gone back and was working on a master's or something.

A laugh rang out. "Hopefully it won't take us that long to figure this out..."

And he had a strange feeling that maybe she was studying something else. Something unrelated to school and higher education.

As a teenager, she'd pulled off some major heists. She would have been able to figure out how to steal those diamonds, especially if she'd studied the security systems that the Payne Protection Agency used.

The floor creaked beneath his weight as he walked into her place. It was small. She was only a short distance away, sitting at a table next to a row of cabinets and appliances.

At the creak, she looked up and froze. Her mouth fell open, and her eyes widened.

She looked nothing like him. Her hair was blond with streaks of brown and red mixed in with it. And her eyes were a very pale gray or blue, it was hard to tell which.

She jumped up from her chair so quickly that it fell back against the cabinets. Then she ran for him, throwing her arms around his neck. "Oh my God! Josh! When did you get out?"

His hands automatically went to her back, to hold her to him for a moment. She was his baby sister, and he'd missed her so much. But part of him also resented her for the sacrifice he'd had to make. And if she'd had anything to do with Henry being taken...

He would never forgive her or himself. He put his hands on her shoulders and pushed her back. "I've been out about eight weeks," he admitted.

Her silver eyes widened. "Eight weeks? That's great. I thought you were going to be in there eight years, so you got out early."

"You would have known if you'd ever come to visit," he said, pain jabbing his heart.

"You told me not to," she reminded him. "And you weren't the only one who warned me to stay away..."

"Luther's dead now," Josh said. "He hasn't been a threat for nearly a year now." So why hadn't she started coming around again?

"Luther's organization and his reach didn't end with his death, and his organization included all kinds of criminals and people you wouldn't expect to be criminals. He had police officers and crime techs and people within the court system on his payroll, too," Sylvie said. "There is still a threat."

Could it have been someone within or associated with that organization who'd taken Henry?

"I need you to tell me the truth," he said. "I need to know if, even though Luther Mills is dead, you're still stealing for Mom, to pay off her debts?"

"Mom's dead, too," Sylvie said.

Pain jabbed his heart, though he shouldn't have been surprised, not with the way their mother had lived her life. But still, she was his mother. She'd given him life. And in giving his father full custody of him, she'd given him a better shot at life than she had his sister. "I'm sorry," he said. "Overdose?"

Sylvie nodded. "She died just a year after you went to prison."

"For something you did," Natalie said, speaking up from behind Josh. "Is that what happened? Is this who the DA thinks you were covering for?"

Sylvie's eyes widened even more as she stared at Natalie. "Who is this? A cop? A lawyer? Why did you bring her here? Are you trying to send me to prison now?"

"We're here because *our son* and my mother are missing," Natalie said, her voice cracking with emotion. "And your brother thinks you might have something to do with it." And clearly Natalie now suspected the same thing.

Sylvie gasped and pressed a hand over her mouth. And Josh didn't know if she was shocked to find out he had a son or shocked because he thought she had something to do with his abduction.

Then tears welled in her eyes, and he felt like he had when she was a little girl. When she would cry every time he left to go back to his dad's, pleading with him to take her with him. Not that he'd gotten to see her that often. But when he had, it had been heart-wrenching, just like it was now.

But he couldn't let her tears distract him from what really mattered now. From whom. Sylvie wasn't a child anymore.

Henry was.

"I need to know, Sylvie," Josh said. "Would anyone from Luther's organization have come after my son? Or those diamonds?"

"What diamonds? And how would they have known about your son when I didn't even know you had one?" she asked.

He hadn't known, either. But he refrained from mentioning that now.

"And I stayed away from you," Sylvie said. "I kept you out of it."

"But not out of prison," Natalie muttered.

"I…" Sylvie swallowed hard. "I didn't know what to do. I still don't."

"What about you, Sylvie?" Josh asked. "Did you take those diamonds? Or my son?"

She shook her head, and the tears slipped free, sliding

down her face. "No, I wouldn't have even if I knew. And I can't believe you would ask me that."

He felt a pang of guilt, but then he reminded himself yet again that she wasn't a little girl anymore. "Can't you understand why I would find it hard to trust you?"

If only Sylvie had told him what was going on with their mother and being forced to steal to cover Monica's debt to Luther Mills, maybe he would have been able to do something before it got so bad.

Before all their lives were in danger...

But clearly, Sylvie wasn't going to admit to anything even if she was involved. He turned to walk away and found that Natalie had already left. He could hear her footsteps on the stairs and rushed after her.

NATALIE WAS IN such a hurry to get away from that apartment, away from Josh and his sister and their lies, that she missed a step. She might have fallen if a strong arm hadn't slid around her waist and caught her. She fell against his body, which fell against the wall.

"Careful," Josh said.

"You weren't," she said. He wasn't careful with her heart all those years ago. "You lied to me."

He hadn't been the thief she'd thought he was, but he'd hurt her all the same. He hadn't deserved his punishment— he'd chosen it. He'd chosen to leave her. And then he'd pushed her away when he'd doubled down on his lies.

Unless maybe it hadn't been a lie when he said he'd never loved her. Because how could he have chosen prison over the life they would have had together if he actually loved her?

"I couldn't tell you the truth," he said. "I know you would have turned her in."

Natalie sucked in a breath. But she couldn't deny it.

"Everything was always so black and white for you," he said.

"It was for you, too," she said. "You were the one with the criminal justice degree. I was just focused on my numbers." And him. He'd been the entire focus of her world that had revolved around her love for him. She'd fallen so damn hard.

So hard that despite how much he'd hurt her, she'd never fully recovered. She'd never really gotten over him, especially when their son reminded her every day of his father.

"It was black and white for me," he said. "Until it came to my sister."

"And you chose her over us," she said. "You chose her over our son."

"I didn't know you were pregnant," he said.

She flinched. But then she reminded him, "You knew that I loved you. You knew that I'd accepted your proposal, your plan for us to get married, and you broke all your promises to me."

"I'm sorry, Natalie," Josh said, his voice gruff. "I'm so sorry. I just didn't know what to do."

"The right thing," she said. "How hard is that?"

"You heard about Luther Mills. He was a ruthless drug dealer with so many powerful people on his payroll that he literally got away with murder for years. You know there were threats. And because of those," he said, "I figured that the right thing to do was to lie and take the blame."

"Then you're not the man I fell in love with after all," she said. "Because he would have known what the right thing really was." She tried to tug away from him, but her foot slipped on another step.

And he pulled her even closer. "I loved you," he said. "I loved you so much, and I hated hurting you. But I couldn't let her go to prison or worse."

"Worse than prison?"

"That man that she was stealing for—"

"Luther Mills," she said. Now she knew why Josh had reacted the way he had when Detective Dubridge mentioned the name.

"Mills would have killed her if he thought she was going to turn on him," he said. "And if she'd been arrested, he might have thought that she would. Potential witnesses to his crimes always wound up dead. Anybody who threatened his operation wound up dead."

Until the Payne Protection Agency got involved. Everybody in River City was aware of what happened from all the news coverage of his arrest and his trial and then his death. River City had seemed like a war zone around that time as Luther tried to take out witnesses and prosecutors and even the judge's daughter.

Luther Mills had failed.

And that was partially why the insurance company had recommended the Payne Protection Agency. Because they'd earned a reputation in this city for getting the job done.

Until now…

Until those diamonds had been stolen.

And their son and her mother.

"I'm sorry, Natalie," Josh said. "I am sorry. And if there was anything else I could have done so I wouldn't hurt you that wouldn't also risk your life or my sister's…"

"It's too late now," Natalie said. "It's too late for us." She believed that he hadn't been a thief then or now. But even though Josh had his reasons for hurting her all those years ago, the past couldn't be undone. He couldn't take back all that pain he'd caused her and all the years they'd lost, not just with each other but with their son.

While she could understand his reasoning, if he'd really

believed that lives were in danger, and even forgive him because of that, she couldn't forget. And because she couldn't forget, she couldn't trust him.

But she couldn't deal with all these feelings, old and new, pummeling her right now, not when she should be focused only on finding her son and her mom.

So while it was too late for them, they had to make sure that it wasn't too late for their son.

HENRY JERKED AWAKE and called out, "Mommy!"

But when his sleepy eyes focused, he could see that he was still in that weird room with the metal walls and the concrete floor. The lamp was burning yet, so it wasn't dark like it had been earlier.

But he was still scared.

And despite the blankets and the air mattress, he was cold and stiff. Even with Mimi's arm around him. She was holding him, but she was asleep again.

And the skin around that cut on her forehead was swollen and bruised, like the worst bruise he'd ever seen. She probably still needed a doctor.

And Henry needed his mommy. But it wasn't Mommy who was supposed to find him. "Daddy…"

He had to find them soon. Henry wanted to go home to Mommy. He wanted to make sure that Mimi was all right, too. Because even when she was awake, she seemed more like Grandpa than herself right now.

Confused.

But she wasn't too confused that she wasn't scared, which made Henry scared, too. She didn't think this was really a game like the person in the mask had told them.

And Henry was beginning to think it wasn't, either.

If it wasn't a game, then were there any rules for finding

him? Even if his daddy found those diamonds, would the person let him know where they were and how to find them? Or would they just leave him and Mimi here forever?

Chapter Eleven

Natalie was right. It was too late for them. Josh had hurt her so badly that he didn't blame her for not being able to forgive him or even to understand why he'd done what he had five years ago. But back then, and even now, he couldn't see another way to keep everyone he'd loved safe. His sister's and mother's lives had been threatened, and his own and even Natalie's, so he'd no choice but to plead guilty.

Now his son's life was at stake, and Josh still wasn't sure if it was because of him or because of Sylvie.

She stood in the open doorway to her apartment, staring down at them on the stairs.

"I'm sorry," she said. "I'm sorry that your son…my nephew is missing." She looked from Josh to Natalie. "And I'm sorry about…everything else."

Natalie stiffened. She was obviously and understandably not ready to forgive his sister any more than she was ready to forgive him.

"Sylvie, if you know anything, please, tell me," Josh urged her.

She held up her hands. "I didn't take the diamonds, I swear. I left that life behind just like I promised you I would. It just took me a little longer, but that's another story for another day."

He nodded because if she couldn't help him, he was just wasting his time here. "Yeah, we really have to get going." Maybe Milek and the others from the Payne Protection Agencies had made more progress than Josh had. Or Detective Dubridge and the River City PD might have figured out something from that video phone call Josh had recorded. He wanted to see it again himself, to search for clues and to see his son again. "We need to go to the police—"

Sylvie gasped again, like she had earlier with a shock that sounded almost painful.

"Not about you," he said. "About Henry."

"Henry," she repeated the name with a sad smile. "That's cute. But if someone's got him, didn't they tell you not to involve the police?"

He shook his head. "There was nothing like that," he said. "No threat to not call the police. Just that I needed to hand over these damn diamonds that I didn't take—"

"Sucks to be accused of something you didn't do," she interjected. Then her face flushed. "I was talking about stealing the diamonds. But you know that better than anyone. I am sorry."

He shrugged off her apology. Just like Natalie had said moments ago, it was too late. Too late to undo what was done, to give him back those five years.

"So where did these diamonds go missing from?" Sylvie asked.

Natalie cleared her throat. "Croft Custom Jewelry."

Sylvie's brow furrowed beneath a lock of tawny hair. "That little family store? They had that much on hand?"

Natalie cleared her throat again. "Not usually, but there is often a rush of engagements around now."

"Wouldn't that be around Valentine's Day, not a month later?" Sylvie asked.

Natalie's lips curved slightly. "There are sometimes more

engagements after, because someone was expecting a ring and was more than a little disappointed with a box of chocolates."

Sylvie chuckled. "Makes sense. So what are we talking about? Diamonds already in rings?"

"No. They were loose stones. Different cuts and carats, ready to be put into rings."

Sylvie whistled slightly. "So worth a lot of money?"

Natalie nodded.

"I might have some idea of how to help you find them," Sylvie admitted.

Josh felt sick. He'd started to believe that she was telling him the truth, that she'd left that old life behind. But obviously she still had connections to it. He wanted to be the protective big brother he should have been for her when they were younger, before everything had gotten so out of hand. But right now, he didn't care about the past or even about the future.

He just wanted to get that little boy and his grandmother back home. He started up the stairs toward his sister. "Okay, tell me how..."

And even if it led to his arrest, like it had the last time he'd listened to his sister and held *something* for her, it would be worth it if they got Henry and Marilyn Croft back.

Natalie was numb with shock and exhaustion. The coffee cup she held had gone cold while Josh's sister sent a flurry of texts and answered some calls, her voice pitched low. One of those texts had probably been to send away whoever was supposed to come over to study with her because nobody else showed up at her place.

Natalie took a sip or two of the nutmeg-and-cinnamon-spiced coffee Sylvie had handed her, but the caffeine churned in her empty stomach. She couldn't think about herself right now, though. She could think only of Henry.

Was he hungry still?

Was he cold?

Was he scared?

Or did he still think this was all some damn game?

Josh had chugged a couple cups of coffee already. But then she remembered that he'd been awake all night, watching her store. Protecting it.

If only someone had been protecting their son...

Mom had obviously tried. How badly was she hurt?

A little cry slipped from her lips as she thought of the blood on the garage floor. Of her mother being drugged and then hurt.

Josh settled next to her on the small sofa and slid his arm around her. "You're exhausted," he said. "Let me get an Uber to drive you back to your sister's place."

She shuddered at the thought of going back there to judgmental Dena and oblivious Timothy. Her father was the least confused of the three of them because he always knew what mattered most. Family.

That was clearly what had mattered most to Josh five years ago when he'd chosen his sister's safety over the life he and Natalie had planned. But he hadn't known then about the life they'd started. What would he have done if he'd known she was pregnant?

Unfortunately, she hadn't found out until after he'd already pled guilty to something he hadn't done. Would he have been able to undo that? Or were he and Sylvie right that Luther Mills would have hurt them more, all of them, if Josh hadn't taken the blame for something he hadn't done?

Luther Mills had obviously wanted Sylvie to keep stealing for him. Or maybe he'd been worried that if she was arrested, she would have turned over evidence against him?

No matter his reason, Luther Mills had had no compunction against killing. He'd killed a young police informant in front of the teenager's sister to send a message to anyone coming after him. And that young man hadn't been his only victim. After Luther's death, countless other crimes of his and of the people on his payroll had been exposed.

But there was speculation that not everybody on Luther's payroll had been discovered. That there could be others. So that danger he'd posed might not have ended even with his death. The man had been that evil.

Knowing that, Natalie couldn't stay angry with Josh if he truly believed he'd been protecting her by pushing her away.

Instead of pulling away from his touch, as she had before, she leaned into him, drawing from his warmth and strength. Her numbness receded as she began to feel again. And it wasn't just the fear this time. She also felt that tingling awareness she'd had from the first moment she'd met Josh Stafford in the college bookstore.

He was so good-looking and strong and warm. Her first impression of him had been right, that he had been protective then. He'd been protective of his sister and mom and even of her.

He just hadn't protected her heart. So no matter how much she'd loved him once, she would be foolish to trust him with her heart again.

She sucked in a breath and eased away from him now. But there wasn't a lot of space that she could get away from him on that small sofa, so she still felt the heat of his body, still felt the awareness in hers.

Maybe she should go back to her sister's. But the thought of seeing Dena again made her stomach churn more than the coffee had.

Maybe Dena had lashed out because she was worried about their mother and Henry. But Josh's sister, who'd just learned of his existence, seemed more visibly concerned about Henry than Dena, who'd been part of his life since his birth. Albeit a small part.

"At least close your eyes for a bit," Josh suggested. "Try to get some rest."

"You were up all night last night, weren't you?" Natalie asked. She'd seen him on the security footage; she knew that he hadn't had any rest.

He nodded. "But I'm used to not getting much sleep."

Maybe that was just because he worked nights, or maybe that was because of being in prison. She couldn't imagine how hard the past five years of his life had been.

"There's no time to sleep now," Sylvie said as she held up her phone. "I have a possible lead. Someone I used to know was approached about a bag of diamonds—"

"Let's call Detective Dubridge!" Natalie exclaimed.

Sylvie shook her head. "You'll never see those diamonds again if you involve the police. And people would probably get hurt as well."

By people, Natalie suspected she meant herself. Or maybe she meant Henry. And if that was the case, then Natalie had to agree with her that it wasn't wise to call the detective no matter how dangerous this might be.

"I'm worried about you getting hurt," Josh said.

"He'll give *me* details about this person, in person, but only me." Sylvie dropped her cell phone into a bag she was draping over her shoulder. "I'll meet with him and let you know what I find out."

"No," Josh said. "If you're really out of this life, I don't want you getting involved in it again. Call him back. Tell him he's going to meet with your brother instead."

"It doesn't work like that," Sylvie said. "You can't just go in my place."

"So it's not like prison," Natalie muttered, her bitterness overwhelming her.

"Tell him I'm an ex-con," Josh said.

"You can go with me," Sylvie said, "since you obviously don't trust me, but you can't go alone."

"I won't be alone—"

"I said no cops."

"Milek Kozminski isn't a cop any more than I am."

"Kozminski?" Sylvie asked, her voice cracking slightly. "What do you know about the Kozminskis?"

"I work for two of them now," Josh said. "Milek and his older brother, Garek, and Garek's wife, too."

"The Kozminskis are thieves. You don't want me in that life, but you're in it?" she asked.

"I work for them at the Payne Protection Agency. They're good guys," he said. "But since you're not aware of that, your fence probably isn't, either."

"He's not *my* fence," Sylvie said, but her face was flushed. "Not anymore…"

"I don't care what he was or is," Josh said. "I just want to find those diamonds, so when the person holding Henry calls back, I can tell them I have what they want."

Sylvie sighed. "All right then. I'll set it up." She pulled her cell from her purse. "What's your number?" she asked him. "I'll forward you the location."

Natalie stood up. "I'll go with you."

Josh snorted. "Not a chance. You should go back to your sister's—"

"I'd rather stay here," she said. With his sister, not her own. Hopefully her father was asleep now. But she wouldn't have been much comfort to him, not with how upset she was.

Then it occurred to her that Sylvie probably didn't want her here. She wasn't sure where else she would go, though, since her home was still a crime scene. "I can go somewhere else…if you have to study."

Sylvie held up her phone. "I sent a text canceling that. This is more important."

Natalie felt a sudden flash of warmth toward Sylvie Combs.

But Josh hesitated a moment, looking from one to the other of them. "I don't think this is a good idea," he said.

"It probably isn't," Natalie agreed. "But if we need those diamonds to get our son back, it's worth it." But he was the one taking the risk, and from the way his sister talked, it might be his life he was risking.

"I don't know if you should stay here with Sylvie," he said.

Which of them was he worried about? He probably thought Natalie was furious with his sister because she'd let him go to prison for something she'd done. And he also didn't trust his sister any more than Natalie did.

"This guy isn't going to wait around for you," Sylvie warned him. "And I'm not going to corrupt my nephew's mother during the short time she'll be here." She must have concluded he was worried about Natalie.

Josh's lips curved into a slight smile. "I'd like to think you wouldn't try, but even if you do, Natalie is incorruptible."

That was why he hadn't told Natalie the truth five years ago. He'd believed she wouldn't let him plead guilty for something he hadn't done, and she would have gone, maybe to the wrong people, to try to save him from prison. And in trying to save him, she would have put herself, him and his sister in danger.

But did he know that she would have done that out of love? Or had he thought she was too judgmental and self-righteous back then?

And maybe she had been. Because she couldn't understand why people would do anything against the law…

But now, loving her son like she did, she knew that she would do anything to keep him safe, even steal some damn diamonds herself.

"Go!" she urged Josh. "We will be fine." She really did feel more comfortable with his sister than her own right now. She couldn't imagine how Sylvie would have gotten inside the store, past the security system and stolen the bag of diamonds. It made much more sense that it was an inside job, which left her family as possible suspects.

Josh hesitated for another moment, and he was standing so close to her that she thought he was going to kiss her, especially when he touched her chin. But he didn't lower his head or tip hers up like he used to. He just ran his knuckle along her jaw. "Be safe," he said. Then he turned and headed out the door.

"You, too," Natalie whispered. But it was too late. He was already gone.

"He's going to be fine," Sylvie said.

"How can you know that?" Natalie asked, and that fury bubbled up inside her again. Obviously, she cared more about him than his sister did. "How could you know five years ago that he would survive prison?" Because it hadn't been just a life-and-death situation for her, it had been for him as well.

Sylvie's pale, silvery eyes widened for a moment. "Oh, we're going to go there…"

"I just don't understand how you could let him take the punishment for something you did," Natalie said.

Tears filled Sylvie's pale eyes. "I didn't know what to do back then. I wasn't even in my teens when Luther made me start stealing to pay off my mother's debts. And he swore if I told anyone, he would kill them and me. Then when Josh was arrested, I didn't know how to get myself out of that situation, let alone how to get him out. I was just nineteen then. For so many years Luther convinced me that there was nobody I could trust, that he had the whole damn police department on his payroll and the DA's office." She blinked furiously at the tears that brimmed over into her lashes. "And maybe I was mad at Josh. He got to live with his dad and his grandma, and I got *her*. Our mother, the raging narcissist. All she cared about was herself, making herself feel better, whatever it took. And it took a lot..." She squeezed her eyes shut. "And maybe back then I was too much like her, too selfish and scared to do what was right for Josh or even for myself."

Sylvie started toward the door then, her hand on the strap of the bag she'd slung over her shoulder. "But now I know that he will be fine because he's not the one meeting with the person who has the actual lead. I am."

Natalie jumped up from the sofa and headed after her. "You can't—"

"I want to help get your son back," Sylvie said. "Don't try to stop me."

Natalie didn't want to stop her, if that was truly what she was doing. But she didn't trust Sylvie Combs. She couldn't trust someone who'd let another person, let alone her own brother, go to prison for something she'd done.

For all Natalie knew, those diamonds might be in Sylvie's bag. She might not be meeting the fence who had a lead on them, she might be fencing them herself.

And then their leverage to get their son back would be gone.

MILEK JERKED AWAKE from the vibration of the desk where he'd lain his head. For a minute. Just a minute...

The vibration was from his cell, the screen lit up with a text of an address. Josh sent him an address. He reached for the phone just as it rang.

"Where is this?" he asked, his pulse quickening with

excitement. "Did you find him and his grandmother? Are they there?"

"No. But the diamonds might be," Josh said. "Or at least a lead to them."

"What kind of lead?" Milek asked. "Is this a fence?"

"I think so. I don't know for sure, though," Josh replied, as if he'd been given information he couldn't trust. "But I'm going there to find out."

"Wait for me." Because whoever had those diamonds wasn't going to give them up without a fight.

With their current market value, the thief would have no compunction against killing to keep them.

Chapter Twelve

Josh pulled up to the alley behind the nightclub. This was where Sylvie had set up the meeting. Not inside the night-club but in the alley.

It wasn't like the alley behind Croft Custom Jewelry. It was too narrow for him to drive into, so he had to park down the block, in the only free spot he'd been able to find. While the club was obviously busy, judging from all the vehicles parked around it and the music booming out of it, the street was dimly lit.

Only one light glowed next to the club's door, so the peo-ple waiting to get inside were lined up in the dark. Josh walked past them, probably as invisible to them as they were to him.

Was one of those people the one he was supposed to meet? Or were they already in the alley?

He just about walked past it like he'd driven past it just a short while ago. It was so narrow and dark, and as he started down it, he nearly tripped and gagged because it was so lit-tered with trash. The acrid smell of it filled his nostrils. He could almost taste the garbage.

Or maybe that was the fear.

Fear that this wasn't going to lead anywhere, that it was a dead end. And not just the alley...

But he had to check it out, just in case it was a viable lead to those diamonds.

Not that he gave a damn about them, but whoever was holding his son and Marilyn Croft cared about them. And so he didn't dare wait for Milek in case whoever Sylvie had set up this meeting with took off with what was his only possible lead to those damn diamonds.

Maybe he would have waited for Milek if he thought it was going to actually be dangerous. Or that it was going to be anything at all.

But he didn't trust Sylvie. She was his sister, and he still loved her. But after what she'd done...

He wasn't sure he'd ever really known her. And maybe he hadn't. While Sylvie was just four years younger than his twenty-eight, they hadn't grown up together. His father hadn't even let him visit her or their mother that often. Every time he had, she would beg to come home with him, and he would be upset to leave her. So his father had started limiting those visits even more.

When they were older and had phones, they texted each other and had video calls. But they were both busy with friends and school. Or so he'd thought.

But she'd been doing other things. Stealing.

He wouldn't have believed her capable of that if she hadn't confessed to him after he'd been arrested with that package she'd asked him to hold for her. He'd been uneasy when he'd done that, wondering if there were drugs inside, but there had been jewels instead and some loose stones like the ones that were missing. And someone had been tipped off that Josh had had them.

Sylvie had been so upset when she'd come to see him in jail. She'd been apologetic then that he was involved, but she'd also obviously been afraid for her life and their mother's and for his. And when she'd confessed that Luther Mills was the one who'd forced her to steal to pay off their mother's debts, he'd understood that fear. And he'd been afraid, too, especially when the officer escorting him back to his holding cell after visitation with his sister had whispered to him that he needed to plead guilty or bad things would happen to a lot of people.

So he'd believed Sylvie. But even though she'd told him the truth back then, that didn't mean she'd told him the truth now about this lead. Was it real or just a wild goose chase?

He and the rats that he could hear scurrying and squeaking in the dark were probably the only living things in this alley.

But then something else moved in the dark, its footsteps heavy. Before he could react, something jabbed into his back. Something cold and hard. The barrel of a gun.

And he realized that soon those rats might be the only living thing in the alley. Well, the rats and whoever was about to shoot him.

FORTUNATELY NATALIE HAD managed to use a charger of Sylvie's to charge her cell some because the minute Sylvie ran out of her apartment, Natalie opened the Uber app to order a car. It probably wouldn't have arrived in time to catch up with her if Sylvie had transportation of her own. But she was waiting outside for a vehicle, too.

Instead of standing in the shadows of the porch like Natalie, Sylvie paced in the street, obviously impatient to get away.

With the diamonds?

Josh wouldn't have come here if he hadn't had doubts about his sister, just as Natalie had doubts about her family. But would any of them risk lives for money?

She cringed as she realized how damn naive she was. So many people did exactly that. They didn't just risk lives,

they actually killed for money. Sylvie was capable of stealing. Was she capable of killing?

A vehicle turned onto the street and then stopped abruptly,
its brakes screeching. Sylvie didn't even appear to flinch as
the headlights illuminated her. She could have been hit. But
she didn't even move now. Then those bright lights flicked
on and then off.

This wasn't a car for hire like the one Natalie had requested. This was someone else picking Sylvie up, someone who knew her.

The young woman ran around to the passenger's side and
pulled open the door.

Natalie's stomach sank with dread that she was going to
lose her. But her phone pinged.

Here.

A car pulled up right as the other one pulled away. She
ran down the front steps and rushed to the vehicle. As she
yanked open the door, she said, "Follow that car. Hurry!"

The older guy behind the wheel laughed. "Seriously?
You're going to Charleston—"

She'd typed in her sister's address on the app. But she
shook her head now. "No, please, follow that car."

"Why?" the guy asked. "Cheating spouse?"

"Cheating something," she suspected. "My little boy is
missing, and I think that person might be able to help me
find him."

"The kid from the news? The cute little guy with dark
eyes?"

She nodded. "Yes, Henry Croft is my son."

The tires squealed as the guy's vehicle peeled away from
the curb. "I have five kids and ten grandkids," he said. "I
can't imagine what you're going through, lady."

"Thank you for doing this," she said. "But please don't get too close. I don't want her to see me."

"Sure, sure. Are you going to call the police?" he asked as he glanced back at her.

She shook her head. "And tell them what? That I have a hunch? I don't have anything more than that."

He nodded. "Okay. We'll follow them and see what's up. But I can already tell from the direction we're heading that it's not to any place good, any place safe."

She'd been right to follow Sylvie. She was meeting with the person who might actually have the diamonds or maybe she even had them herself.

So who was Josh meeting with and was he really in no danger like his sister claimed?

Sylvie had already risked his life once; she probably would have no compunction against doing it again. Sylvie had admitted to resenting her older brother when they were kids, so she might still resent him. Maybe even enough that she would do anything to hurt him.

Like take his son...

Was Sylvie leading Natalie to the diamonds or to her son? And if it was to Henry, then what the driver said scared her. Henry and her mother weren't anywhere safe.

And soon Natalie, and this very kind driver, would not be safe, either. She felt guilty for involving him, but she was desperate to save her son and her mother if it wasn't already too late.

WOODROW WAS USED to getting calls at all hours, not that it was very late right now. But those calls were one of the reasons why he was planning to retire. The other reason was the woman lying next to him. He wanted to spend more time with her.

All the time that he had. He'd come close to dying just a

few short years ago, and it had put into perspective for him what was most important. Family.

And love.

His love, Penny, released a shaky breath. "So they didn't find the boy yet?"

"No." The Amber alert had solicited a lot of calls, but so far all of those suspected sightings of the boy and the vehicle had proven to be of someone else and some other car. No one so far had seen the real boy, except on that recording his father had taken of the video call. And his grandmother and her vehicle were also nowhere to be found.

Penny sighed again. "When the phone rang…"

"I'm sorry that woke you up," he said, and he slid his arm around her, cuddling her close to him. She was so warm and soft, so perfect.

"I was awake," she said. "I don't think I will be able to sleep until that little boy is found safe and sound. I can't imagine the fear and pain his mother is going through."

"Actually, I think you can," Woodrow said. "All of our kids have been in dangerous situations before. We've been lucky that we haven't lost any of them."

"But they were older," Penny said. "They were all able to fend for themselves. He's just a little boy."

"A little boy that a lot of people are willing to do anything to find." Especially his father.

Josh Stafford had just risked his life and his freedom for a possible lead to either the child or the diamonds. He was convinced that he would need the diamonds to get the boy and Mrs. Croft back.

But as a former FBI agent, Woodrow knew that paying the ransom didn't always guarantee the safe return of the hostages. Most kidnappers killed their hostages rather than risk those hostages being able to identify them.

And in this case…

How it was all playing out…

The kidnapper almost had to be someone in the hostages' world. Someone who worked at the store and knew the family. Or maybe even…

One of the bodyguards.

What was certain was that in cases like this, it was really hard to trust anyone and really hard to hang onto hope that the hostages would be returned unharmed.

Chapter Thirteen

Once the police officer who'd nearly arrested him in that alley let him go, Josh headed straight for his sister's apartment. The officer, Sheila Carlson, probably wouldn't have released him if not for Milek showing up and calling the chief of the River City PD.

Officer Carlson had been nearly as desperate for a lead to those diamonds as he was. "Sylvie said you knew something about them."

"Sylvie told me you were the fence," Josh said. Clearly Sylvie had set them both up to waste their time. Or to distract them.

Why the hell was his sister so close with a police officer? And why had that police officer been so quick to pull a gun on him?

Like Sylvie had just reminded him, Luther Mills had had police officers and more on his payroll as part of his criminal organization. Just like that officer so long ago who'd escorted Josh back to the holding cell after Sylvie had come to see him. That police officer had threatened him into pleading guilty, so he'd been on Luther's payroll, too.

Josh really couldn't trust anyone.

He should have been relieved Officer Carlson hadn't pulled the trigger. But whatever the hell else his meeting in the alley had been, it had also been a waste of time. He drove so fast back to Sylvie's place that he was surprised he didn't have the police trying to arrest him again for reckless driving. Because he had a feeling that officer was probably following him…

She hadn't been happy about talking to Chief Lynch. After ending the call, she had made a remark as she uncuffed Josh about having a Get Out of Jail Free card.

Hell, if Josh had that, he would have used it long ago.

Chief Lynch was only giving him leeway because his son was missing. Milek had explained that to Josh and warned him not to push it and not to go off alone again.

But Josh had left his boss dealing with the irate officer and rushed right back here. Not just to Sylvie but to Natalie, too.

He shouldn't have left her with his sister. He should have insisted she go back to her sister's house. Or somewhere else, somewhere she would be safe.

She wasn't safe with Sylvie.

Once he pulled up to the curb outside the Queen Anne, he jumped out and ran up to the porch. He touched the intercom button for 2C, but nothing happened. The door didn't unlock. He pressed it again. Harder.

Still nothing.

The door remained locked.

So he pressed all the other buttons until, finally, someone unlocked it. He pulled it open and rushed inside, running up the stairs.

The door to Sylvie's apartment wasn't locked. It pushed open easily. And he stepped inside to find it empty.

The place was small, just an open area with a bed that folded from a bookshelf and a tiny bathroom. There was no place for anyone to hide in it.

Where the hell were they?

Maybe Natalie had gone back to her sister's. But somehow Josh doubted it, and he didn't want to waste time driving over there if she was somewhere else, somewhere she might need help, like their son and her mother needed help.

Had she been taken, too?

He didn't have her cell number. Why the hell hadn't he gotten it earlier?

So he couldn't call her.

But he had Sylvie's number from when she'd texted him earlier. He tried to call, but it went right to voicemail, a voicemail that hadn't yet been set up for this phone. Was it even her phone or a burner?

How badly had she betrayed him?

And once again he'd risked Natalie's life because of Sylvie. He had to find her and make sure she was all right. His hand shaking, Josh grasped his phone and tried another number. This time the person answered.

"Nikki, this is Josh Stafford," he said.

"I know," she replied. "And I promise I'm not going to stop going over this recording of your son until I can figure out where he and his grandmother are being held. If only—"

"Right now, I need to know where his mother is," he said.

"I thought she was with you," Nikki replied.

He cursed. "I screwed up. I left her alone to chase down a damn dead end. Do you have her number? Can you ping her location?"

"I've got her number and a great program. I'll narrow it down as much as I can."

He heard the stroke of the keyboard and then a curse.

"What?" he asked.

"Her phone must be off—"

Then he remembered that it had died earlier. That was why she had to try to call her sister and brother-in-law from the store phone. While she'd used Sylvie's charger, it must not have been long to keep the battery from draining again.

"I've got another number," he said. And he read off the one from his sister's phone. That was probably off, too, though. "I'm not sure they're together…"

But he had a horrible feeling that they were.

Nikki cursed again.

"That phone dead, too?" he asked. He wouldn't have put it past Sylvie to destroy it even if it wasn't a burner.

"No, I found a location," Nikki replied with a shaky breath.

It wasn't good.

He knew that even before Nikki told him where it was. He knew because of how tightly his stomach was clenching and how the short hairs on the nape of his neck were standing on end.

He'd made a big mistake trusting his sister. The last time he had it had cost him his freedom. This time it might cost a life. The life of the woman he'd never stopped loving and apparently had also never stopped hurting.

THE DRIVER WASN'T wrong about the area. It didn't look safe. People congregated on sidewalks and in the streets, but they didn't do it under the few streetlamps; instead they slunk in the shadows.

"We need to turn around and get the hell out of here," the driver remarked.

"But if this is where my son is…" She didn't want to believe that, though, that her little boy and her mother were somewhere around here. Because it definitely was not safe. She felt bad about pressing the driver to keep following that vehicle, but if she lost it, she felt like she might lose the one chance of finding her son and mom.

"You need to call the police," the driver said. "But I don't think even they come down here. I know we shouldn't be here."

"Thank you for bringing me," she said. "Thank you…" Tears stung her eyes.

"I really want to turn around," he said, his voice trembling with the fear gripping her.

But then the vehicle they were following turned off the scary street. The driver released a slight sigh as he turned to follow it. It went down a few more roads, deeper and deeper into an industrial area.

"This is weird," he murmured.

And then the car they were following seemed to disappear. The lights went off, and it just dropped out of sight.

"I don't see it," he said. "Where the hell…" The road seemed to end at a dock of some kind. "Did it drive off into the water?"

"Where are we now?" she asked.

"The river," the driver responded. "It winds through the whole damn city, but I don't think I've ever been in this area."

There were buildings and shipping containers all around. But few lights and no people.

"We lost them," he said.

"No. No. They have to be here," she murmured. "In one of the buildings or…" Maybe even one of those shipping containers. It would be the perfect place to hide people where no one would see or hear them. Her pulse quickened. "I bet my son is here."

"Then we need to call the police," he said.

"I—I don't think that's a good idea…" If the kidnappers heard sirens, they might get rid of the hostages. She couldn't take that risk. "I'm going to get out," she said. "And just look around."

"Miss Croft, this is a really bad idea," the driver warned her.

She couldn't argue with him. And she couldn't put his life in danger, either, but she was so desperate to find her son and her mom. "You stay here. Or drive off if you want," she said. "I have to look. If my son is here…"

If she did nothing to save him even though she was so close, she would never forgive herself if something happened to him or her mother. She might never forgive herself anyway.

"Be careful," he said.

She pushed open the door and stepped out. Then she started walking toward the building. Maybe the sound of his car engine got quieter because she was walking away from him. Or because her heart was beating so fast and hard that it was all she could hear.

Or maybe the man was driving off like she'd told him he could.

Either way Natalie had never felt as alone or as scared as she did now. But maybe she wasn't alone. Maybe her son and her mother were here, too.

But how the hell was she, on her own, going to save them from their kidnapper?

MILEK HAD JUST sat back down at Garek's desk when his cell rang again, but when he saw who was calling, he breathed a sigh of relief.

"Nikki, I was just going to call you," he said. "I need you to help me find Josh Stafford."

Josh had disappeared so fast from the alley that Milek hadn't even realized he was gone until Officer Carlson had pointed it out to him.

"You shouldn't let him go off alone like that," she'd admonished him. "That guy is so desperate that he's going to get himself killed."

That was what Milek was afraid of.

"Or he's going to get someone else killed," Carlson had added. "And I always heard that the Payne Protection bodyguards were the best."

"We are," Milek had insisted. "But he's not a bodyguard right now. He's a father whose child is missing." And from personal experience, Milek knew how desperate that made a dad, desperate enough to do anything to get him back.

Even give up his own life...

"He just asked me to find someone for him, so I have a pretty good idea where he is," Nikki replied. "And he's going to need backup."

Josh hadn't called for it like he had the last time, though. But he hadn't waited for Milek then, either. Or maybe he didn't trust him to get there in time.

Maybe, after his own sister set him up to either get shot or arrested in that alley, Josh didn't trust anyone anymore. Milek could understand that.

"Who did he have you track down?" Milek asked.

"First he had me try to find Natalie Croft, but her phone is dead," Nikki said. "So then he had me track down another number. The name the service provider has on the account is Sylvie Combs."

Josh's sister. That was who had brought both Officer Carlson and Josh to that dark alley just a short while ago. What the hell was the young woman up to?

She was the one who Amber suspected had really been the thief all those years ago. Was she still?

Or was she more than a thief now?

Was she also a killer?

Chapter Fourteen

God, Josh hoped he was wrong. He hoped like hell that Natalie wasn't with his sister, that she was with her own sister instead. That she was safe with her dad and her brother-in-law in that high-class house that probably had a great security system.

There was no security down here.

Especially not for Josh who couldn't even carry a gun, only the damn canister of pepper spray. Just driving through a neighborhood like this, with gangs and prostitutes and drug dealers, could be a death sentence.

Why would Sylvie have come down here? And why would she have brought Natalie with her?

He hoped like hell that she hadn't. But his gut, his clenched stomach, was warning him that she had.

His cell rang, then connected automatically to the speakers in the SUV.

"What the hell are you doing?" Milek asked him. "Down there? In that area on your own?"

"I'm trying to find my sister and Natalie," Josh said, although he figured that Milek probably already knew exactly what he was doing. "Nikki must be the one who told you where I am and that I'm here because I had her ping my sister's cell."

"Yeah, she also told me about a call she heard on the police scanner while she was on the phone with me," Milek said. "A rideshare driver called in and said that he dropped off a woman near the river just past the area where you are now. She claimed to be Henry Croft's mother."

Josh's blood chilled as his suspicion was confirmed. He shivered.

"He just left her and drove off?" he asked, his heart beating fast and hard with fear for her.

"He wasn't sure what to do," Milek said. "It's a dangerous area."

Josh could see that for himself. "But to leave her alone down here..."

"They were following someone," he said.

"Sylvie..."

"She thought the person might lead her to her son," Milek said.

A place by the river with shipping containers and warehouses. It would be a great hiding place for hostages, especially in an area like this where even if anybody heard or saw anything, they wouldn't tell anyone. They wouldn't want the police coming down here.

"Units are on the way," Milek said. "You need to just stay in your vehicle and wait for them to arrive."

Josh's lights shone on a sign for a shipping company, and he turned onto the street, following it down toward the warehouses, containers and the river.

"Wait in your vehicle," Milek said again. "The police are on the way."

They must have been coming with sirens off because when Josh shut off the SUV engine, he didn't hear anything. It was almost eerily quiet, so much so that he opened his door to listen.

Milek's voice broke the silence, "Josh—"

"What would you do if your son and his mother were in danger?" he asked.

Milek cursed, probably because he knew he couldn't argue with him. He couldn't convince Josh to do something he wouldn't have done himself.

Josh disconnected the call. Then he stepped out onto the cracked asphalt.

There were no other vehicles in sight. Obviously, the rideshare driver had just left her here, but at least he'd made that call to the police.

But where was the vehicle he'd said they followed? Sylvie's vehicle?

He had no idea what his sister might drive. He hadn't even known that she was still in River City for sure until Milek tracked her down. But Josh had had his suspicions when Sylvie stopped trying to visit him that she hadn't held up her end of the deal he'd made with her. Maybe she didn't have a choice, just like Luther Mills had given her no choice when she was just a kid. Or maybe it was all she knew.

Despite what she claimed about no longer stealing, she was all too aware of what was going on in the criminal world. Somehow, she even knew which officer was handling the theft at the jewelry store. And she knew a fence for stolen property, for items of as much value as those missing diamonds.

If that was who she was really meeting here...

At least she hadn't brought Natalie along with her. Natalie had followed her, apparently believing that his sister might lead her to their son and her mother.

Was the little boy here somewhere?

Josh wanted to call out for Henry, for Natalie...even for his sister. But that eerie silence kept him quiet, had him moving slowly toward those buildings. Whatever vehicle

Sylvie had driven here had to be in one of the warehouses or maybe even a shipping container.

Some of the asphalt of the parking lot wasn't just cracked. It was crumbling, and the toe of his hiking boot hit a chunk, sending it tumbling ahead of him to roll against the side of one of those buildings. The bang as the asphalt struck the metal reverberated in the silence.

And then another bang rang out.

A gunshot. But no bullets struck the ground near him. The shot was echoing inside one of the warehouses.

Was he already too late?

NATALIE HAD DONE her best to move quietly. To be careful. To draw no attention to herself as she searched the area for Sylvie and, more important, for her mother and her son. That was why it was a shock when the gunshots rang out, bullets ricocheting off the metal walls of the building she'd entered a short while ago.

Then lights flashed on, and an engine revved.

Natalie had found the vehicle that Sylvie had taken to this horrible area.

Then Sylvie stepped into the beam of the vehicle's head-lights. She wasn't inside it anymore. And this time Natalie wasn't sure that it was going to stop for the young woman like it had in the street outside Sylvie's apartment earlier that evening. It seemed intent on heading directly for her.

Fear welling inside her, Natalie screamed, "Sylvie!"

And more shots rang out.

Sylvie fell.

Natalie screamed again. Then she realized that Sylvie had been knocked to the ground by a body and hopefully not a bullet.

A man with dark hair had pushed Sylvie out of the way of

the vehicle that sped now out of the building, bullets pinging off it.

Natalie recognized the man's dark hair and muscular body. Josh had stepped in front of a speeding vehicle, in front of a barrage of bullets to save his sister. But had he once again sacrificed himself in the process of protecting Sylvie?

"Josh!" Natalie yelled from where she was hidden in the shadows on the other side of the warehouse from them. Her heart hammered with fear for him, fear that she might have lost him again. "Are you all right?"

At the sound of her voice, more shots rang out, chipping away at the wood of the crate she was crouched beside. But at the moment she didn't care about herself as much as she did him. He was the kind of man who kept putting himself in danger to save others. He was the kind of man she'd thought he was all those years ago.

And she wished like hell that back at his sister's apartment she had kissed him before he left. She'd thought for a moment that he was going to kiss her, but he hadn't.

And now he might not get the chance. To kiss her. Or to meet his son.

"Get down!" Josh yelled at her. Then to Sylvie who was struggling to get back up, "What the hell—"

"Let me shoot back at them!" Sylvie said as she pulled something from the bag she'd brought with her. Obviously his sister had a gun.

"Get down!" Josh yelled again.

Natalie wasn't sure if he was talking to her or his sister. And then more shots rang out. Some struck the wood crate, sending chips and splinters raining down on her. She lay flat against the cold concrete now, trying not to get hit. Her heart pounded so hard that she was surprised it didn't crack the concrete.

She wasn't afraid just for herself, but for Josh and Sylvie, too. Because the bullets were flying all around, pinging off the metal walls. Josh or Sylvie must have been firing some, too, because there were so many gunshots. They reverberated inside Natalie's head, ringing in her ears.

But despite the noise inside the warehouse, she could also hear sirens in the distance. Someone had called the police.

But would they get here in time? They had to because this time Josh might be sacrificing more than his freedom to save his sister and her. He might be sacrificing his life.

The shooting inside the warehouse suddenly stopped. She wasn't sure if that was because the shooter had heard the sirens, too. Or it was quiet because the shooter and maybe Josh and Sylvie, too, had been struck.

Was it already too late for help?

WHEN WOODROW RECEIVED a second call that night, Penny had been hopeful that the boy and his grandmother had been found. Woodrow had even seemed hopeful after dispatch let him know that someone called in saying that there was a possible location for the hostages.

Penny jumped out of bed and started getting dressed. She was eager to find out if the boy was okay. Woodrow was, too. He was putting his clothes back on as well.

But then his phone rang again. And as he listened to the caller, his whole demeanor changed. His body was tense again, and when he disconnected the call, he wouldn't meet her gaze.

"What is it?" she asked as she stepped closer to him. "What happened?" Because it was clear that something had. Something bad. She didn't need her sixth sense to tell her that; she could feel it. She could feel it in her husband, in his concern and his dread.

"That location," he murmured, his voice gruff, "where it was suspected the hostages might be…"

"Henry," Penny corrected him. "Henry and Marilyn." They weren't just hostages. They were people. *Real* people. Important people. People who were loved, who were needed, by their family and their friends.

Woodrow nodded. "Yes..."

"What happened?" she asked.

"We don't know yet," he said. "But there are reports of gunfire now at that location."

So if the hostages were there, their kidnapper wasn't giving them up without a fight. Or they were getting rid of them for good...

Chapter Fifteen

Josh couldn't stop shaking even now hours after the close call he'd had. And he wasn't shaking because of how close those bullets had come to him. Though they had come close.

He wasn't the only one who'd nearly been hit, though.

Sylvie had.

And Natalie…

She was shaking, too.

"We'll be safe here," he told her.

Or so that was what Milek had assured him. The condo was tucked away in a corner of the new Payne Protection Agency's office. Also somewhere in this remodeled warehouse was a space Milek used as his art studio.

Josh closed and locked the heavy steel door behind them. He still wasn't sure, despite the security in this building, that they would be as safe here as he'd just told Natalie they would be. But he wanted her to stop shaking.

Back at the river dock, Milek had convinced the police to take Josh and Natalie's statements first, so they could leave the scene of the shooting and get some rest.

Big dark circles rimmed Natalie's green eyes, nearly as black as the frames of her glasses, and she was deathly pale. And shaky…

He was, too, but Josh wasn't sure if he was shaking from

fear and adrenaline or from exhaustion. But as tired as he was, he doubted he would be able to sleep. Not with their son missing.

"What the hell was Sylvie doing?" Josh asked. "And you... I can't believe you put yourself in danger like that!" He could have lost her all over again.

Not that he had her now.

But he wanted to have her, to hold her, to kiss her. He'd missed her so damn much, and tonight...

"You put yourself in danger, too," she said.

He snorted. "The meeting Sylvie set up for me was with an undercover cop, not a fence."

She smiled. "So she told me the truth about that. She assured me she wouldn't put you in danger again."

Something that had felt like a tight band around his heart eased slightly. Maybe Sheila Carlson wasn't one of the cops who used to work for Luther Mills then. Maybe that wasn't how his sister had known her. And she hadn't known that the cop would pull a gun on him like she had.

"But then you were in danger in that warehouse," Natalie said. "You're the one who knocked her down, who protected us both from whoever was shooting at us." She stepped closer to him and wound her arms around him. "I was so afraid..."

He pulled her closer and held her trembling body against his, which was trembling just as much if not more. "I was so scared, too. I was scared that you were going to get hurt, Natalie, seriously hurt."

Or worse. The thought made him shudder.

Her arms tightened around him. "I'm fine," she said. "Not a scratch on me."

He wasn't sure about that. So many of those bullets had seemed to come so close to her. That crate she'd been crouched beside had been riddled with holes.

"What were you thinking?" he asked.

"I was thinking that you sought your sister out because you suspected she might have the diamonds, and then when she hopped in a car with someone right after you left, I had to follow her and see where she was going."

"But you told that driver that you thought she might be leading you to Henry and your mom."

"I wasn't sure where she was going, but I was hoping it was to them." Tears welled in her green eyes. "But they weren't there."

Officers were still searching the area, but Josh doubted it, too. He released a shaky breath that stirred her hair. "And Sylvie claims the person in the car was the fence and the person they were meeting was whoever stole the diamonds." At least that was the story she'd told them and that she was probably now telling Officer Carlson.

Natalie nodded.

"But we have no proof since both the fence and the shooter disappeared before the police arrived."

"Then we need to go back out there," she said, but she didn't pull away from him. She stayed in his arms, almost as if she was leaning on him.

"We need to charge your phone and recharge our bodies," he said. "Food and a quick nap, or we're not going to be any help to find Henry and your mother or of any help to them when they are found."

He was just repeating what Penny and Milek had told him when they'd both showed up by the river. But this time he believed them. Because he was so tired, he could barely stand. Maybe he was the one leaning on Natalie.

"We need to find them," she said, her voice breaking.

"I know."

"You're not going to promise me that we will?" she asked.

She stared up at him, her green eyes so intense behind the lenses of her glasses.

"I think we both know that I've already broken a lot of promises to you," he said. "I don't want to break another one."

"I don't want you to," she said.

He touched her chin then, tipping it up. "I'm sorry, Natalie. I'm so sorry…for everything."

Even if she hadn't already told him that it was too late for them, an apology wasn't going to be enough to make it up to her for how much he'd hurt and disappointed her. He had to do a lot more than just apologize. He had to find their son and her mother.

But he knew that he didn't have the ability to do that right now. He had no idea where to look and was so tired that he could not see…beyond her face.

Her beautiful face.

He wanted so badly to kiss her, but he didn't dare. He'd given up that right long ago.

But then she rose up on tiptoe and kissed him, her lips soft and silky as they brushed across his.

Maybe he was so tired that he'd fallen asleep on his feet because this couldn't be happening. He had to be dreaming. But the dream got more and more vivid. And the feelings, as always when it came to Natalie, overwhelmed him.

THE FEAR SHE'D felt in the warehouse was nothing compared to the fear Natalie was feeling now. What had she done? The kiss went on and on like it had a life of its own. And the passion overwhelmed her. She opened her eyes, and she could see the same passion in his dark eyes.

He pulled back slightly and hoarsely whispered, "Natalie?"

It was as if he couldn't believe it was her, like he was dreaming. And maybe that was all this was. A nightmare at first and now a dream…

She didn't want the dream to end. She didn't want to wake up. "Don't stop," she said, and she reached up to kiss him again. And as she kissed him, she pulled at his clothes, undressing him.

It had been so long since she'd felt passion like this, and it had only ever been with him. After Josh had broken her heart so badly five years ago, she hadn't dared to risk it again. So she'd focused on her son instead, on being a mother to him and a daughter to her parents.

And she'd forgotten she was a woman.

Until that kiss...

Now all the needs she'd denied for so long took over, and after she finished pulling off his shirt, she reached for hers. But his hands were there, pulling up her sweater and then unclasping her bra. And his fingers stroked her shoulders and then moved lower, over her breasts. Her breath caught as need clawed at her. And she unbuttoned his jeans and then reached for the tab, slowly lowering his zipper.

He groaned as she released him from his boxers, stroking her fingers over his engorged flesh. "Natalie," he whispered. "Are you sure?"

"I need this," she said. She needed him. She needed a release from all this tension gripping her. She needed oblivion.

"I can't stop..." He finished undressing her quickly, but as fast as he moved, he also seemed to take his time. He touched every inch of skin he exposed and kissed her everywhere.

Somehow, they made it from the living area into the bedroom, and then he was inside her, and they were making love like they used to. Moving together in perfect rhythm, her meeting his thrusts like this was a dance they'd choreographed long ago and knew by heart.

And her heart... It beat furiously as that tension wound so tightly inside her. And then it broke as an orgasm gripped her. Maybe it was because it had been so long or maybe it was because of everything else, but the pleasure was even more intense as was the passion...

But not love.

She couldn't love him again. Not after how badly he'd hurt her. Maybe she just needed someone to hang onto, something to feel that wasn't fear and pain. But after being with him again, like that, she was even more afraid...that she was falling for Josh Stafford all over again.

His body tensed, and then he found his release. As always, he was considerate of her. Instead of collapsing on top of her, he rolled to his side and kept her clasped against him. The tension drained from his body, and he started to breathe slow and deep and steady.

And something about the rhythm of his sleeping lulled her to sleep, too.

She didn't know how long she slept, but it felt like hours when she jerked awake. But it wasn't like she was waking up from a nightmare but waking up into one as she remembered everything that had happened.

That her son and her mother were still missing, were still hostages.

While she had awakened, Josh continued to sleep. She eased away from his side. They'd fallen asleep in each other's arms. So maybe he'd needed someone to hold onto as badly as she had.

But he must have gotten up sometime after she'd fallen asleep because her phone was on a charger next to the big bed, and she didn't remember putting it there.

All she remembered was how he tasted, how firm his lips were on hers and then on her body. Heat rushed through her, but it wasn't just passion, it was embarrassment and shame. How could she do that when she didn't even know where her son and mother were?

But maybe that was why she'd had to do it, to get her

mind off the nightmare of not knowing where they were. To stop thinking…

Apparently, she'd stopped listening, too, because as she reached for her cell, she could see all the messages and missed calls lighting up the screen.

What if she'd missed a call about Henry? What if he and her mom had been found?

Her hand shook as she grabbed it, but she noted the only missed calls and messages were from her sister. If anyone had found Henry and her mother, she suspected that they would have contacted her directly, not through Dena. They'd had enough trouble tracking her down just like Natalie had.

Why? What was going on with her sister because it was clear that something was.

Natalie's skin, naked beneath the sheets, chilled, goose bumps rising on her flesh. Could her sister actually be involved in the theft or the kidnapping?

Bracing herself, she opened a text message: You need to answer your damn phone.

And another: Where the hell are you?

And another: Why did you leave with him?

And then the last: Dad is missing now. This is all your fault.

Natalie gasped, not at the accusation but at the news.

"What?" Josh asked, and he sounded wide awake. "What's wrong?"

Everything.

Everything was wrong, and she'd been a fool to give in to her feelings last night. Or this morning…or whenever they'd made love.

Heat burned her face now. "My dad is missing." She was fumbling with her phone, trying to call Dena.

It rang several times, but her sister didn't accept the call.

Was that because she was looking for Dad yet? Hadn't she been able to find him?

Or had she found him, and she was just too angry with Natalie to answer her call?

Josh wasn't the only one who had a sister who resented him. For some reason Dena resented her, too. Maybe just because she'd stopped being an only child when Natalie was born.

Then her cell rang, with Dena calling back.

"Yes? Did you find Dad?" Natalie asked her.

"Not yet," her sister replied. "Timothy is out looking for him."

"Dena, when did he go missing? What happened?"

"He was so unsettled last night that he couldn't sleep. He kept trying to get out of our house and was setting off the alarm, so we disarmed it," Dena said. "I don't know when he took off, but Timothy woke up and found the front door open."

"Dena, how could you…" Emotion choked Natalie as she was overwhelmed with concern. Now her father was missing, too.

"You shouldn't have left him here," Dena said, "and you shouldn't have left with *him*."

"My son is missing," Natalie said. "Our mother is missing. Can't you understand why I'm out here trying to find them?"

"Of course I understand, and I'm upset, too, but I don't know where to look for them and neither do you," Dena said. "You could have stayed with Dad. He's used to you being around. He's not used to being here with us."

"Did you call the police?" Natalie asked.

"No. I'm sure he's just off walking. Timothy is looking around our neighborhood for him. He can't have gotten far."

Natalie jumped up and started reaching for her clothes.

"I'll find him." As long as nobody had taken him like her mother and Henry had been taken.

She disconnected the call with her sister and finished dressing to find Josh already dressed, the key fob for the SUV in his hand.

"I'll help you look," he said.

"I'm sure he's fine," Natalie replied. "He does this. He goes walking sometimes..." Especially when he was restless or upset. And not having her mother around made him both unless he was at work.

Josh nodded. "My grandma used to do that, too. She thought she was walking to school, but it was always in the middle of the night."

Despite the medication, night was the worst for her father, too. But she and her mother were used to dealing with him.

"We need to find Henry and my mom, too," she said. "You should focus on that, on them."

"I am. We are," he said. "But we don't have a lead right now. So let's find your dad."

And maybe looking for him was like what they'd done last night, something that would take their minds off their fears over Henry and her mom.

That had to be all that last night was...an escape from reality. Because she knew there was no chance of anything real or lasting between them. She couldn't risk her heart like that again. She couldn't risk getting hurt again.

"CLAUS," MIMI MURMURED in her sleep as she moved on the air mattress next to Henry. "Claus..."

That was Grandpa's name, kind of like Santa Claus, but with a funny-sounding difference, like people were speaking a different language when they talked to him. And people liked talking to Grandpa. He was always so funny and nice.

No wonder Mimi was calling for him.

Henry wanted to see Grandpa, too.

And Mommy.

But he didn't call out for them. He called out for someone else. "Daddy..."

That was who was supposed to find them. Where was he? Why wasn't he here yet? It had to be daytime now. Henry wasn't sure because that lamp was still the only light in the metal building. He just figured it was morning because he was hungry again.

Daddy had to get here soon. He had to get them out of here. Why wasn't he here? Hadn't he found those things he was supposed to find for the person in that mask?

The diamonds?

What would the person in the mask do if Daddy didn't find the diamonds?

What would that person do to Henry and Mimi?

Chapter Sixteen

Josh was furious Natalie's sister had lost Mr. Croft. The last thing they needed was someone else to find. Why hadn't Dena taken precautions to make sure that her dad didn't go wandering in the middle of the night?

It wasn't always possible to prevent that, though. He and his dad had tried with his grandma, but she had become quite the escape artist. When she'd slipped out, she'd always been going to school.

Since Claus had gone to school in another country, he wouldn't be walking there. Maybe he was headed to his home or to the store. Given the early hour, Josh was banking on the house.

As they pulled into the driveway, crime-scene tape fluttered near the side door of the house. Someone had broken it to get inside.

Natalie must have seen it, too, because she released a heavy sigh of relief. "He's here." She didn't jump out before he shut off the SUV like she had the day before.

In fact, Josh reached for his door first. "Are you okay?" he asked.

She nodded. "I don't know what to tell him," she said. "He's most aware in the mornings. He will know we're lying to him. He'll be able to tell something's happened here."

Josh drew in a breath and nodded, too, as he remembered how little patience his grandmother had had when she was lucid and knew she was being humored. "Yes. We'll have to tell him the truth." And hope Mr. Croft could handle that his wife and grandson were missing.

"Thank you," Natalie murmured.

"For what?" he wondered.

"For being here."

He wished he'd been with her the past five years, like they'd planned. That she hadn't had to raise their son without him or handle her dad's diagnosis without him. And no matter how much Josh was with her now, he knew he couldn't make up for not being there then. For choosing to go to prison instead of honoring their engagement.

Even though he'd had his reasons, he didn't expect her to forgive him because he couldn't forgive himself. He pushed open his door and got out.

Natalie rushed around the front of the SUV first and stepped into the house, calling out, "Dad? Dad?"

Josh followed her inside and grimaced. Her dad had been upset with the mess the crime-scene techs had left in the store. But the kitchen was even worse. Since whoever had taken Marilyn and Henry had been inside in order to slip those sleeping pills in the coffee, they'd had to touch things. So most surfaces had been fingerprinted, and the place had been searched.

Natalie ran around the house, calling out for her father. But like the day before, they didn't find a person inside. She turned to Josh with wide eyes. "Where could he be? I thought he was here."

The broken crime-scene tape indicated that he had been. Or at least someone had. Maybe it wasn't Claus. It could have been whoever had taken Henry and Marilyn returning to the scene of their crime, making sure they'd left no evidence behind, or it could have been someone looking for those damn diamonds even.

"Let's check the garage," Josh suggested as he stepped out the patio doors into the backyard.

"We hid the keys to his car," Natalie said. But she followed him across the yard to the side door of the detached structure.

The crime-scene tape fluttered free here, too, broken in the middle. And the door stood open. Josh didn't see anyone standing inside the garage, though, until Natalie bumped his arm and pointed at the Cadillac.

Her father sat behind the steering wheel, his hands gripping it tightly almost as if he was imagining that he was driving. But no sound came from the engine, no exhaust from the tailpipe. It wasn't running.

"Good thing you hid the keys," Josh whispered.

Natalie nodded and drew in a deep breath. Then she crossed the garage, careful to avoid the spot that was marked off where the bloodstain was on the concrete. And she knocked on the driver's window.

Her father jumped and whirled toward her. But he couldn't lower the window since they were power and the vehicle wasn't running.

Josh joined them and opened the door. At least her father had left that unlocked.

Natalie dropped down to her knees, so that she was eye-to-eye with him. "Daddy, where are you going?"

He stared at her and blinked. "I—I…"

"The store is closed today, so you don't have to go to work," she said.

He shook his head. "I—I have to go…" Then he leaned

back and pointed toward the passenger seat where some velvet pouches lay. "I have to put those back in the safe."

Natalie gasped in shock. "Daddy, do you have the diamonds?"

Josh silently cursed himself for not considering it earlier. After he and his dad moved his grandmother into a memory care unit at an assisted living center, they would often find things in her room that didn't belong to her. Like TV remotes, wheelchairs and even a few pairs of dentures, but Grandma had had all of her own teeth.

But diamonds...

How the hell would the older man have been able to bypass the security system and open the vault?

At the moment that was the least of Josh's concerns, though. The only things missing right now had been in a pouch like this, so these were definitely the diamonds.

"We need to get word out that we have them," Josh said, his pulse quickening with hope. He grabbed his phone and started texting.

Not just Milek and Detective Dubridge but also his sister. He wanted everyone to know, so that word would get back to the kidnapper. So that he or she would know that Josh had what they wanted now.

And if they wanted those diamonds, they would have to give him the clue they'd promised that would lead him to where his son and Marilyn were being held. He had to get them back.

WHILE JOSH WAS texting and making calls, Natalie dealt with her dad. She got him out of the car and into a folding chair next to it. Then she reached across the seat for those velvet bags. As she dumped each of them out onto the supple leather of the driver seat, she sucked in a breath.

"This is stuff that went missing before the security system was installed," she said.

These were things for which they'd already filed insurance claims and had been reimbursed. But apparently the items hadn't really been stolen. She dumped out the last bag of small loose stones. There were some diamonds but mostly rubies and emeralds. "This isn't the diamonds that have just gone missing."

"What?" Josh asked.

"They're not here." And she wasn't particularly surprised because she couldn't imagine how her father would have remembered the code to bypass the system. It was changed too often and was too long for her to remember without putting a note in her cell phone.

Josh cursed. "Are you sure? There are a lot of diamonds there."

She shook her head. "Not even close to what was taken." Or to what it would take to get their son and her mom back from the kidnapper.

"It's too late," Josh said. "I've already gotten the word out."

She shook her head. "It isn't going to work. People who actually saw the diamonds and knew how many stones and the size of them won't be fooled."

"I told the detective to let your family know, too," Josh said, "when I texted him."

Her stomach flipped with the fear that her brother-in-law or sister were responsible for Henry and her mom missing. Maybe that was why Dena wasn't as worried as Natalie was. Maybe she knew where they were and that they were safe.

Please, let them be safe.

"This could still be our best shot at getting them back," Josh said.

"Getting what back?" her father asked. "What are you talking about?"

"Nothing, Daddy."

"The diamonds," Josh said, turning toward her father now. He knelt on the floor in front of him.

Her father gestured to his Cadillac. "They're in there. All of it's in there."

"No, Daddy," Natalie said. "There is a big bag of diamonds missing from the vault, remember?"

His forehead furrowed as if he was struggling to find the memory. But then he shook his head. "No, honey. I can't..." He sounded so defeated, and he looked so tired, too, with his suit rumpled, and his white hair mussed. It was so unlike him to not have his hair neatly combed and his suit pressed. He must have slept in it the night before, if he'd slept at all.

Why hadn't Dena taken care of him? Why hadn't she found him some pajamas of Timothy's to wear? And given him a comb?

Maybe he wasn't the one who maintained his meticulous appearance after all. Maybe her mother had been taking care of him more than Natalie realized. Maybe the medication hadn't slowed the progression or reversed some of the damage as much as she'd thought.

She gasped at a jab of guilt with the realization that he hadn't taken his prescription. That was another thing her mother handled and without her there, Natalie had forgotten. Maybe she couldn't judge her sister as harshly as she had.

"Let's get you inside, Daddy," she said as she helped him up from the folding chair. "We'll get you something to eat." And his pills.

"Mr. Croft, where were you keeping these things?" Josh asked, pointing toward the driver seat.

Her father sighed. "The vault, of course."

Natalie shook her head. "No. This stuff went missing a while ago, Daddy. It wasn't in the vault."

He shrugged. "I don't know then, but we better get it back to the store."

"Tomorrow," she said. "It's closed today."

He nodded.

"Let's get you inside…" She pointed him toward the door, but before she could follow him out, Josh caught her hand.

"This isn't right, Natalie," he said.

"I know," she agreed. "I told you. The diamonds aren't there."

"No. This stuff wasn't in here yesterday. We would have noticed or the techs would have noticed when they processed the garage."

"Dad was in the house, too," Natalie reminded him. "Maybe he has a hiding place in there." It made sense. He'd grown up with family who'd gone through the Holocaust and had learned to hide their valuables. "I'll look for it after I get him his medication. Maybe we'll find them yet."

"If we don't, we have to use what we have here," Josh said. "We have to do whatever we can to get our son and your mother back."

She knew he was right, but she was scared they were making a mistake. That instead of getting their son and her mom back, they might piss off the kidnapper and he or she would make certain that they never saw Henry and his Mimi again.

GUILT WEIGHED SO heavily on Milek that he hadn't been able to bring himself to go home the night before. He wouldn't have felt right holding his son and his daughter when Natalie and Josh couldn't hold their child. Natalie had given Henry's picture to the police for the Amber alert, and Milek had a copy of it pinned to the corner of the canvas over which he swept his brush.

The photo was so flat, so two-dimensional. With paint and his brush, Milek could bring the picture to life. And by doing that, maybe he could somehow keep the child alive, too. Because he hadn't done anything else productive.

Garek and Candace were back now and in the office, going over everything with fresh eyes and their expert perspectives. They could do more than Milek could now.

A door creaked open, and he felt her before he saw her. The air seemed to shimmer around his wife; Amber was that full of vitality and ambition and intelligence. And with her vibrant red hair and sharp green eyes, she was stunningly beautiful as well. He still couldn't believe that she'd chosen to be with him.

"I'm sorry I didn't come home," he said. He'd texted her to let her know.

"I didn't expect you," she said. "I know you would be working hard to find the missing child and his grandmother."

Milek sighed. "I tried, my darling. I tried. But I don't know where to look in that world anymore." Last night, slipping back into the ugliness of it had affected him. That was why he was in his studio, with the need to make something beautiful again.

"You were doing everything you needed to," Amber assured him. "Running this agency and coordinating with the police department."

He grinned. "You were keeping tabs on me."

"I am always aware of you, my darling," she said. And she kissed him.

His lips clung to hers for a moment, and he wanted to deepen the kiss. To make love with her. But she was already dressed in a suit and ready for work. And he had work to do, too, more so than just painting. They stepped back, and both released a shaky sigh of regret at ending the kiss.

"How is Josh?" she asked with concern.

"Desperate," Milek said. "He texted. They found some jewels—"

"They found the diamonds?"

He shook his head. "At first he thought so, but Natalie said they weren't the correct ones. He wants to try to use them anyway to get the lead to his son."

"Of course he does. As you said, he's desperate."

"But it might get him killed."

"Josh Stafford has no problem making the ultimate sacrifice for people he loves," Amber said. "Just like someone else I know. He reminded me of you the first time I met him. That was why I knew he was a good man and wanted to help him."

Milek wanted to help him, too, but he didn't know how to save someone from himself. He had a terrible fear, the same one that Garek had shared with him at their grand opening party. He was afraid that they might lose one of their team.

That Josh Stafford would give up more than his freedom this time. He would give up his life.

Chapter Seventeen

Josh's phone vibrated, then lit up with a video screen from an unknown number. "It worked," he whispered to Natalie who stood beside him in her father's study.

If Claus had a secret safe or hiding place anywhere in the house, it would probably be here, but they couldn't find it. And they'd searched pretty much everywhere while Claus was sleeping. This was their second time going through his study.

Natalie rushed to Josh's side and pressed up against him. "Take it, take the call," she urged.

Josh swiped to accept and stared at the face that filled his cell phone screen.

Henry was pale yet with dark circles beneath his brown eyes, like he hadn't slept well. He probably hadn't.

"Hey, there, buddy," Josh said, his heart filling with love for this child he had yet to meet in person. "How are you and your grandma?"

"Daddy?" Henry said, and he blinked and peered at the screen.

"Yes."

"I'm here, too, sweetheart," Natalie said.

"I miss you, Mommy," Henry said, and his bottom lip quivered. Then he glanced up, above the camera lens on the phone, probably to whoever was holding it. Then he looked down at the screen again and, as if he was following orders, asked, "Did you find the diamonds, Daddy?"

"Yes, I did."

Natalie tensed and opened her mouth, probably ready to tell the truth, like she always did.

But Josh grabbed one of her hands with his free one and gently squeezed. He hated that he was lying to his son, too, but they couldn't waste any more time. They needed to get him and his grandmother home.

"How is Mimi?" Natalie asked.

And Josh realized the boy hadn't answered his first question. He hadn't told him how they were.

"She wants Grandpa," Henry said, his voice breaking with tears. But then he glanced up, probably at the masked person again.

At least Josh hoped the person was still wearing their mask, that they hadn't let Henry or Marilyn see their face. As long as they couldn't identify them, their kidnapper didn't have any reason to kill them.

But that still didn't guarantee that he or she wouldn't. There were no guarantees even if Josh had the right diamonds for the ransom.

Henry's long dark lashes fluttered as if he was blinking away his tears, or maybe he was just that nervous. That scared. "Did you really find the diamonds, Daddy?" he asked.

Glad now that he'd brought in those bags from the car, Josh handed the phone to Natalie. He pulled the bag of loose stones from his pocket and spilled the diamonds into his hand while leaving the other stones in the bag, making it look full. Hopefully the kidnapper would think the rest of the diamonds were still in the bag.

He nodded at Natalie, who focused the camera on his

hand and the bag. Her throat moved as she swallowed hard, as scared as he was that this might not work.

"I have them right here," he said, "but if that person with the mask wants to get them, they're going to have to let you and your grandma go." Then he reached out with his free hand and disconnected the call.

Natalie fumbled with his cell, as if trying to get the call back. "What the hell are you doing!" she exclaimed. "We're not going to get them—"

The cell vibrated, and a text lit up the screen: Don't play games with me.

"They know," she whispered as if the kidnapper could still hear them, as if Josh hadn't disconnected the call.

Hanging up on his son was like punching himself in the gut. He hated to do it. He wanted to stare at the little boy as long as he could. But he knew this was the best way to deal with the kidnapper, to keep them off guard, to make them mess up.

He dumped the diamonds back in the bag and shoved it in his pocket. Then he took back his cell and typed a response.

I have what you want. You have my son and his grandma. Give them back if you want the diamonds.

The phone was still for several long moments. Natalie began to cry, tears sliding down her face.

Then the text came back:

No police. No games. In an hour I will text you an address where you are to come. Alone. With the diamonds or the hostages die.

"It's too dangerous," she whispered again.

"It's too dangerous to bring the police and have the kidnapper run off without letting me know where our son is," he said.

"It's too dangerous to try to pass off that bag as the missing diamonds."

"Then let's add more to it," he suggested. "Let's get some of these other diamonds out of the settings and go to the store and get some, too. Whatever we have to do."

She sucked in a breath, but then she nodded. "Yes, whatever we have to do…"

THEY'D SPENT MOST of the past hour at the closed store with her dad, taking apart whatever piece of jewelry they could to add more diamonds to the bag. Though he hadn't understood what they were doing or why, her dad had helped.

And then Josh's phone vibrated. "This is it," he said. But he didn't pull it out. He didn't look at the address.

"Tell me where," Natalie said.

He shook his head. "No. And you can't try to follow me like you did my sister."

"But—"

"No, Natalie," he said. "You need to stay here with your dad. I can't protect myself if I'm worried about protecting you, too."

That was true. He could have died the night before in the warehouse, with the shooter firing at him, Sylvie and her. She didn't want him alone in a situation like that again. But she didn't want her son and mother in it, either.

Tears stung her eyes. "At least tell me where—"

He shook his head. "No. I can't risk you getting nervous and contacting the police."

"Josh—"

"I have to go, Natalie. I have to try…"

To get their son back and her mother. He had to try even though he was risking his own life for theirs. Damn him.

She was starting to fall for him all over again, no matter how badly he'd hurt her five years ago.

As he headed toward the back door and the alley where he'd parked the SUV, she stepped in front of him and kissed him. Their lips parted, their breath combined, and the passion ignited. But then she pulled back and whispered, "Be careful, please."

While she wasn't sure she could ever trust him again with her heart, she didn't want to lose him again, either.

He nodded. But he didn't promise.

And she had no doubt he would do whatever he had to in order to get their son and her mother back. As the door closed behind him, she felt like she had when she left the prison after visiting him that last time. Like she might never see him again...

The thought had a tear spilling over and rolling down her cheek.

Her father put his arm around her. "Don't worry about him, honey," he said. "That man of yours is a good one. You can trust him."

Her father had no idea who Josh was and how badly he'd already broken her heart. But she hugged her dad tightly, taking the comfort he offered as well as giving some.

After he'd showered, eaten and taken his medication, he seemed like his old self again. Almost as if he knew what was going on, but she couldn't be sure.

"We better get this stuff back in the vault," he said, pointing toward the bags lying around that contained the stones and other items they hadn't used. The things that had gone missing before the new system.

"Let me get the lock," she said.

But he opened the middle drawer of the desk he had in the backroom. Then he pulled out some folded slips, sales invoices, but the numbers scrawled on them weren't item numbers or orders. They were the codes that changed every day or so.

"Dad," she gasped. "I didn't realize you were writing those down."

Every time it changed, she had shared the new code with him because she'd known he wouldn't remember it. It had seemed respectful to include him, to act like he was still running the store. He was already losing so much that she hadn't wanted him to lose his pride, too. So she'd just read them off to him, and while he usually had a pen on him and a pad of invoices nearby, she hadn't thought he would have been quick enough to write down the whole series of numbers.

"It's my vault," he said with that pride. "My store…until it's yours."

"Mine?"

"Your mother had the lawyer draw up papers to turn ownership over to you. I already signed, and she was waiting just a bit longer before she signed. I can't remember why."

"Mine—"

A floorboard creaked.

Natalie tensed, hoping that it wasn't Timothy or Dena out there. They must have unlocked the front door. Usually, they would have come through the alley, though, like Hannah, but it was her usual day off.

"Hello?" Natalie called out. "Who's…" She started toward the showroom door, but it opened before she reached it. She stumbled back a step as Sylvie Combs walked into the room. "What are you doing here?"

"Don't worry," Sylvie said with a smile. "I'm not here to rob you."

Her father chuckled. "You would be the prettiest thief ever if you were."

Natalie smiled at her father's flirting. Even if he wasn't trying to sell something, charm and flattery were such ingrained parts of his personality that she doubted even the progression of Alzheimer's would change it. "This flirt is my dad, Claus Croft. Dad, this is Josh's sister, Henry's aunt, Sylvie."

Sylvie let out a little gasp. "Oh, it didn't even occur to me that I'm an aunt."

"Yes, you are." Natalie hoped that the young woman would be able to meet her nephew soon. But most of all she hoped Henry would meet his dad. That Josh would bring their child and her mother back home.

And himself.

"I—I saw Henry's picture on that Amber alert," Sylvie said. "He looks just like Josh."

Natalie smiled and nodded. "Yes, he does."

"That must have been hard," Sylvie said. "After what happened…" She trailed off with a glance at Natalie's dad, as if wondering how much he knew.

Even before his early on-set diagnosis, Claus hadn't known much about Josh. But he was still pretty perceptive. "I'll leave you two lovely ladies to your conversation, and I'll spruce up the showroom." He stepped out the door that Sylvie had just entered.

"How did you get in here?" Natalie asked. She knew she'd locked up last night and had engaged the alarm on the front door. "Was someone else out there? Did someone let you in?"

Sylvie smiled. "Nobody has to let me in."

"That's a really good security system," Natalie said. It wasn't as high-end as other models Garek Kozminski had showed her, but it was the best they'd been able to afford. Apparently, it wasn't enough to keep out diamond thieves and Sylvie Combs. Were they one and the same?

"It is a really good system," Sylvie agreed.

"Have you been in here before?" Natalie asked with suspicion.

Sylvie shook her head. "No. I haven't. I was just curious

how good the system was and what kind of thief it would take to bypass it. Now I've confirmed it would take either a really good thief or someone who didn't have to bypass it, someone on the inside."

That was Natalie's fear, too. She closed her eyes and nodded. "I know…" That her sister and brother-in-law were possible suspects.

"It could also be someone on the inside of the company that set it up," Sylvie continued. "The Kozminskis have a reputation in this town, Natalie. And Josh is the only one of their employees who didn't actually commit the crime he served time for."

"What are you saying? You think it's one of his coworkers or his bosses?" Natalie asked with sudden alarm. "They've been tracking his whereabouts." Even though he hadn't told her where he was going, his company would know. She wasn't going to get her son and mom back, she was going to lose Josh too.

Fear struck her so hard that she dropped into the chair behind her father's desk and knocked the sales slips onto the floor. "Oh my God…"

Sylvie knelt down in front of her. "What are you talking about? Where's Josh?"

"He left to make the exchange," Natalie said.

"He has the diamonds?" Sylvie asked. Then she glanced around the backroom, at the items strewn across the surfaces. "What's going on here? What is he really trying to exchange for the hostages?"

The kidnapper had to believe that he had the real diamonds. And Sylvie…

Could she still be part of it? Should Natalie trust her? Josh's sister had already put his life in danger before; Natalie didn't want her putting him in danger again. But he was already in danger, maybe more than Natalie had realized if he couldn't trust his bosses and coworkers.

"Tell me what's going on," Sylvie urged her. "You can trust me, and you can definitely trust my brother."

Tears stung Natalie's eyes now as all her doubts and uncertainties and fears overwhelmed her.

"Now you're scaring me," Sylvie said with a shaky sigh. "He's doing something stupid, isn't he?"

"Do you mean like when he took the blame for you?" she asked. Sylvie was the thief. Josh was a man who sacrificed himself to protect those he loved, like a child that he hadn't even known he had.

"Exactly like that," Sylvie said. "If he's trying to convince the kidnapper that he has the diamonds, his bluff is going to get called."

"Why are you so certain that he doesn't have them?" Natalie asked. "Do you have them?"

Sylvie shook her head. "No. You know I don't."

"I wouldn't be asking if I knew," Natalie said.

"You wouldn't be asking if my brother actually has them," Sylvie said. "And look at this mess..." She picked up the sales slip from the floor and used them to gesture around the place. "It's obvious what you're trying to do."

"I'm trying to get my son and my mother back," Natalie said.

"That's what my brother is doing," Sylvie said. "And I'm afraid he's going to get himself killed."

She wasn't the only one afraid...

"Because you know he doesn't have the diamonds," Natalie said. Maybe Sylvie had just figured it out from the mess in the backroom. But still... "On your brother and your nephew's lives, do you have them?"

"I swear I don't," Sylvie said. "I was with the fence who

was supposed to be meeting with the person who actually has them."

"I don't really care about the diamonds," Natalie admitted, even if her father and mother were going to give her the store. "I just want my son and my mom safely back." And Josh.

Sylvie unfolded the slips she'd picked up from the floor, and her pale eyes narrowed. "What are these?"

Natalie snatched them from her hand. "Sales slips. My dad still uses the paper invoices. He hates the computer." So he had a pad of invoices...that had carbon between them for duplicate copies for the buyer and the retailer and in some cases the finance company. She unfolded each slip that was only the top sheet. What had happened to the other two?

Even if he'd thrown them out...

"What?" Sylvie asked. "What's wrong?"

Natalie let out a curse. "I think I know who has the diamonds."

But there wouldn't be time to get them back. Josh was already on his way to make the exchange. And when the kidnapper realized he'd lied, would that wind up costing Josh his life and their son and her mother's theirs as well?

MIMI WAS STILL sleepy today, but Henry was excited. Too excited to sit on that air mattress, so he walked in circles on the concrete floor, never going much beyond the glow of the lamp.

"Daddy's coming," he told her. "He found the diamonds. And now he's going to find us."

Mimi pushed herself up, but then she closed her eyes again, and her face scrunched up like she had a bad headache. She was even holding onto her head, like it was too heavy for her neck. "Sweetheart," she said, "we don't know for sure that person in the mask is going to tell your daddy where we are."

"But that was the rule of this game," Henry said. "Daddy had to find the diamonds, and then he would get a clue to finding us."

Mimi nodded, but then a little groan slipped out of her mouth. "I know. But sometimes people break rules."

"Like Chelsea Oliver." She broke the rules all the time. She cut in line. She never waited until she was called on, and she would just walk out of class without asking for permission to leave. He really wasn't sorry he'd accidentally spit his gum into her hair. But she sure had told on him quick even though she got mad every time someone told on her for breaking rules.

"Yes," Mimi said. "Like little Chelsea."

"Daddy won't break the rules," he said.

And his grandmother made that face again, like she was in pain, but she hadn't moved.

"He won't," Henry said. "He'll find us."

"I hope he does," Mimi said. "But we have to try to find our own way out, too."

Henry liked that idea. He really wanted to get out of this place. Even with the lamp, it was dark, and it was cold when he wasn't under those blankets with Mimi. He wanted to go home.

Chapter Eighteen

Josh didn't have to glance into the rearview mirror to know he was being followed. The kidnapper might be back there, but he knew for certain who else was following him. Someone from the Payne Protection Agency.

He wasn't so naive that he didn't realize that his phone was being monitored. Probably not just by the Payne Protection Agency but also the River City Police Department. Milek wasn't going to let him get himself killed like he nearly had the night before.

But their presence made that more likely to happen than if he went alone. Even worse, it might cause the kidnapper to get rid of their hostages.

So he called his boss now, who sounded a bit distracted as he answered with rustling noises more so than his voice.

"Milek?"

"Yes, what are you doing?"

"I think you know."

"Getting yourself killed?"

"Better me than whomever you have following me," Josh replied. "Tell them to back off, or they're not going to get just *me* killed."

"You're making an exchange for the hostages right now," Milek concluded.

"I hope so," he said.

"Or you're walking into a trap," Milek said.

"Either way I have to risk it. But I don't want to risk Henry and Marilyn's lives because the kidnapper spots someone else. Tell Dubridge that, too."

"He knows," Milek said. "He has a child now, too. He gets it."

Josh was only just *getting* it. He'd given up a lot for his sister, but that might have been partially out of guilt that he hadn't been there for her when she'd needed him. But with Henry…

It wasn't just guilt driving Josh, although he felt some of that, too. And it wasn't just love. It was something even more primal. He knew he would do anything for his son.

"Just please, keep everyone back and out of sight," Josh implored his boss. "Don't make it so that I lose my son before I ever get a chance to meet him."

Milek released a sigh that rattled the speaker. "Okay. Just be careful."

Josh wasn't going to make his boss a promise he couldn't keep—he'd already made too many of those. So he disconnected the call.

The area for this meeting wasn't as dangerous as where Natalie had followed Sylvie the night before. This was a hiking trail, but it was a busy one, with several vehicles parked at the head of it. People were coming and going, alone, in pairs and groups, with strollers and dogs.

This wasn't going to be dangerous at all. So maybe whoever was holding Henry and Marilyn wasn't dangerous, either.

Hopeful now, Josh jumped out of his SUV with the bag of diamonds zipped into one pocket of his leather jacket, and the pepper spray zipped into the other.

He started off, walking fast, hurrying past hikers to where

the trail came to a fork. One side was the easy trail which was wide and obviously well trod. The other led uphill, over tree roots that made the ground uneven. This was where he had to go.

He was the only one who took that fork as the others continued on with their dogs and strollers on the easier path. He had to find another fork between this trail and what was essentially an animal track. And along that track, he was to leave the bag on the other side of a fallen tree.

Ordinarily he would have enjoyed the day, which was unseasonably warm this early in the spring. The sun beamed down through the trees that were just budding leaves. He missed the fork to the animal path at first and only turned back when he noticed a deer standing above him on the trail.

The animal path went uphill before going down to where a fallen log lay across it. Josh's heart was pounding hard with anticipation more than exertion, and he glanced around him. But even the deer was gone now. And the birds and squirrels had gone quiet as well.

He was close. Not just to the log but to the kidnapper, too. They had to be somewhere nearby, watching him. And so he did what he'd been ordered to do. He unzipped his pocket and pulled out the velvet bag. Then he crouched down and leaned over the fallen tree, tucking the bag onto the other side of it. He pressed his palms against the rough bark to push himself back up. But before he could stand, something struck him hard across the back of his head.

Pain radiated throughout his skull, but he clung to consciousness. He blinked and tried to clear away the black spots blurring his vision. And he rolled over to stare up into a hideous face... That mask...

The one his son had been talking about.

And he reached out, trying to grab the kidnapper, trying to hang onto them.

"Where is my son? Where…" Josh whispered, his voice draining away along with his consciousness. His last thought before everything went black was that he'd failed Natalie once again.

"WHY HASN'T HE CALLED?" Natalie asked as she paced the cramped backroom of Croft Custom Jewelry. She should have insisted on going with Josh, although she wasn't sure what she would have done with her dad if she had.

Claus had already set off the alarm twice since they'd arrived at the store. Maybe he wasn't doing as well as she thought. Or maybe her restlessness was making him restless.

"You said he left right before I showed up, so he hasn't been gone that long," Sylvie pointed out. "And you don't know where he was even going for the drop-off. It could have been a long drive to it."

Natalie had told Sylvie how he hadn't shown her the address. "But what if some of his team or his bosses aren't to be trusted?" she asked her deepest fear aloud. "Then he has no backup. He's all alone, just like he was in prison…" Her heart ached thinking of how it must have been for him, of how much he'd given up. And now he might be giving up his life.

Sylvie reached out then and clasped her hands. "I am so sorry, Natalie. What he did for me hurt so many more people than I knew." Tears shimmered in her eyes. "Not that it matters. Just hurting him was bad enough."

"It was," Natalie agreed.

"But you and Henry suffered, too," Sylvie said.

"And now my little boy is out there, and my mother…" Natalie was so scared for them, for Josh and for herself. She was falling for him again even though she knew she shouldn't.

"Josh is going to do his best to get your son and your mother back," Sylvie said.

"But what if the kidnapper knows that he doesn't really have the diamonds they want? What will they do to him?"

Sylvie released a shaky breath. "I don't know. But let's focus on what we do know." She tapped a finger on the sales invoices that sat on top of Natalie's desk now. "Your father was writing down the security codes. Whoever saw these or got ahold of the other copies of these invoices probably has those diamonds. Who could have seen them?"

Natalie felt that surge of urgency and anger again as she'd realized who the prime suspects were. "I think it has to be one of the other sales reps." She'd already called them. Timothy had been short with her, saying he'd been up all night looking for her father, so he was taking the day to rest. Hannah had promised to drop by before she headed to a class. This would have been her usual day off. And Natalie felt a pang of guilt for suspecting them. "But then I guess that even a customer might have wondered about those numbers, someone perhaps casing the place…"

Sylvie shook her head. "I don't know. I think Payne Protection would have picked up on someone casing the place."

"My brother-in-law thought that Josh was when he saw him on the surveillance videos from after hours."

"He was guarding it, though?"

Natalie nodded.

"He wanted to go into law enforcement," Sylvie said. "I'm glad that he is…in a way."

"Because the diamonds were stolen, I think he feels like he failed," Natalie remarked. "Like he felt he failed you."

"I failed me," Sylvie said. "Though it was easier to blame him. I guess I picked that up from my mother, not taking any responsibility for my actions and blaming everyone else."

Natalie's heart softened toward the younger woman.

"I failed him, too," Sylvie said. "And you and my nephew. And I really want to do whatever I can to help now."

"Then let's find him," Natalie said. Because the longer she waited to hear from him, the closer she was getting to losing her mind.

When the alarm went off again, she cursed and rushed out to the showroom. But it wasn't her father who'd opened the door this time; it was Hannah.

"I'm sorry," the young woman said. "I saw Mr. C and thought it was unlocked."

"No, we're closed for the day," Natalie said as she quickly punched in the code again to shut off the alarm.

Hannah tilted her head, and her long dark ponytail swung across her slender shoulders. "Then why did you want to see me?"

"Geez, you have to know about her son," Sylvie remarked as she joined them in the showroom. "How can you ask?"

"Who are you?" Hannah replied. "And I'm sorry about the kid and Mrs. C, but I don't know how to help."

"You can answer a question," Natalie said.

Hannah nodded. "Yeah, but I already answered everything the police and those bodyguards asked me." She yawned as if she was tired.

Natalie was tired, too, tired of people who didn't care about other people. Like her sister and brother-in-law and this young, carefree woman. "Well, I am damn sorry to inconvenience you, but two people I love are missing, and I will do anything to find them!" Three. Maybe.

Why the hell hadn't Josh called?

Hannah's thin throat moved as she swallowed. "I—I get that. I do, but I don't know how to help you."

"Tell me the truth," Natalie said. And she laid the sales invoices on the showroom case between them. "Do you have the other copies of these?"

Hannah didn't even look at them. "I do everything on the computer. Those are Mr. C's."

"I know. But the other copies are missing."

Hannah shrugged. "I don't handle the paperwork. You do."

"These aren't real sales," Natalie said. "They're the codes to the security system."

Hannah sucked in a breath. "Oh. I didn't know…"

She hadn't even looked at them, or she would have known that the figures jotted down on them weren't item numbers.

"So if the police are searching your place right now, they won't find copies of these?" Sylvie asked as she stared intently at the woman who was probably just slightly younger than she was.

Hannah snorted. "The police aren't searching my place. They have no reason to do that, and even if they were looking, they wouldn't find anything. I don't have the code to the vault."

"Maybe you didn't keep the copies," Sylvie began. "But—"

"If you really want to find out who's been taking things," Hannah said and she was looking at Natalie instead of Sylvie, "you need to look closer to home than me."

That was what Natalie had been afraid of. "So you do know something?" Natalie asked.

"I know that there are things happening around here that I don't want to be part of anymore," Hannah said. "Let's consider this my last day. I'm not coming back to work here even if you manage to reopen." She whirled around and rushed out the front door, setting off the alarm once again.

While Natalie was able to shut off the security alarm, another one kept raging inside her. Alarm for her son and mother and for Josh.

"What the hell did she mean by that?" Sylvie mused aloud. "Even if you manage to reopen?"

Natalie shrugged. "The store is the least of my concerns right now."

"I know," Sylvie agreed. "But she knows more than she told us or the police."

"But why wouldn't she share it?"

Sylvie sighed. "She's either afraid of incriminating herself or she's just afraid."

Natalie could relate to the latter. She was so very afraid.

DESPITE EVERYTHING ELSE going on around him, Milek was inspired to keep working on his painting of the little boy. Something about it called to him as if he could find answers within the portrait.

As if he could find the child and his grandmother…

"Are you going to the hospital?" Garek asked.

Milek hadn't heard his brother come into the studio, but he didn't jump. He expected him. "Josh won't be there long."

"He got knocked out. He needs a CT scan."

"He won't be there."

Milek's cell rang, but Garek was the one who answered it, putting it on speaker. They looked so similar that Garek was able to open it with face recognition.

"He's gone," Ivan's voice rumbled out of the speaker.

"Who?" Garek asked.

"Josh took off from the hospital. I thought he was in radiology, but he just left." The big man cursed. "First I lose sight of him on the trails, and he gets hurt, and that bastard kidnapper gets away, and now this."

"He wasn't going to get treatment," Milek said. "He's not going to do anything until he finds his child."

"And, boss…" Ivan continued, his voice gruff with either concern or embarrassment.

"What?" Garek asked.

"My truck keys are missing. I think Josh took it."

Milek chuckled. "Of course he did." Josh had taken his vehicle once, too, but he wasn't about to admit that in front of Garek. Josh was more resourceful than even Amber had realized. But then he'd probably had to be in order to survive five years in prison.

"What do I do now?" Ivan asked.

"I'll have Nikki see if she can track his phone," Garek said.

"He left it here," Ivan replied.

Garek cursed. "I'll get back to you," he said and disconnected the call. He stared at the portrait for a moment. "Man, you've really brought him to life. It's like he's here in this room with us."

"I wish he was."

"Do you think he's dead?" Garek asked. "Do you think it's too late for him and his grandmother? The kidnapper got away with the diamonds."

"Not the ones he or she wanted," Milek said.

"Yeah, exactly," Garek said. "Either way it doesn't look good for the hostages."

And it didn't look good for Josh Stafford, either.

Chapter Nineteen

Josh hadn't found the slip of paper in his pocket until he was getting ready to change into a gown for the CT scan. It was in the pocket where he'd had the velvet bag of jewels he had stashed in the fallen log.

The masked person had taken the bag after knocking him out. And they'd gotten away before the bodyguards and the police officer who'd been close to him had been able to see them. Ivan, Viktor, and Officer Carlson had all missed the person in the mask.

Was that possible?

Or was more than one person involved in the kidnapping? Maybe someone close to Josh or within the police department. He couldn't trust anyone.

There was definitely already more than one person involved since the person who'd stolen the diamonds and the one who'd taken his son and the boy's grandmother couldn't be the same. So maybe there was another…

Someone helping the kidnapper escape.

That was why Josh told nobody what he found in his pocket, and he left his cell behind, too. He regretted that now since he hadn't had a chance to talk to Natalie, to tell her what was going on. She was probably going out of her mind with concern for their son and her mother.

He needed to bring them back to her. It was the least he could do to try to make up for all the other ways he'd disappointed and hurt her.

She was such a loving and beautiful person that she deserved to be happy. He knew that she probably wouldn't ever find happiness with him again, if she could ever bring herself to forgive him, but he had to try to get her back the people who made her happy, the people she loved like he loved her.

So he slipped out of the hospital with that note in his pocket along with the keys to Ivan's vehicle.

It wasn't a Payne Protection Agency SUV. Because those were so easy to spot, Ivan had used his personal vehicle to follow Josh, an older truck with a lift kit and oversized tires on it. The thing was big and loud, which was unfortunate because the kidnapper was going to hear him coming.

If this was a trap...

It probably was a trap. But Josh didn't care. He didn't care about himself at all. He cared about Natalie.

No. He still loved her. He cared about her mother, too. And he loved his son already. He'd told his son that he would find him, so he had to try. He had to follow every lead to wherever he was being held.

But were the little boy and his grandmother here?

It was surprisingly close to where Josh and Natalie had spent the night, in the condo attached to the office of the newest Payne Protection franchise. The area had once been a booming industrial district but was pretty much abandoned now but for warehouses being converted into businesses and living quarters and artist studios.

But this wasn't an address for a warehouse, Josh saw as he drew closer. It was for an old storage facility. The place had been abandoned long ago, probably when the factories and other things had gone out of business around it.

It would be the perfect place to hold hostages. Or to kill someone.

The short hairs on his nape tingled as he feared that someone was watching him. But he didn't notice any other vehicles parked on the cracked asphalt. Unless it was parked inside one of the storage units like that car Sylvie rode in had parked in the warehouse the other night.

Was Sylvie part of this?

Did she resent him that much that she would hurt him like this? That she would hurt his son? He wasn't sure how she would have even known about him, though, but Sylvie had somehow known which officer was investigating the diamond theft. She had connections. Was it still through Luther Mills's criminal organization?

Josh shut off the loud engine of the truck, and an eerie silence enveloped him. He was just far enough outside the part of town that was starting to come back that there were no sounds here. No engines. No voices. Not even birds or animals made a peep around here.

He pushed open the truck door, which creaked slightly, and jumped down. The movement jarred his body and his head, and he flinched at the pain that shot through his skull. Whatever the masked person had struck him with had been hard enough to knock him out.

A branch or a gun?

Had nobody else really seen the person? Josh wasn't sure he could trust the other bodyguards or now even his bosses. But maybe the kidnapper had quickly taken off the mask and tucked it and the bag of diamonds inside one of those strollers. That would have been a great way to blend back in with the other hikers.

But around here there was no one to blend in with and escape unseen. There were just the metal walls of the storage units that cast shadows all around. Some of them had doors that opened to the outside. Those all stood open and were obviously empty. The other units' doors opened off a wide walkway that ran between the middle of two separate buildings. The walkway had a roof over it and a metal floor that creaked beneath his weight and echoed with his footsteps. If someone was here, they would hear him coming.

And just like them, Josh really had nowhere to hide.

But now, he realized, someone could be hiding inside one of the units, ready to jump out at him as he drew near. So he pulled out his can of pepper spray, the one he should have had ready back in the woods.

But each unit he passed was either locked or stood open and empty. Until…

Some light filtered through a hole in the metal roof and shone into the shadows of one unit, glinting off metal and glass. A vehicle. The same make and model of Marilyn Croft's missing vehicle.

This was where the kidnapper had brought them. Were they still here?

Unconcerned about his own safety, he called out, "Hello? Henry? Marilyn?"

His voice echoed off the metal. Maybe they weren't here anymore. Or they were tied up and gagged.

Or…

He didn't even want to consider the thought that flitted through his mind, that brought him such pain and dread. No. He couldn't consider that possibility…that he was too late.

That they were dead.

NATALIE NEEDED TO find Josh and her son and her mother. After that conversation with Hannah a short while ago, she suspected her sister and brother-in-law might know how.

"Can you stay here with my father?" she asked Sylvie. He was in the backroom again, fiddling with some of the empty settings.

Maybe he was wondering the same thing Hannah had been, how they would open again with so much of their stock gone. The insurance company would probably reject a claim for those diamonds, and they wouldn't pay twice for the other items. So how would they replenish their inventory?

Sylvie narrowed her silvery eyes. "Why? Where do you think you're going?"

"I have to talk to my sister," Natalie said.

"Not alone."

"She's my sister," Natalie said. "She won't hurt me."

"If she's been stealing from you and has something to do with the disappearance of your son and mom, you can't trust her even though she is your sister," Sylvie said. Then she grimaced. "Yeah, I heard the hypocrisy in that."

Despite herself, Natalie smiled. There was something about Sylvie Combs...something that made it impossible to dislike her. "How are you going to protect me?" she asked the younger woman.

Sylvie wriggled her brows, which were a darker blond than her streaked hair. "I am the one who is armed," she said.

Natalie remembered that she'd had the gun the other night, the one that Josh had taken to fire back at whoever had been shooting at them. She'd seen him hand it back to her before the police arrived.

"I should have made him keep it," Sylvie said. "But if Officer Carlson knew he'd touched it the other night, he would be in violation of his parole. And she would probably be only too happy to put him back in prison."

Natalie flinched with the realization that not only had Josh gone off alone, he'd gone off unarmed. "I really need to find him."

The alarm rang out from the showroom again.

"Speaking of unarmed," Sylvie said. "You really should have just disarmed that thing."

She probably should have, but she'd wanted to keep the store closed and her dad safe. So maybe leaving him alone in a jewelry store with a thief wasn't her smartest option. She glanced at the monitor for the camera in the front and saw Mrs. Lynch standing inside, but she wasn't alone. A blond man messed with the control at the front door, and the alarm stopped.

Natalie rushed out to join them, anxious for news. That had to be why they were here. Something had happened.

"So someone else knows how to disarm that system," Sylvie remarked. She'd followed Natalie.

Garek Kozminski turned toward her, his silvery eyes narrowed. Then they widened with surprise. "Who are you?"

"Sylvie Combs," she replied.

"Josh's sister," Natalie said. "Why are you here? Has something happened to him?"

Garek tensed and cleared his throat.

Natalie turned to Mrs. Lynch. "Please, tell me what you know." She trusted the older woman to share everything with her. She'd been so empathetic and comforting the day before.

"We don't know much," Mrs. Lynch replied.

"Josh made the drop," Garek said.

"And?" Sylvie prodded.

But Natalie's stomach was tightening with dread. She knew. "He was hurt."

Mrs. Lynch nodded. "Yes. But not so badly that he didn't leave the hospital on his own before he was even treated."

"Treated for what?" Natalie asked.

"Was he shot?" Sylvie asked, her voice sounding as if she was being strangled.

Garek shook his head. "He got hit over the head during the drop. But he was well enough to steal a vehicle."

Natalie gasped while Sylvie chuckled.

"His coworker won't press charges," Garek assured her. "We just don't know where he went. He left his phone behind, so we weren't able to track his whereabouts through that. And Ivan's truck is too old to have GPS. He was using it instead of one of the company SUVs so the kidnapper wouldn't notice it."

So they had been following him, just like Natalie suspected. But to help him or to hurt him? He'd been hit over the head and the jewels taken, but even though he was injured, he'd rushed off again without telling anyone where he was going. Because he didn't trust them, either...

"I don't know where he went," she said. "He didn't call me." But she suspected they already knew that, too, that they were monitoring her phone calls. To help them? Or to make sure they didn't figure out what was really going on?

"We think he may have gotten a lead to where your son is," Penny said.

Garek's phone vibrated, and he pulled it from his pocket to look at the screen.

"What? What is it?" Natalie asked. "Have you found him?"

"Uh...someone might have spotted Ivan's truck," he murmured. "I'm going to check it out."

"I want to go—" Natalie began in unison with Sylvie.

But Garek ignored them both and rushed out the door. They started to follow him, but Penny stepped in their way. "He must think it's dangerous," she said. "And he doesn't want you getting hurt and anyone getting distracted. You need to stay here."

Natalie shook her head. It was dangerous because Josh couldn't trust his boss or coworkers, and now they knew where he was. "I have to go," she insisted. She had to follow Garek to make sure he didn't do anything to Josh or to her son and her mother.

"We can head down to the police department or the bodyguard headquarters," Sylvie said. "Maybe we can find out from someone there where Josh is headed. Or, after what Hannah told us, your sister and brother-in-law might know, Natalie, if they actually have something to do with all this."

"You should just wait for news," Penny said.

But Natalie had been standing around and waiting for news for the past two days. "No. Penny, can you stay here with my father? He's in the backroom."

But she didn't wait for the older woman to agree. She just rushed into the backroom, grabbed her purse and kissed her father's cheek. "I'll just be gone a little while, Daddy," she said. Then she pushed open the back door to the alley and started toward her SUV. Fortunately, she and Josh had taken separate vehicles to the store that morning.

She clicked the fob and unlocked it. As she jumped in on the driver side, Sylvie jumped in the passenger side.

"Kozminski was driving a long black SUV," Sylvie said. "Maybe we can catch up with him. But you need to hurry."

Her hand shaking, Natalie pushed in the ignition and then shifted into Reverse. She coasted back a bit before shifting into Drive and heading toward the mouth of the alley. The road it opened onto was a busy one, so she started braking. But the pedal kept going down...all the way to the floor.

And nothing happened.

"I can't stop!" she yelled.

The SUV kept going, directly into the traffic racing along the busy road. Either she screamed or Sylvie did. Then horns blared, brakes squealed, and metal crunched as they were struck...several times.

"Henry!"

That wasn't the person with the mask calling his name.

Henry didn't know why Mimi was holding her finger against her lips, shushing him like Miss Howard shushed their class when they were getting too loud.

"Henry, it's…" The deep voice trailed off for a moment before getting louder, closer. "Henry, it's your dad. Let me know if you're here. Help me find you."

Henry started to open his mouth, but Mimi covered it with her hand. And she shook her head. Then she used her other hand to shut off the lamp.

Didn't she want his daddy to find them?

"Mrs. Croft, Natalie sent me," the voice continued. "She and your husband are really worried about you both. He's confused and…"

She gasped then. "Josh?" she called out. "Is that really you? Josh Stafford?"

That was his daddy's name?

She slipped her hand down from Henry's face.

He called out, "Daddy?" Then he called out even louder, "Mommy?" Was she with him?

As much as he wanted to meet his daddy, he really wanted to see his mom. To hug her and have her hug him. Her hugs always made him feel better. Safer…

Happier…

Chapter Twenty

Josh could hear them, but he couldn't see them.

Henry banged on the door from the other side, calling out to him, "Daddy! Daddy! We're in here."

"There's a lock," Josh said. A padlock held the sliding door shut on what must have been one of the bigger storage units. "I have to find something to break this lock." Maybe Ivan had something in his truck, some tool that Josh could use to snap the padlock loose. "I'll be right back," he said. "I promise."

But when he started toward the exit, he heard the rumble of an engine. And another.

Then a shadow fell across the entrance.

"Damn…"

He had the pepper spray canister. But obviously more than one person had driven up since there was more than one vehicle. And they were probably armed with more than pepper spray.

What the hell was he going to do?

Whatever he had to in order to protect his son.

He headed toward the exit but kept close to the side of the walkway, in the shadow of the units. But then shadows blocked the exit, making it even darker around him. Despite the dim lighting, he noticed the glint of a gun.

He wasn't going to be able to do much to protect himself against bullets. He didn't have Sylvie with him today. He didn't have her gun to use to fire back.

"Josh?" a familiar voice called out. "It's Garek and Ivan."

It sounded like Milek, but it was his older brother.

Josh would have preferred that it was Milek. Of everyone in the agency, he trusted Milek the most. But he wasn't going to be able to take out Garek and Ivan with his can of pepper spray. So Josh braced himself and stepped out of the shadows. "I'm here."

Garek's gaze went straight to the canister he clasped. "Did you think we were the kidnappers coming back?"

"Just because it's not, doesn't mean you're safe," Ivan said, his voice gruff.

Josh started to raise the canister. Ivan was the only one of his coworkers who was allowed to carry a weapon. Pepper spray wouldn't protect Josh from bullets, but it might buy him some time. "What do you mean?"

"You stole my truck!" Ivan said.

"You need to get better at your job," Josh said, and he wasn't really teasing.

But Ivan laughed anyway, and some of Josh's tension eased. There really was a kindness in the big man that made Josh want to trust him. And Garek was Milek's brother, and they seemed much more alike than Josh and Sylvie were.

Josh drew in a breath, then released it along with his mistrust. "Do you have anything in your truck that would break a lock?"

"You found them?" Garek asked.

Tears burned Josh's eyes as he nodded. "I found them." He headed back toward the big storage unit with the locked door. "We need to get them out."

"Daddy?" Henry called out, his voice quavery.

"Yes, I'm still here. Some friends are here, too. They're going to help me get you and your grandmother out of there."

Garek looked at his gun before holstering it again. He knew what Josh did, that the risk of one of the people inside getting hit with a stray bullet was too great. "I never met a lock I couldn't pick," Garek admitted. And he reached into his pocket and pulled out a small case.

Ivan ran back from wherever he'd gone, his big body hitting the walkway so heavily that the metal bounced beneath Josh's feet. "I have a tire iron."

Garek snorted. "This'll be faster." A phone buzzed, but he ignored it while he used two small metal picks on the padlock. Within seconds, it popped open.

Josh's hands shook as he pulled at the handle. Ivan reached over his head and shoved it open.

The little boy standing on the other side stepped farther back into the unit, as if scared. He had every right to be after the ordeal he'd endured.

To seem less intimidating, Josh dropped down to his knees. "It's me, Henry. I'm your dad."

Henry hesitated another moment, his dark eyes wide in his dirt and tear-smeared face. Then he rushed forward and threw his arms around Josh's neck, clinging to him, as his little body shook.

Josh shook, too, with relief and with rage for the monster who'd put a child through such fear. Who'd put him and Natalie through such fear.

Henry pulled back to look over his shoulder. "Where's Mommy?"

"She's at the jewelry store with your grandpa," Josh said. "She can't wait to see you, though." Because he hadn't trusted his team, he hadn't brought his phone. But now that it seemed like Ivan and Garek were really here to help him, he would use one of their phones to call her.

The two of them had rushed over to Mrs. Croft, who was sitting on an air mattress in a corner of the unit. Her hair was stained with blood, and her face was deathly pale.

While his boss and coworker were checking her out, Josh cupped Henry's face in his hands and studied him. "Are you okay? Did that person hurt you?"

Tears welled in the little boy's eyes, but he shook his head. "No. Mimi got hurt though when she fell…or maybe that person pushed her…" His bottom lip quivered.

Josh hugged him again. "You're safe now, honey. You and Mimi are safe."

"Did that person get in trouble for making us play their stupid game?" Henry asked as his lip quivered again. "For Mimi getting hurt?"

"Not yet," Josh reluctantly admitted. "But soon. Soon." He silently cursed himself for letting that monster get away with the jewels.

"We're going to call in paramedics," Garek said, "For Mrs. Croft. We don't want to move her until we know how badly she's hurt." He pulled out his cell. As he glanced at the screen, his mouth fell open with a soft gasp.

"What is it?" Ivan asked.

Garek glanced at Josh and then at the boy. "Let me make this call…" He called 9-1-1 and reported Mrs. Croft's head wound and that she'd been held for a couple of days in an old shed and wasn't treated for her injuries. Then he added that he also had another person with a head wound.

Josh looked at him in alarm, concerned for Henry, but then realized that his boss meant him. His head was pounding, but he'd figured that was just with the adrenaline coursing through him. And the fear…

Ivan rushed out to his truck and came back again with bottles of water and some candy bars. While the big guy chatted with the little boy, Garek gestured Josh out the open door.

"What is it?" Josh asked with dread. Because he knew that Garek had seen something on his phone, either a text or a voicemail transcript that had unsettled him before he'd called for help.

Garek's throat moved as he swallowed. "I left Mrs. Lynch at the jewelry store with Natalie and your sister."

"My sister? Sylvie was with Natalie?" That alone was cause for concern. The last time Josh left them alone together he could have lost them both. "What happened?" Because he knew from the tense look on his boss's face that something had.

"I think they were leaving to try to follow me here, and they were involved in an accident," Garek said.

"Accident? What the hell did Sylvie do now?"

"She wasn't driving. Natalie was," Garek said. "But I'm not sure how much of an accident it was. Mrs. Lynch thinks the brake line was cut. There was a puddle of fluid in the alley where her SUV was parked."

Josh bit back a curse. "Just…how badly are they hurt?"

"They're at the hospital. They're being treated," Garek said.

Which meant they were hurt.

Josh's heart had filled with love and relief just moments ago when he got to hold his son. But now… Now fear gripped it again, so tightly that he could barely breathe.

"Daddy," Henry called out to him, as if he too sensed that something was wrong. Then he pushed past Ivan and ran out to join him in the walkway. "Daddy! I want Mommy. I want to see Mommy."

"Me, too, buddy," Josh said, and he picked him up, holding him close against his hurting heart. "Me, too."

She had to be okay. For her sake. For their son's sake and her parents' and for Josh's.

NATALIE NEVER LOST CONSCIOUSNESS. Maybe it would have been easier if she had, if she'd had a moment in which she wasn't worried about her son and her mom and her dad, too, and the store.

And Josh…

Maybe she was worried the most about him right now. He'd left the hospital with a head injury. He could have crashed, too, or worse.

Head injuries were so serious. She didn't have one. Just some bumps and bruises. The airbags had saved her and Sylvie from the worst of it. But the vehicle had been damaged so much that it had taken a while and the jaws of life for firefighters to extract them from the wreckage. She and Sylvie had talked a lot then, and Natalie understood her better.

But Natalie couldn't understand what had happened with her SUV. Just that morning the vehicle had been fine, but as they'd left the alley, the brakes had gone out, making it impossible for her to stop.

"We're really lucky we didn't get killed," Sylvie remarked from the gurney on the other side of a heavy curtain that separated her ER bay from Natalie's. Then Sylvie reached out and jerked back the curtain.

"I'm sorry," Natalie murmured.

"Sorry that I didn't get killed?" Sylvie teased.

"Sorry that it happened," Natalie said.

"You're really sweet," Sylvie said with a smile. "And like my brother, you try to take the blame for things that aren't your fault. Someone must have cut the brake line."

The thought had occurred to Natalie, too. It was the only thing that made sense since she kept her vehicle properly maintained. She wouldn't drive her son in a vehicle that wasn't. She wouldn't risk his safety in any way.

Yet Henry and her mother were in danger. She'd thought

it was because of Josh at first, but now she realized it had to do with the store. With the jewelry and the money...

"Someone tried to kill you," Sylvie said.

What if Henry had been with her then?

"We need to get out of here," Natalie said.

"Go," Sylvie urged her. "I'm going to wait for that prescription for painkillers the doctor promised. I know when the adrenaline wears off tomorrow, we're going to feel like a semi hit us."

"I think it did," Natalie said. She already felt the pain as she swung her legs over the side of the gurney.

Her feet had just hit the floor when she heard a voice call out, "Mommy? Where's Mommy?"

There could have been a bunch of other mommies in that ER, but she knew this child was calling for her.

"Henry!" she yelled. Had she hit her head after all? Was she imagining this? Because all she could see in front of her was that curtain.

Then a small body wriggled under it, and Henry ran to her, winding his arms around her legs. "Mommy! Mommy!"

Her legs weakened, and she sank to the floor, clutching him in her arms while tears rolled down her face. "Oh, my sweetie, I love you so much! Are you okay?"

He leaned back and nodded. "Yeah, Daddy found me, Mommy. Just like he promised."

And more tears spilled over with gratitude and with love. She was falling for Josh all over again.

"Where is your daddy?" Sylvie asked, her voice cracking.

The curtain that Henry had crawled under was pulled back, revealing Josh standing there. He looked beyond exhausted with dark circles beneath his eyes and blood staining the collar of his shirt. He'd never looked better to Natalie. Just that he was here...

She picked up Henry in one arm and wrapped the other

around Josh's neck, holding him close and said, "Thank you. Thank you so much."

Sylvie sniffled and muttered, "I'm not crying, you're crying."

Josh chuckled as he pulled back from Natalie.

"What's so funny?" Henry asked.

"Your aunt is funny," Natalie replied.

"Auntie Dena isn't here," Henry said, and he glanced around as if to make sure. Then his face twisted into a grimace. "And she isn't ever funny."

"This is your aunt Sylvie," Natalie said, pointing toward the woman on the gurney. "She's your daddy's sister."

"And she is funny," Sylvie said of herself. "Nice to meet you, little man."

Henry smiled shyly at her.

"My mom?" Natalie asked. "How is she?"

"She's here," Josh said. "She's being treated, but she was conscious and seems to be doing well."

Some of the pressure on Natalie's chest eased a bit. "That's good."

"What about you two?" he asked, his voice gruff. "I heard about the accident."

"That isn't what I would call it," Sylvie said.

"Detective Dubridge has some questions for you about that," Josh said.

"He probably has some for you, too," Sylvie remarked.

Josh nodded. "And for Henry. They need to figure out yet who the person in the mask is."

Henry shuddered at just the mention of his kidnapper, and he hugged Natalie tighter. "I didn't like that game, Mommy. I don't want to play it again."

"You're not going to play it," she assured him. "That person is not going to bother you again." But as she said it, she heard the hollowness in her own voice, the lack of conviction.

"If you see that person again, you scream your head off," Sylvie told him. "You kick them. You punch them. You don't go without a fight."

"Fight?" Henry asked.

Sylvie nodded.

"But I won't get in trouble?"

"No," Natalie replied. And she wondered now if this abduction was partly her fault, that she'd taught her son to be too polite, to play too much by the rules.

Sylvie nodded. "Don't ever let someone take you where you don't want to go," she said.

"But I'm little, and that person was big," Henry said.

"But you're tough," Sylvie said, and her voice cracked a bit. "You're really tough, Henry."

The little boy sent his aunt another shy smile. But then he whispered in Natalie's ear, "I was really scared, Mommy."

"That's okay," she said. "I was, too."

She was scared when he and Mother were abducted. And she was scared in that warehouse and when her brakes didn't work. And she was still scared that that person might come back for her son or for them.

She was also scared that Josh might leave again. Just as she was realizing how much she still loved him. But could they have a future if she couldn't bring herself to fully trust him with her heart again? Could they have a future with so much still up in the air about the diamonds and whoever had abducted Henry and her mom?

Or was that person going to come back and come after them again just like Henry seemed to fear?

GAREK WAS PISSED, not because his and Candace's getaway had been cut short but because his brother hadn't called him sooner. From the first moment they'd opened their own agency, he'd worried about something like this, about losing one of their employees. Or their family...

Family made him think of his dad, who'd died a few years ago serving time in prison for a crime he hadn't committed. Like Josh Stafford.

Patek Kozminski spent fifteen years in prison for murder until a fellow inmate killed him, coerced by the man who'd really committed the murder. That was all over now. His father was gone. But for some reason Garek was thinking about him since meeting Josh's sister.

Sylvie Combs looked more like Garek's sister than she did Josh's. With her pale, silvery eyes, she looked more like a Kozminski, which made sense since Amber was pretty sure she was the one who'd stolen the stuff that Josh had gone to prison for stealing. While Garek's father hadn't been a killer, he had been a thief.

A thief was still on the loose now. The original bag of diamonds was missing as well as those other pieces Josh had used in exchange for his son.

But the thief was the least of Garek's concerns right now.

He was worried about the kidnapper and about the person who'd cut the brake line on Natalie's vehicle. It hadn't taken a crime-scene tech long to confirm what had caused the wreck. Nikki had pulled up the security footage from the alley that showed someone dressed like a vagrant in a ratty old parka lurking around Natalie's SUV. The vagrant had known to keep their face away from the camera, well aware of where it was, but it was clear they'd messed with Natalie's vehicle.

She and Sylvie Combs could have been killed. So yeah, a thief was the least of his concerns.

Garek had a would-be killer to find before the person tried to kill again.

Chapter Twenty-One

That first day when Josh and Natalie had searched her house for Henry and her mother, Josh had been looking for people, so he hadn't paid much attention to the furnishings and the decorations. But now, standing in the doorway to Henry's room, he could see that Natalie had taken care to make the place perfect for their son.

Henry had blue-and-green-striped walls decorated with *Toy Story* decals that matched his curtains and blankets. Stuffed animals took up more of the bed than he did, tucked as he was under the covers.

"I can stay in here with you," Natalie said.

"No, Mommy. I'm tough, like Auntie Sylvie says," Henry insisted. "I'm not scared."

Then he was the only one in the house who wasn't, because Josh was scared, and he could tell that Natalie was, too. Her parents were staying at the hospital. Her mother had a concussion and was seriously dehydrated and anemic. After his sleepless night and his worries, her father's blood pressure had been so high that they'd wanted to keep him for observation as well.

Natalie had considered staying at the hospital, but Penny Payne-Lynch and Sylvie had sworn that they would keep watch on them.

Josh still wasn't sure that he could completely trust his sister, but he loved her and appreciated that she was trying to help as much as she could. He just hoped that was out of love and not guilt.

"He's fallen asleep," Natalie whispered, and she backed slowly toward the door, as if worried that a sudden movement might awaken him. And after what the poor kid had been through, it might.

"Leave the door open," Josh said when she joined him in the hall. The two of them stood there for a long moment, just watching him. Love filled Josh's heart, but it wasn't just for his son.

Their son.

They'd made that perfect little boy together. And he could just about pinpoint the night they'd done it, probably the night they'd gotten unofficially engaged.

"I'm sorry," he whispered to her. But the words weren't enough, they would never be enough.

"You're sorry?" Natalie asked. "You found our son and my mother, just like you promised. You brought them back."

"I was talking about everything else." Everything Josh couldn't take back, that he couldn't undo. All the pain he'd caused her.

"Tonight…" Her throat moved as if she was struggling to swallow. "Tonight, let's just be grateful that we're all okay and that Henry is home where he belongs."

Josh nodded. "I'm staying, too," he said.

He knew that Garek had posted bodyguards outside, but he didn't care. He wasn't leaving Natalie and Henry. Not again. If he had his way, it would never happen again. But that wasn't his decision to make; that was hers.

"I want you to stay," Natalie said. And then she reached out and entwined her fingers with his. In her other hand she held a monitor that matched the one on Henry's nightstand.

She clearly intended to make sure that she was always connected to their son now, no matter where they were.

"I want you to stay with me," she said, and she led him down the hall toward another bedroom.

With its soft pink walls and white lace curtains, this room was clearly hers. And instead of leaving the door open, like she had Henry's, she closed it behind him, shutting them inside together.

NATALIE HAD SO many reasons to be afraid. So many reasons to be upset and even angry after what had happened over the past couple of days. But at the moment, like she'd just told Josh, she wanted to focus on gratitude.

And on him.

"Thank you," she said, "for bringing back our son at the risk of your own life. And I'm grateful for your sister, too."

"You've nearly gotten killed with her twice now," Josh said with a shudder. "I don't think she's very good for you."

She smiled. "Actually, she is. She's made me laugh despite all the stress of the past couple of days. And she's staying at the hospital with my dad and mom. My own sister and brother-in-law can't be trusted to do that."

She couldn't trust them at all right now. She really couldn't trust anyone but Josh. But she had called Dena and Timothy and let them know their parents were at the hospital. She'd assured them there was no need to come down, that they could wait until morning, since their parents were sleeping. Timothy and Dena had readily agreed to wait.

And Natalie's doubts about them had increased. Where had her father found those missing jewels? Did he have a secret stash in the house? Or had he walked to the store first before going home?

But she didn't want to think about the store or her sister. Or even Josh's sister right now. She didn't want to think at all right now.

"Thank you," she said again. And she slid her arms around his neck, careful of the bandage on the back of his head, and stretched up his body to press her mouth to his.

His lips clung to hers in nibbling, caressing kisses, but he pulled back with a shaky sigh. "Natalie, you're hurt, and you must be exhausted."

She shook her head. "I'm a little bumped and bruised, but so are you. And I'm not tired at all." She was wound up from the rush of adrenaline from the crash but mostly from getting Henry back home.

Josh had done that. And she loved him for it. She loved him. If only she could trust him again…

"I don't want to take advantage of you," he said. "Of how high your emotions are right now. I feel badly that I might have the other night."

She chuckled. "If anything, I'm the one taking advantage of you…" She reached for the hem of his shirt, pulling it up over his washboard stomach. He was lean, but he was also all muscle.

So damn sexy…

His dark eyes got even darker as passion flushed his face. "I want you so badly, Natalie."

"Then make love with me," she urged as she stepped back and pulled her sweater over her head. She flinched as she did it, though, her sore muscles protesting.

Josh cursed. "I can see the bruises from the seat belt. I don't want to hurt you."

It was already too late for that, but she didn't want to dwell on the past anymore. She didn't even want to worry about the future. She wanted to be only in the moment, in the now. So she ignored the pain and her bruises, and she finished undressing until she stood naked before him.

"Natalie…" He groaned as if the sight of her brought him pain. She could see the tension in his face and his body. A muscle twitched in his cheek. "I want you so badly." He touched her then, running his fingertips along the bruise over her shoulder. "But you've been through so much."

She smiled and offered him the same assurance their son had offered her. "I'm tough."

"Yes," he said, his voice gruff with awe. "You are incredibly tough."

She wasn't, though. She'd nearly lost it so many times over the past couple of days. And she undoubtedly would have if he hadn't been there for her, for them.

He yanked off his shirt and shucked off his jeans and boxers so that he was naked, too. His body seemed to pulsate with the passion that coursed through her as well. He kissed her with all that desire, his mouth moving hungrily over hers. But he touched her gently, like she was made of glass.

But if she was, she would have broken before now. She would have broken five years ago when he went to prison. She hadn't entirely believed it herself when she'd claimed just minutes ago that she was tough, but she was. And even if Josh hurt her again, she would survive.

But she didn't want to miss another chance to be with him, to feel the passion and the ecstasy that he brought her.

Though his touch was gentle, it drove her mad. The way he ran just his fingertips over her skin, over her breasts, over her nipples which were so incredibly sensitive. She moaned as the tension built inside her, winding so tightly through her that she worried she might break.

Then his hands moved down her body, over the most sensitive part of her, and her knees began to shake. She moaned again, nearly reaching a release. But she didn't want to go without him. So she touched him as tenderly as he was touching her, gliding just her fingertips across his skin, over his muscles.

He groaned. Then he guided her toward her bed, laying her down atop her quilt. And he made love to her with his mouth.

She couldn't hold out. The tension broke as an orgasm quivered inside her. And she shook from the force of it. And then he was moving, sliding in and out again. Thrusting as gently as he'd touched her.

That tension built again, bringing back the desperation and the desire. She arched and moved, meeting those slow thrusts, clutching him with her inner muscles.

He groaned again. "Natalie…" He started moving faster now. She matched his rhythm.

He lowered his head and kissed her lips, nibbling at them. Then his tongue slid into her mouth, mimicking the movements of their bodies.

A madness overtook her. She wrapped her legs around his body and held on as she moved her hips. The tension broke again, this orgasm more powerful than the last. She muted her scream of pleasure against his mouth.

She swallowed his groan as his body tensed and then convulsed.

He murmured something against her lips, something she wanted to pretend she hadn't heard. Something she didn't want to acknowledge even though her heart yearned to be his again. She loved him.

Natalie had never stopped loving him, and she didn't think she ever would. But that still didn't mean she would ever be able to trust him again not to hurt her or, worse yet, to hurt their son.

HIS BED WAS so soft and warm that Henry wanted to snuggle even deeper under the covers. He wanted to sleep and dream only good dreams.

But something was waking him up. Some noise, some movement.

And he opened his eyes to find that he wasn't alone. It wasn't Mommy or Daddy in his room, though.

It was the person in that mask.

He remembered what Auntie Sylvie told him. To scream. To kick and punch. To not let that person take him anywhere again without a fight.

But Henry didn't feel tough like she told him he was. He felt scared and almost as if he couldn't even move as that person reached out for him again.

Chapter Twenty-Two

As exhausted as Josh was from the past couple of days and from making love with Natalie, he couldn't sleep. Even though they had Henry back and Marilyn was being treated, Josh couldn't relax.

Because he couldn't be sure that, even with the bodyguards outside, they were safe. If only he hadn't lost that bastard on the trail. But he had, and then he'd nearly lost Natalie and his sister, too, when the brakes were cut on her SUV. Someone was deliberately targeting her.

But why?

Natalie was the sweetest, most selfless person he'd ever met. Such a good mother and daughter…and lover. As passionately as they'd just made love, he was tempted to reach for her again, but she'd fallen asleep. And he wanted to let her rest.

But he couldn't. He was restless instead, his stomach muscles tight, his nerves on edge. Then he heard something sputtering out of that monitor. A creak of a door or a floorboard.

Was Henry up?

The poor kid was probably having a nightmare after the ordeal he'd gone through, after that abduction. The thought made Josh more uneasy, and he slid quietly out of bed and quickly got dressed. He grabbed the monitor, taking it with him as he carefully turned the knob and opened the door just wide enough to squeeze through before pulling it closed behind himself.

He didn't want to disturb Natalie's sleep. She had to be exhausted, emotionally and physically. And yet she'd made love to him with so much passion.

And love?

Did she love him yet?

He'd told her he loved her, in that moment when he felt the pleasure he'd only ever felt with her, so intense that it was almost painful. So intense that it shook him to his core. He loved her. But he couldn't expect her to give him another chance. He couldn't expect her to ever trust him again after how badly he'd hurt her.

He closed his eyes for a moment and then opened them again. That was when he saw the shadow down the hall, standing inside Henry's open doorway. Had one of the bodyguards come inside the house to check on them?

"Hey," he called out softly, not wanting to wake up Natalie but also wanting to know what was going on.

The person turned toward him, and he saw the mask, the mask Henry had talked about, the mask Josh had seen for himself after he'd been struck over the head.

And then he heard Henry scream.

"I told you not to play games," the person said to Josh, the voice raspy and strange yet almost familiar, too.

"Who the hell are you?" Josh asked, and he rushed forward, closing the distance between them.

But the person was closer to the stairs and half fell, half ran down them and then through the kitchen and the open patio door.

Josh followed, reaching out, trying to catch them.

Where were the others? The bodyguards who were supposed to be guarding the place? Had this person hurt them?

Had he or she hurt Henry? He'd screamed, but that had sounded more like out of fear than pain.

Still, Josh was torn between wanting to go back and check on his son and wanting to catch the kidnapper and end this once and for all.

NATALIE WASN'T SURE if she actually heard the scream or if it was part of her dream. But then she heard the pounding footsteps on the stairs. "Josh?"

She reached for him, but the bed was empty and already cold on his side. How long had she been asleep?

And what had happened? Where was the monitor she'd put on the nightstand? It was gone with Josh.

She jumped out of bed, dragged on some clothes and then ran out into the hallway.

It was empty now. Those footsteps must have been pounding down the steps, not up. On her way to the stairwell, she stopped in front of the open door to Henry's room. The blankets were pulled back, some of the stuffed animals and pillows lying on the floor.

But not her son.

He was gone.

"Henry!" she shrieked. "Henry!"

Oh God, no...

That kidnapper shouldn't have been able to get to him again. There were bodyguards outside. They were supposed to be protecting them, though she should have known better than to trust them. But she had that monitor, too. How hadn't she heard the person on it? She never should have left Henry alone.

But maybe he wasn't alone. Josh was gone, too. He must have heard something before she had, or he'd reacted faster.

"Henry! Josh!" she yelled their names as she ran for the stairs. Where were they? What had happened to them?

Once she hit the bottom step, she felt the cold breeze blowing through the open patio door. The curtains danced on the wind, flapping against the walls and the glass. They slapped at Natalie as she passed through them, as if slapping her for being a bad mother, for putting her own desires over the safety of her son.

"Henry!" she called out again. "Hen—"

A big hand covered her mouth, muffling her cry. And a heavy arm wrapped around her, holding her, imprisoning her. This wasn't Josh's body; she knew his too well.

No. This was a stranger.

The intruder? The kidnapper? Was he going to take her now?

Better her than her son.

Please. Henry had to be safe.

MILEK HAD SPENT too many hours awake over the past couple of days. He wasn't sure if he'd ever slept at all, but even with the little boy found, he hadn't been able to rest. So he was driving over to check on the overnight guards who were making sure that Josh, Natalie and that precious little boy stayed safe.

Ivan and Viktor were there. They were bigger than he was. Younger. Stronger. But they hadn't been bodyguards very long. And their actual jobs were to protect things, not people, so he called them on the radio as he headed over.

"We just heard something down the street," Viktor said. "Sounded like a scream. Maybe somebody saw someone lurking around. I'm going to check it out."

"I can," Ivan chimed in on the radio.

"Just one of you," Milek said. "And I'll be there soon." He drove up just seconds later, but he didn't see anyone near the front of the house.

He called them up on the radio, but neither guard answered. Had they both gone to check out that noise? That could have just been a distraction to get them away from Josh and Natalie and Henry.

Milek knew it when he heard a scream through his open SUV window, this one coming from inside the house. He threw open the door and jumped out. As he was rushing toward the house, he tripped and fell over a long, hard body. "Ivan!"

He'd been so worried about losing Josh that he hadn't considered the risk to the others. To Ivan and to Viktor.

Milek felt the man's neck and found a pulse. He was alive, just unconscious like Josh had been earlier that day when the kidnapper had struck him.

Knowing how dangerous the kidnapper was, Milek drew his weapon from its holster. His finger slid off the safety because he knew he needed to be ready. He was a good shot, and he had no compunction against killing if it was to save someone else. As a teenager he'd killed…to protect his sister.

And he would do it all over again if he had to.

Anything for family. And his employees were family, too. He had to find Viktor and Josh and that little boy and Natalie Croft.

He started toward the house. The side door was closed and locked. But then he heard movement coming from behind the house. And he rushed around the corner, his gun drawn and pointed. He wasn't going to get hit over the head and disarmed. He was going to shoot to kill.

But when he stared down the scope on his barrel, the gun was pointed at a boy. A little boy whose wide eyes stared at him in horror and fear.

Chapter Twenty-Three

Josh had pursued the kidnapper down the stairs and through the backyard to an alley that ran between the houses in this area. He was gaining on him, and when he extended his arm, he was nearly able to reach him. But he grabbed the back of the hood instead, pulling it down, snapping the string of the mask that fell away to the ground. The hood slipped through his fingers.

Josh was so close. He nearly had him. He pumped his legs to run faster, to close the distance between them again.

But then he heard another scream. Henry's.

The little boy sounded terrified.

Josh had assumed there was only one kidnapper, only one intruder in the house. But it made more sense that there were two or even three. How else had the bodyguards been disarmed?

Or were they in on it?

And Josh had left Natalie and Henry alone with them in that house. He turned around to run back toward them.

But he felt a flurry of movement behind him, like the person he was pursuing was going to become the pursuer again.

When Josh turned back, he caught a glimpse of a face before the man reaffixed the mask he'd picked up from the ground. But it was too late.

After hearing the terror in Henry's scream, Josh hoped that it wasn't too late for Natalie and their son, too. He ran back toward them as fast as he could.

And he could only hope that he made it to them in time. He couldn't lose either of them, and he certainly couldn't lose them both and survive.

NATALIE'S HEART WAS pounding so fast and hard that Henry had to be able to feel it, too, as she held him tightly in her arms. "Are you okay?" she asked him again.

His last scream had terrified her. And she'd managed to wrest free of the man holding her to find another man trying to hold her son.

"Mommy!" Henry had screamed before running into her arms. She'd been holding him ever since, and this time she never intended to let him go.

"I didn't know he was the one in the backyard," Milek said, and his face was nearly as pale as his silvery eyes. "After I found Ivan unconscious on the front lawn, I had my gun drawn and pointed it at him."

"Is Ivan okay?" asked the man who'd caught her as she slipped out the patio doors. "He offered to check out that noise down the street. I shouldn't have let him go alone. I knew it, I started after him…"

And that must have been when the man in the mask got into the house.

"Ivan has a pulse, but he needs an ambulance. You call for one, Viktor," Milek said. His hands were shaking.

"Where's Josh?" Natalie asked, her voice cracking.

"Daddy chased the person in the mask out of my room and out of the house," Henry said. And the little boy must have followed them both out.

"Of course Josh went after him on his own," another man

said. He came around from the front of the house, holding his head.

Viktor smacked his shoulder. "You're all right?"

Ivan nodded. "Yeah…son of a…" He glanced at Henry. "Person got a jump on me."

"Did you see who it was?" Milek asked.

Ivan shook his head and grimaced. "I was walking toward that noise we heard, sounded like a woman screaming. And then someone must have rushed out of the shadows, got me from behind like they got Josh. I didn't see anything."

"I saw someone in a mask coming out the patio door," Viktor said. "Josh was right behind them. And the boy and then someone else came after him." He turned toward Natalie. "I thought you were an accomplice chasing the kid."

So he'd been protecting her son from her. She nearly smiled. She would have if Josh was back. But he'd gone after the kidnapper alone.

Where was he?

"THERE'S DADDY!" HENRY exclaimed when his father ran into the backyard.

"Oh, thank God," Mommy said, her voice all soft and shaky.

Maybe she thought the person in the mask was going to take Daddy away like they'd taken Henry and Mimi. Was that why they came back tonight?

"Daddy protected us," Henry said. Because they were all here, and the masked person wasn't.

"Did he get away?" one of the big men asked. He had really, really short, really, really pale hair, and he kept rubbing his head and making the faces like Mimi had made after she fell. He was the one who'd helped him and Mimi at the metal building. He'd had candy bars.

Daddy nodded. "This time."

Henry's heart started beating as hard as Mommy's was against him. "Is he coming back?" he asked, and his voice was all shaky like hers. "I don't want him to come back." Tears filled his eyes.

He wasn't as tough as Auntie Sylvie said. After feeling like he was frozen at first, he had tried to fight off the person when they started reaching for him, trying to pull him out of his bed. But he knew that if Daddy hadn't shown up when he had, he wouldn't be here now. He would have been back in that cold building, on the hard concrete floor. And Mimi wouldn't have been with him this time because she was with Grandpa and Auntie Sylvie.

"He's not coming back," Daddy said, and he reached out and patted Henry's back, rubbing it like Mommy did when he didn't feel good. "He's going to go to prison where he belongs."

"He?" Mommy asked. The other men said it at the same time she did.

"You saw him," said the man who had eyes just like Auntie Sylvie's. And he was smiling like he already knew Daddy's answer.

Daddy smiled back, but then he looked at Mommy and his smile slipped away.

"I don't care who it is," she said. "I just want them behind bars where they can't hurt us anymore."

Josh nodded, and then he walked a short distance away with the other men. And they lowered their voices, probably so that Henry wouldn't hear them. They didn't want him to be scared. But he was.

Especially when he heard Daddy say, "He knows I saw him. He's going to run. We have to hurry."

"If he knows you saw him, you're in danger," the bigger guy with the longer hair said. "You need to lie low with protection. Let us handle this."

But Daddy shook his head. "No, I want to see this through. I want to watch them put handcuffs on him and take him away."

Henry would have wanted that, too, but he really didn't want to see that masked person ever again. He just wanted him gone.

And for Daddy to stay forever.

Chapter Twenty-Four

Josh did as Milek told him—he called Detective Dubridge. But they were already in Milek's Payne Protection Agency SUV, heading over to the house the masked man owned to make sure that he didn't get away before the police arrived. They were definitely going to beat the detective there, which was good because Josh was really tempted to beat the man who'd terrorized his son.

"Don't do anything stupid," Dubridge warned through the speakers of the SUV as if he'd read Josh's mind. Or maybe he just knew what he would do if someone had done to his child what this bastard had done to Josh's.

The masked man had put Henry and Natalie through hell.

Milek drove the SUV up to the monstrous concrete-and-glass house at the end of the cul-de-sac. Instead of pulling into the driveway, he pulled across it, blocking the entire width of it so that the Lincoln parked in the open garage wouldn't get past them. The trunk lid was up, some things spilling out of it like someone was packing in a hurry.

Just Timothy, or was Dena involved too? Viktor and Ivan had heard a woman's scream; it was what had lured them away from the house. So Timothy had to have a female accomplice.

Josh reached for the door handle.

"Stay here," Milek said. "Let's wait for the police like Detective Dubridge told us to."

"But he could run."

"I've got him blocked in, and he won't get far on foot," Milek said.

"You don't know that," Josh said. He'd barely been able to catch the guy earlier that evening. Timothy was much faster and stronger than Josh would have thought. "He could call an Uber. We need to get out. We need to hold him until the police get here." Because he wasn't letting him get away again.

He wasn't giving him another chance to abduct his son.

And he wasn't wasting time arguing with his boss about it, either.

So Josh opened the door and stepped out onto the driveway. Just as he headed toward the Lincoln, the door to the house opened, and Timothy, arms loaded with suitcases, stepped into the garage. He must not have been able to see over the pile of luggage because he kept coming toward the open trunk and dumped the load onto the other stuff.

"Going somewhere?" Josh asked.

Timothy fell back against the car. "You son of a bitch."

Josh shrugged off the insult. It was the truth, after all. "It's over, Timothy."

Timothy turned and reached into the trunk. And Josh heard the sound of a gun cocking.

"I will shoot you," Milek said almost matter-of-factly. "I've killed before, another creep like you who terrorized a kid."

Josh glanced at his boss, and he could see that Milek wasn't bluffing. He would kill, and he very clearly had.

Timothy must have realized it, too, because he pulled his empty hands out of the trunk and held them up. "You've got this all wrong," he said. "I didn't hurt anyone—"

"Was it your partner who hurt Mrs. Croft then?" Josh asked.

"Partner?"

"You can't have done this all on your own, Timothy," Josh said. "Who are you working with?"

"With or against…" Milek muttered.

"I don't know what you're talking about," Timothy said, and he was clearly bluffing. "You have no proof of anything."

"We won't find those diamonds you took off me on the trail around here somewhere?"

"Those weren't the right ones," Timothy said, his voice shaking with fury as his face flushed. "You think you're so damn smart playing that sick joke on me…"

Sirens wailed in the distance.

"Who are you working with?" Josh persisted. Because clearly Timothy wasn't smart enough to have pulled off the kidnapping on his own. He was barely making any sense right now.

"I'm not saying anything else without a lawyer present," Timothy said.

"We're not the police," Josh said. "It doesn't matter what you say to us."

Timothy snorted. "No, it doesn't. So I'm not saying another damn word to you." But then he must not have been able to help himself because he continued, "She'll never forgive you, you know."

"Forgive *me*?" Josh asked. "What are you talking about?"

"Natalie, she's never going to forgive you."

"For figuring out that you kidnapped our son and hurt her mother?" Josh asked. "I don't think she needs to forgive me about that."

"For breaking her heart," Timothy said. "She was devastated and embarrassed. Her baby daddy went to prison as a thief, leaving her to raise her son alone. She had to live with her parents. She had no life, nothing, after you left. You think I'm the bad guy here? You're the bad guy, Josh

Stafford. And while she might be happy with you now for finding Henry, it won't last, not when she remembers how horribly you disappointed her."

"I guess you would know something about disappointing people," Josh said.

Timothy nodded. "I do, and I know how it feels to be disappointed by people. It's not something you get over easily if ever at all."

The sirens grew louder as the police vehicles turned onto the cul-de-sac and drowned out whatever else Timothy was going to say.

But Josh didn't need to hear the rest of it to know that the guy might be right.

Natalie might never forgive him.

NATALIE WANTED TO get Henry back to bed, and she wanted to be alone for a moment. But the two big bodyguards were both still here, inside the house with her. She wished they would have gone with Josh and Milek instead.

But Josh and Milek were going to call the police. They'd promised. Had they?

"You should take him to the hospital," she told Viktor as she pointed at Ivan, who had one hand on the back of his head as he grimaced. "Head injuries are serious."

Her mother was still in the hospital because of hers. And Josh probably should have stayed as well after he got hit over the head earlier today.

But instead he'd been here with her and Henry, saving them both again.

"I'm fine," Ivan insisted.

"No, you're not," she said. "But I am. Henry and I will be okay. Timothy won't come back here." Before they'd left, Josh had told her whom he'd seen. And Timothy knew that

Josh had seen him, that he knew who he was. He had to be on the run now.

A knock rattled the side door that opened onto the driveway. Henry, who'd been nearly falling asleep at the table, gasped. And the two men tensed. Then the knob started to turn. Was it unlocked?

Or did this person have a key?

The door opened. But Natalie couldn't see who'd entered because Viktor and Ivan put themselves between the door and her and Henry. Just like Josh, they were willing to give up their lives for her.

She'd been wrong to doubt them. They were good men. Like Josh…

"Who the hell are you?" Dena asked. "And where's my sister?"

"I'm here," Natalie said. "And this is my sister," she confirmed for the guards.

"I wish it was Auntie Sylvie," Henry muttered. He'd only met her once, but he'd had an immediate connection with her like he had with his father. Like Natalie had had with his father all those years ago, a connection that heartbreak and five years apart hadn't severed.

"Who's Auntie Sylvie?" Dena asked. "Some female bodyguard?" She shrugged. "Never mind. I don't actually care."

Of course she didn't.

"I want to speak to my sister alone," Dena told Ivan and Viktor.

But Ivan shook his head, which made him wince again.

"I will be safe with my sister," Natalie said, though she wasn't totally sure about that. "Henry, why don't you take Mr. Viktor and Mr. Ivan upstairs and show them your stuffed animals?"

"I am a big bear guy," Viktor said. "And maybe a teddy would help Mr. Ivan feel better."

"You can lay down in my bed," Henry offered. "Mimi slept a lot after she fell in the garage." He took one of Ivan's big hands in his and tugged him toward the stairs.

Natalie smiled as she watched the three of them climb the stairs. She didn't have to worry about anyone getting close to Henry, not with those two gentle giants guarding him.

"What the hell is going on, Natalie?" Dena asked.

"You tell me," Natalie challenged her sister. "I am really curious how much you know, how involved you are."

"Involved in what?"

"Henry and Mom's kidnapping," Natalie said. "The diamonds—"

"Like I told the police, I have no idea about any of that, and I still don't know what's going on," Dena said. "Timothy grabbed his passport and is throwing all of his stuff in his car right now, and he won't answer any of my questions."

"And you thought I would have the answers," Natalie said. "So you must know—"

"He told me to come here, that you would be able to explain everything," Dena said.

"He's the one," Natalie said. "He took Henry and Mom. He hurt her."

Dena shook her head. "No. That makes no sense."

"Josh caught him in here tonight, trying to take Henry again."

"He doesn't even like kids," Dena said.

"No, but he likes money," Natalie said. "Or maybe you're the one who likes money."

"Most people like money, Natalie," Dena said. "Stop being so naive for once."

Natalie had been through so much the past couple of days that her patience had run out, leaving her temper to snap. "Stop being such an uncaring bitch for once, Dena."

Instead of being offended, Dena smiled. "You should

be more like me," she said. "Then you wouldn't get hurt so much."

"Just once," Natalie said. Just Josh.

"But it was enough that you never tried to get in another relationship," Dena said. "You were afraid to get hurt again. But you wouldn't if you just wouldn't care…"

"But I want to care," Natalie said. "I want to be able to love, to care about the people close to me, like my son and our parents…and you."

Dena chuckled now. "I'm surprised you managed to spit that out. We've never been close."

"Whose fault was that?" Natalie asked.

"Mine," Dena admitted. "I hated you from the day you were born because Mom and Dad loved you so much."

"They love you, too."

"They're not giving *me* the store."

"You've never shown any interest in it," Natalie said. Then she stepped back. "You knew it. You knew about their plans."

Dena snorted. "Mom warned me because she was worried that I would be mad at you. That I would think you put them up to it. She didn't want to cause any more friction between us."

It had always bothered her mother, much more than it had ever bothered them, that they didn't have a close relationship. But because of who Dena was and how she'd always treated Natalie, Natalie had given up trying to have a close relationship with her sister.

"She didn't want you to be spiteful," Natalie said. And she remembered how many times Dena had ruined the cake for Natalie's birthday, how many times she'd ruined the surprise about what her present was. "I'm shocked you didn't tell me what they were doing."

Dena shrugged. "I didn't care."

Natalie snorted now. "Yeah, right. Is that what this is all

about? You and Timothy stealing from the store and then kidnapping my son when those diamonds disappeared before he could get to them."

"I told you *I* didn't care," Dena said.

"But you knew what he was doing," Natalie surmised.

Dena shook her head and then laughed. "I actually thought he was having an affair. The late nights, the sneaking around…" She laughed again.

"And you didn't care about that, either?" Natalie asked.

Dena shrugged. "It would have been kind of hypocritical of me."

"You're having an affair, too?"

Dena smiled now, and her blue eyes lit up. "Yes. I was planning to divorce Timothy anyway. But I really had no idea what he was doing, that he was even capable of such things. I guess that just goes to show that you really can't trust anyone."

Natalie understood that all too well.

Dena studied Natalie's face for a moment. "I actually thought Timothy might be having the affair with you."

"What?" Just the thought had bile rising up the back of Natalie's throat.

Dena shrugged. "All he does is work. Who else is at his work besides you and Dad?"

"Damn!" Natalie and Sylvie had been right to suspect Hannah.

"What?"

"Maybe you should have spent more time at the store," Natalie remarked. Because her and Sylvie's instincts had been right. No matter what she'd claimed, Hannah was involved in the thefts and probably with Timothy as well. Co-conspirators or ex-co-conspirators who had double-crossed each other?

If the latter was the case, then surely Timothy would give

her up, would provide evidence against her, and this would all be over soon.

If Timothy had been caught…

Had Josh and Milek arrived in time to stop him from getting away? Timothy had already had his passport and been packing his things when Dena left their house.

"Mommy!" Henry called down from the top of the stairs. "Mommy!"

Scared by the urgency in his voice, she ran halfway up toward him. "What? What's wrong?"

"The big guy fell down," Henry said. "He's sleeping like Mimi was."

"We do need that ambulance," Viktor called down from behind Henry. He stood at the top of the stairs with his cell phone pressed to his ear. "And you and Henry are going to need to come to the hospital with us," he said, "so that we can make sure you stay safe."

"We'll be fine," Natalie assured him. "My sister is here with us."

"No, she's not," Henry said as he peered down the stairs. "Auntie Dena left."

For where? To go back home? Or to her lover?

Or to find her husband's lover?

Because if that was the case, Dena was putting herself in danger. And while her sister made her crazy, Natalie still loved her and didn't want anything to happen to her.

MILEK HADN'T EXPECTED to be brought down to the police station along with the suspect he and Josh had stopped from fleeing the country. But when he arrived at Timothy Hutchinson's house, Detective Dubridge insisted that both Milek and Josh give their statements immediately and in person at the police department.

Milek could understand needing Josh's statement since he

was the one who'd seen the intruder without his mask and could identify him. But Dubridge had also wanted Milek's.

He'd put them in separate rooms, and he hadn't asked them about just tonight but all the events that had gone on leading up to tonight. Dubridge started with his and Garek's agency being hired by that insurance company to investigate all the claims they'd had recently.

Clearly Dubridge suspected that Timothy wasn't the only guilty party in this case. And Milek had no doubt that he was right about that.

Someone else was definitely involved. They'd stolen the diamonds that Timothy wanted, and he'd been so desperate to get his hands on them that he'd kidnapped Josh's son to get them.

So who had stolen the diamonds?

And was that the same person who shot at Natalie and Sylvie in that warehouse?

Was it the person who'd cut the brake line on her car?

Even with Timothy in jail, Natalie and her son were still in danger. So Milek and Josh needed to get back to them and out of the police department before something else happened to them.

Chapter Twenty-Five

Josh hadn't realized when he'd gone to the River City PD to give his statement that Timothy might not be the only one who needed a lawyer. He probably needed one, too, because Detective Dubridge was keeping him there, drilling him with questions that had more to do with the thefts than with the abduction of his son and Marilyn Croft.

And he even left Josh sitting in that interrogation room while he questioned Timothy, too. Like he was checking to see if their stories matched.

"What's going on?" Josh asked when the detective returned. "Do I need to call a lawyer?"

"That's up to you."

"I didn't do anything wrong," Josh insisted. Though he had gone a bit rogue a couple of times, it had been to make certain he got his son back safely. "Timothy is the one you need to be questioning."

"I have been questioning him, too. We found enough evidence in his car and house to link Timothy Hutchinson to the abductions," Dubridge agreed. "But we didn't recover the real diamonds. He admitted that's why he went back tonight to grab Henry again because you didn't give him the diamonds he thinks you'd taken. You gave him back the things he already stole that disappeared from his house when you were there a couple of nights ago with his sister-in-law and father-in-law."

Josh sucked in a breath. "That's where those came from… his house."

"What?"

"Natalie's dad came up with the jewelry that had gone missing before the Payne Protection Agency was even hired, the jewelry the insurance company had already paid them for," Josh said. "He must have found them in Timothy and Dena's house."

"Hutchinson admits to taking them," Dubridge said. "After he learned that his in-laws were going to give the store to his sister-in-law, he was hell-bent on getting every-thing out of it that he could."

Josh cursed. "To hurt her. That must be why he took Henry, too."

"He took Henry because he really believes you have the diamonds," Dubridge said. "You're a convicted jewelry thief, and you had the security codes to the store. That's why he's convinced you have them."

"He's wrong. I don't have them."

Dubridge stared at him through narrowed dark eyes. "I'm beginning to believe you."

"I really don't care whether you believe me or not," Josh admitted. "I care about finding out who tried to hurt Natalie. Her brake line was cut. You confirmed that. And some-one shot at her and my sister the night before that. Was that Timothy?"

Dubridge sighed. "I really don't think so."

"But he resented Natalie getting the store," Josh reminded him. "Maybe he thought he would inherit it if something happened to her."

"But he wouldn't inherit it, his wife would," Dubridge said. "And it doesn't sound like they're on good terms. She wasn't at the spa the other day. She was in a hotel with another man. I personally confirmed her alibi with him and the hotel staff."

"Natalie's relationship with Dena isn't good," Josh said. It was even worse than his relationship with Sylvie. "Even though she had nothing to do with the abduction, Dena could have been the one who tried to hurt her. And who might still try to hurt her…" He jumped up then. "I have to get out of here and make sure Natalie is safe. If you want to keep me here, you're going to have to arrest me."

Dubridge didn't stop him from walking out. Josh found Milek waiting for him in the hall outside the door. The older man looked tense and exhausted.

"Are you okay?" Josh asked. "What's going on?"

"Ivan passed out," Milek said. "The head injury was worse than he would admit."

"Is he okay?"

"He's at the hospital getting treated. An ambulance brought him there, and Viktor followed it with Natalie and Henry, too, to make sure they stayed safe."

The pressure on Josh's chest eased a bit. "That's good." They still had protection.

"But they disappeared on him once they all got to the hospital," Milek said. "He can't find them. And in the rush to leave with Ivan being hurt, they left Natalie's cell at the house."

Josh cursed. But then he remembered the last couple of times that Natalie had gone off on her own that she hadn't actually been alone. "Do you still have my sister's cell number?" Josh asked.

Milek nodded.

"Call her."

When Sylvie picked up, she sounded groggy like she'd been sleeping. "Hello?"

Milek had his cell on speaker, so Josh spoke, "Are Natalie and Henry with you?"

She hesitated a moment.

"Sylvie? Are you there?"

"Yeah," she said. "I didn't want to wake up the Crofts. I'm out in the hall now. What's this about Natalie and Henry? I haven't seen them since they left with you."

"You're still at the hospital?"

"Yeah, Mrs. Lynch was exhausted, so I told her I had this watch. But I fell asleep, too."

"So you didn't see Natalie and Henry at the hospital?"

She gasped. "Are they hurt? What happened?"

"They were fine, but Natalie's brother-in-law tried to grab him again tonight."

"Son of a bitch!"

"He's in police custody now." And Josh had nearly been as well.

"That's good."

"But I don't think he's the one who cut the brake lines or shot at you both," Josh said. "So someone else is still out there trying to hurt her. I think it could be her sister, trying to stop Natalie from inheriting the store."

Sylvie whistled. "And I thought I was the worst sister ever..."

"Sister?" Milek asked. "Viktor said Natalie's sister was at the house when Ivan passed out. But then she just disappeared."

That didn't mean that Dena had left, though. Maybe she'd hung back and followed them to the hospital.

Josh cursed. "We have to find them."

Because he had a horrible feeling that Dena was going to kill Natalie and Henry both. That way she could make certain that she was the only heir left to the jewelry store.

HAD SHE MADE a big mistake leaving the hospital with her sister? Viktor was with Ivan in radiology, so Natalie hadn't had the chance to tell him where she was going.

She probably should have woken up Sylvie, though, but the young woman had been sleeping so hard in a corner of the room that Natalie's parents shared. Even Henry, as happy as he'd been to see her, hadn't wanted to wake her up. And Natalie hadn't felt comfortable leaving him with her while she was sleeping. Her parents were sleeping, too.

So she and Henry had gone back into the hall with Dena, who'd been standing in her parents' room when Natalie and Henry had come by to check on them.

"They're getting so old," Dena had mused.

Natalie hadn't known if she was surprised or appalled or sympathetic. "Midsixties isn't old," she'd said. Mom looked great, usually, but she'd been through a hell of an ordeal. And sixty-seven was much too young for her dad to already be getting dementia. She hated that, hated that they were already starting to lose him.

"It is, really," Dena had insisted. "I always thought Timothy and I would be like them and stay together forever."

But Timothy was going to prison. On the way to the hospital, Viktor had confirmed that Natalie's brother-in-law had been taken into custody. He couldn't try to hurt Henry or her again. He had to be the one who'd cut her brake line and shot at her and Sylvie in the warehouse, too. He had to be furious that she was going to get the store that he worked at for so long.

Dena wasn't, though. She wasn't mad at her or jealous, so Natalie had no reason to suspect her of anything anymore.

"Who is he seeing? You know," Dena had prodded her.

"If what you say is true, and he only works and comes home, it would have to be Hannah."

"Hannah?"

"She's a young woman who works as a salesperson," Natalie had explained. "Worked. She quit the other day." When she and Sylvie had confronted her with those sales slips with the passcodes on them.

Dena nodded. "She must have known that Timothy would screw up and get caught. She's probably already out of the country."

"With the diamonds," Natalie said. "She must have been the one who took them and then double-crossed him."

"Let's go to the store and find out where she lives," Dena said.

"Why? She's probably already gone."

"What if she's not?" Dena asked. "And I want to see the woman my husband was having an affair with. You must have a photo ID or something of hers around the store, something with her picture on it."

"I thought you didn't care," Natalie reminded her.

"I'm curious."

Natalie should have reminded her that curiosity killed the cat, but she didn't want to say that in front of Henry. He was so tired that he was nodding off. She'd sighed and agreed to go to the store as long as Dena brought them home after so that Henry could go back to sleep in his own bed.

But once Dena parked her vehicle in the alley, Natalie had an overwhelming sense of foreboding like she'd made a mistake. A horrible mistake.

Was the mistake leaving the hospital with Dena? With trusting her? Or in coming to the store?

Dena herself had called Natalie naive and admonished her for trusting anyone. Had she been warning Natalie to not even trust her?

Dena pushed open her door and then glanced across the console at Natalie. "What's wrong?"

"This is probably a mistake."

Dena shrugged. "Why? I'm not going to fall apart seeing his affair partner. I just want to know what she looks like, how young she is…"

Natalie sighed. "What do you care when you have an affair partner of your own?"

"He's old," Dena said dismissively. "He's rich. But he's old. And I just… I don't know." She shrugged again. "Yes, I know. As you and Mom would point out, I'm vain and shallow. And I just want to know…"

"Dena, you're beautiful…"

"And impatient," Dena said. "Just let me in, and you can come back out here."

Natalie glanced at Henry who was sleeping in a booster seat in the back. Apparently, her sister knew someone with a kid. Maybe her affair partner. "Okay. Henry is exhausted. Let's leave him here."

Dena glanced in the back, as if she'd forgotten he was even there. "Sure."

"Just lock him in." Natalie did not want to risk losing him again. That was why she wanted him in the vehicle. In case this was a mistake. In case Dena wanted to do more than look at a picture of her husband's affair partner. She stepped out of the car and waited until Dena locked it before she opened the back door to the store.

"There's a picture of Hannah on the wall in the showroom," she told Dena. But then she turned on the lights and found the woman herself standing in the backroom. The vault door was open, and she was emptying it out.

"God, you're a pain in the ass," Hannah said. "If only I would have killed you when you and that blond woman messed up my meeting with the fence." She reached for something else in the vault and then turned back toward them with a gun in her hand. "I'm not a great shot at distances, though. But up close…" She stepped closer to them.

Dena moved closer to Natalie. "Hey, what's going on? Who is this?"

"This is her," Natalie said. "The woman having the affair with your husband."

Dena snorted. "No, it's not."

Natalie's heart was beating even faster and harder with fear. What was her sister doing? Were they in on this together, Dena and Hannah?

Had it been a setup bringing her here?

"This woman is too young for Timothy, too pretty," Dena said, and she edged a little closer to Natalie.

She felt the tool that Dena was slipping into her hand, behind their backs. It was one of the sharp chisels Natalie, Josh and her dad had used to get some of the diamonds out of their settings.

Hannah smiled. "And he said you were a bitch."

"Oh, I am," Dena said. "I'm just not stupid. There's no way you would ever fall for my idiot husband. You were just using him."

"Yes, but he's not such an idiot that he must not have had some doubts. He held onto everything we stole, saying we'd cash it all out at once and run away together."

"That's why you took the diamonds," Natalie said. "You didn't want to wait for him."

"I didn't want to go away with him, especially not where he's going now," Hannah said. "He's such an idiot. He hasn't figured out I've had the diamonds the whole time I've been *helping* him try to get them back. Like tonight, I distracted the bodyguards, and he still nearly got caught trying to abduct your son again. He knows he was seen and that he will be arrested if he sticks around."

"That's why you're here," Natalie surmised. "You're taking everything you can to run away."

"He promised he won't implicate me," Hannah said. "But I knew you were already figuring out what he hadn't."

"That you stole the diamonds."

Hannah laughed. "He really believes your baby daddy has them. He told me all about him when he saw him on the security footage."

Josh hadn't taken them, just like he hadn't taken the things he'd gone to prison for stealing.

"Maybe whoever finds your bodies here will believe the same thing, and nobody will be looking for me," Hannah said with a smile.

"You think you'll be able to blame our murders on a guy who isn't anywhere around here?" Natalie asked.

"I don't care who they blame as long as it's not me," Hannah said. Then she swung her gun barrel toward Dena. "Now hand over the keys to your vehicle."

"Why?" Natalie asked, thinking with horror of Henry sleeping in the back seat. If Hannah was heartless enough to kill her and Dena, she wouldn't hesitate to kill him as well.

"Well, I know your vehicle is out of commission after I cut the brake line," Hannah admitted. "You should have died in that crash. You and your blond friend. Where the hell is she?"

"At the hospital still," Natalie said. "But why do you want my sister's vehicle? Didn't you drive yourself here?" She didn't want Hannah anywhere near the alley and her son.

"It's getting light out," Hannah said. "I don't want anyone to see me leaving the front of the store. I'm going out the back, and since that's where you came from, you must be parked in the alley."

"Who cares why she wants it?" Dena asked. "Let's just hand her the damn keys." She reached behind Natalie again and took the chisel from her. Then she stepped toward Hannah, like she was going to hand her the keys. But instead Dena swung her arm, with that tool in her hand, toward the girl's face.

Natalie didn't know if Dena hit Hannah or not...before the gun went off.

The blast echoed off the walls of the small room and knocked Dena back into Natalie. And she didn't have to wonder if she'd been hit or not. Her sister had obviously been shot.

And now Hannah swung the gun barrel toward her.

THE SOUND OF a blast woke Henry up to darkness. "Mommy!" he cried out. "Daddy!"

But they hadn't been with Daddy. He'd gone after the person in the mask. He was going to make sure that person didn't ever play games with Henry again. But Henry felt like someone was playing a game now. Cops and robbers?

That was what Chelsea played with him sometimes, and she pointed her finger at him like it was a gun. Then she yelled really loud, "Bang, bang, you're dead!"

He wasn't sure that she sounded like a real gun, though. She didn't even sound like the ones on TV. But whatever he just heard had sounded like the ones on TV.

Was that what that noise was? Not Chelsea but a real gun?

Lights flashed in his face as another vehicle pulled into the alley. It was that long black vehicle that Daddy had left in with his boss.

"Daddy!" he yelled. Henry unbuckled his seat belt and went to the door, but it was locked. So he had to scramble over the seat to the one in the front, behind the steering wheel to unlock it. Then he pushed open the door and jumped down. "Daddy!"

He was right. Daddy was here, and he wasn't alone. Auntie Sylvie was with him. He was so happy to see them, but he wanted Mommy, too.

And so did Daddy. He hugged Henry tight and asked him where she was.

"I don't know. But I heard something… I think I heard a gun…"

"You stay here with Auntie Sylvie," Daddy said. And he handed him over to her, like Henry was a baby that couldn't walk.

Henry didn't care, though. Auntie Sylvie was warm and smelled really good. And he snuggled close to her.

"You can't go in there if someone has a gun," Sylvie said. "Let me. I'm armed."

Daddy took Aunt Sylvie's purse and said, "Now I'm armed. Get in the SUV and call the police."

"Just wait for them—"

Another *bang-bang* echoed around the alley. Daddy pulled open the back door to go inside the store. That had to be where someone had a gun.

And it also had to be where Mommy and Auntie Dena had gone when they left him sleeping in Auntie Dena's car. But Mommy didn't have a gun.

Did Auntie Dena? Or was there someone else inside with them?

Someone like the person in the mask who played games that weren't fun and hurt people?

Chapter Twenty-Six

Screaming and swearing greeted Josh the second he stepped inside the back of the jewelry store.

"You bitch!" a woman shrieked.

But it wasn't Dena. It was the younger woman, the sales-clerk, and she held a gun, pointing the barrel at Dena with one hand while she held the other over her eye. Blood trailed down from beneath her hand.

"You already shot her," Natalie said as she leaned over her sister who was lying on the floor. "Twice."

"The first shot didn't kill her because she got me again!" the woman said. "She got my eye!" She gestured toward her face with her gun before swinging the barrel back toward Dena and toward Natalie, who was much too close to the object of Hannah's wrath.

"You'll shoot your eye out," Dena muttered and then laughed.

"She's crazy!" Hannah shrieked. "She's a crazy bitch! No wonder Timothy cheated on her with me."

It was all making sense to Josh now, though he wasn't sure why or how all the women had wound up here. But Sylvie had been right when she'd figured that this was probably where they were.

"Somebody will have heard the shots," Natalie said. "The police will be on their way. You should get out of here."

"She never gave me her keys," Hannah said. "But it doesn't matter now. You're going to have to drive me. Get her keys and the bag."

A big bag lay on the floor next to her, jewelry spilling out of it. She must have dropped it when she fired at Dena or when Dena had attacked her.

"But before we leave, I'm going to put a bullet in this bitch's brain," Hannah said, and she stepped even closer to them.

"No!" Natalie screamed. "I won't drive you anywhere if you hurt her."

"You're going to do what I tell you," Hannah insisted. "I am the one with the gun."

"You're not the only one," Josh said, and he stepped out of the shadows with Sylvie's gun clutched in his hand.

But he hadn't moved fast enough because Hannah grabbed Natalie with her bloodied hand and kept her between them. "Put it down, or I'll kill her right here!" she yelled.

Josh didn't lower the weapon, not yet, but he moved farther into the room, trying to get closer to her. Trying to get between them.

But Hannah was moving, too, jerking Natalie with her toward the door he'd stepped through just moments ago, like the three of them had done a little turn to switch positions in the room.

"Let her go," Josh urged Hannah. "I'll drive you. My vehicle is right outside."

"Give her your keys," she said.

"They're in it. It's running," he said. "I think you could drive yourself. Leave her here."

"If I leave her here, she'll be dead. Just like you and that bitch on the floor," Hannah threatened.

But if she took Natalie with her, she would definitely kill her, too, once she no longer needed her. He willed Natalie to duck, to do anything to let him take a shot.

But Hannah held the gun so close to Natalie's head as she dragged her to the door. It must not have shut tightly behind him because it was open now. Before Hannah could step through it, though, something swung. Something long and shiny and hard. It struck Hannah's head, and she fell to the ground with a clank.

"I know, I know," Sylvie said. "You told me to wait in the car with Henry." Instead, she'd gotten a tire iron out of it. "I locked him inside it, and I did call the police."

Sirens wailed.

Natalie was back on the floor next to her sister. "Help's coming, Dena. Hang in there."

Dena nodded. "She just hit me that first time," she said. "It hurts like a bitch, though. Guess it takes one to know one…"

Sylvie chuckled. "Henry's wrong," she said. "Auntie Dena is pretty funny, too. And pretty tough."

"Henry has a lot of strong women in his life," Josh remarked with awe over how fearless they'd all been.

He was also awed by how much he loved Natalie. He hoped so damn much that Timothy was wrong and that she would be able to find a way to forgive him for hurting her and give him another chance to prove how much he loved her and that he would never hurt her again.

NATALIE HAD NEVER been so afraid as when she'd stared down the barrel of Hannah's gun. She'd thought for sure that she was going to die. But that hadn't scared her as much as the thought of that heartless monster leaving with her son sleeping in the back seat of Dena's car. Hannah would have killed him, too, just as she'd tried to kill Dena.

Dena had been wrong—Hannah had struck her twice.

Once in her side and the second time in the shoulder. But she'd probably already been in shock and hadn't felt it. Both bullets had gone straight through her, and while the surgeon had to stop some internal bleeding, he had assured them that Dena would be fine.

Natalie wasn't fine. She was still scared. And not just over what could have happened but over what would. It was all over now.

Hannah had been treated and taken into custody. Timothy was already in jail. It was over.

Did that also mean that Natalie and Josh were over? She was pretty sure that he would want to stay a part of their son's life. They were together now while Natalie had stayed at the hospital with Dena and their parents.

Natalie left her parents standing over Dena's bed and stepped out into the hall. She needed a breather. And she needed to see her son and Josh.

She wanted him to not just be part of Henry's life but part of hers, too. But she'd been grappling so much with her own feelings, with falling for him all over again, that she wasn't sure what he wanted.

"There's Mommy!" Henry said, and he let go of Josh's hand to run up to her.

She dropped down to gather him into her arms and hug him tightly. "I thought you two went home," she said. That was what she remembered telling Josh to do when the ambulance arrived. She'd ridden in it with Dena to the hospital, and she'd told Josh to take Henry home.

"We wanted to be here for you," Josh said, answering for them both.

But did he mean it? Did they both want to be there for her or just her son?

"Hey, Henry," Sylvie said as she walked up behind Josh. "Your daddy's boss is painting a picture of you, and he wants to see you up close to make sure that he got you just right." She held out her hand. "Let's go talk to him."

Henry wriggled away from Natalie to rush over to his aunt. But Sylvie pointed him back toward the waiting room. "He's right there. The one on the left." She made an L with her left hand to show the boy which was which. "Cuz they both look so much alike."

"They look like you," Henry said.

"Uh…yeah…"

Once the little boy scampered away, Sylvie turned back toward them. "Milek has time yet. He could add the two of you to that portrait and make it a family one. Please, don't let my mistakes mess up the rest of your lives. You belong together." Then she blinked furiously and turned away, heading off after her nephew as she muttered under her breath, "I'm not crying. You're crying."

Natalie smiled, but her heart was beating fast and hard after Sylvie's pronouncement, especially with the way Josh was looking at her. So intensely. "What?" she asked.

"Could you do it?" he asked.

"Do what?" Be a family with him and their son? She would love to do that.

"Could you ever forgive me?" Josh asked. "Could you ever trust me again after what I did?" He sounded so tortured, like he was in more pain than Dena after she got shot.

"I didn't think I could," Natalie admitted.

He flinched. "Giving you up was the hardest thing I've ever done. But I didn't know how to save Sylvie. She was working for a monster who threatened her life and our mom's…"

"And yours," she said. "That was why she didn't take the blame because he said he would kill you. And why she kept stealing. He told her that if she didn't, he would get to you in prison. Someone else she cared about died in prison, so she knew he could do it." Sylvie had explained all that to her while they'd been trapped in the wrecked SUV.

Josh sucked in a breath. "That explains her actions. Can you understand and forgive mine?"

"I know that you were worried about the same things she was, about her life and yours and even mine," she said. "But you could have told me the truth."

"You never would have let me go to prison for something I didn't do," Josh said. "And if you had started making noise about the charges and the conviction, I was sure that he would go after you next."

Josh had already told her as much, but she needed to confirm. "So, you were trying to protect me, too?"

He nodded. "I would rather lose you that way, to never see you again, than for you to lose your life."

"It wouldn't have been just my life," she said. Henry would have died, too. She'd been pregnant then. "You did the right thing. We're all alive. You, me, Henry, Sylvie…"

He released a breath like he'd been holding it a long time, maybe five years. "Yes, that is all that matters. That we're all alive."

"And you're out now," she said. "You have a chance at a new life."

"I want a chance at the life we would have had," he said. "I want to marry you. I want to be a family. I love you, Natalie. I never stopped loving you."

"I never stopped loving you," she admitted. "Even when I hated you for what you'd done, I still loved you."

"And now?"

"Now?"

"Do you still hate me?"

She closed the distance between them and wrapped her arms around him. "No. Now I love you more than ever."

"So you can forgive me?"

She nodded. "Can you forgive me?"

"For what?"

"For not telling you that I was pregnant."

"I didn't give you much of a chance to talk that day," he admitted. "I had to get you to leave before I told you the truth."

"The truth is that everything you did, you did out of love," she said. "I was angry."

"You had every reason to be."

She kissed him. "You are the most amazing man, Josh Stafford, and I can't wait to be your wife."

"I hope Sylvie is right and Milek has time to add us to that portrait of Henry. We all belong together," he said. "For the rest of our lives." And then he kissed her back.

"ARE WE CRAZY?" Garek asked his brother. He'd come so close to having all his fears realized about starting his own branch of the Payne Protection Agency.

Their employees had been hurt and could have died. They could have lost members of their team. Now they were considering adding another one.

Milek let out a shaky breath. "No. It has to be her. She looks exactly like Stacy."

"Oh God, we have to tell Stacy," Garek remarked.

"Who is Stacy?" Sylvie asked. "And why are you two talking about me like I'm not here?" Her nephew had run back to his parents, but she'd stayed in the waiting room with Garek…because he had asked to talk to her.

But all he could do now was stare at her.

"Stacy is our sister," Milek replied.

She nodded. "Okay…what does any of that have to do with me?"

"Because we think you're our sister, too."

She chuckled. "I'm Josh's sister."

"And yet you look more like us," Garek said.

"Well, Josh and I had different fathers. He looks like his dad, and I…"

"Look like yours," Milek said. "Our father."

"I don't know," Sylvie said. "I was really little when he went away, so I don't remember much about him…except his eyes." She looked at the two of them then. "My mom didn't tell me much either except that he was a criminal who went to jail. Even on her deathbed, she wouldn't tell me his name, just that he died in prison."

"He was murdered," Garek said.

"I know that," she said.

"How?"

"Luther Mills told me that," she said. "He also knew who my father was. And he mentioned the name to me once, but I was never certain if he was telling the truth or just messing with me."

"Patek Kozminski was our father," Milek said. "I think he was yours, too."

She shrugged. "I don't think it matters much. He's dead."

"It matters to us," Garek said. "You're family."

"Josh is my only family. And Henry…and hopefully Natalie will be soon."

"We're family, too," Milek said.

"But you don't even know me."

"We'll get to know you when you're working with us."

"What are you talking about?"

"We're offering you a job with our branch of the Payne Protection Agency," Milek said.

She laughed. "That's like having the fox watch the henhouse, isn't it?"

"We've heard that before," Garek admitted. "We're former foxes ourselves. That's what you are, too, right? You told Josh that you're not stealing anymore."

"Not since Luther died," Sylvie said. "I swear."

"Yeah, we'll have to work on that," Garek teased her. "You do swear a lot. We'll have to give you some training, too. I hear you're a lousy shot. But we do need some employees who are actually allowed to carry firearms. Most of ours would violate their parole if they did."

She laughed. "Okay, I'm beginning to see the family resemblance now. You're both smart-asses."

"And so are you," Garek said. "You're very smart. Josh told us that you already figured Hannah was involved. And then you were the one who knocked her out. You'll be an asset to the team, Sylvie."

"So, this isn't a pity job offer?"

"I didn't know there was such a thing," Milek said.

"Uh, that's why you work for the Payne Protection Agency, out of pity," Garek teased. "God knows you couldn't support yourself let alone your family on what you make as an artist."

Milek was probably a millionaire several times over, but he just nodded. "That makes sense," he agreed. "Because I'm not very good with firearms, either. We can work on that together, Sylvie." He held out his hand.

She shook it. Then she shook Garek's. "All right," she said. "I'll take this job. I just hope we all don't come to regret this."

Garek remembered his fear from the opening, that he would lose one of his team. With Josh and Ivan getting hurt, he had come close, but they'd all survived.

But what if something like this happened again? Now their own sister was a team member, they could lose her again after they just found her.

They wouldn't put her right on any cases, though. They would train her first.

And they would focus on the rest of the team. On Blade and Viktor and Ivan…

Josh had already earned some time off to be with his son and the woman who would hopefully be his wife soon.

* * * * *

COMING SOON!

We really hope you enjoyed reading this book.
If you're looking for more romance
be sure to head to the shops when
new books are available on

Thursday 27th March

To see which titles are coming soon, please visit
millsandboon.co.uk/nextmonth

MILLS & BOON

LET'S TALK
Romance

For exclusive extracts, competitions and special offers, find us online:

- **f** MillsandBoon
- **X** @MillsandBoon
- **◉** @MillsandBoonUK
- **♪** @MillsandBoonUK

Get in touch on 01413 063 232

For all the latest titles coming soon, visit
millsandboon.co.uk/nextmonth

Afterglow Books is a trend-led, trope-filled list of books with diverse, authentic and relatable characters, a wide array of voices and representations, plus real world trials and tribulations. Featuring all the tropes you could possibly want (think small-town settings, fake relationships, grumpy vs sunshine, enemies to lovers) and all with a generous dose of spice in every story.

♪ @millsandboonuk

⊙ @millsandboonuk

afterglowbooks.co.uk

#AfterglowBooks

For all the latest book news, exclusive content and giveaways scan the QR code below to sign up to the Afterglow newsletter:

SCAN ME